THE RUBY

OTHER BOOKS AND AUDIO BOOKS
BY JENNIE HANSEN:

Abandoned

All I Hold Dear

Beyond Summer Dreams

The Bracelet

Breaking Point

Chance Encounter

Code Red

Coming Home

The Emerald

High Stakes

Macady

Some Sweet Day

The Topaz

Wild Card

THE
RUBY

a novel by

Jennie Hansen

Covenant Communications, Inc.

Cover image *The Ruby* © Dave Malan

Cover design copyrighted 2008 by Covenant Communications, Inc.

Published by Covenant Communications, Inc.
American Fork, Utah

Printed in Canada
First Printing: October 2008

15 14 13 12 11 10 09 08   10 9 8 7 6 5 4 3 2 1

ISBN 10: 1-59811-661-4
ISBN 13: 978-1-59811-661-8

There are so many people to thank each time I write a new book: my husband, my family, my editor, my beloved "goosies," and all of the Covenant staff, but there are four people I wish to particularly mention this time. They are my "new" sisters: Pat Hansen, Theda Smith, Peggy Smith, and Jean Smith. I've learned from you and thank you for the joy you've brought my brothers.

PROLOGUE

Nauvoo, 1846

KRAFT RUNDELL SAT at his desk staring at two brilliant stones centered on its polished surface. He couldn't begin to estimate the value of the jewels: the most flawless diamond he'd ever seen, large enough to grace the crown of a monarch, and a perfectly cut Burmese ruby with the illusion of a star perfectly centered in it. Each jewel was worth far more than the wagon and supplies he'd given the Mormon woman in exchange for them. He subdued a twinge of conscience by reminding himself that he had offered far more before his financial situation had become dire. And he had allowed her to keep the sapphire and the emerald. Anyway, it was because of the Mormons that his business was in ruins and his wife had left him, taking their child with her.

He'd leave tomorrow morning to begin his journey to New York to exchange the gems for enough cash to launch his business anew. By the time he returned, the rest of the Mormons would be gone, and it would be safe for Claire and the baby to return.

He caressed each stone, putting off leaving his office for his empty house. Light from the lantern resting on one corner of the desk reflected off the jewels, the beauty of it giving Kraft an excuse to stay lost in his dreams a little longer.

1

Illinois, 1846

"CHARLOTTE MAE RIGGINS, git in the house this minute!"

"Yes'm, Granny." Charlie Mae gave a longing glance toward her brothers who were just disappearing over the split-rail fence behind the barn. *It ain't fair. Boys do their share of dirtyin' the house and eatin' vittles. They oughtta do some of the cleanin' and fetchin'.* She didn't dare say the words out loud. If Pa heard her, he'd whip her.

Mr. Sawyer had been by earlier, and he and Pa had sat out on the porch talking most of the morning. She heard them plain as day while she washed breakfast dishes, helped Granny dress, and swept the house. The boys had listened too, the older ones lounging around on the porch and the younger ones hiding behind the bushes that grew along one side of the house. She was about to set an extra plate for lunch when Mr. Sawyer said he would be moseying on. He had a few more folks he meant to talk to about plans for that night.

She ate her lunch standing up in the kitchen. Granny always ate her meals in the kitchen at the pine table, but Charlie Mae found it simpler to stand. That way she didn't have to keep jumping up and down when she had to fetch things for Pa and her brothers. She could hear them talking about Mr. Sawyer's visit. She pretended she wasn't interested each time she carried more biscuits and gravy into the front room where the big oak table sat, the one that Pa had hauled from Tennessee to Arkansas, then all the way from Arkansas to Illinois. He and her four brothers gathered around it, arguing and shouting uproariously as they ate. They ate so much, especially Irwin, so that at most meals there was scarcely anything left for Charlie Mae and Granny.

"There ain't enough salt in the gravy," Granny complained as Charlie Mae returned to the kitchen from one of her trips to the front room. She handed her grandma the salt shaker. It did no good to argue with Granny. She'd taught Charlie Mae how to cook and clean, and Charlie did it just the way Granny said, but it never satisfied the old lady. Charlie Mae was pretty sure Granny hadn't always been ornery and complaining. She had vague memories of Granny holding her in a big rocking chair and making humming sounds in her ear. Charlie Mae lifted a forkful of biscuit soaked in milk gravy toward her mouth.

"Charlie Mae, fetch another crock of buttermilk," Pa shouted. Charlie glanced at the food she was about to eat and set her fork back down. Best she get the buttermilk. Dawdling would bring her a switching at best.

She ran as fast as her thin, brown legs beneath her too-short dress could go to the cold cellar and returned, panting with the heavy crock clasped in her arms. Pa took it from her to pour himself a glass then set it on the table where Deke and Irwin both reached for it. They poked each other and wrestled over it for a few minutes. Deke won because he was the biggest. She waited for the scolding that always followed anytime she had to make a trip to the cellar during a meal. She never could run fast enough. The scolding didn't come, so after waiting a few minutes more, she crept back to the kitchen, figuring Pa was in a good mood because Mr. Sawyer said the last of the Mormons were finally moving on— with a little help from him and some of his friends. It seemed to Charlie Mae that all Mr. Sawyer ever talked about was how much he hated the Mormons. Pa was almost as bad.

She wasn't sure why Pa and Mr. Sawyer hated the Mormons. From what she'd seen of them, they were a hard-working lot. Their kids got to go to school too. Pa said they had dangerous ideas and were heretics, whatever that meant. He said they were trying to run the whole state and free the slaves. Deke said the Mormons had their own Bible too, though she couldn't see why any of that mattered. Deke couldn't read any more than Pa or her other brothers could, and they didn't own any slaves.

Her lunch was cold, and there was no way she could eat the congealed gravy. She scraped at it with her fork, then swallowed a few bites of her biscuit. Pa's hounds would be pleased to get the gravy; they never minded if it was cold and lumpy. She didn't have to worry about her greens; Granny had snitched those off her plate and eaten them while she was in the other room. She didn't care. Cold greens weren't any better than cold gravy. Someday, when she was grown up, she was going to fix a whole dinner just for her to eat while it was hot, and she wouldn't jump up to fetch anything for anyone.

Deke and Clyde, her oldest brothers, left with Pa, riding on three of Pa's four mules right after supper that night. She suspected they'd been drinking Pa's corn liquor, which meant they wouldn't be home before morning. They'd sleep past noon and wake up meaner than skunks. She sighed in resignation then set to work gathering up dishes. She carried them to the bench where the dish pan sat. She poured hot water from the teakettle over them and resisted the urge to stomp her foot. It didn't seem right that womenfolk always had to work while menfolk went places and got to sleep late.

Through an open window she could hear Irwin and Sander. They weren't happy either. They sounded mad as hornets because they got left behind. From where she stood washing dishes, she could hear them complaining.

"I can ride and shoot as well as Clyde, mebbe better," Irwin whined. "'Sides, last time Pa went, he came back with a silver dollar."

"We can still go," Sander suggested in a sly whisper. "I been sneakin' into that Mormon town to throw rocks at windows and swipe stuff most all summer. I know a shortcut. We could go watch the fun."

"If Pa catches us . . ."

"He ain't gonna catch us. By the time he and that bunch git finished with their business and celebratin', we'll be sound asleep in our beds."

"Do you think we'll get a chance to swipe any of them gold plates Old Man Sawyer said they claim to have?"

"Naw," Sander chuckled, "but you might git a few chickens or a new shirt. That one you're wearin's more holes than shirt."

Charlie Mae fumed as she listened to Irwin and Sander make their plans. She never got to go anywhere, and she never got anything new. Sometimes Pa let Sander go to the store with him, but he never took her, and Sander was only a couple years older than she was. She'd grown a lot since they'd left Arkansas, and her dresses were all so small she couldn't do them up anymore, so she had to wear Granny's dresses with a piece of rope around her middle to keep them from dragging on the ground. She suspected she was a little bit taller than her closest brother too. Sander didn't like that. Irwin was at least four inches taller than Sander, and Deke and Clyde were practically grown men. Deke had turned eighteen last spring and was now taller than Pa.

Charlie Mae brushed a strand of frizzy curls off her forehead. The combination of summer heat and the pan of hot dishwater made her straw-colored curls coil tighter and stick to her face and neck. She wished she were outside on the porch with her brothers instead of up to her elbows in dishwater in a hot kitchen. Better yet, she wished she could go with them through the cool woods and along the river to watch the fun in Nauvoo.

An idea began to form. Why shouldn't she go? Granny's rheumatism had been acting up all day, and she'd fixed her bedtime toddy with more of Pa's moonshine than usual. She'd be asleep by the time Charlie Mae finished the dishes, and once Granny fell asleep, there was no waking her until morning. She could follow Irwin and Sander. She'd be really quiet, and they'd never know.

Once the last plate was stacked in its place and the kitchen floor swept, Charlie Mae hurried outside to gather clothes from the line that stretched between two trees behind the house. She noticed that Irwin and Sander hadn't left yet, but they appeared to be fixing to leave right away.

Bringing in the wash gave her an idea. She slipped into Sander's clean shirt and overalls. A hat one of her brothers had left behind completed her disguise, though it took longer than she liked to stuff her snarled curls inside it where they couldn't be seen. She used her dress and the rest of the clothes she'd taken from the line to create a lump beneath her quilt in the corner behind the cookstove where she slept each night. She took the precaution in case Pa returned before she made her way back. Hopefully, it would appear she was sleeping beneath the ragged quilt.

She let herself out the back door and edged her way along the row of bushes until she could see the front porch. It was empty.

Cutting across the yard, she skirted the barn and headed for the river. She'd listened to her brothers enough to know which direction they meant to go. Following the path to the river was easy, but once she turned north, the trail wasn't so well-marked, and some places were nothing more than swampland.

Each rustle had her looking around fearfully. For as long as she could remember, she'd been nervous about going into the thick trees alone. Deke had warned her about bears in the woods, and she knew gators liked to hide in wait for their prey in swamps. She hadn't heard about any gators in Illinois, but she wasn't about to take the chance of stumbling onto one.

The snapping of brush a short distance ahead almost convinced her to turn back, but then she heard Irwin's voice and figured her brothers weren't far ahead. Knowing they were close by made the rest of her trek through the woods and along the river bank almost pleasant.

She liked the flexibility wearing Sander's britches gave her, and she'd been avoiding Pa's bursts of temper and severe punishments so long, she'd gotten good at moving quietly so that she didn't draw attention to herself. These two factors combined to aid her in silently moving a short distance behind Irwin and Sander, who were making no effort to be quiet or to conceal their movements. They talked and laughed as they moved swiftly toward town.

Charlie Mae knew little about towns other than that the houses were crowded close together and that there were stores where anyone who had enough coins could buy flour or other fixin's. They'd passed through a few towns on their way from Arkansas more than a year ago. They'd even passed right through the Mormon town of Nauvoo. It had seemed like a nice place with houses in neat rows and garden spots and fruit trees in the backyards. Several people had smiled and waved when she poked her head over the end of the wagon in order to see better, but Pa said Mormons were wicked people who needed to be taught a lesson. She wasn't sure what kind of lesson he and Mr. Sawyer meant to teach 'em.

Through the trees, she caught glimpses of the stark silhouettes of abandoned farms. She didn't know why the people had gone off and left perfectly good houses and land or why some of the houses and barns had been burned. Pa planned to farm the forty acres next to his corn patch next year. He said he had as much right to it as the Mormons that had been driven off. He told Deke, "'Sides, they ain't comin' back, and it wouldn't be right to let that land go to waste."

Irwin and Sander were slowing down, and their voices were getting softer. They were probably getting close to town and didn't want anyone to catch them spying at the goings-on Pa and Mr. Sawyer had planned. Charlie Mae didn't exactly know what those plans were, but from what she'd overheard earlier, it was bound to be exciting, and Deke said it was going to be fun. She moved forward slowly, keeping an eye out for her brothers. She didn't want them to catch her and send her back to the house. She didn't want Pa to whip her either.

Stepping off the narrow trail, she walked in the grass to muffle the sound of her steps. Through the trees, she caught sight of pinpricks of light. She figured the lights came from the town houses. Evidently Irwin and Sander thought the same thing because they weren't talking anymore. She was close enough to them now to detect two dark shapes moving stealthily up the trail. Keeping to the shadows, she followed.

Somewhere in the distance, a dog howled. Charlie Mae shivered. She hadn't figured on the Mormons having dogs. She was glad Pa had shut his hounds up in the barn before he left. If they'd been loose, they would have howled back and probably picked a fight, spoiling everything.

When her brothers reached the edge of town, they darted down a dark alley. Charlie Mae hesitated, uncertain whether to follow. At last she squared her thin shoulders and plunged into the dark space between two buildings. She inched her way with care until she reached the end of the alley, where it intersected with a wide street. No matter how hard she stared in either direction, she couldn't tell which way Irwin and Sander had gone. The street was unlit and the buildings were dark, leaving her wondering if she should retrace her steps to a stand of trees on the edge of town where she could watch for whatever was going to happen.

This might be her only chance to see the town, though. Even though the night was dark, with only a crescent moon and a few wispy stars, she didn't want to miss this opportunity. If she stayed on the side of the street where the shadows were the deepest, she could still explore a bit. With her back against the nearest building, she sidled along, feeling her way. The planks beneath her bare feet were still warm from the afternoon sun and worn so smooth there were hardly any splinters. She passed five or six buildings in this cautious fashion before noticing a sliver of light showing beneath a lowered blind of the building behind her.

Her heart beat faster with the realization that someone was awake. *What if it's a Mormon and he catches me?* Another alley opened at the side of the building, and she ducked into its welcoming blackness. She stood still, listening intently until her heart settled to its usual steady rhythm. No sound came from the building where she'd seen the light, but her ears did pick up the pounding of horses' hooves coming down the street she'd just left.

She shrank against the brick wall at her back. As the beat of hooves grew louder, she retreated from the street, hoping that this alley, too, ended near the stand of trees beside the river where she'd first entered town. Her toe struck something hard. She clapped her hands across her mouth to keep a scream from escaping. Once the pain ebbed to a steady throb, she reached out with her hands to discover what she had run into. It only took a moment to learn she'd careened into a barrel. Exploring with her hands, she discovered a second barrel and a door stoop.

The horses had reached the opening to the alley, and now she could hear riders on their backs, whooping and hollering. She could see the riders, too, by the light of their half a dozen or more flaming torches. The man leading the ragtag mob looked like Mr. Sawyer. Frightened, she crowded into the narrow space behind the barrels.

She could see now that there were more than a dozen dark-faced riders on the horses and mules that raced up and down the street. One rider drew his mount to a stop then hurled his torch toward the window where she'd seen a sliver of light. A whoosh of sound followed, and flames leaped skyward. She figured the torch had struck a kerosene lantern.

Her fear grew as she realized the building a few feet from where she crouched was on fire, and when the flames reached the back of the building, she would be in danger of being caught by the fire. The alley was narrow, and though the building she crouched beside was brick, the flames would reach her anyway if she stayed where she was. She started to rise, ready to risk being seen running toward the back of the alley and into the woods. Two large animals charged past her, startling her into remaining behind the barrels.

Charlie Mae noticed Pa and Deke sneaking away from the screaming, yelling mob, leaving Clyde behind. He started to follow, but the fire was jumping between buildings by the time he reached the alley where they'd disappeared. Charlie Mae watched him rein in the mule he rode and turn the animal's head and kick its side, urging it toward another alley farther down the block.

Brilliant light filled the alley, and Charlie Mae looked up to see the roof of the neighboring building covered in flames. Scrambling from her hiding place, she ran. When she reached the back of the buildings, she stopped. Seeing nothing of the men and horses that had dashed down the alley minutes earlier, she eased herself around the corner of the brick building. Spotting a stack of wooden crates, she crouched low and ran behind them.

From behind the crates, she looked back once more at the burning building. Flames leaped from the roof of the frame building to the roof of the brick building. Her hiding place wouldn't be secure for long. She'd have to make a run for the shadowy row of trees she could just see in the distance.

A shout had her twisting her neck to look back toward the burning building. A man stood framed in the rear doorway. Flames formed a vivid orange backdrop behind him as he clutched at the doorjamb with one hand and held his other hand in a raised, clenched fist.

A slight movement in her peripheral vision drew her attention to a man who stood with a raised rifle at his shoulder. Thunder boomed from the long rifle, and the man in the doorway crumpled face-first in the dirt. A triumphant shout rose above the crackling flames, and the rifleman, followed by another figure, darted toward the fallen man. The one toting the rifle stood by, while the second man kicked at the fallen man until he flopped over on his back. The kicker then knelt to search the dead man's pockets.

Charlie Mae knelt, frozen in terror. A terrible memory played at the edges of her mind. She'd seen someone else fall just that way long ago. Something white had fluttered briefly near the still form. Her mind would go no further.

A section of the nearby roof fell with a resounding crash. Flames leaped into the air, illuminating the scene as brightly as though the sun had suddenly risen. Charlie Mae watched, too stunned to run for her own safety. Pa, holding his deer rifle, stood over the man who had been shot. Deke knelt beside the body. Burning gorge rose in her throat, threatening to strangle her.

Pa killed that man like he was a deer or a squirrel. She'd seen enough game killed by her father and brothers to know what dead meant. *Was this why Pa and her brothers and Mr. Sawyer came to Nauvoo tonight?* She watched Deke search the man and had to stifle an urge to scream at him to leave the poor dead man alone. Her stomach hurt.

The ground rumbled as the building the dead man had left minutes earlier collapsed, raining sparks across the victim, Pa, and Deke. It reminded her that the fire was now raging inside the building just behind her too. She needed to leave her hiding place. But Pa might shoot her too if he caught her sneaking away. She'd always known Pa was mean, but now she knew he was even meaner than she'd believed him to be. Her brothers, except Sander and sometimes Irwin, were just like him. Sometimes Sander was nice to her. Irwin wasn't nice to her, but he wasn't mean either. Mostly he paid her no mind. She wondered where Irwin and Sander had gone and if they'd seen Pa kill the man. She didn't feel well, and she needed a drink of water. She hoped the flames would die down soon so she could sneak away in the darkness.

While she hesitated, Pa and Deke ran toward the mules she could now see were tethered to a post. The animals were snorting and kicking, making mounting them difficult. Once they were both astride the animals, Pa whooped and Deke echoed the cry. They both savagely kicked the animals' sides, urging them to a run. From across the fiery rubble she could see shadowy figures racing about on the other side of the flames and hear distant screaming and gunfire.

She stood and looked longingly toward the distant trees, then back at the still figure lying on the ground. Some force seemed to draw her toward the fallen man. She took a step toward him, then fearing she might be seen by the men on the other side of the fire, she dropped to her knees to crawl the rest of the way. When she reached him, she looked at him for a long time. He was neatly shaved and wore the finest clothes she'd ever seen. One hand, doubled into a fist, was tightly closed. The other lay open across the gaping wound in his chest.

"I'm sorry," she whispered. "Pa shouldn'ta done that."

A shower of sparks fluttered to the ground. She brushed several from the man's shoulders and felt the sharp sting of one striking her cheek. She stood, poised to run. Again she hesitated, feeling a great sadness and a strange sense that she had stood there before. She couldn't move the man, and she couldn't keep sparks from landing on him. Soon his clothes would catch fire, and he would burn.

A large piece of burning debris landed at her feet. She watched it sizzle brightly, then turn black. As she shifted her eyes from the black lump, she saw a large red coal lying next to the man's closed hand. Without thinking, she reached down to brush it aside.

Something registered dimly in her shocked brain. The coal should have been hot, but it wasn't. It was smooth and cool between her fingers, and it didn't fade to a charred, spent lump. She clutched the strange coal tightly in her small hand, then holding it close, she turned to run toward the trees as though Pa's hounds were nipping at her heels.

* * *

WHEN SHE REACHED the trees, she paused to look back, regretting leaving the dead man amid the flames. She saw someone ride toward the body. Just as a shower of sparks rained from the burning building onto the man sitting astride a mule beside the fallen figure, she recognized Clyde. She hoped he hadn't observed her hurried departure.

His attention seemed to be focused on the man on the ground. Kicking the mule's side, he urged him forward. The animal balked, stubbornly refusing to get closer to the burning inferno. Clyde dismounted. Taking time to tie the mule's reins to a post, he stood eyeing the flaming timbers tumbling around the body and then sprinted forward. Like Deke, he riffled through the man's pockets then stood as though disappointed.

Before regaining his feet, something drew his attention to the dead man's clenched hand. He stooped to pry the object from the man's lifeless fingers. Clyde stood for several minutes, still looking down at the object he'd taken. Something startled him, and he dashed toward the mule. After mounting in one wild leap, he kicked the animal's sides. He disappeared into the darkness, traveling fast in the opposite direction Pa and Deke had taken.

Charlie Mae ran. Heedless of her surroundings and oblivious to the sharp tree branches that slashed her face, she ran deeper into the trees.

2

CHARLIE MAE DROPPED to the ground in a dark thicket. The odor of rotting leaves and rich, dark dirt assailed her nose, but she paid it little attention. Vivid, confusing pictures flashed before her eyes like bursts of lightning. Something hovered at the edge of her mind—so terrible it tore at the center of her being. Deep, wracking sobs spilled from her throat, blending with the rush of the river. She cried for a long time. Then she slept.

The excited chatter of birds awakened her as the first gray light of morning filtered through the trees. She opened her eyes and found herself staring into eyes almost the same shade of green as her own. They belonged to a boy whom she assumed was a little younger than she was.

"Why are you sleeping here?" he asked. "Aren't you cold? And wet? Where's your mama? Are you lost?"

The questions came at her more quickly than she could absorb them. For just a moment, she wondered, too, what she was doing sleeping on the ground in a grove of trees. Then it all came back: the dead man, Pa with his rifle, Deke searching the man's pockets, blood everywhere, the strange images—the red coal that didn't burn her hand.

Her hands fluttered to her pockets until she found the hard lump lodged in a deep pocket of the overalls she'd borrowed from Sander.

"What are you looking for? Do you need a handkerchief? Is that blood on your hand? Does it hurt?" She wished the boy wouldn't ask so many questions. She couldn't think what to say, and she needed to get home before she was missed. The sun was up, so she was probably already in trouble.

She attempted to sit up, but she felt wobbly and dizzy. Her hand went to her head, and she had trouble focusing. When she was finally able to see through her swollen eyes, she found that the boy, in addition to green eyes, sported a thatch of pale red hair and the most freckles she had ever seen. He wore faded, patched pants and a plaid shirt. Both were too short for his slender limbs. A leather belt, many times too large, was cinched around his waist with one end dangling nearly a foot from the buckle. His feet were as bare as her own.

Running her fingers through her mop of tangled, frizzy curls, she was vaguely aware she'd lost her hat. Taking hold of a sapling to steady herself, she dragged herself upright. She knew she needed to hurry, but her head hurt terribly, and she didn't know which way to go. The path had disappeared, and she couldn't hear the river. Turning from side to side, searching for a clue that might tell her where to go, she felt panic rise like bile in her throat.

A small hand took one of hers. "Don't be scared," the boy said. "I'll take care of you." His hand tugged at hers, indicating she should follow him. Not knowing what else to do, she let him lead her through the woods.

Pa would whip her for sure. The scars on her back weren't completely healed from the last time he'd struck her with the buggy whip.

"There it is." The boy pointed to the smallest house she'd ever seen. "That's where I live. Grandma will fix your hand and help you find your mama. I don't have a mama. She went away to heaven. There's just Grandma and me, and we don't have enough money to buy a wagon and flour. Did your mama go to heaven?" He began walking faster toward a shack made of mismatched boards. A goat grazed in the yard, and several chickens scratched in the dirt. A curl of smoke rose from a crooked chimney, and a tiny, doll-like figure stood in the doorway. She could tell the person was old because her skin was wrinkled like Granny's and her hair was white, but she was no bigger than Charlie Mae.

"That's Grandma," the boy said.

"Who is this, Spencer?" The woman smiled at Charlie Mae. No one had ever smiled at her like that before. It made the woman's wrinkled, papery skin look young and pretty. And it made Charlie Mae feel welcome and safe.

"I don't know her name," the boy said to the woman. "She doesn't talk."

"Goodness! Where did you find her?" The woman took an unsteady step toward Charlie Mae, holding out her arms in a welcoming gesture. It seemed the most natural thing in the world to step forward to meet the woman. As the old woman's arms folded around her, Charlie Mae had one more flash of memory—of being held against someone soft and warm who smelled like summer.

"Can you tell me your name, dear?" the woman asked after a moment, holding her at arm's length.

Tears came to Charlie Mae's eyes, and there was a big lump in her throat. She shook her head.

"That's all right; you can tell us later." The woman drew her close again, giving her another gentle hug.

Without being exactly sure how it happened, Charlie Mae found herself inside the little house with the woman clucking over her scratched arm and counting the burn marks in her shirt. Sander was going to be mad when he saw his shirt.

It seemed strange to look into the face of an adult without kinking her neck to look up. The little woman sent the boy, Spencer, to fetch a tub. Then she poured a kettle of hot water into the tub and added almost a whole bucket of cold water. When she was satisfied with the water temperature, she sent Spencer to fetch more water and to search for eggs while she helped Charlie Mae divest herself of her clothes and urged her into the tub.

It never occurred to Charlie Mae to protest the woman's actions, and there was something soothing about sitting in a tub of warm water. Spencer's grandma knelt beside the tub to give her a gentle scrubbing. She even washed her hair without getting any of the suds in Charlie Mae's eyes. When she finished, she wrapped the child's shivering body in a big piece of flannel to dry her, then produced the loveliest clothes Charlie Mae had ever seen. There were white lawn drawers, a lacy camisole, a frilly petticoat, and a white gown that swished when Charlie Mae moved.

The lady seated Charlie Mae on a low stool before the fire and began to brush her hair. Sometimes the brush caught in the tangles, and it took considerable patience to work the snarls free. After awhile, the snarls were gone, but the lady continued brushing Charlie Mae's hair so that it curled around her bent, gnarled fingers, then fell in long, springy curls over her shoulders.

She learned the woman's name was Sister Pascal. While Sister Pascal worked, she talked or hummed. Charlie Mae had never heard the songs before, but she liked the way they sounded.

Spencer came back into the house carrying a basket with a few eggs. He set them down and tilted his head to one side while he studied Charlie Mae.

"I reckon you're right pretty," he pronounced. His blunt appraisal made her feel strange. Nobody had ever said she was pretty before. He turned to his grandma. "She's wearing your baptism dress. Is she going to be baptized?"

Charlie Mae didn't know what *baptism* meant, but she figured the dress was good enough to be an angel's dress. Granny sometimes talked about Ma becoming one of the "blessed angels" in heaven. Charlie Mae didn't blame Ma for leaving, and she scarcely remembered her, since she'd only been four when her mother went away, but sometimes she wished Ma had taken her with her.

"Breakfast is ready," Sister Pascal told her. "Sit yourself down right here on this chair." She pointed to a straight-backed chair, one of a half dozen gathered around a matching table. Spencer was already seated across from the chair his grandma indicated.

Charlie Mae didn't know what to do. She was awfully hungry, but she needed to find her way back to the house where Granny, Pa, and her brothers would be waiting for her to fix their breakfast. She was already in big trouble and bound to get a whipping, but if she hurried, she might make it before Pa woke up if he'd been drinking with Mr. Sawyer last night—and if Sander and Irwin didn't tattle on her.

She opened her mouth to protest, but nothing came out. The harder she tried to talk, to explain, the tighter her throat became. Tears filled her eyes. What if she couldn't ever talk again? She shouldn't have followed Irwin and Sander. She wished she hadn't seen Pa shoot that man. She'd been bad and was almost burned. Now she couldn't talk.

"Sit down, dear." Sister Pascal urged her toward the chair. Charlie Mae sat on the edge of it. Through watery eyes, she saw a small mound of scrambled eggs and a biscuit. She nibbled at the eggs and noticed that Spencer had already eaten his breakfast. It wasn't much breakfast for a boy. No wonder he was so little.

"Here," she tried to say as she scooted her plate toward him. Again no sound came out. She leaped to her feet and ran toward the door, flinging it open.

"Don't go," Spencer called. He left the table to run after her. He caught her hand as she was stumbling through the door.

"We want to help you." Sister Pascal was beside them now. "We'll figure something out. I know . . ." she picked up a stick that had been lying near the step. She handed it to Charlie Mae. "Can you write your name?"

Charlie Mae shook her head. She didn't know anything about writing. Granny could write her name. Charlie Mae wanted Granny to teach her how to write her own name, but Granny didn't know all the letters. She had a big, old Bible that had been her pa's, but she didn't know any of the words in it.

"Oh, dear, I wish you could tell me where you live so we'd be able to help you find your way." Spencer's grandma looked concerned.

Charlie Mae didn't know how to write words, but she sometimes drew pictures in the sand down by the river. They weren't very good pictures, but maybe she could draw the river and the Pascals would show her the way to it. She began making lines in the dirt. From the puzzled look on Spencer's face, she could tell he didn't know they represented a river, so she made a few more lines, forming a crude paddleboat.

"Is that your house?" Spencer asked. She shook her head.

"I think it's a boat on the river," his grandma said slowly, uncertain of the guess she had ventured.

Charlie started to nod her head, but Spencer demanded to know if she'd fallen off a boat, leaving her unsure whether to nod or shake her head.

"If this is the river," the old lady said, taking the stick from Charlie's hand, "this is where we are." She touched a spot a short distance from the river Charlie Mae had sketched in the dirt. She drew a little box. "Nauvoo is the closest town. Did you come from Nauvoo, dear?" She touched a spot on the dirt map.

Well, at least she was on the right side of Nauvoo, and if she walked due west, she'd reach the river. Still unable to speak, she patted the woman's hand and pointed, trying to convey the message that she appreciated her help and that she'd be going toward the river now. She stood and prepared to begin walking. She'd only taken a few steps when she remembered Sander's clothes. She hurried back to the small house and gathered up the clothes that lay neatly folded on a stool near the fireplace. She rolled them into a tight bundle, feeling the lump of strange coal through the stiff fabric.

She stepped quickly past the Pascals. Leaving the clearing, she turned to wave to the kind old lady and found Spencer running toward her. "Grandma said I could walk with you as far as the river," he said. "She wanted to come too, but she can't walk very well."

Charlie Mae really didn't mind Spencer's company. He talked an awful lot, but he was much nicer than her brothers. Sometimes it got awfully lonesome being the only girl in the family. Granny was a girl, but she didn't talk to Charlie Mae much, except to tell her to do chores. She'd been nicer when they lived in Arkansas. Granny hadn't wanted to come to Illinois, but Pa had made her come.

The sun hadn't been up long, and the morning still had that bright, new feel that seemed full of promise. She could smell the river before she actually saw it. Rounding a bend in the path, she caught her first glimpse of the mighty river that spread so far she could scarcely see the opposite shore. It would take considerable walking to reach the path she'd followed the night before on her way to Nauvoo. During the scary, dark night, she'd strayed a long way from the path in her flight. She began to walk faster.

"Will your ma be worried about you?" Spencer panted, trying to keep up with her longer steps.

Charlie Mae shook her head without trying to explain.

The grass and trees along the overgrown trail were damp with dew, and patches of fog hung over the river. They came upon a swampy area Charlie Mae recognized. If she turned left, she could skirt the bog and enter the path just a short distance from Pa's farm. She turned to bid Spencer farewell.

With Charlie Mae's few gestures, the boy seemed to understand. He looked at her sadly, and she understood that he was as lonely as she was. Someday, if Pa didn't beat her too hard, she'd come back.

The sun was bearing down, turning the day hot, when she hurried up the path leading from the river to the house. All looked peaceful. She could see the mules grazing in the pasture behind the barn and chickens scratching near the hen house. Pa's hounds lay sleeping on the front porch. Old Peach lifted her head but didn't bay a greeting. Instead, she lowered her head and went back to dozing. There was no sign of her brothers or of Pa.

She ran across the clearing and eased open the backdoor, wincing as it squeaked in its usual fashion. Granny looked up from her chair beside the table. She opened her mouth, but minutes passed before she spoke. Charlie Mae waited for the scolding she knew would be coming.

"Be you dead?" Granny asked, her hand fluttering to her chest.

Charlie Mae remembered the white dress she wore and shook her head. She wanted to explain, but she knew it was impossible. She went to her pallet behind the cook stove, where she removed the white dress and slipped her own frayed and patched dress over her head. She rolled the pants and shirt she'd borrowed from Sander into a tight bundle and stuffed them beneath her quilt. She'd wash and mend them later.

Picking up the dress and petticoat, she held them for a moment, wondering at their softness. They were the prettiest clothes she'd ever worn. She supposed she should wash them too and then take them back to Sister Pascal when she could sneak away without Pa knowing.

Thinking of Pa brought a tremble to her limbs, and she found herself in need of sitting for a spell. Sinking down on a low stool beside the stove, she held her head between her hands. She was surprised to feel the touch of a hand on her head a moment later.

"You ain't a ghost, I reckon, but I thought for sure you was an angel," Granny said. "I been 'spectin' an angel to come for me most any day, and I thought you was your angel ma come to take me home. Where'd you git that purty angel dress? And how'd you git your hair all soft and shiny with curls what look like sausages?"

Charlie Mae lifted her head, pointing to her mouth, then shook her head. It took awhile, but finally Granny understood that she couldn't speak. Granny insisted on checking Charlie Mae's throat then ordered her to bed. The old woman bustled around the kitchen, preparing a potion that burned all the way to Charlie Mae's stomach when she swallowed it.

She didn't mean to fall asleep, but when she awoke it was to the sound of voices coming from the next room. Pa was shouting. She cringed beneath the quilt, never doubting that Pa's anger was directed at her.

"You both oughtta be whipped for what ya done!" Pa bellowed. "When I find . . ."

"What do you suppose he took?" Deke asked. "I searched those pockets good, an' I gave ya the few coins I found."

"Did ya check to see if he had a watch? I bet he took the fella's watch," Irwin said.

"He won't git far on what he'll git fer a pocket watch." Deke sneered.

"Sometimes rich folks' watches are made outta gold and 'stead of numbers, they has diamonds where the numbers orta be. Sometimes they's even got jewels on the outside of the watch." The sound of Pa's fist striking bare flesh and Deke's yelp of pain accompanied Pa's scornful words to his oldest son.

"Where do you think he went?" Irwin asked.

"You should've watched to see which way he went." Charlie Mae heard another loud smack and figured Pa had thumped Irwin.

"What about that kid? The one Sander and Irwin saw afore they hightailed it back here?" Deke spoke again.

Charlie Mae felt faint. She hadn't figured she might have been seen.

"He was just a little kid. Probably heard the noise and sneaked out to see what was going on. It didn't appear he even touched the body on the ground," Sander said.

"What else did ya see?" Deke taunted.

"Gimme back my vittles," Irwin whined. Charlie Mae surmised Deke had taken his brother's plate and was holding it out of the boy's reach to torment him into telling what he knew.

"We weren't close enough to get a good look, hidin' in the trees like we was, but it 'peared he crawled from the other building what was burning, took a good look, then stood up an' ran like he was skeered. We figgered he was just one of those Mormon brats. I was gonna foller him, mebbe throw a few rocks to make him run faster, then we saw Clyde come sneaking outta the other alley farther down the street, leading old Bertha. He stopped by the body like he knew it was there. He searched the dead man's pockets just like Deke did, and he reached down and pulled on one of the Mormon's hands. We figgered he found somethin 'cause he tucked it in his pocket afore he jumped on Bertha and lit out, headin' north." Irwin's voice was sullen, but he doggedly shared all he knew. There was a clattering sound Charlie Mae figured was Deke setting Irwin's plate back on the table.

Charlie Mae's prospects brightened. Clyde was in bigger trouble than she was. Seemed she hadn't been missed like he had been. Her whole body shook when she thought about Sander and Irwin seeing her in Nauvoo. It was no surprise that Irwin hadn't recognized her. He was never really quick to figure things out, but she couldn't believe Sander hadn't recognized her.

"Better git outta that bed and get some vittles on the table. It's almost noon," Granny warned her.

Charlie Mae scrambled to her feet and set to work at once. While assembling the ingredients for biscuits, she asked, "What about breakfast? What did you tell Pa?" The sound of her own voice caught her up short. She could talk, even if it was only a hoarse whisper.

Granny's smile was sly. "He didn't git up 'til a few minutes ago, and his head hurt so bad, all he wanted was some o' my special recipe. He and Deke didn't git home 'til almost sunup."

"And the boys; didn't they come lookin' for breakfast?"

"They slept kinda late then was real quiet so as not to wake their pa and Deke. 'Course, first thing they done when your Pa woke up yellin' 'bout not bein' able to find Clyde afore they rode home last night was to tell him they saw Clyde run off."

Charlie Mae figured Clyde was smarter than Pa had ever figured him to be, and she silently wished him luck. She suspected he'd lucked onto finding some money, a gold watch, or a ring Deke had missed. If she were seventeen like Clyde, she'd run off and never come back. Someday, when she was grown, she'd run away too. She'd go some place where she could sit down to eat her dinner, wear pretty clothes like Sister Pascal's baptism dress, and no one would ever hit her again. Her shoulders sagged; she didn't figure she'd ever be brave enough to try to leave.

Granny's smug look convinced Charlie Mae that Granny wasn't any too fond of Pa, even if he was her own kin. That's probably why she hadn't raised an alarm when she discovered Charlie Mae wasn't in her bed.

Pa didn't notice her voice was kind of scratchy. He didn't expect her to say anything anyway. And in a few days, she awoke with her throat feeling much better and discovered she could manage more than a whisper. A few days later, her voice was back to normal. She never told Granny what she had seen in Nauvoo nor about Spencer and his grandma. Granny didn't ask either, but while Charlie Mae worked, she sometimes found herself humming the song she'd heard Sister Pascal sing. When that happened, Granny would get that sly look on her face and tell Charlie Mae she best forget singing and just do her work. Some nights she dreamed about the dead man, but he had on a calico dress and a white petticoat. Then she'd awake shivering in the dark.

Things were different with Granny after that, though Charlie Mae never understood why the old woman changed. She helped Charlie Mae more with the household chores, and sometimes she talked to her about her ma and spoke in whispers about "woman things."

Irwin was spending more time with Pa now that Clyde was gone, and Irwin was growing more surly and difficult. Deke went off on his own sometimes. Granny said Deke was courting the Sawyer girl. Sander was different too. He spent most of each day by himself, fishing or hoeing the garden. Sometimes he fingered the tiny holes in his shirt and watched Charlie Mae with an odd look in his eyes. That look made her heart beat faster, and she suspected he knew more than he was letting on about the night Clyde rode away and she had found the strange red stone she kept hidden behind a loose brick in the fireplace. Something told her that look was a warning that he was just biding his time. Sander was too smart to tell on her if there wasn't anything in it for him.

Sometimes she took out the strange stone and just looked at it when she was alone. Oddly, she felt a kind of peace when she held the stone. It almost seemed to be a kind of assurance that she wasn't alone, that somewhere, someone watched over her.

3

THERE WAS ALWAYS work to do on the Riggins farm, but as summer drew to a close, there came a day when Pa set Charlie Mae and her brothers to picking apples while he rode off to town on one of the mules. As soon as he left, Deke borrowed another mule and headed for Sissy Sawyer's home with Irwin riding behind him, his long legs hanging below the work animal's belly.

Sander and Charlie Mae picked apples for awhile, filling two large baskets, which they hauled to the cellar.

"I ain't pickin' no more apples," Sander announced as they set the heavy baskets down in the cool cellar. He stomped up the steps and headed for the barn. Charlie Mae trailed behind him, watching him gather up his fishing rod. She knew he'd return with a string of fish for her to fry for supper. He always caught enough for supper when he fished, and when she had fresh fish to fry, fixin' supper took no time at all. She wandered back to the small grove of apple trees, set her basket down, and began to pick the bright red fruit, feeling resentful. It wasn't fair that she had to pick apples while everyone else sneaked off. Her fingers grew slower and slower as an idea came to her.

She couldn't lift the heavy basket by herself, and since her brothers had all taken the day off, she would too. She finished filling the basket before returning to the house. Just as she expected, Granny was asleep in her chair.

Taking the white dress and petticoats she'd carefully washed weeks earlier from their hiding place in the back of a cupboard, she secured them in a bundle which she strapped to her back. Soon she was on her way toward the path that led to the river. She passed the cellar and detoured to fill her pockets with apples. Keeping an eye open for Sander, she stepped onto the faint trail that led to Nauvoo.

The distance seemed far shorter than it had the morning she'd hurried in the opposite direction. When she reached the swampy place, she started up the hill. Reaching the clearing where the small house sat, she called, "Hello! Spencer! Sister Pascal!"

Spencer's face appeared at the house's one small window, and he began to whoop and holler. "Grandma! It's the girl. She came back." He ran from the door with the elderly woman hobbling after him, clutching a heavy club she used for a cane.

"I brought your dress back," Charlie Mae said as she went to meet the woman. Sister Pascal put her arms around Charlie Mae and gave her a hug. Charlie Mae didn't know how to react. Demonstrations of affection were completely foreign to her.

"Dear child, I am so glad to see you are safe and well."

"She can talk!" Spencer shouted with a happy grin.

She turned to him, responding to his smile with one of her own. "My throat hurt for a few days, then it was good as new. I can talk fine now."

"Do you live near here?" Sister Pascal asked.

"Down river, near the big bend. We been there more'n a year now. Pa bought the farm from Mr. Sawyer."

"That used to be George Anderson's farm." The elderly lady looked sad for a moment. "Well, never mind. That's all in the past. Come in the house. I was reading a story to Spencer, and he was practicing his letters."

"Would you like an apple?" Charlie Mae asked Spencer as they made their way to the house.

"Oh, yes," he answered eagerly. She handed one of the red beauties to him then offered one to his grandma.

"I'll save mine for later." She smiled as she accepted the fruit.

"We've got lots of apples," Charlie Mae told her. She unloaded her pockets and lined up six apples on the table.

"I helped Lottie Anderson plant those trees from seedlings when we first came to Illinois," Sister Pascal said, dabbing at her eyes with a handkerchief. "I miss that dear woman."

"Why did she go away?" Charlie Mae asked. Grandma looked hesitant, but Spencer felt no qualms about answering her question.

"Some bad people came to their farm in the middle of the night. They tarred and feathered Brother Anderson and shot their cow. They said they'd burn down their house and shoot them if they came back. The Andersons went to Nauvoo where they bought a big wagon so they could go to the far mountains with Brother Brigham."

Cold shivers ran down Charlie Mae's back. Something about Spencer's story rang warning bells in the back of her mind. It reminded her of the night she'd followed Irwin and Sander to Nauvoo.

"Sit here beside me, one on each side," Sister Pascal encouraged the children. "I think you'll like this story." She began to read from a well-used volume of children's stories.

Charlie Mae was entranced. She didn't remember ever being read to before, but there was something strangely familiar about it. She already knew some people could read and write marks on paper, but she hadn't suspected it could be so thrilling to hear someone read the marks, turning them into words.

When the story was finished, Sister Pascal asked Spencer to show her how well he could write his name. Charlie Mae couldn't believe how nice the letters looked. And Spencer was younger than her. After he erased his name, he handed the slate to her.

"I never learned no letters," she mumbled, feeling embarrassed.

"I'll show you." Sister Pascal took the slate from her hand. "You haven't told us your name," she prompted.

"My whole name is Charlotte Mae Riggins, but most folks call me Charlie Mae." She looked down at her dusty toes peeking from beneath her hem.

"We'll start with C." The elderly lady drew a large C, then she handed the stylus to Charlie Mae, who laboriously copied the letter.

"That's a really good C," Spencer pronounced approvingly.

Charlie Mae proved an apt pupil, and before she reluctantly began her return journey, she had mastered all of the letters in her name. It was with reluctance that she set down the slate. The sun was far to the west, and she'd be in trouble if Pa's supper was late.

As he had before, Spencer walked with her as far as the low-lying, swampy area beside the river. He didn't do all of the talking this time, and Charlie Mae found it rewarding to find someone who wanted to listen to her. They paused on a hill overlooking the marsh and the river beyond. As they stood awkwardly saying their good-byes, from farther up the river came several deep booms. The children paused to listen but were unable to identify the source of the sound.

"I better get back to Grandma," Spencer said, digging his toe into the soft dirt and glancing over his shoulder in the direction of the sound. "If she heard those booms, she'll be worrying about me."

Charlie Mae nodded, feeling a strange reluctance to return to the farm. That afternoon at Spencer's small house had been about the best time in her whole life.

"Will you come again?" She could tell Spencer was reluctant to end their time together as well. She nodded her head. Somehow she'd find a way to visit him and Grandma Pascal again.

She had almost reached the place where the path entered the clearing behind the Riggins' house when she heard whistling, and Sander stepped from the bushes to walk beside her, carrying a string with two catfish. He didn't say anything to her, though he looked like he might. She kept walking.

For the next week all Pa talked about was "lickin' them Mormons." Deke and Irwin had ended up going along with what Irwin called "the army." Pa did a lot of strutting and crowing, but from the bits and pieces she heard, it sounded like he and her brothers had joined up with a bunch of hooligans who had got their hands on a cannon. They'd attacked Nauvoo again and scared a lot of women and children. Deke boasted of beating up some farmers outside of town who were harvesting a field of grain. Irwin mostly seemed proud of the fact he'd swiped a pie off some Mormon woman's window ledge. Sander didn't say anything, but Charlie Mae didn't think he regretted that he hadn't been included in the foray.

In the coming weeks, she found several opportunities to make the long trek to the Pascal house. A magic world opened up to her as she learned the shapes of the various letters and that each had its own peculiar sound, running together to make words. She was so excited by the lessons she received there that she gave little thought to the way Sander always appeared along the path to walk with her the last short distance from the river to their house. She was simply grateful that his presence kept everyone else from questioning her absence.

* * *

ONE MORNING A cold wind blew in from the north, making Charlie Mae aware that few leaves remained on the trees and winter was coming. With the coming of winter, it became harder to slip away unnoticed, but she visited the Pascals as often as she could and was pleased when each visit included another reading lesson. The hike from the Pascal house to the path was one of her favorite parts of the visit because it was a time when she and Spencer could laugh and share confidences. She quickly noticed that Sister Pascal and Spencer didn't talk the same way she did, and she began a conscious effort to speak the way they did.

As she prepared to slip away from the farm one blustery, cold November day, she figured this would likely be her last visit to her friends, the Pascals, until summer came again. Spring always brought additional labor and chores, making a few hours' escape impossible. She usually took some small gift of apples or fresh rolls on her trips to the little house, but this day she was in a hurry and only took time to remove her red stone from its hiding place. She wanted Spencer to see the coal that looked fiery hot but didn't burn or blister her fingers.

She walked with rapid steps along the path to the river and slipped into the woods before she reached the trail. She was careful not to walk in the same place each time she turned onto the faint path. She didn't wish to make a trail that might ignite any of her brothers' curiosity should they wander that way. Drawing an old shawl that had been her mother's tighter about her shoulders, she moved with rapid steps, anxious to get inside the little house and out of the wind. She thought longingly of the small room with its brightly colored curtains and pretty tablecloth, chairs gathered closely around the table, and a multicolored, braided rug on the floor. She wished her own kitchen was as pretty and welcoming. A sound brought her to a stop. She whirled around, searching the trees and shrubs for anything out of place. All was still.

Just some woodland animal, maybe a possum or a crow, she attempted to reassure herself, but she couldn't shake the feeling that something much bigger was following her.

When she reached the little house that lay almost hidden in a deep copse of trees, she found everything in turmoil. A horse and mule were tied to a tree beside the door, and Spencer was dragging a heavy sack toward them. Several other bundles were tied to the pack frame on the mule's back. A big man walked out of the house. Beside him was Sister Pascal, hobbling along with the help of her walking stick. She stopped frequently to sniff and to wipe her eyes.

Spencer saw her first. "Charlie Mae!" he shouted. He released the bag he was dragging and ran toward her. He grasped her hand. "Charlie Mae, I thought I wouldn't get to say good-bye to you." There were tears in his eyes.

"You're going away?" Charlie Mae felt bereft. The future dimmed as she contemplated never seeing her friends again.

"Brother Anderson came to get us. He says Brother Brigham sent him and some other folks to get the old and poor Saints out of Nauvoo before the mob kills us all."

"But you don't live in Nauvoo."

"We didn't move to Nauvoo because we thought we were safe in Grandma's house hidden in the woods—and Nauvoo was too great a distance for her to walk. But with the Andersons and Bishop Partridge gone, there's no one to help us anymore. It isn't safe for anyone to bring us food, and Brother Anderson said we will starve or the mobs will find us if we stay, so we must go."

"I won't ever see you again, will I?" She stood as though rooted to the ground with bits of ice crystals blowing across the clearing and lifting her tangled curls free of the tears streaming down her face. The years ahead stretched bleak and lonely before her.

Spencer wrapped his arms around her. Tears wet his cheeks too. "When I'm grown up, I'll come back for you," he promised. "I won't ever stop being your friend."

She felt a hand brush her hair. Sister Pascal's thin, blue lips touched Charlie Mae's forehead. "We shall miss you, Charlotte Mae. Your visits have brightened our days, and the gifts you brought may have saved our lives." Charlie Mae blinked in astonishment. How could a few apples and biscuits save anybody's life?

"They're coming! You better git!" A figure dashed into the clearing, waving his arms. Recognizing her brother Sander, Charlie Mae's mouth gaped open.

Brother Anderson scooped up Sister Pascal, as though she were a child, and set her on his horse. Before Spencer could follow them, Charlie Mae fumbled in her apron pocket for the red stone. Gripping it tightly, she thrust it into Spencer's hand. "Take this and don't ever forget me."

"I won't forget," the rusty-haired boy vowed, dropping the red stone into his pocket just before the man picked him up. He tossed Spencer on top of the load lashed to the pack mule's back, then stepped into his horse's stirrup. He swung up behind the elderly woman, who sat straight and tall in his saddle, blinking back tears.

"Hang on tight." He turned his head to offer instructions to Spencer, who sat amid the bundles on the mule's back, then glanced back toward Sander, giving him a curt nod. "Thanks, boy," he said in a grim voice before digging his boot heels into his horse's sides.

With both hands gripping the rope lashing, Spencer sent Charlie Mae one last smile before the mule loped out of sight, trailing Brother Anderson's horse.

Charlie Mae couldn't move. She couldn't even send Spencer one last wave of her hand before he was gone.

"Come on." Sander gripped her arm, dragging her toward the trees. "They mustn't catch you here."

Listlessly, she let him pull her behind him. Branches tore at her hair, and dry leaves crackled beneath her feet. Sometimes Sander ran and sometimes he slunk through the trees as though playing at being an Indian. Mindlessly, she followed.

"Git down!" He hissed a sudden command while shoving her toward the ground. She scraped the palms of her hands as she fell. She lay sprawled in the dirt and debris, gasping for breath. A sense of reality began to intrude on her numb senses.

"Sander—"

"Shh," he whispered. She was about to protest when she heard a sound she'd heard once before and had hoped to never hear again. Horses' hooves were pounding their way closer, accompanied by the whooping and shouting of drunken men. It was that summer night all over again. She cringed lower into the dead grass and bushes not far from where she'd lain that awful night. Her hands and feet grew cold.

Sander left her side to creep toward a pile of brush and stones. Suddenly afraid, she followed him. He frowned when she knelt beside him, but he didn't send her back. From their position behind the pile of rubble, they had a clear view of the trail she'd followed a short time earlier while happily anticipating a few stolen hours with Spencer and his grandma.

A horse raced into view, followed by a familiar mule. She recognized Mr. Sawyer and Pa. A few other horses and mules clattered up the path, then came Deke and Irwin riding double on one of Pa's mules. With dread filling her heart, she watched them until they were out of sight.

She knew by the shouting and cursing up ahead that Pa and his friends had reached the Pascals' little house and had found it empty. After a little bit, a wisp of smoke drifted toward the leaden sky. She listened for gunshots. Not hearing any, she hoped that meant Spencer and Sister Pascal were still safe and getting farther away.

As she knelt watching the smoke turn blacker and thicker, a new wave of sadness filled her heart, and all of the things she should have seen before began to fall into place. She should have guessed the Pascals were Mormons. And she should have guessed Pa had lied about the people he said were wicked. Pa was the wicked one, the one who lied and burned houses and shot people. Mr. Sawyer was wicked too. She knew now why Sister Pascal's friends had left their farm. She wondered if Pa knew Mr. Sawyer didn't own the farm he'd sold to him. Pa and his friends were thieves and liars. She didn't want to live with thieves and liars and cook their dinners anymore.

"We'll have to run for it." Sander pulled Charlie Mae to her feet. "When they don't find any Mormons, they'll be mad. We best be back at the house doin' our chores when Pa gits there."

He was right. It would be dangerous to hang around the Pascals' house. This time Sander didn't have to drag her. She matched his running strides step for step.

Before they reached the house, Sander caught at her arm, bringing her to a stop beside him. "You can't ever tell anyone you been visitin' Mormons," he warned. She felt a wave of relief. If he was cautioning her against telling, it wasn't likely he meant to tell either.

"How did you know?" she mumbled with her head down. "They was good to me. Honest, I didn't know they was Mormons 'til today."

"I seen ya come home one mornin' in a white dress an' then I found holes in my shirt like I'd got too close to a fire. I figured that boy Irwin and me seen the night Pa shot that trader in Nauvoo was you, so I fallered ya when you took the dress back. I ain't like Pa, hatin' folks just 'cause they're different. I could see that old lady and the little boy weren't a danger to nobody, and she started in teachin' you letters. I allus wanted to learn to read, but Pa's dead set aginst book learnin'. He hated that Ma could read. And, well, I figgered if I let you be when you got a chance to learn, you'd teach me." There was something hopeful in Sander's voice.

"I didn't learn enough, but I'll tell ya everything Sister Pascal taught me," Charlie Mae promised.

"I already know a little bit 'cause sometimes I listened under the window." There was pride in Sander's voice.

"Them Mormons ain't bad like Pa said." She felt a need to stand up for Spencer and his grandma.

"I know, but don't never say nothin' good 'bout the Mormons to Pa. Irwin tole me that just before Ma took off, a couple of them Mormons come around to our house in Arkansas. They left a book with Ma, and Pa gave her a thrashin' when he found her readin' it."

"Sander, what about the Pascals' chickens? They didn't have time to catch 'em and take 'em along. It would be a shame for the foxes to git 'em."

"I 'spect Irwin will be bringin' a couple of 'em home fer you to fry up for supper." There was a tinge of bitterness in Sander's voice.

4 ❧

Spring 1848

IT WAS THE day Granny was buried that Sander caught up to Charlie Mae as she walked along the dusty road that led to the house, walking with her for a mile before he spoke.

"I'm leaving," he blurted without preamble. She'd been expecting to wake up one morning and find him gone for almost a year now, ever since Deke married Sissy Sawyer and took over a farm two miles away that had been abandoned by the Mormons. Sander had finally got his growth and now towered a good foot over his sister. He leaned toward her, bringing his mouth closer to her ear.

"I tried. I tried real hard to stick it out until you reached sixteen and could find a husband to look after you, but I can't wait any longer."

She shivered in spite of the warm March day. She didn't fancy finding a husband to take care of her. She wasn't impressed by the way the few men she knew took care of their women. She supposed she'd have to marry someday, but it wasn't something she looked forward to. She didn't want to live in Pa's house one day longer than necessary either, so she figured that if she got a chance to get married, she'd have to take it.

Charlie Mae knew that with Deke and Clyde both gone, the bulk of the farmwork now fell to Irwin and Sander. Irwin didn't seem to mind as long as Pa left him a jug and he had plenty to eat.

He'd changed over the years from the youth eager to please Pa and be included in his and Deke's activities. Now he seldom spoke to anyone other than Sander, and he'd become something of a loner. He did whatever work was asked of him, then disappeared into the woods. He started each day with slow sips from the jug Pa gave him once a week, and by the time supper was served, he was sullen and moody.

Pa liked to drink with his friends, not by himself like Irwin, and the more he drank, the louder and meaner he became. On good nights he came home to fall across his bed and snore until noon the following day. On bad nights, he broke things, picked fights, and shouted obscenities. He'd broken Sander's collarbone the night before Granny died.

Sander had taken to the little bit of book learning Charlie Mae had been able to teach him. In no time, he could sound out words and read Granny's Bible. Granny had caught them one night with their heads together, studying out the sounds of her big book. Instead of being angry over their borrowing her book without asking, she'd been excited by the discovery that they could read. She never questioned how they'd gained the skill, but each night before drinking her toddy and stumbling off to her bed in the narrow space beneath the stairs, she demanded that they each read a page aloud to her.

In time, Sander had begun spending the meager coins that fell into his hands on books, slender volumes of poetry, newspapers, and an occasional dime novel which he kept hidden from Pa. Charlie Mae never questioned where he got those few coins but was grateful he shared his books with her. They opened a whole new world of words and ideas, places and dreams.

One terrible night Pa came home early and unexpectedly stormed into the kitchen to find Sander lying before the fire with a book propped before him. Pa snatched the book from Sander's hands and slammed it into the fire, then he grasped the poker.

Holding the heavy piece of metal with both hands, he'd lurched toward Sander, swinging it wildly.

"I shoulda knowed whar ya wuz gittin' all that sissy talk. Ain't no son o' mine gonna waste his time stickin' his nose in devil books. I'll whup it outta ya like I whupped it outta yore ma."

Charlie Mae cowered against the wall, hearing a strange buzzing in her ears and thinking she might faint. She wanted to go to Sander's aid but knew Pa would beat them both if she did, and the beatings for both of them would be more severe.

Sander ducked and tried to slip away, but Pa followed, swinging and cursing. The poker struck Sander's shoulder with a loud cracking sound, and Sander's face turned as white as new milk. He didn't scream but made a gasping noise like he wanted to cry. He wouldn't let himself. The noise awakened Granny from her alcohol-induced slumber, and she stumbled into the room with her long, gray braid coming unwound. She clasped her Bible to her bony chest and pulled herself up in majestic splendor.

"Eustace, put that poker down!" she ordered in a voice Charlie Mae had never heard the old woman use before.

Pa shook the poker at her then tore the book from her arms, tossing it carelessly toward the open fire. She screamed and scrambled toward her precious Bible as Pa turned again to Sander, who stood looking sick, with one arm hanging uselessly at his side and water and mucous running from his nose and eyes. Pa raised the poker high over his head, and as he began to swing it toward Sander's head, Granny slapped him across the side of his head with a heavy iron skillet. Pa wilted toward the kitchen floor while Granny calmly brushed off her Bible. And once more clasping it in her arms, she tottered back to bed.

Charlie Mae had ripped up a sheet to bind Sander's arm to his chest to prevent him from accidentally moving his shoulder. Irwin came creeping down the stairs. He made a rude sound deep in his throat then helped Charlie Mae and Sander drag Pa to his room.

Most of the pulling and tugging fell to Irwin as Sander could only use one arm, and each time he pulled on Pa's suspenders, little prickles of perspiration popped out around the sides of Sander's mouth where the skin looked a bit green. They left Pa lying face-down beside his bed and then crept to their own beds.

In the morning, Charlie Mae found Granny had stopped breathing sometime during the night, still holding her tattered, charred Bible in her arms. Pa wept and moaned, then went to town to arrange for a proper burial for Granny. He didn't notice Sander's bandaged shoulder nor say anything about the previous evening's altercation. Charlie Mae figured he didn't remember much of what happened while he was drunk, which was probably just as well, because if he remembered Sander could read, he'd want to know who had taught him, and he'd find out she could read too.

"I can't take more than one or two books with me, so the rest are yours," Sander told her. "I hid Granny's Bible along with the other books I've collected in the top of the barn in a hole beneath the loft floor. There's a keg of rusted nails and harness pieces sitting on top of it. Just be careful Pa don't catch you reading."

"I'll be careful," she promised. She wanted to beg him not to go or to take her with him, but changing his mind was useless, and he'd be fortunate if he was able to take care of himself. She couldn't burden him with taking care of her too.

Pa and Deke had ridiculed Sander for months for the fine way he talked, and she supposed she and Sander should have both been more careful not to let their book learning show. She never said much, and Pa didn't expect any talk from her, so she'd been safe, but Sander thought it was important to practice talking the way people in his books and some of the people in town said their words. She'd never heard real people talk the way book people did—except for the Pascals, and that was a long time ago, going on five years, but it had seemed mighty fine.

Sometimes she thought about Spencer and his grandma. Their memory was like a pleasant dream: not real, but comforting. Occasionally she thought about the strange stone she'd found the night Pa had killed that trader in Nauvoo and wondered if Spencer kept it and if he ever looked at it and thought about her.

Only Irwin showed up for breakfast the next morning. Pa hadn't staggered in until nearly dawn and had immediately fallen asleep. She didn't ask about Sander, and Irwin didn't offer any information. He ate his breakfast in silence before picking up the milk bucket and heading for the barn. When he returned, he was carrying one of Pa's jugs.

Two days passed before Pa noticed Sander was missing. He flew into a rage, throwing his tin plate at her and aiming a blow to Irwin's jaw before storming out of the house to ride his mule into town. For two days Irwin was unable to eat, and there was something frightening in the hate and misery she could see in his eyes.

* * *

Illinois, 1850

IT FELL TO Charlie Mae to help Irwin plant the corn. Irwin worked steadily, but there was no pleasure in working with him. Surprisingly, he drank less, but his usual calm demeanor seemed to be a cover for something dark and seething. She missed Sander's stories and the little courtesies he'd sometimes performed for her like helping her carry heavy baskets and throwing corn to the chickens. Often she wondered where he'd gone and if his collarbone had healed.

Irwin grew thin, and his eyes smoldered with anger as spring gave way to summer and another winter came. Some days he'd leave the house with Pa's rifle right after the milking was finished in the morning and wouldn't return until time for supper and the evening milking. His trousers would be wet to the knees from tramping through the snow. Sometimes he carried a brace of geese, and sometimes he'd tote a gutted deer carcass across his wide shoulders. He wasn't friendly with her like Sander had been, but he wasn't mean like Pa and Deke either. Charlie Mae found herself sympathizing with Irwin as Pa left more of the farmwork to him. Knowing that his only pleasure came from eating and Pa's jugs, she made a special effort to cook the foods he particularly liked.

As winter drew on and the temperature dropped further, the Riggins' house grew increasingly dismal. Loneliness and hard work ate at its inhabitants, and days would pass without a word being spoken among them. Charlie Mae cooked and cleaned, and when she dared, she visited the barn, ostensibly to search for eggs, but she always returned with one of Sander's books hidden in her pocket. When she wasn't reading the book, it rested behind the loose brick where she'd once hidden the red stone.

Irwin milked and fed the stock and felled logs which he stacked for firewood. Pa spent little time at home and was frequently gone all night. Only a handful of Mormons remained in Nauvoo, and the few remaining homes and businesses had been taken over by new owners. The city had taken on a rundown, seedy appearance. Saloons had sprouted up. Only one wall remained of the once-magnificent Mormon temple, and there was talk of knocking it down before it fell on someone. So far no one had aroused enough ambition to get the job done. Without a focus for the hatred that had driven men like Pa and Mr. Sawyer, the whole county seemed to hang in limbo, with little for the once-fomenting firebrands to do. Some of the men and boys had gone west, while others vented their useless rage on politics and the future of the slavery issue. Neither Charlie Mae nor Irwin questioned where Pa spent his time or what he found to do; they were simply pleased that he stayed away.

One morning in early February, Pa rose earlier than usual and seemed to be almost cheerful. The weather was cold, but there had been no new snow for more than a week, so the road was open and the snow on it well-packed. He hitched the mules to the wagon and drove off without a backward look.

Irwin chopped wood for awhile. When the axe grew silent, Charlie Mae saw him disappear into the woods with a jug and Pa's rifle. Facing the prospect of being alone all day, Charlie Mae mixed bread and set it on the hearthstone to rise, then scrubbed floors. She cleaned the small space under the stairs that she had inherited from Granny. She'd saved Granny's dresses. Two were worn, but the other one looked as though it had hardly been used, and Charlie Mae didn't remember seeing it before.

When the dough threatened to overflow the mixing bowl, she pinched off enough for three loaves and saved back enough to make cinnamon rolls. Cinnamon rolls were a treat especially favored by Irwin. She didn't know why she made an effort to please Irwin, who rarely even acknowledged her existence. Perhaps it was because she understood his misery and felt guilty because she had the respite of Sander's books while he had nothing but Pa's jugs.

With stew bubbling in a large pot, the house clean, and the smell of baking bread and cinnamon hanging in the air, she sat down to read. She was startled midafternoon to hear the creak of a wagon approaching over the frozen road.

Rising to her feet, she went to the window to peer out. To her astonishment, she saw Pa's wagon approaching. By the time the wagon reached the barn and Pa began shouting for Irwin to put up the mules, the book was hidden and the table set.

Knowing Irwin was out of earshot, she pulled Granny's old cloak, which she now claimed as her own, from its nail behind the door and hurried outside. The sun's bright reflection coming off of the snow nearly blinded her, but she hurried to the barn. Stepping from the bright light into the darkness of the barn brought total blindness for several seconds.

When her eyes began to adjust, she was at first astonished to see Pa releasing the mules from their harnesses himself. Then her eyes focused on a small, plump figure still seated on the wagon seat. Pa had brought a woman home with him!

Charlie Mae eyed the woman, uncertain whether she should introduce herself or wait for Pa to make introductions. The woman's brown hair was pulled back in a careless bun, and she wore a large cape that appeared to have once been lavender but was now mostly faded to gray. Her eyes were small and closely set while her mouth was full with thick lips that appeared to have been smeared with rouge earlier in the day that had since nearly rubbed off.

"Don't stand there gawkin', Charlie Mae. Take Agnes and the little ones to the house and show 'em around." Pa's order caused Charlie Mae to jump. She glanced at him and back at the woman she assumed was Agnes. The woman was climbing down, using the wagon spokes as a ladder. A parade of shabbily dressed little boys followed. The youngest was little more than a baby.

"Cletus and Dwight can stay here and help with the chores," Pa announced. Two more boys emerged from the dark interior of the barn wearing scowls. Charlie Mae guessed the older one was nineteen or thereabouts, same as Sander, while the younger one was a little younger than her own sixteen years.

Before she could start for the house, Charlie Mae got another surprise. Agnes reached over the side of the wagon and drew out a clumsily wrapped parcel. She passed it to one of the children, then reached for another. When all but the toddler were loaded down with bags and parcels, Agnes hefted another large bundle and thrust it toward Charlie Mae. Caught off guard, she accepted the large, canvas bag. She hesitated only a moment before hurrying toward the house with it.

With each step, Charlie Mae's mind whirled. *Who were these people? And why had Pa brought them to the farm?* Thanks to her brothers' efforts and her own, the farm produced well, but it provided little beyond food for their table and just enough apples to keep Pa and Irwin in cider. The little cash Pa got went for store-bought liquor. Sander had always figured Pa got more for the crops he hauled to town than he let on, but she'd seen no evidence of Pa squirreling away any funds.

"Charlie Mae," Pa yelled, and she stopped in her tracks. "Tell Irwin to git his lazy carcass out here."

"He went hunting. Said he saw deer tracks down by the river."

She waited for an explosion, but Pa merely grunted. She continued her trek toward the house.

Opening the kitchen door, she set the heavy canvas bag down and held the door wide as Agnes and her brood marched inside. As one, the children dropped their parcels and swarmed across the room. Opening drawers and cupboards, scuffling and fighting, they reminded Charlie Mae of a swarm of locusts.

"Sugar buns!" one boy shouted on discovering the cinnamon rolls she'd baked for dinner to cheer Irwin.

"Mine!"

"I found 'em!"

She watched in alarm as fists flew and the boys shoved the rolls into their mouths and trampled fallen bits under their boots. Undaunted, the toddler scraped the smashed chunks off the floor and into his mouth.

When an enterprising five-year-old spotted the loaves of freshly baked bread cooling on the window ledge and started for them, Charlie Mae leaped into action. Reaching the window first, she barred his way.

"The bread is for supper." She glared at the child. "You've already ruined dessert. You can't have bread too."

"But I want . . ." the boy whined.

"I'm hungry," a second boy chimed in.

"Your sister will share the bread with you after your pa and brothers are through doing the chores," Agnes said. It seemed to be a warning directed toward Charlie Mae, who was struggling to make sense of the woman's words.

"You may show the boys their room now," Agnes informed Charlie Mae.

"Their room?" Charlie Mae stammered. A sinking feeling in the bottom of her stomach was warning her there were big changes coming her way, changes she wasn't going to like. "My brothers have always shared the big room at the top of the stairs," she offered.

The boys were off like a whirlwind. They darted through the door leading to the front room, found the stairs, and fought their way to the top, screaming and yelling every step of the way. She cringed at the thundering steps overhead.

"This will do nicely." Agnes stood with her hands on her plump hips, surveying the huge, round table with a dozen straight-backed chairs that occupied the center of the main room. There was little else in the room other than a stone fireplace and a highboy that had belonged to Granny. Agnes looked toward the stairs and got a sly expression on her doughy face. "It'll be up to you to git the boys straightened out up there. Them stairs are too much fer me in my condition."

Charlie Mae stared at Agnes in consternation. Was the woman saying she was expecting another child? "I need to finish fixing supper. Pa will be hungry when he comes in." She had no desire to venture upstairs, where, judging from the sounds floating from the floor above, Agnes's boys were demolishing the roof and killing each other.

"I'll take care of supper," Agnes informed her. "It's a wife's duty to fix her man's supper."

"Wife?" The word came out in a strangled gasp.

"Eustace and me were married in town by the new preacher this morning."

She'd almost forgotten Pa's name was Eustace. "He didn't say anything," she managed. She wasn't really surprised that he hadn't told her his plans. He seldom spoke to her at all, but she was surprised that Pa had married a woman with so many mouths to feed.

"Eustace said that with all but one of his first batch of boys grown and gone, and the one what's left not worth much, it was time to make an honest woman of me an' teach our boys to farm."

Charlie Mae was speechless. She couldn't believe Pa had a whole other family. She wondered if Deke knew. It would be just like Deke to know all about Agnes and her passel of brats and not say a word to her or Irwin.

"You might jist as well take some of your little brothers' bags upstairs as you go." Agnes stood in the doorway, pointing to the pile of makeshift luggage the children had dropped on the kitchen floor.

What choice did she have? Charlie Mae gathered up the first couple of bags she came to and trudged with them up the stairs. She stood at the top of the stairs, aghast at the chaos the boys had created in the few minutes they'd been in the attic bedroom. Something snapped inside of her. She'd spent her entire life picking up after, cooking and cleaning for, and taking orders from four older brothers; she wasn't going to put up with similar treatment from this herd of new brothers.

"Stop!" she ordered, clapping her hands for emphasis.

Startled, five small faces turned toward her. "There aren't enough beds for all of you, so the younger ones will have to double up. That bed," she pointed to the one closest to where she stood, "belongs to Irwin. Stay off of it. Your brothers who stayed in the barn with Pa are too big to share a bed, so the next two beds are theirs. That leaves three of you to share the biggest bed by the window, and the two smallest boys can share the mattress on the floor under the eaves. Now march downstairs to collect your bags. You can store them beside your beds."

"We don't have to mind you," the oldest boy replied. "You ain't our ma."

"No, I'm not your ma, but it seems I'm your big sister. And boys that don't mind their big sister don't get any dinner." There was no arguing that the boys weren't her brothers. Every last one of the five little boys bore a remarkable resemblance to Pa.

5

A LOOK OF awe and fear crossed the little boy's face. He darted from the room, and his brothers followed him, clattering down the stairs. They returned moments later, dragging their various bundles. Charlie Mae took advantage of their absence to straighten the coverlet on Irwin's bed and return his few possessions to the wooden box where he kept them. She had a hunch Irwin wasn't going to be pleased with the new arrangement.

Arguments erupted as the boys claimed their places, but eventually each boy had staked a claim to a place to sleep.

"All right, let's go downstairs and wash up for supper. Line up right here." She put out a hand to prevent a wholesale plunge down the stairs. Amidst plenty of grumbling, she led the way.

On reaching the front room, a fight ensued over who would sit where until Charlie Mae assigned them each a seat. From the sideboard, she collected a mismatched array of dishes until each place setting had either a plate or a bowl and at least one eating implement.

"You haven't set enough places." Agnes stood in the doorway, surveying the table.

"There's nine. That takes care of your seven boys, Irwin, and Pa."

"Set a place for me opposite Eustace," Agnes instructed.

"Pa says women should eat in the kitchen after he and the boys have finished," Charlie Mae tried to explain.

"He has a wife now, so there will be some changes. Fetch me a plate."

"All right." She had no intention of arguing with her step-mother. "Boys, while I set a place for your ma, you can wash up at the wash bench beside the kitchen door."

The boys raced to do her bidding, and Charlie Mae pretended she didn't see the black look Agnes directed toward her. Inside, she struggled to control a faint queasiness. She strongly suspected there were stormy days ahead.

A commotion at the door heralded Pa's arrival. He was followed closely by Cletus and Dwight. Irwin lagged a few steps behind, a deep scowl darkening his face.

Charlie Mae hurried to the kitchen. She reached for the kettle of thick stew she'd left simmering all afternoon over the fire. Setting the lid aside, she thrust a ladle into the pot, then carried it to the table. She returned for the bread and was dismayed to discover only two loaves on the shelf where she'd set them to cool. Two loaves would be barely enough for a taste around. She'd like to shake those greedy little boys.

She sliced the bread thin before carrying it to the table. When she returned to the kitchen, she pulled out a large mixing bowl and began stirring up a batch of biscuits. If she could get them baked and to the table before Pa discovered there wasn't enough bread to go around, perhaps he'd go easy on the boys.

She'd just thrust the biscuits in the oven when an angry roar came from the other room.

"Charlie Mae, git in here," Pa roared.

Slamming the oven door closed, she hurried to where the rest of the family was gathered around the oak table. Her limbs trembled, and the dizziness that made her weak when Pa yelled at her threatened to overcome her.

"What kind of stew is this?" Pa's voice sounded narrow and mean. Startled, she glanced at his plate where two small chunks of potato floated in a sea of pale, watery liquid.

"I don't understand—" Pa's hand struck the side of her face, and she staggered backward. "But I made it just like always. Perhaps Agnes added some water to make it stretch for eight more mouths." Her hand went to her face, and she looked beseechingly at the other woman. Agnes ignored her and instead slurped the stew from her spoon with complete concentration.

"Bring some more bread and a crock of apple butter. I don't aim ta starve 'cause you're put out with havin' a new ma to answer to." It would do no good to point out how unfair Pa was being. Defending herself would only bring more blows.

"I'll get the apple butter from the cellar." Charlie Mae returned to the kitchen where she snatched her cloak from the nail behind the door and hurried outside to the cellar. The air was sharp and cold, and she shivered as she lifted the doors and hurried down the stone steps of the cellar. It only took a moment to find the crock. Since she was already in the cellar, she snatched up a smaller crock of pickled peaches. They'd have to do for dessert.

As she thrust the kitchen door open a few minutes later, she was surprised to see Agnes leaning over the open oven door. The woman whirled around to face Charlie Mae. Her mouth was full, and she clutched a half-eaten biscuit in her hand. Charlie Mae noted the biscuits could have done with another minute of browning time.

"You were gone so long, I came to see if I could help." An ugly picture came to Charlie Mae's mind. She pictured the untidy woman wolfing down the missing loaf of bread and devouring the meat and vegetables from the stew, then filling the kettle with water.

"Here, carry this to the table," she thrust the heavy crock toward the woman. "I'll finish the biscuits." As she lifted the biscuits to a platter she noted that the pan was short four of the biscuits she'd placed there. She glanced up just as Agnes swiped a finger through the crock of apple butter and thrust it into her mouth.

When the others finished their meal, Charlie Mae approached the table to clear away the dirty dishes and was appalled at the mess she found. Ma's few glass dishes were chipped or broken, glasses and cups had been spilled, leaving puddles beneath the table, crumbs littered the floor, and greasy fingerprints covered every surface. Agnes didn't join her in the kitchen to help wash the dishes, but she supposed she couldn't rightly blame Pa's new wife. It was her wedding day.

Charlie Mae was drying the last dish when she sensed someone behind her. A hand slid down her arm, taking the bowl from her fingers. "I'll put that on the shelf for you." Cletus leaned across her to set the bowl on a shelf above her head.

"Thank you," she muttered as she hastily moved away. Something about Cletus's nearness made her uneasy.

He smiled and touched her chin with his finger. "Just bein' brotherly," he said. "I think I'm going to enjoy havin' a little sister."

She wanted to tell him to return to the other room, but she didn't want to be rude. He might be trying to be kind, but something about the young man caused the hair at the back of her neck to rise.

"Charlie Mae!" Irwin swung open the door connecting the two rooms. For once, she was happy to see her brother. Irwin looked from her to Cletus, then back to her. The scowl that had become a permanent part of his face deepened. He stood with his arms folded, neither approaching nor retreating.

"We'll talk later." Cletus directed his words at her, and she sensed a deeper meaning behind them. He strolled from the room whistling.

When the door closed behind Cletus, Charlie Mae turned to Irwin. "You know I don't scare easily, but something about that boy makes me plumb nervous."

Irwin glanced at the closed door then down at his feet. "I 'spect you best be keerful," he mumbled. "His ma ain't the respectable sort, and I figger the apple don't fall far from the tree."

"If Agnes isn't respectable, then why did Pa marry her?" Charlie Mae asked.

"There's things I 'spect you don't know." His face turned red, and even his ears flamed with color. "The young'ns are Pa's, and likely he figgers to git some work outta Dwight and Cletus 'til the little boys are big enough to run the farm fer him."

"Well, you could sure use the help. Pa expects you to do all your work and what our brothers left too."

Irwin looked ill at ease. He took a couple of steps as if about to leave the room, then he lifted his head to say, "Jist don't let Cletus put his hands on ya."

"I know more'n you think, Irwin. Granny said I needed to know enough to protect myself from the wrong sort of fellers, and Sander did some plain speaking afore he left."

"I wish Sander hadn't up an' left." She was surprised to see a watery brightness in Irwin's eyes. She should have known he missed Sander too, and not just for the work his brother did around the farm. They were nearly inseparable for the longest time.

"Pa didn't leave him much choice." She didn't attempt to hide the bitterness she felt toward Pa for making it impossible for Sander to stay.

"Then you don't blame Sander none?"

"Heavens no! I don't blame Clyde none either. Livin' with Pa ain't easy."

Irwin didn't respond, but she noticed a strange glint in his eyes. She also noticed he wasn't drunk, though she would have sworn he had been a short time earlier at the supper table. It occurred to her that this was the first real conversation she could recall having with Irwin. She remembered, too, that he'd had a reason for coming to the kitchen and it wasn't likely that reason had been to talk to her.

"Were you looking for something when you came to the kitchen?" she asked.

"That was a mighty poor supper tonight, and when I came in from outside, I thought I smelled cinnamon." He hung his head. "I was hopin' . . ." His voice trailed off, but she knew what he'd been hoping. More than once she'd held back a piece of pie or some other treat from supper for him to wrap in a piece of linen and take with him hunting the following day. He'd never said thank you, but he'd started cleaning the fish and small game he brought her to cook before setting them on her work table.

She shook her head. "I baked cinnamon rolls." His face brightened then fell when she went on. "The moment those boys entered the house, they devoured every roll before I could stop them. I think Agnes ate the other loaf of bread and picked the best pieces from the stew."

That night as she lay exhausted on the cot beneath the stairs, where she'd moved her sleeping quarters after Granny died, she found sleep impossible. She tried to look on the bright side of the upheaval in her life. With another woman and all those children in the house, she wouldn't be lonely anymore. She'd had little experience being around other women and had often longed for a female friend, but she suspected Agnes wasn't the friend she'd hoped for.

Granny had been company of sorts, and though she had been bossy by nature, she'd been kinder to Charlie Mae after she'd mistaken her for an angel that long-ago day when Sister Pascal had loaned her the baptism dress. She wished Granny were present now to tell her what to do. She lit a lantern and pulled Granny's Bible from beneath the cot. If she read Granny's book, she'd feel closer to her. Anyway, sometimes she felt more at peace when she read the big book, and a few times it had given her ideas for dealing with Pa and her brothers.

She read until she thought she might be able to fall asleep. After snuffing out the lantern, she lay still, thinking about Joseph, the boy who had been sold by his brothers. She felt a great deal of empathy for the boy who was hated by his brothers and slandered by his master's wife. She felt almost a personal vindication when he became rich and powerful. It had been one of Granny's favorite stories too. Sander had read it aloud to Granny many times, and

Granny had said Joseph won in the end because he remembered to say his prayers. Sander had argued that the story didn't say anything about praying, but Granny insisted the praying was there if one looked carefully. She knew Granny prayed, but Charlie Mae never did. If Granny was right—and she usually was—then Charlie Mae should try it.

She crawled out of bed to kneel. There was barely enough room for the cot, and she had to twist sideways to bend her knees. She closed her eyes tightly and then stopped. She didn't know what to say. Finally she whispered, "God, my name is Charlotte Mae Riggins. I could use some help about now. Amen." She remembered the *amen* part from one of Sander's books. She crawled back in bed, and eventually she slept.

She awoke once. Someone was moving stealthily about the kitchen. She heard the big tin dipper strike the side of the water bucket, followed by footsteps scampering up the stairs. Figuring some of the boys had gotten thirsty during the night, she drifted back to sleep.

The following morning, Irwin surprised her by appearing in the kitchen before doing his chores. He carried a hammer and didn't speak, not even to wish her good morning. While she set water to boil for oatmeal porridge and sliced salt pork into a large cast-iron skillet, she heard hammering coming from the alcove under the stairs that had been Granny's room and was now hers. When she returned from gathering eggs, Irwin was gone, but a sturdy wooden peg that twisted to secure the door had been added to the inside of her door. She appreciated the small amount of privacy the narrow alcove gave her, but she'd never considered the need for a lock to bar intruders. She remembered the footsteps during the night and felt a chill run down her back. Other than cleaning his catch before bringing it to the house, this was the only kind thing she could recall Irwin ever doing for her.

That night she awoke to stealthy steps again. After a few moments, there was a tug on her door, followed by a string of curses and a not-so-stealthy retreat up the stairs.

Charlie Mae guarded her kitchen jealously in the coming days. She had no intention of giving Pa an excuse to strike her again. Resorting to threats, she made the big room off limits to the boys. They whined and cried when she chased them from the room until she devised a plan whereby she provided them with an apple, a handful of dried apricots, or a cookie each afternoon if they stayed out of the kitchen the rest of the day. She noticed Agnes was always on hand to claim a share when she gave the treats to the boys. It was more work to prepare the treats, but it kept their fingers out of the food she was preparing for meals.

Dealing with Agnes wasn't so easy. She felt a constant tug-of-war between herself and Agnes, whom she had to watch more closely than the little boys. Anytime Charlie Mae turned her back, Agnes gorged herself on food meant for the meal Charlie Mae was preparing. She constantly stole pies or puddings set aside for dessert. She never assisted in cleaning up the messes she and her sons made or volunteered to help with the mammoth pile of dishes after meals. Pa lectured and stormed over the poor meals Charlie Mae too often served, but he didn't strike her again.

It soon became obvious the other woman was filling Pa's ears with lies—accusing Charlie Mae of rudeness and of preventing her from preparing better meals. Pa blamed the two women's differences on Charlie Mae.

"She's your ma now," Pa snapped at Charlie Mae. "And you best mind her."

Charlie Mae couldn't think of Agnes as her ma, but she doubled her efforts to get along with the older woman and to invite suggestions from her for meal preparation and the tasks necessary to running the household. Her efforts only brought added work to her already work-laden days. Agnes took to sleeping late and ordering Charlie Mae to look after the boys and prepare her favorite dishes. Her forays into the kitchen were never to assist with preparations but consisted of raids on the dishes her stepdaughter was about to serve.

Pa resumed his trips to town as spring approached, and some-times he took Agnes with him, leaving Charlie Mae to watch the little boys. One day after he and Agnes had stayed up late drinking from one of Pa's jugs, and it was nearing time for the midday meal, he staggered to the table with a throbbing head, expecting dinner. The boys raced around the table and up and down the stairs screaming and fighting. Charlie Mae rushed to the kitchen to find Agnes sampling the venison pie Charlie Mae had left baking in the oven.

"That's for dinner! Keep your fingers out of it!" Charlie Mae shouted. Pa would more than beat her if there wasn't enough of the pie for him to get his fill for dinner.

"Don't tell me what I can do, Miss Uppity! This is my house, and I can do what I want!" Agnes's shrill voice berated Charlie Mae right back.

Shoving open the kitchen door, Pa thundered, "Quiet! Git the food on the table, and it best not be skimpy!" He raised a threat-ening fist.

Charlie Mae shrank back. One of the venison pies she'd baked was missing, but she feared riling Pa even more if she accused Agnes of eating it. Agnes had no such qualms; she launched an attack.

"Charlotte is holding food back, hiding it for her and that worthless Irwin to eat later," she whined. "That's why there ain't enough vittles to go around." She marched to an overturned pot. Flipping it over, she revealed the missing pie while Charlie Mae stared in shock, unable to speak.

Pa turned on her in a fury. "Git out of my sight, girl. You and that worthless, no-account Irwin can be the ones to go without dinner. From now on your stepma can do the cookin', and you best stay out of the kitchen."

Charlie Mae fled to the barn, seeking the loft and Sander's books as she wept and steeled herself for the gloating taunts Agnes would direct toward her when she returned. She also expected meals would soon become less appetizing as the gluttonous woman gorged herself on the nuts, raisins, and jellies Charlie Mae used to add pleasant variations to meals.

A rustle of sound brought her head up. She was startled to see Cletus's head peering over the edge of the loft floor. He grinned when he saw her and scrambled toward her over the hay stored in the loft. He sat down much too close to her, and she edged away, hiding the book she'd been reading beneath the loose hay. He reached for her arm, and she jerked it out of his grasp and attempted to stand.

Cletus lunged toward her, tackling her and causing her to lose her balance. She tumbled into the hay, the rough stalks scratching at her face and hands.

"Leave me alone!" She slapped at his hands and attempted to twist away. He imprisoned her slender hands in one of his large paws and threw a leg over hers to prevent her escaping.

"Stop pretending you don't want it. I seen the way you look at me." His face was right next to hers, and the look on it was as mean as any she'd seen on Pa's.

Charlie Mae was scared. Cletus was much bigger than her. She opened her mouth to scream. The sound echoed through the barn, but Cletus only laughed.

"Ain't nobody goin' to come. Nobody cares anyway. Your Pa said it might settle ya down to git hitched." He pressed his mouth over hers. Bile rose in her throat, and she began to gag.

Fight! An almost-forgotten voice seemed to shout in her ear. Charlie Mae hadn't grown up in a houseful of quarreling, fighting brothers without learning a few things. She bit down on Cletus's lower lip until she tasted blood. At the same time she forced her free knee into his chest with all the fury he inspired in her. He yelled and jerked back, freeing her other leg and her hands. Gathering her feet together, she thrust them into his abdomen, knocking him backward before scrambling to her feet. Once on her feet, Charlie Mae continued to attack, scoring his face with her nails and aiming her thumbs toward his eyes. A real fear that she would die if she didn't keep attacking kept her kicking and striking out. Mindless anger drove her on.

Spitting and snarling, Cletus attempted to ward her off. Blood ran into his eyes from a deep gash near his right eye, and blood from his lip dribbled down his chin. Doubling up a fist, she aimed for his larynx.

"You'll pay for this!" he screamed. His windmilling arms landed a blow to the side of her head, making her dizzy. One of his hands grasped her dress, tearing at the bodice until the fabric hung in shreds. This only accelerated her adrenaline.

She didn't dare let up. He was between her and the ladder. As soon as he could regain his equilibrium, she knew he would resume his attempt to force himself on her. He'd likely beat her senseless too—or kill her. Gradually she moved closer to the edge of the loft. When the hay beneath her feet became so thin she could feel the wood planks, she tried to feel for the ladder with her feet.

"No you don't, you little witch." He lunged toward her, screaming obscenities. She sidestepped and watched in horror as Cletus teetered on the edge of the loft. Just when she thought he would regain his balance, he made a desperate grab for her skirt. Clutching the fabric in his fist, he attempted to steady himself but only pulled her closer to the edge.

Granny's much-abused old skirt ripped off, sending Cletus tumbling backward, still clutching the faded gray cotton. The sudden release of the fabric caused Charlie Mae to fall backward onto the hay, where she lay gasping for breath.

A scream rent the air just before a sickening crunch sounded, followed by silence.

6 ⤳

No sound came from below. Was Cletus lying in wait to jump on her when she tried to descend the ladder—or was he dead? With hesitant steps, she made her way to the side of the loft. Dropping to her knees, she peered over the edge.

Cletus lay unmoving far below. She watched for several minutes, fearing he might jump to his feet and come after her. At the same time, she feared he was dead and that the sheriff would hang her for murdering him.

She crawled to the ladder. After climbing down, she studied Cletus to see if he had moved. At last she stood and began a circuitous route around the sprawled body that lay half in and half out of the gutter that hadn't been cleaned that morning, a job she'd heard Pa assign to Cletus. A pool of blood spread out from where his head lay, and one leg was twisted at an unnatural angle.

Charlie Mae had almost reached the barn door when a dark shape strode inside. A hand grasped her upper arm before she could run.

"What's going on?" Deke roared. "What happened to your dress? I'll beat you proper if you shame the family by gittin' yourself in the family way."

"I think I killed him." Shrinking back from her brother, Charlie Mae blurted out her fear.

"Who? You best tell me what's goin' on."

"It was Cletus," she gasped, struggling to keep herself from collapsing in tears. Deke never had had any patience with tears. "He kept trying to get in my room at night 'til Irwin put a peg on the door. Today he . . . he tried to . . . he ripped my dress . . . and . . . he fell from the loft."

Deke looked at her then at Cletus lying on the floor. He walked over to the fallen youth and ripped the torn skirt from the lifeless fingers that still clutched it tightly. Carrying it back to Charlie Mae, he said, "Put this back on."

While she struggled with trying to wrap herself in the tatters of her skirt and hold the cloth in place with a torn strip of her petticoat, Deke returned to Cletus. He knelt down and laid his head against Cletus's chest. He listened a moment then rose to his feet. "He ain't dead, but I oughtta put him out of his misery, the worthless piece of dung." He strode back to Charlie Mae. "I 'spect it's true then. I heerd in town that Pa married the Widow Scranton and brung them whelps out here to the farm."

"It's true. Pa said he and Agnes are married," Charlie Mae mumbled in a shaky voice.

"I ain't likin' bein' at the beck an' call of my wife's pa, but he's been sick most all winter, and when he keels over, his farm will be mine. Pa said he was savin' the money from last year's cash crops to buy the Grant farm that lies between our places and that we'd join the three farms together into the biggest farm in the county. Soon Pa and me was gonna be rich. Those plans don't include sharin' nothin' with the widow's brats." He paced back and forth, the scowl on his face growing darker.

"Pa and half of the men in the county have been keepin' company with the Widow Scranton since Parley Scranton got shot for cheatin' at cards. I ain't havin' that passel of brats cheat me outta what's rightly mine."

"What about Irwin?" Charlie Mae asked hesitantly. She wasn't exactly standing up for Irwin, but he had put that lock on her door, and it didn't look to her like Pa and Deke had given much thought to Irwin in their plans—or to her.

"Irwin ain't smart enough to run a farm. He's the only brother I got left, and I figure I can always find a bed and a jug to keep him happy."

"Deke, what am I going to do? I can't be here when Cletus wakes up. Cletus said Pa wants me to marry up with him."

"Pa's just worryin' about his belly. He knows the widow can't cook nothin' fit to eat. If you was to marry Cletus, he could keep you here cookin' fer him."

"But he told me a little while ago to leave the kitchen to Agnes."

"You ain't half bright. He's just gittin' her off his back and tryin' to make ya think ya hafta work harder to git on his good side. Tomorrow he'll be orderin' her outta the kitchen, an' if she fixes her usual slop for supper, she'll be black 'n' blue." It crossed her mind to wonder how Deke knew so much about Agnes.

"I won't marry Cletus!"

Deke laughed. "You will if Pa says so. 'Sides, it's likely the only chance you'll git."

"If she was to marry Cletus, in no time there'd be a whole lot more brats havin' a claim to the farm." Neither Charlie Mae nor Deke had heard Irwin enter the barn. Charlie Mae felt a pang of pity for Irwin. He'd likely come to the house expecting dinner and been turned away. "Seems it would be in your best interest to help Charlie Mae git far away from here." Irwin went on speaking to Deke. "Pa took the mule I tied to the porch and left for town. This would be a good time for her to go."

"Women ain't worth nothing 'cept keepin' a man's bed warm and his belly full, so it was bound to happen sooner or later, and it's just like Cletus to be lookin' out fer himself." Deke seemed to be considering Irwin's suggestion. A crafty look entered Deke's eyes. "Pa married the widow without talkin' it over with me. It would serve him right to hafta eat her slop. We ain't got no kin to send Charlie Mae to visit, so she's goin' to need someone to look out fer her iffen she leaves. I cain't leave Sissy with a babe on the way. Irwin, you'll have ta go with Charlie Mae."

Maybe Irwin was a whole lot smarter than either Deke or Pa gave him credit for.

Irwin didn't seem the least bit perturbed by Deke's suggestion. "I was thinkin' the same thing," he said in a bland voice. He turned to Charlie Mae. "You cain't go ta the house lookin' like you been in a fight. I'll go find a few things fer both of us while you collect the vittles we'll be needin' from the cellar."

"All right," she stammered. She couldn't imagine depending on Irwin to take care of her, but he seemed to have some sort of plan which was more than either she or Deke had. Cautiously she crept toward the cellar. She returned to the barn a short time later with her arms full just seconds ahead of Irwin, who strolled back into the barn with a heavy bundle in his arms.

"I told Agnes I was plannin' on going hunting with some friends and that I'd be campin' out fer a spell," Irwin said when he dropped a few items at Charlie Mae's feet. "Best you put these things on."

She picked up the pile of clothing and darted into a stall, where she quickly stripped off her torn dress and pulled on a pair of Sander's outgrown britches, a flannel shirt, and boots her brother had outgrown and left behind. When she stepped out of the stall, Irwin handed her several small bundles.

"How are we going to carry all of these things?" she wondered aloud.

"I figure Deke's horse can carry everythin' as far as that burned out shack in the woods, and we can handle it from there."

Deke didn't appear pleased at the prospect of loaning them his horse, but eventually he agreed, no doubt because he'd calculated the advantage of getting rid of his last remaining brother.

"What about him?" Charlie Mae shivered as she pointed to Cletus.

"Dwight sneaks off to the barn about this time every afternoon to smoke and steal a few pulls from the jug he keeps hidden in the manger. He'll find Cletus. If not, Deke will be returning this way in an hour or so and can just happen on him." Irwin didn't sound overly concerned.

* * *

DEKE AND IRWIN unloaded their supplies while Charlie Mae watched. She felt strangely disoriented, as though the sun had come up over the river instead of setting there. Her mind could scarcely grasp what Cletus had attempted to do to her, and she ached physically from the fight. No doubt the aches and welts would soon turn to bruises. She had no illusions about Deke's self-serving greed being the major factor in his agreeing to help her escape. It was Irwin who astonished her. She was beginning to suspect he'd been planning to leave for some time. It was discovering he was capable of planning such a venture and his willingness to take her along that was astonishing. She stamped her feet to dislodge the snow that was making them cold.

"We'll stay in the shed over yonder for tonight," Irwin told Deke, pointing to the hut that had once housed the Pascals' chickens. Charlie Mae feared she and Irwin would freeze before morning, but that was preferable to facing what she'd left behind at the farm. Deke nodded his head from where he sat on his horse. There was no mistaking his anxiousness to be on his way.

Once Deke was out of sight, Irwin turned to her. "There's a stream the other side of the clearing. It's frozen over, but there's a sledge in the shed we can pile our supplies on. It should move easily over the ice until we reach the river."

Charlie Mae's mouth gaped open. "But you told Deke . . ."

"I lied," Irwin confessed. "I don't trust him, and the less he knows, the better."

Charlie Mae followed Irwin to the shed and was amazed to find it quite comfortable. It also confirmed her suspicion that Irwin had been planning his escape for some time. A small, dented stove that looked like the one Sister Pascal had cooked on stood in one corner, and she suspected it had been used recently. There was a chair and a workbench. It was clear that many times when she thought Irwin was hunting, he had been fixing up the shed and constructing the sledge in preparation for running away.

It was an odd-looking sledge built of logs lashed together and mounted on runners. The front was narrower than the back, and it had a large cargo area which she could see contained a number of canvas-wrapped items.

It didn't take long to add the supplies they'd brought with them to the items already on the sledge. The task of dragging the unwieldy conveyance to the creek was much harder, and it required all of their combined strength, but at last it was in place. With both of them pulling on the rope handle, the heavy contraption glided with ease over the ice.

When they reached the river, Charlie Mae viewed the wide expanse with trepidation. A ledge of ice clung to the shoreline and in some places extended some distance out into the dark water. Chunks of ice floated in the current.

"It would've been best if we could've waited another week or two until more of the ice was gone," Irwin muttered as he nudged the awkward sledge closer to the water. A cracking sound came from below the sledge, and the ice grew more slippery as pockets of water formed around the cracks.

Charlie Mae eyed the water through narrowed eyes before looking back at the sledge. *It's a raft! Irwin planned all along to turn his sledge into a raft.* The thick double layer of logs and the high sides made some kind of sense now, but Irwin knew nothing about boats. It probably wouldn't even float. Her hesitation lasted only a moment. She didn't want to drown in the icy river, but even that would be preferable to spending one more night under the same roof as Cletus and Pa.

"Climb in," Irwin yelled, and she scrambled to do his bidding. She nearly landed on her face as she pulled herself over the side and tumbled inside the boxlike boat. Straightening, she was in time to see Irwin make only a slightly more graceful arrival. He staggered to keep his balance. Once steady, he grasped two long poles. He handed one to her.

"We need to push ourselves clear of the shore." He demonstrated by poking the pole against the icy bank behind them. A deafening crack sounded, and the boat lurched to one side. She lost her footing and slammed against the side.

"Push!" Irwin shouted.

Pulling herself upright, she stuck one end of the pole over the side, where she shoved awkwardly against anything she could reach with it. The boat lurched again, wobbled from side to side, then with a screeching sound broke free of the ice and began to drift south.

Charlie Mae held her breath. They were actually floating. She glanced at the floor and saw no seeping water. She began to feel slightly more optimistic.

"Ice on the right! Shove it away with your pole," Irwin shouted, and Charlie Mae turned her attention back to the river. The smaller chunks of floating ice weren't difficult to deflect and probably wouldn't cause any damage anyway, but the large chunk bearing down on them could do a great deal of damage. It hit her pole, sending vibrations up her arms.

"I can't turn it," she panted.

Irwin rushed to her side. With their combined effort, they were able to stave off the ice just enough to keep it from crashing into them, though it made a fearsome sound as it scraped the side of the boat.

When the danger was past, Irwin returned to the opposite side of the boat. It occurred to Charlie Mae that having two poles, moving the sledge from the shed to the ice, and a number of other small things she'd noticed, indicated Irwin had planned all along for a second person to accompany him. She wondered if he'd meant for that second person to be her. The thought filled her with unusual comfort.

Charlie Mae was so busy watching for ice and warding off potential threats she didn't even notice when they passed the point where the path from the farmhouse reached the river. They passed numerous small towns, but she paid them little heed. The sun was beginning to set, and clouds were piling up to the west when she became aware of the deep ache in her arms and a rumbling in her stomach.

"How are we going to get back to shore?" she asked. "We're not staying on the river all night, are we?"

"There's a big sandbar a few miles up ahead. I heard the riverboat captains in Nauvoo talking about it. The current will carry us nigh the Missouri side just before we reach it. We'll go aground there." Irwin's answer invited more questions than it gave answers, but Charlie Mae didn't ask them. It appeared to her that Irwin knew what he was doing, and she'd just have to trust him for a spell.

The boat struck the sandbar with a resounding smack, nearly causing her to drop her pole.

"We have to hurry afore the raft breaks loose," Irwin warned. "Gather up everything ya kin carry." He piled two of the canvas parcels on his back and tucked the bag he'd carried from the house under an arm. Using his free hand, he swung over the side of the boat.

Not wishing to be left behind, Charlie Mae swept the other canvas pack onto her back and picked up the two bags of food she'd taken from the cellar. When she reached the side of the boat, she looked down fearfully. The raft shifted, and she guessed that without Irwin and the supplies he'd carried, it was riding higher in the water and would soon break free.

"Come on, hurry!" Irwin urged. She could see the water didn't reach to his knees. He reached for one of her parcels, and with a hand freed, she slid over the side of the boat. Shock nearly caused her to collapse when her feet touched the icy water.

"Stay on the sandbar," he warned and led the way, splashing through shallow water to a cut in the bank that would be filled with spring runoff water in a few weeks.

Charlie Mae stumbled as she stepped onto shore. She could scarcely feel her feet, and the ground seemed to sway beneath her.

"Git a fire started while I fetch the rest of our supplies." Irwin dumped one of the parcels at her feet and turned to splash his way back to the boat.

Opening the canvas pack, Charlie discovered dry kindling and flint. It only took her a moment to select a spot, sheltered from the wind, to start the fire. Irwin was back by the time it was burning nicely and she was beginning a search for larger pieces of wood. He merely grunted his approval and joined her in her search for wood.

Irwin discovered a sizable log and dragged it near the fire. Retrieving an axe from one of his bundles, he began chopping it into thick chunks which would burn for hours. While he chopped wood, Charlie Mae searched through the bundles of supplies until she found a skillet and a knife. Soon salt pork, beans, and biscuits scented the air. Charlie Mae wasn't sure which she appreciated the most: the prospect of filling her stomach or the heat of the cooking fire warming her frozen feet and hands. Irwin clearly favored filling his belly.

They ate in silence then crawled inside the tent Irwin had constructed from the canvas he'd wrapped around the firewood. They only removed their boots before wrapping themselves in their quilts. Irwin had built up the fire with several large logs, and the opening of their tent faced the warmth. The leaping flames caused strange shadows to dance on the canvas walls. Charlie Mae didn't figure sleep would come soon, even though she was more tired than she could ever remember being.

"Irwin, how long you been planning this?" she asked.

"Me 'n' Sander saw Pa shoot a man a long time ago. Deke was with him, an' he didn't care none. Clyde took off, an' fer awhile I thought I could take his place with Pa and Deke, but I soon learned they figgered I was a no account 'cause I didn't have the stomach for the mean things they done. Sander said we'd have to leave one day too. At first we just talked about it, but after awhile we remembered that the Mormons' shed in the woods was still standing. It even had a few tools in it, so we started building the sledge. We made up our minds that one day we'd have lots of money and no one, least of all Pa, could call us 'no accounts.'"

Charlie Mae wondered if she should tell Irwin that she'd witnessed the shooting too, but before she could make up her mind, Irwin went on. "One day afore Granny died, she gave Sander and me each a gold piece she'd kept hid from Pa and made us promise to look after ya after she was gone. When Sander took off, he said he feared Pa would kill him if he stayed, so it was up to me to look after ya."

Tears dampened her eyes. She'd never been sure Granny or her brothers cared about her, but it appeared they did, at least a little bit.

"Thank you," she said—words that were unheard of in the Riggins family.

"At first me and Sander figgered we'd find a fella who needed a wife who could cook right good and get him ta marry ya. It weren't 'til you started savin' rolls an' pie fer me that I started thinkin' about bringin' you with me," Irwin admitted.

"There hasn't been much of that lately."

"That weren't your fault. I knowed that."

"I promise when we get settled someplace, I'll bake all the pies and rolls you want."

"I don't 'spect we'll be settlin' anywhere soon. Once we reach St. Louis, I aim to sign us up with one of those wagon trains headed for California. We'll be livin' in a tent 'til I get enough gold to build a house. Some day I aim ta be rich."

7

CHARLIE MAE DIDN'T reckon she'd sleep that night, but exhaustion eventually claimed her. She awoke when Irwin crawled from their tent to stir up the fire, and she soon discovered a fine dusting of new snow covering the ground.

By the time they finished their breakfast, the snow had melted, and the sun was promising a warmer day than the previous day. Irwin walked down the streambed to the river and returned to tell her their raft had broken free and drifted away during the night. He didn't appear unduly alarmed, so she waited for him to go on. She was discovering a new side to this brother who had always been silent and seemingly detached.

"We passed a farm late yesterday. I'll see if they have a horse they'll sell me," he announced before starting to walk back the way they'd floated from the day before.

"How will you pay for a horse?" she called after him, running to catch up. He stopped and turned to face her with a frown.

"I ain't going to steal one," he said. "I got money."

"I wasn't suggesting you'd steal one. I just didn't know you had any money. You still have Granny's five-dollar gold piece?"

"That and the money I been gittin' for Pa's whiskey."

"Pa counts those jugs. How'd you get some to sell?"

Irwin chuckled. "He's been givin' me a jug several times a week ever since I turned sixteen. I been sellin' the shine an' fillin' the jugs back up with well water." Irwin almost smiled. "I been lettin' him think I was drinkin' all that rotgut."

Laughter bubbled from Charlie Mae's throat. Irwin was providing one surprise after another. It appeared Sander wasn't the only smart brother in the family.

"You stay here," Irwin told her. "Git packed back up, and I'll come fer ya soon's I can."

She watched him lope off into the trees and felt a kind of panic rising inside her. She wondered if he would really come back. Forcing herself to be calm, she turned back to survey their camp-site. The fire needed more wood, and it was time she discovered what kind of supplies Irwin had brought along.

An hour later, she leaned back against a tree and cataloged the items she'd found. It appeared to her they had food for about a week. There was a cast-iron skillet and a battered tea kettle, no doubt rescued from the burned-out Pascal home. There were four flannel shirts and a change of britches for each of them, all made by her and Granny. She didn't recognize the quilts; they'd likely been snatched off of some unwary woman's clothesline. There were extra socks, underpinnings, and Granny's lace-trimmed, best blue dress that Irwin had gathered up for her on his last trip to the house. Charlie Mae hadn't worn the blue dress yet, and she'd never seen Granny wear it; it was too fancy for cooking and gathering eggs.

At the bottom of the bundle of clothing, she'd encountered a surprise. Irwin had brought along Granny's Bible. He couldn't read, so she wondered how he'd known the book was the one thing it had pained her most to leave behind.

Before she packed up their food supplies, she prepared a lunch they could eat cold along the way. Taking down the tent, she wrapped their quilts inside part of the canvas. Then she searched for enough fire kindling to pack. When all was in readiness, she seated herself on a large stone near the fire and waited. The trees loomed large around her, and strange sounds caused her to jump.

She couldn't help wondering what would become of her if Irwin didn't return.

As the morning dragged on, she fought not to lose faith that Irwin would return for her. To keep herself occupied, she opened the Bible and began to read. A verse in Romans stood out: *For whatsoever things were written aforetime were written for our learning, that we through patience and comfort of the scriptures might have hope.* A light seemed to come on inside her. God knew there would be times when people would feel lost and lonely with nowhere to turn. He'd had his prophets write the scriptures so she and Granny and all the other people who were facing difficulties would know they weren't alone. *He knows where I am.* The thought gave her comfort just as the words written long ago eased her mind.

Absorbed in her reading, she almost missed the sound of shod hooves. She stood, clasping the book to her chest, prepared to run if the figure emerging from the trees proved to be someone other than Irwin.

Her brother arrived, riding on a big, black mule. The animal took its time sliding to a stop when Irwin yelled whoa. Leaping from the animal's back, Irwin took care to keep the animal's reins in his hand as he continued on to stand facing Charlie Mae.

"The farmer wouldn't part with one of his horses," he stated in a belligerent tone.

"A mule will be fine." Charlie Mae gave him a hesitant smile. "You've been riding mules all your life."

"Not like this one. He don't like me." He glared at the mule. "'Sides, I always fancied ridin' a horse."

Charlie Mae reached up to pat the mule's neck. The big animal arched his neck and rubbed his head against her shoulder as she watched Irwin improvise a pack frame.

"He bites," Irwin warned. "But he's big and strong. Let's get our things loaded and git as far as we can before dark." He fastened the reins to a sapling and moved to the bundles Charlie Mae had ready. As he swung the bundle holding the tent and quilts over the animal's back and tied them to the frame, the mule bared its teeth and attempted to take a bite out of his back.

"That wasn't nice," Charlie Mae scolded. She patted the side of the mule's head and murmured in his ear to keep the animal distracted as Irwin loaded the other bundles. When he finished, he hurriedly stepped back before the animal could attempt another nip.

With the absence of a riding saddle, Irwin stood on a rock to scramble onto the mule's back; he then reached a hand down to assist Charlie Mae. When she was settled behind him with the canvas wrapped bundles at her back, he slapped the reins, signaling for the mule to move forward.

The mule didn't move. Irwin dug in his heels and yelled louder with the same results. Charlie Mae giggled.

"All right, you give it a try," Irwin snapped. "This black devil seems to like you better'n me."

Charlie Mae gave a clicking sound from one side of her mouth followed by, "Giddyap, Sugarplum." The mule stepped out at once.

"Sugarplum?" Irwin snorted.

"I think he's a really fine mule."

"He seems to think you're pretty fine too," Irwin grumbled, conceding the mule accepted her commands better than his.

They covered a considerable distance before Irwin spoke in a musing voice. "Ma had a way with mules too. They allus liked her better'n Pa."

"Do you remember our ma?" Charlie Mae asked in a hesitant voice. She'd asked Pa once about her mother, and he had clouted her upside her head.

"Yeah, I remember. She was purty and right sassy. She yusta make molasses cookies just 'cause they were the kind I liked best."

"Was she sick a long time afore she died?"

"She warn't ever sick! She runned off." Irwin kicked the mule's side to get him to move faster, and the scowl on his face said he was through talking.

* * *

CHARLIE MAE LOOKED around in awe as the mule, with its long-legged gait, traversed a St. Louis street. She'd never seen so many people or buildings before. The city was filled with mostly men, though she spotted a few calico skirts and poke bonnets. She gaped at men dressed in buckskins with hair as long as that of the ladies. Farmers and gentlemen in fancy suits and tall hats were in equal supply. Boys and dogs raced at will, and horses, mules, and oxen were common sights. The air had turned warmer, melting the streets into aromatic sludge.

Irwin found a spot a short distance out of town to set up their tent. While Charlie Mae prepared a stew using almost the last of the supplies they'd brought, Irwin set off to discover what he could about the parties preparing to head west in the next few weeks. She knew he had some money left after purchasing Sugarplum, but she wasn't sure how much. Along the way, they'd discussed a number of things, and she was relieved to learn he'd put a lot of careful thought into their journey. He also treated her better than she'd ever known any of her menfolk to treat her before. They'd talked again of their ma, and Charlie Mae discovered Irwin wasn't angry with her because she'd run off but that she hadn't taken him with her.

Her confidence in Irwin grew as she watched him meet each challenge they encountered. They would need more supplies, and she couldn't see how they could pack enough on the mule to last them all of the way to California and for them to still be able to ride the animal, but by now, she felt confident that Irwin had something in mind.

Charlie Mae took advantage of a day in camp to wash their spare sets of clothing. While the wet clothes she'd spread on nearby bushes were drying, she wandered toward some of the nearby campsites. She discovered that most camps were larger than hers and Irwin's, though she glimpsed an occasional solitary campsite that looked as small and bleak as their own. Some groups of travelers were composed of family members, but others were made up of mostly men, usually trappers or those who were banding together for protection as they journeyed to the gold fields in California.

She'd been pleasantly surprised to learn Irwin wasn't as taciturn or unfeeling as she'd always supposed. She'd gathered hints that he was concerned that the other prospectors preparing to go west wouldn't accept a female in their company. She couldn't help worrying about this too, since how could she survive if Irwin's money ran out or if the only group that would take him wouldn't take her?

It was late afternoon, and the smoke from dozens of cook fires filled the air when Irwin rode up on Sugarplum. She rubbed down the big mule and fed him an apple core while she waited for her brother to speak. He looked near to bursting with excitement.

"If the rain holds off another week, we'll be leaving on the last day of April with the biggest freight train to ever leave St. Louis and the first headed west this spring. The best part is we won't have to buy our own flour and other supplies. I hired on to drive one of Captain Walker's freight wagons in exchange for meals and a grub stake when we reach Sacramento."

"Is he willing to take me too?" She bit her lip and gazed up at him anxiously.

"You was the clincher what got me hired. Captain Walker is takin' his wife and children with him. His wife is ailin', and he's been lookin' for a respectable woman to help her and look after their two young'ns. I told him you'd been looking after our Pa's house and doin' the cookin' since our ma died. Told 'im too that Pa got married agin to a widow with a passel of youngsters you been helpin' her raise."

"That's wonderful." Charlie Mae swallowed hard. "I could almost be grateful to Agnes for giving me experience taking care of small children."

"He said he's prepared to pay ya ten dollars an' feed fer cookin' an' helpin' Missus Walker. We'll need trunks and another change of clothes . . . food to last us 'til we leave . . . a rifle . . ."

"Come eat your supper," she urged.

He accepted a steaming plate of stew. "We should get enough from sellin' that blamed mule to purchase what we need."

"Sell Sugarplum?"

"I didn't want to tell ya, but it took almost all o' the money I had to buy that mule. The farmer knew I didn't have any choice but to pay what he asked. That much coin should a paid fer two mules at least."

"I'll miss him." She said the words softly. She would miss the big animal that was always eager to do her bidding. She couldn't recall receiving much in the way of obedience before from man nor beast.

"Someday I'm gonna be rich enough to buy a dozen horses if I've a mind to. I'm gonna have a big house and all the vittles a man can eat, too." He scraped the bottom of his plate with his spoon and swallowed a long draft of water.

It was strange, she thought, that during all the years she and Irwin had lived under the same roof, she'd never considered that he might have dreams and plans for the future. Her own dreams had consisted of little more than getting through her days without being whipped or beaten by Pa and of stealing a few minutes to read. Only recently had she begun thinking about her chances of escaping the farm and having a home like the ones in books, where folks talked nice to each other and there were pretty curtains on the windows and rugs on the floor.

"Do ya think ya might read from Granny's book tonight?" He leaned back with a contented sigh. "Ma used to read to us. Sander used to read to me sometimes, too, from the books he bought, and I miss hearin' them stories. He told me the Mormon lady what lived in the woods taught ya yer letters an' you teached him." There was something humble and childlike in the simple request that touched Charlie Mae's heart.

"Yes, I'll read to you," she said. "And tomorrow, if you like, I can start teaching you your letters."

"Sander taught me to write my name already." There was a note of pride in his voice. "He said folks think more of a man who can write his name than one that has to scratch his mark."

Charlie Mae read until the fire burned down to coals and the light grew too faint to see the words any longer. Closing the book, she stared at the red coals for a time, remembering the coal she'd found that awful night in Nauvoo and the young boy who had been her friend. That was another thing she would add to her list of plans for the future. She'd have friends, and she wouldn't ever be lonely again.

* * *

CHARLIE MAE MET Sylvia Walker the following day. Irwin insisted she wear Granny's good dress for the meeting and tame her frizzy curls into a bun at the nape of her neck. The dress was too large around the middle and she had no way to take it in. She added a needle, thread, and scissors to the mental list of supplies she and Irwin needed to acquire before leaving St. Louis. She needed a hairbrush too. Granny's brush had been left behind. Her thick curls hadn't taken well to hasty finger combing the past week and were now refusing to stay in the bun she'd labored to form.

Irwin made awkward introductions when they reached the Walker camp then hurried away to assist Captain Walker, who was inspecting the wagons and meeting with a group of prospectors who wished to join his train for greater protection on the westward journey.

Mrs. Walker turned out to be thin and pale but of a cheerful nature. She confided that the recent loss of a stillborn infant had ravaged her health. The boy and girl who stood solemnly beside the wagon were introduced as Andrew, seven, and three-year-old Abby. Andrew resembled his mother, while Abby's hair was nearer red than gold, and her chubby cheeks attested to a healthy appetite.

"You're awfully young." Mrs. Walker eyed her as though doubting her ability to do the job. Charlie Mae wasn't tall, and she'd never gained much weight, making her appear closer to twelve than almost seventeen. The oversized dress hid the few curves that had appeared in recent years, adding to her youthful appearance.

"I'll be seventeen the day we set out for California."

"Have you really had as much experience cooking as your brother claims?"

"Yes, ma'am. If you'd like me to stay here today and cook supper, I'd be pleased to show you what I can do."

"It's a deal! And from now on you must call me Sylvia, and I shall call you Charlie Mae." Mrs. Walker clapped her hands in delight. "My husband is right tired of the sorry meals I prepare, but he's too loyal to partake of a decent meal at one of the hotels in town."

She showed Charlie Mae where the various supplies were stored and offered her a voluminous apron to cover her dress. Charlie May set to work. Soon a large piece of beef was sizzling in a heavy kettle, and potatoes were roasting in the coals of the fire. She wished for fresh greens, but she'd already searched along the river and in the wooded area surrounding the camp and found nothing had come through the ground yet, or if it had, it had been trampled and eaten by the large number of cattle and horses preparing to go West. She prepared a skillet cake, pouring sweet batter over canned peaches, and kneaded dough for raised biscuits.

When all was ready, Mrs. Walker sent Andrew to fetch his pa. Irwin accompanied the wagon master back to the Walker wagons and was invited to remain for supper. Irwin accepted with enthusiasm.

The captain ate with obvious enjoyment, and when he reached for his fourth biscuit, Charlie Mae felt certain the job was hers. She looked over at Mrs. Walker, who merely winked. It was enough.

Charlie Mae basked in Captain Walker's praise of her culinary skills as she and Irwin walked back to their camp. Her brother didn't comment on her successful dinner, but she knew he was pleased that her efforts were acceptable to the Walkers. She suspected he was also well-pleased by the opportunity her demonstration had provided for filling his own belly. They'd had to keep their food consumption low while traveling to avoid running out before they reached their destination, and meals had been less than satisfactory ever since Pa married Agnes.

"No!" Irwin shouted and began to run.

Startled, Charlie Mae looked around wildly. They were almost to their campsite, but it was far from the way they'd left it. Their tent was down, and their few belongings were scattered about. Her first thought was that Cletus had followed them, then she realized it probably wasn't Cletus but simply a thief who had ransacked their camp. She stooped to pick up Granny's Bible that lay face-down in the mud.

Irwin's steps didn't slow as he raced past their trashed tent. Peering into the darkness, she saw why. A figure was galloping away on Sugarplum.

8

THE MULE WAS racing toward town with Irwin in pursuit. It was obvious Irwin couldn't possibly run as fast as the mule, but with so much at stake, he had to try. Without hesitating to think of a plan, Charlie Mae began to run too. Instead of following Irwin, she raced at a diagonal toward the road, cutting through camps hoping she could head off the animal before it disappeared into the maze of city streets thronged with men and animals. She never thought as far as what she'd do if she managed to intercept the thief.

"Stop! Thief!" she shouted, collecting a string of men and boys who raced after her. The few dogs in camp joined the chase. A pain grew in her side, and her lungs felt near to bursting, but she wouldn't give up. The mule was the only thing of value she and Irwin owned. Giving up the animal to provide themselves with necessities for their journey was only tolerable because it was necessary to their survival. Losing Sugarplum to a thief would be unbearable.

Charlie Mae had narrowed the distance between her and her quarry but wasn't close enough to intervene. She was close enough to see that the rider was kicking furiously at the mule's sides and using a quirt to urge greater speed. The mule was about to disappear from sight when Charlie Mae stopped. Putting two fingers to her mouth, she released a shrill whistle, then began to scream, "Sugarplum! Whoa! Come back!"

The animal stopped so that the man riding Sugarplum flew over his head. The black mule changed course to run at full charge toward Charlie Mae. Men and boys scattered, but Charlie Mae held her ground until Sugarplum's thundering hooves stopped inches in front of her, and the mule nudged her shoulder with his big head.

"Sugarplum." Her arms circled the long, black head, and tears ran down her cheeks. Fumbling in her pocket, she produced a biscuit, which Sugarplum accepted. Charlie Mae didn't often give way to tears, but there was no holding back this time. Her shoulders shook, and tears coursed down her cheeks. A crowd gathered around her, marveling that she'd thwarted the theft. She ignored them until Irwin limped up beside her.

"Blamed thief got away," he muttered. "I was too winded and too far back to lay hold of him."

"Never seen a girl call a mule like that," a man spoke admiringly.

"I didn't know he would come when I called, or I would have called sooner," Charlie Mae whispered to Irwin.

"Let's git back to camp and see what we can salvage."

Captain Walker made his way through the crowd.

"I saw what happened. Bring your mule and whatever isn't ruined over to our camp," Captain Walker said. "Your employment might as well start now. You can begin getting used to my animals, and Mrs. Walker will be happy to have your sister's help and company before we leave."

"Ain't nobody gonna buy that mule off ya now, boy," a man familiar with Irwin's attempts to sell the mule that day hollered. "Word'll spread like wildfire that all your sister hasta do is whistle, an' that black devil will run back to her."

"I'm afraid he's right, son," Walker said quietly. "He looks like a strong animal, but no one's going to pay good money for a mule that's likely to run back to its previous owner. Would you consider loaning him to me until we get to California? I'll trade you a rifle and five dollars for the use of him."

Charlie Mae was pleased when Irwin accepted the deal. They wouldn't have as much cash to purchase necessities, but when they reached California, she suspected he'd be glad they kept the animal to haul their supplies to the gold fields.

* * *

THE DAYS UNTIL their departure passed quickly, and Charlie Mae was amazed by how much she learned each day from Sylvia, who had been educated at a fashionable girls' school. She helped Charlie Mae select two gowns suitable for their journey, helped her with her unruly hair, and when she discovered Charlie Mae's interest in books, Sylvia included Charlie Mae in her son's daily school lessons and loaned her a book from her box of carefully packed books to read during her free time. Sylvia took pains to correct Charlie Mae's grammar, too, when they were alone.

"It's a shame there aren't more ladies traveling with us this trip," Sylvia said as they sat quietly on the shady side of one of the Walker wagons. "You and I shall be each other's sole friend during our journey, and I am sincerely grateful to the Lord for your arrival. I would prefer that the children have other children about, but their lack of playmates will not deter their spirits so severely as I expect my own would be without the companionship of another woman."

"My brother said settling land isn't the purpose of this train and that your husband's intent is to travel quickly and to make his fortune from selling those things miners need." Charlie Mae spoke slowly and distinctly.

"That's right and well said, too," Sylvia said, complimenting Charlie Mae on her careful diction. "My dear husband traveled west last year with just eight wagons and sold his supplies, the wagons, and all of the mules for a goodly sum before he had time to pitch his tent. He traveled back to Ohio on horseback, making excellent time after he reached the Salt Lake Valley by riding with a band of Mormon missionaries who were traveling all the way to New York."

"Wasn't he tempted to stay and try his luck finding gold?"

"No, he wished to be with me and the children and couldn't see himself as a miner. He learned that thousands of men and boys and a few women have traveled to California from all over the world to make their fortunes panning and digging for gold. But not many of them are adequately supplied. The miners have to eat, and they need blankets, picks, pans, tents, and all kinds of things. With the abundance of gold they're finding, they can afford to pay much higher prices than what the items are worth in the East. Being an experienced freighter, John disposed of our home and his freight yard in Ohio. Then using his profits from last season and the sale of his property, he purchased supplies to freight to California, where he feels there are better opportunities."

"Do you plan to live there?" Charlie Mae asked. It seemed unlikely that a cultured woman like Sylvia Walker would be content to live in the tent cities of either San Francisco or Sacramento.

"It may be difficult for a time." Sylvia sighed. "But we do not wish to be separated for months or years. John has assured me that the next wave of travelers to California will be farmers and merchants who will carry civilization with them, and he wishes to be there to provide plows, seed, and furnishings for them."

* * *

CHARLIE MAE DISCOVERED that young Andrew was nothing like the young half-brothers she'd left behind. He was quiet but protective of his fearless little sister. He also preferred reading a book to accompanying his father and Irwin when they saw to the mules. Abby giggled and played cheerfully inside the wagon or in the thick dust that had replaced the mud around her mother's wagon. Charlie Mae added one more item to the growing list of plans for her future—she hoped to have children: happy, well-behaved children like the Walker children, not rude tyrants such as

Agnes's boys. She'd rather be a mother like Sylvia, too, who played with her children, told them stories, and spoke softly to them than be like Agnes, who shouted and belittled her boys.

Each afternoon, Charlie Mae took the children for a long walk, allowing their mother to rest for an hour or two. On their return, Abby would be ready to crawl into the wagon for a nap beside her mother while Charlie Mae and Andrew read and began supper preparations. This time of preparation became a pleasant interlude in a life that had known little pleasure and fostered a deep friendship between the two women.

On the morning their trek began, Charlie Mae couldn't hide her excitement. Captain Walker and two scouts dashed about the encampment on horseback, shouting orders and helping the teamsters get their wagons and animals in order. First came the wagon the Walkers would share at night and which held Sylvia's personal possessions. It would be pulled by four mules. It was to be followed by two wagons connected together that contained cooking supplies and the Walkers' personal furniture. Irwin was assigned to drive the six-mule team pulling those wagons. Sugarplum was harnessed with the mules beginning the trip under Irwin's charge. A short, bandy-legged man who had been hired to cook for the teamsters would drive the Walker family wagon. At night, one cook wagon would be Charlie Mae's bedroom, which she would share with the children. The other would be shared by the camp cook and Irwin.

Following the family wagons were forty heavy freight wagons with their loads tightly lashed under canvas. Some of the freight wagons were hitched together and pulled by eight to sixteen mules while the heaviest wagons, those carrying rifles, ammunition, cook stoves, and plows, had their own teams. The mules, for the most part, settled into their traces without any problems, but a few acted up, exhibiting the temperamental tendencies long attributed to the breed. Such occasions excited the half dozen dogs that were part of the train, occasioning a great deal of barking and shouting from both the mule skinners and the dogs' masters. A dozen lighter wagons followed the freight wagons, some pulled by mules and some by horses. They were manned by miners and trappers wishing the protection of the large train on the hazardous trek.

Charlie Mae stood in the wagon, surveying the string of wagons stretched out behind them, awed by the impressive sight. Far in the distance, she caught sight of two wagons she hadn't seen before. It looked as though they were being pulled by horses, and the rising sun was making their canvas tops appear pink. They were too far away to pick out details. Following them was a herd of extra mules, horses, and a small number of cattle being driven by riders on horses. Prospectors mounted on horses or mules were strung along the length of the train, which stretched for more than a mile.

"It's an impressive sight." Sylvia stood beside her with one hand shading her eyes. "I asked John why he was using mules instead of the oxen he has depended on for years to pull his freight wagons. He said that though oxen are stronger, mules are faster and more sure-footed, and he wishes to reach California as quickly as possible. That's also why we won't be required to walk as much as women on other wagon trains do." Sylvia's willingness to share her knowledge was one of the things that endeared her to Charlie Mae, who knew little of the world beyond the farm but was eager to learn all she could.

"Me see!" Abby held up her arms in an impatient gesture to be picked up. Charlie Mae was quick to oblige, hoisting the child in her arms so she could see the long line of wagons stretched out behind them. Andrew stood on his toes atop a box for a better view. Sylvia stood beside him.

"You best get inside," their driver said. "Looks to me like the captain is about to signal the beginning of the march." Sylvia jumped down to the main portion of the wagon, and Charlie Mae handed Abby to her. They all moved to the back of the wagon, where the canvas was rolled back, affording them a view of the long snake of wagons. A shrill whistle sounded, followed by the sharp sound of whips cracking in the air. One after another, the wagons lurched into motion, and the constant squeak of harness leather formed a steady rhythm.

The children were excited, and settling Andrew to his studies took a great deal of persuasion. Following a brief nooning, Charlie Mae decided to walk for a time with the children to afford their mother a chance to rest and to give them a chance to work off their wiggles. It felt good to stretch her legs, and Andrew seemed to enjoy physical movement as well, but it didn't take long until Abby was signaling that keeping up with the long-legged mules was too much for her chubby, short legs. Charlie Mae carried her for a time. Eventually she set the toddler inside the wagon with instructions to curl up beside her mother to rest.

Late afternoon brought clouds streaming across the sky, and a breeze ruffled the manes of the mules. As evening drew near, the wind gusts became stronger, and the clouds formed gray under-bellies. Captain Walker called the train to a halt and instructed the drivers to form a double circle, securing the stock inside for the night, where they would be easier to control should the impending storm frighten any of the animals. As they were the first large train on the trail, there was adequate feed for the animals inside the circle, and the drivers took turns leading their teams to the nearby stream. Tents began to sprout up all the way around the inside perimeter of the wagon circle.

As soon as the Walker wagons were in position, Charlie Mae began supper preparations. From the corner of her eye, she saw someone coming toward her and flinched. Cletus! Fear rose in her throat, and she looked around for a place to hide then back to the approaching man. As he came closer, she could see he wasn't Cletus and felt foolish for allowing the long, stringy hair and the man's lanky form to mislead her. As he came closer, she could see he carried an armload of firewood and that he was the driver who had been assigned the task of fetching wood for her cook fire that night. He dumped the wood not far from the wagon, and she was grateful she didn't need to scour the trail for wood as Pa would have expected her to do. Captain Walker's efficiency and thoroughness was completely foreign to her experience. If she ever decided to marry, she'd look for a man who thought ahead like Captain Walker.

Before the stew and biscuits were quite ready, long slants of rain began to slash their way toward the ground. Worried that the meal would be ruined and that her first night on the trail would prove a disaster, she looked around for a way to keep the rain off the campfire. She noticed that the camp cook who had set up his wagon some distance away had a wide, canvas awning stretched from the side of the wagon over his cooking area.

Rushing to the wagon, she searched for a similar awning to cover her cooking area. The rolled canvas was easy to spot, but it was large and awkward to handle. As she struggled to unroll the canvas and wondered how to set it up, she felt the weight lifted from her arms. She looked up to see a young man grinning at her. A wide-brimmed hat nearly hid his face, but she could see straight brown hair poking from beneath its brim and hazel eyes sparkling with laughter. He wasn't a great deal taller than she, but he had wide shoulders and heavy arms. He handled the heavy canvas as though it weighed no more than a broom handle. In moments he had the awning set up.

"Thank you," she said, looking shyly at her feet. Then remembering her stew, she rushed to give it a vigorous stirring.

"Ain't you the gal what saved your brother's mule from a thief?" he asked.

Blushing furiously, she nodded her head. She wanted to explain that she hadn't done any more than shout the mule's name and that she didn't know why Sugarplum had taken a fancy to her and came when he heard her voice.

"Funniest thing I ever seen! One minute that fella was grinnin', thinkin' he'd get away easy; the next he was flyin' over that black mule's head like a pesky fly." He chuckled, then added, "My name's Chester Gafton." He looked at her expectantly, and she realized he was waiting for her to introduce herself.

"I'm Charlie Mae Riggins." She should have said Charlotte, she chided herself.

"I reckon we'll be seeing each other around." He looked pleased by the prospect and stood smiling longer than necessary. "I better get back to my own supper," he said, ending the awkward pause. He touched his hat brim, and she watched him hunch his shoulders to keep the rain from pouring off the brim of his hat to slide down his collar as he dashed into the storm.

Irwin ate with the other men, but Captain Walker appeared out of the rain for a hasty meal with his wife and children. When they finished eating, he left to issue last-minute instructions to the men who were assigned to guard the camp that night. While Charlie Mae cleaned up the cooking utensils and placed everything in order for the next meal, Sylvia got her children ready for bed and tucked them in for the night. When they were asleep, she rejoined Charlie Mae beside the smoldering fire under the canvas awning.

"You look tired," Charlie Mae said, looking toward Sylvia. "You better get in bed before you catch cold." The rain had given the night air a chilly edge.

"I shall." Sylvia sighed with weariness. "In California the sun shines almost every day. I expect I will grow stronger there." She stood on shaky legs.

"Here, let me help you." Charlie Mae put her arm around the other woman and walked her to her wagon. "Get beneath your quilts quickly."

"You must rest too." Sylvia smiled wanly.

"I shall," Charlie Mae promised. She turned away to return to the fire, but Sylvia's voice stopped her, causing Charlie Mae to look back.

"I didn't forget," Sylvia said quietly. "This is for you." She held out a parcel. "Today, you are seventeen. A woman. What a wonderful day to begin a journey and a new life."

Sylvia drew back inside the wagon, and Charlie Mae carried the parcel to her stool beside the dying fire. She simply looked at the package for a long time. She didn't remember ever receiving a gift before—except for a borrowed white dress. Finally her fingers untied the string securing the brown paper. Spreading the paper apart, she stared in awe at a thick shawl painstakingly made from dark maroon yarn.

Burying her face in the soft garment, she felt the prickling of tears attempting to force their way to the surface. Pulling the shawl across her shoulders, she marveled at its warmth and beauty. She didn't know it was possible to be so happy. She stood, preparing to make her way to the wagon where she was to sleep. As she walked, a gentle touch on her back caused her to turn, thinking Irwin had come to tell her good night on their first night on the trail, she was surprised to find herself looking into Sugarplum's big, brown eyes.

"Oh, Sugarplum," she whispered. "I'm glad we weren't forced to part. It'll be glorious to go to California together."

Lying on a thick feather tick atop the barrels stored in the Walker's second wagon, Charlie Mae lay awake for a long time listening to the steady beat of rain striking the canvas top. She listened to the children's soft breathing nearby and the stomping of hooves beyond the wagon. She was almost asleep when she remembered the horse-drawn wagons. With all the rushing to make camp and prepare supper in the rain, she'd forgotten the wagons that had sparkled pink in the early morning light. Tomorrow she'd ask Sylvia about them.

9

FREQUENT RAIN SQUALLS slowed the train as the wagons crawled across Missouri. Mud clutched at wagons and mules alike while the men struggled with fevers and sniffles. The showers seemed to hit the hardest about the time they made camp each evening, and many evenings, dinner was almost ready by the time the last stragglers made their way into camp. She understood that the first wagons moved with greater ease than the latter ones, because being early in the season, the mules found grass to walk on as they pulled the wagons, but the later wagons, even though they spread out across a half-mile-wide swath, sank into the black, muddy tracks left by the lead wagons.

Charlie Mae kept busy cooking and trying to keep the children warm and dry, leaving her little time to pay attention to anything else as they set up camp each evening. At first she'd been apprehensive whenever any of the men approached the Walker wagons, but as the men merely touched their hats then continued about their business, she'd begun to feel safe. The courtesy shown her by Captain Walker and the older man who drove the cook wagons went far toward easing her concerns as well.

The mornings usually saw the end of the rain, but the puddles and Missouri mud brought their own misery. Even as she huddled in her shawl and carried heavy cooking pots to and from the wagon, she didn't regret leaving the farm. She was accustomed to hard work, but the discovery that all men were not like Pa and Cletus made her burdens lighter.

She and Irwin usually managed to exchange a few words before
they started out each morning and again when they set up evening
camp as he released the mules from their traces and as she collected
supplies for supper from the wagon he drove. She always patted
Sugarplum's neck and whispered in his ear before Irwin led him
away, and sometimes she slipped the mule an apple core.

Chester Gafton became a frequent visitor, and she learned he
was twenty-two, just a year older than Irwin. He said he'd been
working for Captain Walker since he was fourteen, at first feeding
and brushing the stock, then making short deliveries. This was his
first long trek, but since his widowed mother had remarried and
his sisters were all wed, there was nothing to hold him in the East.
He, like thousands of other young men, hoped to make his fortune
in California.

Chester took upon himself the responsibility for setting up the
canvas rain shelter over her cooking area each night, and he
usually lingered to talk to her while she prepared supper. She
figured he was lonely without the company of his mother and
sisters and that being on his own was as new to him as her own
freedom was to her—and she understood about loneliness.
Though she and Irwin had undertaken this journey together,
Irwin wasn't given to small talk or sharing his feelings. Chester's
friendly conversation became something to look forward to each
day—and he made her laugh. When he discovered she'd had little
to laugh about in her life, he doubled his efforts to tease and
acquaint her with humorous anecdotes.

On the first evening without rain, Chester arrived as she was
scrubbing out the cooking pots. Seating himself on one of the
camp stools, he said, "I would have been here sooner, but one of
the wagons broke an axle, and I was needed to hold up one corner
of the wagon while a new one was put in place."

She handed him a plate of the cobbler she'd baked that evening,
and he dug in with relish. After a moment, he wiped his mouth

and said, "I thought *my* Ma was good at making cobblers, but this'n is the best I ever ate."

"You miss your family, don't you?" Charlie Mae asked.

"I reckon so. I been lookin' after Ma and my sisters a long time, and it seems right strange not to be worryin' about earnin' enough money to keep 'em fed and whether they be meetin' the right kind of fellas."

"And what kind of man do you consider the right kind of fella?" she asked.

"One just like me." He chuckled, and she joined in his laughter.

"Who's he?" A suspicious voice interrupted.

Charlie Mae looked up to see Irwin standing at the edge of the light given off by the dying cook fire. He didn't look pleased to see Chester.

"My name's Chester Gafton, if it's any business of yours." Chester set his plate aside and rose to his feet. He wasn't as tall as Irwin but easily outweighed him. While Irwin was tall and wiry, Chester was as solid as a young bull. He thrust out his heavy chest much as Charlie Mae had seen young roosters do when challenged by the flock's patriarch.

"Anybody pesterin' my sister is my business." Irwin wasn't intimidated.

"He isn't pestering me," Charlie Mae was quick to say. "That first night when it rained, he showed me how to set up the canvas awning to keep the rain from putting out my fire. He stops by sometimes to talk."

Both men relaxed somewhat, though they kept a wary eye on each other. Charlie Mae scraped out the last of the cobbler and thrust the plate toward Irwin. He accepted it eagerly. When he finished, he wiped his mouth with the back of his sleeve. "Cookie does all right," he said, "but he don't make cobblers."

Charlie Mae smiled. She knew that was as close as Irwin would come to offering her a compliment. Tall and lean, most folks would never guess her brother had a sweet tooth.

"Mighty tasty." Chester sighed, giving his plate one last scrape.

Charlie Mae took their plates to wash and listened as they began a stilted conversation.

"You a mule skinner?" Irwin questioned Chester. "Can't say as I rightly like the idea of my sister seein' a mule skinner."

"I drive mules and horses, oxen too. Been doin' odd jobs for the captain since I was a lad."

"You're younger than the other mule skinners. Most looks to be at least thirty."

"You ain't thirty, and ain't you drivin' mules?"

"I'm only drivin' mules to git to California. When I git there, I mean to look for gold."

"I'm workin' for a grubstake too," Chester admitted. With the mention of gold, both young men relaxed and soon discovered they shared a common dream. They were still sitting beside the fire that had burned down to coals, arguing the merits of panning versus building a sluice box, when Charlie Mae bid them both good night and made her way to her wagon. *Men!* She grumbled under her breath, feeling vexed even though she really had nothing to be annoyed about. It was just that she grew weary of all the talk about gold, and she felt cheated out of the time she and Chester might have gotten to know each other better and laugh together over some small incident in their day.

* * *

SHE WAS AWAKE before daylight the next morning. She dressed quietly and made her way out of the wagon without disturbing the children. The air carried a hint of summer warmth and was rich with the scent of rain-washed earth. She paused a moment to breathe deeply and thought about spring planting, feeling a moment's sadness for her old life. Then she remembered Pa and Cletus and put thoughts of the past behind her. She and Irwin were doing fine. They were traveling with friendly folks and on their way to a new life that promised to be much better than the old one. Granny had been fond of saying, "God helps them what helps theirselves," and that's what she and Irwin meant to do.

A faint hint of light was beginning to herald a new day as she set to work preparing breakfast. Captain Walker climbed down from his wagon, carrying his boots. He smiled but didn't speak before seating himself on a stool to pull on his boots. Soon men were going about the business of watering mules, and the morning's silence was broken by the braying of animals, the barking of dogs, and the shouts of men.

The morning took on the sense of urgency she'd become accustomed to with everyone anxious to complete breakfast and routine chores in order to be on the road as soon as possible. With the sun shining brightly and a haze of steam rising off the damp ground, there was a general air of cheerfulness as they went about their tasks. It seemed she scarcely had time to clear away the breakfast dishes before the call came to move out.

That day, Charlie Mae found concentrating on Sylvia's lesson difficult. Her eyes kept wandering toward the patch of blue framed by the opening in the canvas at the back of the wagon. After lunch she decided to walk for awhile, and Andrew asked to walk with her.

"All right," Sylvia told her son. "You may walk until Charlie Mae becomes tired or she finds you can't keep up."

Charlie Mae enjoyed the steady pace the mules set. She felt almost like a child, playing with Andrew, skipping puddles and racing ahead, then waiting for the wagon to catch up. Andrew spotted a lizard scurrying through the grass, and together they followed it for a short distance. Where it disappeared through a crack in a pile of rocks, they spotted a patch of pale lavender May flowers. It was all new and wonderful to Charlie Mae to play with such abandon. They gathered a handful of blossoms to take back to Sylvia.

"We'll have to run now," Charlie Mae announced, pointing to the wagon train. Their wagon was almost out of sight. Stuffing the flowers into her pocket, she took Andrew's hand and began to run.

After a few steps, Andrew pulled his hand free. As he did so, he shouted, "I'll race you."

Charlie Mae and Andrew ran toward the wagons. She paced herself so that she neither passed the child nor lagged behind. She enjoyed the sensation of the warm spring air rushing past her face and the exertion of muscles that had received little exercise during the past week. As they neared a freight wagon, she shouted, "We'll have to slow down now before we frighten the mules."

With a show of reluctance, Andrew slowed to a trot. Able to look around as they moved at the slower pace, Charlie Mae discovered they'd fallen far behind their own wagon but were only a little more than halfway back the long line of freight wagons. Some of the drivers smiled and waved to them, their attention recalling her earlier fears. She slowed down, keeping as much distance as possible between her and the wagons until she remembered Chester drove one of those wagons. She found herself searching the faces of the drivers to see if she might see him. If Chester were near, she'd be safe.

She didn't discover Chester, but she saw something that amazed her. Bringing up the rear of the long train of wagons were the two pink wagons she'd noticed the first day. They really were pink! The canvas was rolled up to allow air to circulate through the wagons, but there was no mistaking the color.

Even more startling was the sight of six women riding on the wagons or walking beside them. They were arrayed in gowns as colorful as their wagons' canvas tops. She stood still, staring in shocked surprise until Andrew tugged on her hand.

Reminded of her responsibility, she turned away from the curious women and made a game of taking giant steps until a horse pulled up beside them. She looked up as Captain Walker tipped his hat toward her before greeting his son.

"Would you like a ride back to the wagon?" he asked the boy.

Andrew nodded his head, exhibiting his eagerness. Charlie Mae wasn't certain whether the boy was eager to ride with his father or if their excursion had tired him, but once Andrew was settled in front of his father and he'd waved farewell, she set out with long strides, relishing both the freedom of movement and freedom from responsibility for a brief time.

A commotion a short distance ahead caught her attention, and a black-and-white dog streaked in front of her. It was closely followed by a larger, yellow dog with bared teeth. The second dog caught up to the first animal, and a snarling, biting fight erupted.

Stepping back to stay out of their way, she looked around for the dogs' owners. Seeing no one hurrying forward to stop the fight, she picked up a stick and took a step toward the rolling pile of fur.

"Stop that," she ordered, shaking the stick at the animals. They paid her no heed. The smaller, black-and-white dog seemed to be getting the worst of the battle. Fearing it might be killed by the larger animal, she moved closer, hoping to insert the stick between the two dogs.

"What do you think you're doing?" An angry voice came from behind her. A hand snatched the stick from her grasp.

Without taking her eyes from the dogs, she shouted back, "That yellow dog is trying to kill the smaller one."

"Who cares? He's just a stray."

Shocked, she whirled to face a tall, lean, unshaven man wearing ragged overalls who had pulled his wagon out of line. "I care!" Without thinking, she attempted to wrestle the stick away from him.

"I ain't got time for this!" He jerked away from her and gave a sharp whistle. The yellow dog left the fight to dash to his side.

"He's your dog?"

"Best coon dog in the whole of Missouri," the man boasted, but Charlie Mae was no longer listening. She knelt beside the other dog that was still lying on the ground. She noticed he was thin and dirty, his matted coat streaked with smears of blood. His sides were heaving, so she knew he was alive.

"Nice dog," she whispered in a tentative voice. She'd always liked dogs, even Pa's lazy hounds. Behind her she heard the driver urge his mules on and issue a command to his dog as he moved back into the line of wagons. A feeling of panic struck her. If she didn't hurry to catch up, she'd be left behind.

The afternoon was far spent, and it wouldn't be long before the wagons circled for the night. She could easily catch up then, but there would be no hot evening meal started for Sylvia and the children. Even now, Sylvia was probably awake and wondering about her, but her tender heart wouldn't permit her to walk off and leave an injured animal.

She stretched the back of her hand toward the dog's nose. She couldn't tell whether he sniffed it or not, but she continued her reach until she could pat the back of the dog's head. Since he still offered no objection, she parted his tangled coat to examine what appeared to be the worst of his wounds. Her examination revealed that in addition to a dull coat and emaciated body, his footpads were worn and tender. Several of the larger wounds needed to be tended but didn't appear life threatening. She tried to think of a way to get him back to the wagon, where she could tend to him and start dinner. She wasn't sure what breed the dog was, but it wasn't as big as a hunting dog. Perhaps she could carry it.

Bending, she struggled to lift the animal. When she straightened, she was surprised to discover the dog was no heavier than Abby, though certainly much more awkward to carry. The poor thing was nothing but bones and hair.

She set out with the dog in her arms, moving as rapidly as she could. No matter how hard she tried, though, she couldn't seem to keep pace with the mules and kept falling farther behind. The dog occasionally whimpered, and she feared she was hurting it.

"Don't worry, dog," she tried to reassure the animal. "We'll catch up. Then I can take care of you and find you something to eat."

"What happened to the dog?" It was a woman's voice. She was surprised to find two of the women from the mysterious pink wagons walking beside her.

"A big dog attacked him," she answered.

"Is he seriously hurt?" one of the women asked. She seemed to be examining Charlie Mae, not the dog. She was dressed in a bright yellow gown with a low-cut, ruffled neckline. Charlie Mae averted her eyes, looking back down at the dog she carried.

"I don't think so. He has a couple of bite wounds that need attention, but mostly he seems exhausted and hungry. The owner of the other dog said he's a stray."

"I've heard of dogs that have been left behind trying to catch up to their masters and some that have accompanied their masters so far, then deciding they've had enough, they turn around and try to make their way back home," the other woman said, averting her eyes. Charlie Mae turned to her and was glad to see that her deep green gown had a higher neckline than that of the first woman. She appeared to be younger too, about her own age or a bit younger, and shy. She had long, chestnut curls and warm, brown eyes framed by the longest, thickest lashes Charlie Mae had ever seen. She also had an impossibly small waist.

"You'll never catch up to your wagon carrying the dog," the woman in the yellow dress said in a practical voice. "Give him to me, and I'll see that his wounds get treated."

"But he's bleeding and dirty," Charlie Mae protested. "He might ruin your dress."

"No more than yours, and I have others." Charlie Mae flushed, sensing the two strange women knew her selection of gowns was severely limited.

"I think you better do as Miss Louisa suggests," the woman in green said in a soft voice. "Mrs. Walker won't be pleased if you introduce a dirty, flea-ridden dog to her children."

"She won't take kindly to the dog either if dinner is late." The other woman looked pointedly toward the wagon train where the freight wagons had all passed them.

She knew the women were right, but she hated to shift a responsibility she'd taken on to other shoulders.

"Don't worry. If you want him back after he's well, you can have him. And you can visit him as often as you like." Louisa reached for the animal, and Charlie Mae surrendered him reluctantly. Louisa promptly deposited the dog in the younger woman's arms.

Charlie Mae patted the dog's head. "Take care of him," she whispered. She clutched her skirt and ran, though she suspected Sylvia would say her behavior wasn't ladylike. It wasn't until she slowed with a stitch in her side that she remembered she'd talked back to the man with the yellow dog. Her audacity stunned her, and she began to tremble. In her experience, talking back to a man meant a beating.

She was almost to the Walker wagon when parts of her conversation with the brightly dressed women began to sink in. She knew nothing about them, yet they seemed to know who she was and that she worked for Sylvia Walker.

10 ❧

INSTEAD OF RETIRING to her wagon, Sylvia rejoined Charlie Mae near the campfire after the children were settled in their bed that night. It wasn't long before both Irwin and Chester appeared.

"Did you hurt yourself?" Chester suddenly asked. It took a moment before Charlie Mae realized the question was directed toward her.

"No," she responded in a puzzled voice.

"That looks like blood on your collar and cuffs." He frowned as he scrutinized her.

"I found an injured dog while walking today." She glanced quickly toward Sylvia then down at the stains on her formerly white cuffs. "I tried to help him . . ."

"Did he bite you?" Sylvia cut in.

"No, he was emaciated and weak, but another dog attacked him and some of the wounds were bleeding. I must have gotten blood on me when I picked him up."

"You shouldn't have taken Andrew anywhere near that dog. He's quite terrified of dogs." It was the first time Sylvia had spoken to Charlie Mae with sharpness. For a moment she was too stunned to consider defending herself, then she remembered that Andrew never shied away from the dogs that accompanied some of the mule team drivers. It was more likely that Sylvia was the one who was afraid of dogs.

In a quiet voice Charlie Mae said, "Andrew and I walked almost to the rear of the wagon train. We'd started back when the captain came along and offered Andrew a ride on his horse. I didn't find the dog until after Captain Walker rode off with Andrew." That seemed to soothe Sylvia's concern but also confirmed what the two women who had taken the dog had said about Sylvia not welcoming the injured dog. She wondered how they knew about Sylvia, since Sylvia had never mentioned them.

"Where is the dog?" Irwin asked. "I didn't see you carrying it when you caught up to the wagons just before we stopped for the night."

"Two ladies saw me carrying him. They offered to take the dog and care for him until he's better." She turned to Sylvia. "I thought you and I were the only ladies on the wagon train."

"Those women aren't ladies." Sylvia drew herself up, appearing both indignant and embarrassed. Charlie Mae glanced with questioning eyes toward Irwin and Chester. Neither would meet her eyes. There was something about the women Sylvia and the two men didn't want her to know. Slowly, understanding began to enter her mind. She'd heard Pa and her older brothers discuss wicked women who accepted money to do things Granny said were evil.

"Oh." She didn't know what to say. Except for their flamboyant dresses and the pink canvas of their wagons, the two women she'd encountered hadn't seemed any different from other women she'd met in St. Louis. They were much nicer and prettier than Agnes, and from what Deke had said about her stepmother, she'd gotten the impression that women of that type tended to be plump and rude. Of course, she didn't have much experience with the female gender other than what she'd gleaned from books, two elderly women, and her friendship with Sylvia.

Chester and Irwin bid her good night shortly after Captain Walker joined the small group gathered about the dying campfire.

Charlie Mae rose to her feet also. She was tired from the day's exertions and anxious to find her own bed.

"I'll walk with you." Sylvia rose to her feet and took her arm. When they reached the wagon where Charlie Mae slept, Sylvia spoke in a quiet voice.

"Since you weren't privileged to be reared by a mother who could teach you such things, I feel I must warn you not to have anything to do with those women at the rear of the wagon train. If your paths cross again during this trip, pretend you don't see them."

"I didn't know . . ."

"I'm sorry you had to find out in such an awkward manner that there are women of low character on this train. I was angry with my husband when he informed me that they would be following at the rear of his wagons. He said that women of that sort always follow where there are large numbers of men and that if he didn't allow them to follow his wagons, they would attach themselves to a train made up of families and cause contentions that could endanger marriages or even lives. I suppose he's right— and they paid well for the privilege. They also agreed not to . . . well—*work* until we reach California."

"It shames me to admit I know little about what a proper woman should do, having grown up in a house full of males, but it seems unkind to snub those women when they only attempted to aid me." Charlie Mae couldn't meet Sylvia's eyes. Instead, her gaze went beyond her friend and employer to a distant small fire at the far side of the ring of wagons. She imagined the grateful dog snuggling in the arms of the woman who had carried him away and the various women feeding him choice scraps from their evening meal. At least she hoped they were caring for him in a kind manner. "I must check on the dog from time to time since I said I would," she mumbled.

"Good women do not associate with women who . . . have relations with men who aren't their husbands," Sylvia said stiffly.

"It just won't do for you to have anything to do with them, and I cannot understand why you wish to bother yourself over a filthy dog. Nevertheless, I'll discuss the matter with John and see what he might suggest." Sylvia's voice was softened.

* * *

IN THE COMING weeks, the weather continued to improve, and the wagons made rapid progress. They left Missouri, crossed Nebraska, and were soon approaching the high Wyoming plateaus. Grass was plentiful, and they made good time. They didn't meet any Indians, though Captain Walker's scouts reported that they'd crossed Indian signs a few times and that he felt confident the tribes were aware of the large number of men in the party and would not attack.

Charlie Mae enjoyed caring for the children and relished her first friendship with another woman only a few years older than herself. She received daily reports from Irwin and Chester concerning the dog she'd rescued, and one evening Chester strolled to her campfire leading the dog by a length of rope. He'd fashioned a collar from a piece of worn harness and attached the rope to it.

Seeing the dog, Charlie Mae dropped to her knees and reached out a hand to the animal, wondering if he might remember her. He ignored her hand and eagerly jumped nearer to run his tongue across her cheek. She wrapped her arms around his furry neck that now gleamed from good health and attention. She buried her face in the animal's thick fur for a moment before looking up to smile at Chester.

"Thank you," she said. "I've longed to see for myself that he is really well again."

"Doggie!" Abby escaped from her mother's grasp to run toward them.

"No, Abby," Sylvia screamed. "Dogs bite."

Charlie Mae looked up in time to halt the child's mad dash. She took Abby's little hand and showed her how to approach the dog and pet his fur instead of pulling it. "Nice doggie," the child crooned.

Charlie Mae looked up to see that Sylvia had turned white and that Andrew cowered behind his mother's wide skirt. She suspected his fear came more from seeing his mother frightened than because he feared the dog. "He won't hurt Abby," she said, attempting to soothe the other woman's fears. Sylvia didn't appear convinced.

"Ma'am," Chester slowly rotated his hat between his fingers, "I didn't mean to scare you none. I just came to see if Miss Charlie Mae would like to take the dog for a walk. I'll bring her back afore it's dark."

"Yes, yes. Go." Charlie Mae suspected Sylvia would have agreed to almost anything that would put distance between her baby and the dog.

"Me go!" Abby reached for the rope.

"Not today, Sweetie." Charlie Mae picked her up and returned her to her mother.

"My doggie. Mine," the child screamed in protest, kicking her legs and demanding to be set down.

"That is not your dog," Sylvia scolded. "Now I must wash you again." She carried her protesting daughter toward the nearby stream.

Chester turned the dog's rope leash over to Charlie Mae, and they began a leisurely stroll in the opposite direction from that which Sylvia and her daughter had taken. They wandered for several minutes before she asked, "Does he have a name? I mean, what do . . . *they* call him?"

"Since no one knows what his real name is, Miss Bonnie calls him Mr. Rags." Chester scuffed a toe in the dirt. "She's real good to him, feeds him the best scraps and lets him sit on the wagon seat when it's her turn to drive."

Charlie Mae stopped to pat the dog's head. "I'm so glad you're feeling better, Mr. Rags."

The dog tried to lick her face, causing her to laugh. There was something about the dog's exuberant display of affection for her that touched a need seldom filled in her life. "I wish I could keep him with me now."

"The captain arranged for your brother and me to take turns meeting Miss Bonnie some distance from Miss Louisa's wagons each night to check on the dog for you. I don't reckon his missus would welcome Mr. Rags living with you." Chester sounded sympathetic.

"No, Sylvia has made it plain she doesn't care for dogs. Pa's hounds weren't friendly like Mr. Rags," Charlie Mae went on to confide. "Mostly they slept in a pile on the porch and barked their heads off if someone came calling. They only ever minded Pa, and they tolerated me because I was the one to carry bones and scraps to them after Pa and the boys finished eating." Charlie Mae began walking again, and Mr. Rags danced at her side.

Chester walked closer than necessary on her other side. She wondered if he liked her the way young men in some of Sander's books liked special girls and if maybe he was courting her. She liked him, and he didn't scare her like most men did. He never made romantic speeches or quoted poems, but Granny said courting usually began with walking out together, and she'd warned Charlie Mae not to get discouraged if she didn't have a beau by the time she was sixteen, when most girls were wed. "Some girls take their time findin' a man what suits 'em. Why, some girls don't get hitched afore they's eighteen, and with your pa bein' unfriendly and all, it might take longer for the young men to larn about ya." Charlie Mae had sensed Granny had meant her words as consolation for her lack of marriage prospects.

Chester found a spot beside the creek where they could sit. He alternated tossing sticks into the water and throwing them along the bank for Mr. Rags to retrieve. After a few minutes, he spoke of his plans to search for gold when they reached California. He said he'd discussed the matter with Irwin, and the two young men had decided to become partners.

"I heard that most of the streams close to settlements are getting played out and lots of folks are giving up, but with the two of us working together, our chances of success will be better than most," he said. "Captain Walker has promised to outfit both of us, and with Irwin's mule to carry supplies, we can go to more remote areas than other prospectors. With you to cook for us and your dog to warn of trespassers, we'll be in good shape."

"Perhaps I can learn to pan, too." Charlie Mae didn't relish being confined to the cook fire while Irwin and Chester searched for gold. She wasn't as set on getting rich and owning a big house as Irwin was, but she didn't want to spend her whole life at the beck and call of other folks either. She'd like to have a home of her own and be surrounded by people who laughed and talked with her.

"I'll teach you." Chester smiled at her. "But if you don't find any gold, I'll share mine with you." He ducked his head, and his ears turned red. "It'll be dark soon. Best we move along." He stood and held out a hand to help Charlie Mae rise to her feet.

"Mr. Rags!" Charlie Mae called, and when the dog came running to her, she fastened the rope to his collar again. He trotted at her heels as she and Chester continued their walk. She mulled over Chester's offer to share his gold with her. A pleasant feeling filled her heart. She was almost certain Chester's offer meant he was courting her.

Mr. Rags perked up his ears and began tugging at his leash. Charlie Mae walked faster, putting aside thoughts of courting. Ahead, she could see someone seated near the small stream where they were camped for the night. As they drew closer, she could see the seated person was a woman. In fact, she was one of the women who had taken Mr. Rags to care for him. Instead of a green dress, the woman wore a deep navy blue shirtwaist that came almost to her chin. Brilliant red buttons extended the length of the dress from her neck to her hem. Long dark ringlets, glinting red in the setting sun, cascaded over her shoulder as she watched their approach.

Charlie Mae was uncertain what her course of action should be. She certainly didn't wish to imply approval of the woman's profession. Neither did she wish to go against Sylvia's counsel, but it wasn't in her to be rude to the person who cared for the dog she'd found.

Chester's steps began to lag, and she sensed he wasn't comfortable with the situation. Taking matters in her own hands, Charlie Mae stepped forward, extending her hand. "Thank you for caring for Mr. Rags. He seems perfectly happy now and quite attached to you."

The other woman glanced around, as though nervous, before taking the hand Charlie Mae offered. "He's been a perfect gentleman, and I enjoy his company immensely."

"I don't believe I introduced myself the day I found him. I'm Charlotte Mae Riggins, but most people call me Charlie Mae."

"I go by Miss Bonnie."

"And I'm Miss Louisa." Charlie Mae hadn't noticed the other woman's arrival, but she extended her hand to Louisa as well. Louisa's grip was as firm as that of a man's.

Feeling a slight pinch, Charlie Mae glanced down at Miss Louisa's hand and swallowed an exclamation of surprise. On the woman's finger was a ring with a red stone that looked much like the stone she'd found by the dead man more than six years earlier. It was smaller, and though it glimmered like a live coal, it lacked the perfect star in its depths that she'd glimpsed inside the other stone, but it was the same blood-red color.

Seeing Charlie Mae's interest in her ring, Miss Louisa appeared sad for a moment, then she gave a small tinkling laugh. "The ring was given to me when I was but an innocent girl like you by a young man who wished to make me his bride. The ruby is a precious jewel, and he said its fiery color was to remind me of his feelings for me. His papa forbid our courtship and demanded he reclaim the ring. My beau refused and ran from his father's house. The next day his horse returned without him, and many days passed before his broken body was found at the foot of a steep path. When his father came to my house demanding the return of a valuable family heirloom, I said I'd already returned it to his son. It was a lie, of course, the first of many." Her tinkling laugh sounded rehearsed. "It was also the first of several fine pieces of jewelry I've collected to see me through the years when I can no longer work." There was a smugness to her knowing smile.

Charlie Mae was taken aback. She wasn't certain whether she believed Miss Louisa's sad story, but she suspected she was telling the truth about the gemstone. Somewhere deep inside she supposed she'd always known that the stone she'd given her friend was valuable. It was probably far more valuable than Miss Louisa's ruby. She felt a moment's regret for having given up the jewel then was filled with warmth knowing she'd given the two people who were so kind to her something of great worth.

"We better go back," Chester said. He glanced over his shoulder and shifted from one foot to the other, signaling his unease with the situation.

"Shall I take Mr. Rags now?" Miss Bonnie asked him. "It will save you making another trip."

Chester readily agreed, and Charlie knelt to hug the dog and bid him farewell. Mr. Rags's pink tongue swiped her face, and Chester saved her from sprawling backward in the dust. He helped her to her feet before taking her arm to escort her back to the Walker wagon.

They walked companionably for several minutes before Chester stopped and faced her. "It would be best if you don't mention Miss Bonnie and Miss Louisa to anyone. I should have taken you another way as soon as I saw who was there."

"I'm glad I could thank them for caring for Mr. Rags."

"Still . . ."

"It's all right. I won't say anything." She hesitated before asking, "Do you think Miss Louisa's ring is as valuable as she said?"

"Yes, I've heard some jewels like rubies and diamonds fetch more money than gold. If that red stone is a real ruby, there are folks that would pay all they've got to own it. And she ought to be careful 'bout flashin' it around and temptin' robbers to steal it."

Charlie Mae almost told Chester about the stone she'd found and now suspected was a ruby. She thought about holding it in her hand and hiding it behind the fireplace brick until the day she'd given it to Spencer, the young Mormon boy who had been kind to her. She'd never told anyone, and she wasn't certain why she said nothing to Chester now.

11 ବ

"IT MIGHT BE safer to go on to Fort Hall than turn south," one of the teamsters said as nearly two dozen drivers sat around the campfire discussing their proposed route with Captain Walker. They'd reached Fort Laramie earlier in the afternoon and had set up camp.

"I heerd Mormons are near as dangerous as Injuns," another said.

Charlie Mae stifled a snort of derision, and Irwin glared at her. She wasn't part of the discussion and was only present because she'd helped the camp cook carry the coffee pots from the cook fires to where the men were assembled.

"The Army wishes to purchase four wagonloads of supplies to replenish depleted supplies for the trains following ours. They won't pay as much as we can get in California, but with four empty wagons we can lighten all of the wagons and purchase barrels in Salt Lake to fill with water. I believe that carrying extra water will get us across the Humboldt Basin faster and in better shape than anyone else has ever made it," Captain Walker explained, wishing to take the South Pass route into Salt Lake City, the Mormon stronghold.

"Ain't the Humboldt Basin jist forty miles? Our mules are in good shape, and we can make that in two good days if we push. Ain't no reason to worry about extry water," one of the prospectors said.

"I've been across that stretch of desert," a veteran driver interjected. "It ain't like the prairie or brush land. It's forty miles of blistering sun and sand. The sand makes it nigh impossible fer the best teams to pull ordinary wagons, and we got heavy freight wagons. There's very little water twixt Salt Lake and the Humboldt Basin, so the mules will already be thirsty afore we git there."

"The trail is littered with bones bleaching in the sun," the captain continued. "Our best chance of getting all of our teams and wagons through is by carrying extra water, and the only place we can purchase water barrels is from the Mormons. We can replenish other supplies from them too."

The seasoned driver backed up the captain. "The Mormons do a brisk trade with wagon trains and won't bother us none if we keep to ourselves and don't bother their women."

"We'll only stop there long enough to purchase barrels, then we'll be on our way," the captain promised.

"They was right nice to us when we passed through last year," another teamster who was making his second trip to California said. "Sold us fresh milk, baked goods, and garden greens."

The talk went on long after Charlie Mae retired to her wagon. The next morning, she learned that Captain Walker's proposal had been accepted by most of the party, and the train would be journeying through Salt Lake. A few of the prospectors chose to take the Oregon Trail route and departed on their own.

She felt a shiver of excitement. She'd never heard any good about the Mormons, but she'd liked Spencer and his grandma. They'd been nothing like the lawless savages Pa and his friend Mr. Sawyer said all Mormons were. Thinking back to the night that led to her meeting the Pascals, it seemed to her that all of the fighting and shooting had been done by Mr. Sawyer, Pa, and their friends. The man Pa shot hadn't even drawn a weapon.

Captain Walker and a handful of drivers drove four wagons inside the fort, and Charlie Mae learned that the wagon train wouldn't move on until the following day. It was good to have a day off from the constant traveling. She and Sylvia took advantage of the stop to wash clothes and spread them on bushes to dry.

When their chores were finished, Sylvia declared she was exhausted and planned to spend the afternoon resting. She took Abby inside the wagon for a nap, leaving Charlie Mae and Andrew on their own.

"Could we go see the fort?" Andrew asked. Charlie Mae could think of no reason why she and the boy shouldn't visit the fort. Pausing only to brush her unruly hair back and fasten it in place with a leather thong and to slick back Andrew's hair, she took his hand, and together they made their way through the big double gates.

They paused to look around at the rows of barracks and small houses. The buildings close at hand resembled a small town, with a blacksmith shop and a general store. Farther away were stables and a large corral. Soldiers in uniform and bearded men in buckskins seemed to be hurrying from one place to another. Some eyed her in a manner that made her uncomfortable. Andrew gripped her hand tighter and walked so close he nearly tripped her when he spotted an Indian woman wrapped in a blanket striding toward the gates with three small, naked, bronze children following like a row of ducklings. One of the women from the pink wagons passed them on the arm of a soldier.

"Miss Charlie Mae," someone called, and she turned to see Chester hurrying toward her.

"Hello, Chester," she said as he stopped beside her. Before she could think of anything further to say, Irwin caught up to them too.

"We were on our way back to camp to see if you wanted anything from the post store," Chester told her.

"Oh, we aren't shopping," Charlie Mae said. "We just wanted to see the fort."

"There are a lot of soldiers and trappers hereabouts. A few Indians, too. You better stay with us," Irwin ordered. She didn't argue, though being told what to do annoyed her. She was getting used to making her own decisions and had discovered she liked having a say. The bustle and crowds inside the fort were a little overwhelming, and she was glad to have Chester and Irwin's escort. She just would have preferred being asked instead of ordered to remain with her brother and Chester.

To Charlie Mae's surprise, Irwin boosted Andrew onto his shoulders for a better view as they walked about the fort. She glanced toward them at frequent intervals and was pleased to see that the perpetual scowl she'd long associated with Irwin was nowhere in sight. They ended up at the post store where Chester purchased peppermint sticks for everyone. Sucking on the sweet candy, they strolled slowly back to camp in time for Charlie Mae to begin supper preparations. Chester and Irwin left to take their turn watching the stock. She watched them walk away, deep in conversation. Chester was good for Irwin—and for her too, she concluded. She discovered she couldn't wipe the smile from her face.

* * *

CHARLIE MAE WALKED with Abby on one hip and Andrew trudging beside her. She swept damp, sticky curls from her face and longed for a dipper of fresh, cold water. Crossing the plains had been relatively easy compared to the long, sandy slope they now faced. With a worried glance at the wagon she trudged beside, she hoped Sylvia would feel better once they reached the coolness of the mountains. Her employer had been weak and was annoyed by the children's voices ever since they left Fort Laramie.

Some of the mules turned temperamental when the wagon train started up the steep slopes leading from the prairie to the mountains. Charlie Mae felt she couldn't fault them. As they toiled up a slope, Abby begged to be carried, which wasn't unusual. She usually started out wanting to walk, then as the trail grew steeper, begged to be carried.

Spotting their father riding toward them, Andrew called to him. The captain reined in beside them, then took Andrew up before him.

"Sylvia would have my hide if I let Abby ride on my horse," the captain said by way of apology. "Perhaps you can catch up to your brother. You have my permission to ride with him or on any of the other wagons if you wish."

Chester must have observed their exchange and caught the gist of it. He beckoned to her and slowed his wagon so she and Abby could scramble onto the seat beside him. "Whew!" She brushed her hand across her damp forehead and settled Abby on her lap. "It's too hot to walk today. Thank you for giving us a ride."

"My pleasure." He grinned and slapped the reins across the backs of the closest pair of mules to urge them to pick up their pace again. It made little difference. All of the wagons had slowed as the hill grew steeper, and the mules strained to pull the heavy freight wagons through the sand.

"I hear there's just this one bad stretch of sand before we reach the pass," Chester said. "But after we leave Salt Lake, there's more than forty miles of sand. I'm not looking forward to that."

Charlie Mae shuddered. "I feel sorry for the mules; it's really hard to walk in sand."

"The captain said we'll be laying over a few days in Salt Lake. He plans to buy water barrels and see if there's a doctor who will look at his wife."

"Good. I'm worried about Sylvia. She doesn't seem to care about anything, and the children's noise makes her head ache. Staying in one place for a couple of days might help her feel better."

"You're not worried about the Mormons?"

"I grew up near the Mormon town of Nauvoo. They were never any bother. It was men like my pa who caused all the trouble. There was an elderly Mormon woman and her grandson who lived a short distance up the river from us. They were kind to me, and I'd love to see them again." She stared wistfully into the distance.

"Do you plan to find them when we get to Salt Lake?"

"I wouldn't know how to go about it," she admitted.

"If I get a chance, I'll ask around for you. What are their names?"

"The woman's name was Sister Pascal, and the boy was Spencer."

The mules topped the ridge and began to move more quickly.

"This is the continental divide," Chester explained. "From here on, all the streams flow to the Pacific instead of back east to the Atlantic."

"It doesn't look any different."

"No, it doesn't. We probably won't notice any difference until we reach a river or stream of some kind."

"Does the continental divide mean that we're almost to Salt Lake City? We've been climbing for a long time, but I can still see higher mountains ahead."

"That's South Pass ahead, and it's miles wide. But it ain't the worst part. Captain says it's just the beginning of the worst."

* * *

THE GOING WAS slow as the train wound its way toward the mountains. A cloud of dust drifted behind the wagons, and there was little vegetation alongside the trail. Occasionally Charlie Mae spotted fleet-footed antelope in the distance. Chester complained that the antelope weren't worth bothering with since they weren't much bigger than the gray jackrabbits that the dogs chased. Even Mr. Rags proved adept at catching the rabbits to supplement his diet.

Captain Walker had a different attitude toward Mr. Rags than that of his wife, and he encouraged Charlie Mae to keep the dog near her when she walked with the children, suggesting the dog would provide an early warning should they encounter a snake. Abby particularly grew attached to the little black-and-white dog that proved to have an uncanny ability to herd cattle. Charlie Mae soon learned that Mr. Rags was adept at keeping the children from straying as well. More than once the little dog dragged Abby away from a dangerous ledge or from getting too near the straining mules.

Two days out of Fort Bridger, they met a small train composed of Mormon men driving buggies. Both parties stopped for a short time to exchange trail news. The Mormons passed on word that a large number of ships had arrived along the California coast, laden with goods, which were being sold to the miners for outrageous prices and saturating the market. With a glut of supplies, prices would soon drop. This news served to dampen spirits, but the captain was determined to press on.

The next day, a sharp wind swept across the high plateau they were crossing, bringing rain that struck with stinging force. The trail grew slick, and it took considerable persuasion to keep the mules moving.

Hearing Sylvia cry out, Charlie Mae left the children in the second wagon with Irwin to watch over them, while she pulled her shawl over her head and splashed and slipped through the mud to Sylvia.

"What is it?" Charlie Mae knelt beside the other woman's bed in the back of the wagon.

"I'm just so scared," Sylvia whimpered. Crawling on the bed beside her, Charlie Mae wrapped her arms around her friend.

"It's just a summer storm," she said, attempting to comfort Sylvia.

"I've always hated thunder and lightning," Sylvia said.

"This storm is pretty bad," Charlie Mae conceded, "but the mule drivers are all experienced men, and they have everything under control."

Sylvia continued to cry, and Charlie Mae stayed with her until the storm lost its fury and her employer fell asleep. When she was sure Sylvia was sleeping soundly, Charlie Mae covered her with a quilt and watched for a few moments longer. Sylvia seemed to alternate between fever and chills. She seldom left the wagon and had long since ceased the lessons she'd been giving Andrew. Of late, she'd shown little interest even in her children.

Slipping from Sylvia's wagon, Charlie Mae dodged mud puddles as she hurried to the wagon where she'd left the children. She hoped they hadn't been as frightened by the storm as their mother had been. She peeked in the wagon, and a slow grin spread across her face. There, lying on the narrow mattress she shared with them each night, Abby and Andrew slept soundly. Snuggled between them was Mr. Rags. He opened his eyes, yawned widely, and lowered his head once more onto Andrew's thin chest.

Instead of clearing the air, the storm seemed to make the air muggier. The mules were damp and hung their heads when they halted each night. Sylvia became so listless Charlie Mae feared for her life and kept the children in the second wagon most of the time. One late July night, Charlie Mae could detect a different odor in the air. A breeze drifted from the cut between the steep columns of rock that soared toward the sky behind the campsite, and it was laden with the scent of pine. When the sun disappeared, the temperature dropped, and everyone felt refreshed. Even Sylvia was persuaded to leave her wagon to join her family for supper. Before morning, the air turned sharply cold, and blankets were drawn closer. The following day the heat was back, but now the wagons traveled between cliffs that offered occasional respite from the sun, and the nights brought welcome cooler temperatures.

But there was no respite for the mules. Charlie Mae pitied them and took Sugarplum the last withered apple when they stopped for lunch. The train passed through Echo Canyon with its towering red cliffs, then topped two more mountain passes before starting its way down Emigration Canyon. Sylvia lay listlessly in her wagon in spite of the refreshing dippers of cold water Charlie Mae and the children carried to her.

"Look!" Andrew stood on the wagon seat and pointed ahead. Charlie Mae followed his excited gesture. There at the foot of the winding trail was a large settlement. In the distance, far beyond the large collection of houses, was a shining lake. A shout went up as wagon after wagon began the last leg of their journey out of the mountains. Even the mules became excited at the prospect of reaching the settlement, and the teamsters had to rein them in with sharpness and brake their wagons to prevent a disaster.

Before they reached the bottom of the incline, three riders approached their train. They spoke briefly with Captain Walker, then one rode back toward the city, and the other two escorted the wagons into the frontier city.

Charlie Mae stared in awe at houses and neat yards. Businesses lined the street, and men and boys watched the wagons proceed down the main street of the town. She caught an occasional glimpse of a face peering through a window or a skirt disappearing around a corner. Eventually they reached a grassy area just beyond the city where they were told they could make camp. Captain Walker selected two men to accompany him, and they rode off with the escort riders.

As the wagons were circled and fires were lit, Charlie Mae heard a rumble of voices as several men voiced their distrust and animosity toward the Mormons. Uneasiness crept over her. The drivers were mostly Missourians. The Mormons had no reason to welcome or trust them, and they might even see the Missouri men's arrival as an opportunity to seek revenge. If the teamsters carried their grudges into town, they could be placing the entire wagon train in danger.

* * *

"CHESTER AND IRWIN invited me to accompany them on a walk through town. Are you feeling well enough for me to leave you for a little while?" Charlie Mae directed her question to Sylvia, who reclined against a large pillow inside her wagon. The canvas had been rolled up to allow any stray whispers of air to find their way to the woman, who sat fanning herself and looking wan. Abby lay beside her mother, sleeping soundly. Andrew had accompanied his father on a jaunt into the Mormon city, and it would be several hours before she would need to start dinner.

"Even with two escorts, I'm not certain it is safe for a lady to wander the streets of this heathen city. I've heard the men lure women here from as far away as England to force them to become their wives." Sylvia looked peeved.

"That's likely just one of the nasty rumors people like Pa's neighbor spread about the Mormons. Though you can be sure neither Chester nor my brother would permit anyone to take advantage of me." Charlie Mae surprised herself by speaking in defense of the Mormons. Before their journey began, she would not have expressed an opinion aloud, especially one favorable to the Mormons.

"I'm sure you're right. They're both dependable young men, and I suspect Chester has his sights set on making you his wife. Go and enjoy yourself, but do be careful." Sylvia leaned back against the pillow with one hand fluttering futilely.

Charlie Mae felt her cheeks go hot. It seemed that almost everyone assumed she and Chester would marry, though Chester hadn't broached the subject once. And Sylvia didn't look well; perhaps Charlie Mae should stay and try to coax her friend to eat. Though surely rest was what Sylvia needed most, and there was little Charlie Mae could do to help her if she remained at camp.

"I'll be back in plenty of time to begin dinner," she promised before turning away to join the two young men who were waiting for her.

"Just a minute," Sylvia called out to her. "I've heard the Mormons sometimes sell fresh fruit and vegetables to travelers. If you pass a market, would you be so kind as to inquire about the prices of various kinds of produce? If they aren't asking too much . . ." She handed Charlie Mae a silver dollar.

"Yes, ma'am." Charlie Mae accepted the coin. She'd never had any money of her own, but she knew a dollar was a great deal of money. She'd see that Sylvia got good value for her coin.

"New potatoes and greens would be most satisfying for supper." There was a hint of longing in Sylvia's voice.

Charlie Mae would scour the entire settlement for fresh produce to tempt Sylvia's palate and put a little color in her cheeks. She tied the coin in one corner of her handkerchief and tucked it in her apron pocket.

12 ⟡

CHARLIE MAE HAD little with which to compare Salt Lake City, but it seemed to her a grand place. The streets were wide, and neat plank walkways kept her skirts from dragging in the dust. There were a few large buildings that surely had some public purpose, and more were under construction. Some of the houses were the mere cabins she had expected, but many were fine homes. Young trees lined the streets, and numerous fruit trees could be seen behind the houses. Children played in neatly fenced yards, and several ladies nodded politely to her as they passed.

Entering a general store, she was surprised to see Captain Walker conversing with a group of men in dark suits. On seeing her, Andrew ran to greet her and show her the peppermint stick his papa had purchased for him. Seeing the sweet, Chester stepped to a counter where a woman in a dark skirt and white shirtwaist stood. Charlie Mae inquired of her about fresh produce and was told the store didn't have any because nearly every house in the city had its own garden plot.

Chester purchased peppermint sticks for the three of them. Minutes later, sucking on the candy like children, they continued on their way. Charlie Mae lightly rested one hand on Chester's arm as they walked. They spotted a number of well-tended gardens as they strolled down the street but hesitated to knock on doors and inquire about purchasing vegetables.

Rounding a corner, Charlie Mae spotted a small, gray-haired woman bending over a row of beans in a generous-sized garden. Her heart leaped. For a moment she thought she'd found Sister Pascal. But when the woman glanced up and drew a sleeve across her damp brow, it became obvious she wasn't the woman Charlie Mae had once known. Nevertheless, she stepped to the fence to call in a polite voice, "Good day, ma'am."

"Good day," the woman returned the greeting, though she looked hesitantly at the two strong, young men standing beside her.

"I wonder if you might be willing to sell some of those beans." Charlie Mae stepped close to the neat board fence that bordered the vegetable garden. "Our employer's wife is ill, and we've been traveling since early spring. It might be that the fresh beans would perk up her appetite."

"Oh, I've been hoping to sell my excess produce to the wagon trains passing through here, though you're the first this season. I have corn, beans, potatoes, cucumbers, and this morning, I discovered the first ripe melon."

Charlie Mae clapped her hands in excitement then drew the dollar from her pocket, unwrapped it, and held it out on the palm of her hand. "I shall take as much as this coin will purchase."

The woman smiled. "If one of the gentlemen would be so kind as to assist me in digging a few potatoes . . ." Before she finished speaking, Irwin stepped over the fence and picked up a fork he saw lying on the ground. A quarter of an hour later, the three young people left with Charlie Mae's apron filled with beans and cucumbers, Irwin's hat heaped with stubby red potatoes, ears of corn protruding from Chester's pockets, and a medium-sized melon tucked under his arm.

When they reached camp, they found a flurry of activity. Two wagonloads of barrels were being unloaded, men were shouting instructions, mules were braying, and the dogs were barking and running about in a frenzy of excitement. The women from the last wagons were peering out of the back of their wagon but staying mostly out of sight as Captain Walker had ordered. Charlie Mae had overheard him explaining to Miss Louisa and the other women that the Mormons didn't take kindly to females of their profession, and they should keep out of sight to avoid trouble until the wagon company's business in Salt Lake City was completed.

A black-and-white streak raced by them, nearly knocking Charlie Mae off her feet as she struggled to hang onto the contents of her apron and absorb Mr. Rags's exuberant greeting.

"No, no," she scolded the dog, but even Mr. Rags knew her heart wasn't in it. Bunching the apron together with one hand, she patted the dog's head.

"Next time I go for a walk, I'll take you with me," she promised. After a few moments, Irwin led the dog back to Miss Bonnie. He stood talking to her for several minutes, and Charlie Mae saw him offer her a few of the potatoes from his hat. She wished she'd thought to share with the woman who cared for Mr. Rags.

Continuing toward their own wagons, they passed Cookie and observed that he too had found an abundance of garden produce and was busy slicing potatoes and onions into his biggest pot.

Sylvia and little Abby were still asleep when they reached the area where the Walkers' personal wagons were set up. Irwin volunteered to fetch water for his sister and hinted he'd be eating with her that night instead of with the mule drivers. Chester looked with real regret at the melon he set down, and Charlie Mae promised to save him a slice.

"I best go help with the water barrels," Chester said. He took a few steps before looking back to ask, "What did you say was the name of those Mormons you knew back in Nauvoo?"

"Spencer Pascal and his grandma, I don't know her given name. I only heard her called Sister Pascal."

"I'll ask around, see if any of these fellows delivering barrels know of them." Chester whistled as he hurried away.

Charlie Mae seated herself on the grass on the shady side of the wagon to snap the beans. She was more than halfway through the task when Sylvia and Abby climbed down from the wagon.

Sylvia appeared pleased with Charlie Mae's purchases. Seating herself on the grass beside her young cook, she picked up a long, slender green bean and began a slow, awkward attempt to copy Charlie Mae's nimble actions. After a few moments, her hands fell idle, and she leaned back against a wagon wheel, seemingly exhausted. Abby picked up a small fistful of the beans too but seemed to think them some kind of new toy.

"I brought an extra bucket of water." Irwin set two heavy buckets down near the women. "I figured you might want to put the melon in one of them to get it cold."

"Thank you." She smiled at her brother and marveled at how much Irwin had changed from the sullen boy she'd once thought she knew. In one way he hadn't changed though. He still liked to eat, and he appreciated his sister's culinary skills.

Captain Walker took pity on Chester and invited him to join his family and the Riggins siblings for supper. He accepted with alacrity and held out his plate twice for Charlie Mae to fill with the little new potatoes. Even Sylvia seemed to have found her appetite, sampling each of the dishes Charlie Mae had prepared and seeming to savor each bite of cold melon. The melon was attacked heartily by the children too, and Charlie Mae wished she'd been able to secure two.

They lingered over their supper long after everyone had eaten their fill. Finally, Charlie Mae rose to her feet. If she didn't begin scrubbing the dishes soon, darkness would fall before she finished the task.

"Charlie Mae?" The soft voice startled her so much she nearly spilled the kettle of hot water she was preparing to pour into the tin dishpan. Slowly she turned to see a tall, thin boy of about fourteen or fifteen who looked vaguely familiar. A smattering of freckles covered his face, and his gangly arms and legs appeared to have outgrown his shirt and pants. A mop of red hair curled against his neck and nearly covered his ears. He smiled a sweet, sad smile and for a moment she thought she couldn't breathe.

"Spencer?" she gasped.

He nodded his head, and a wide grin spread across his face. "Brother Haslam stopped by the house to tell me someone from the wagon train was enquiring about me on behalf of a girl by the name of Charlie Mae Riggins."

Setting the kettle back over the fire, she reached out her hands to the boy. He took them, and she gulped back tears. "I've wondered if you and your grandma found your way safely to the Rocky Mountains," she said.

A shadow crossed the boy's face. "Grandma died the night we crossed the Mississippi. I came on with Brother Anderson."

"Oh! I'm so sorry. Your grandma was awfully good to me."

"She was good to everyone. She was about as close to being an angel as I ever hope to meet."

"Who is this fellow?" Chester came to stand beside her. Possessively, he reached for her arm. She wasn't sure she liked his proprietary stance.

"This is Spencer Pascal," she introduced. Impulsively, she stood on her toes to deliver a kiss to Chester's cheek. She had no call to be angry with him; he'd shown her a kindness in asking after the Pascals. "Thank you for asking after him for me."

Chester's chest puffed out, and Charlie Mae felt herself blush. Looking quite pleased with himself, Chester held out a hand to the boy, and Spencer shook it.

Irwin came forward and looked Spencer up and down with a hint of his old scowl on his face. "You've grown a mite since I last saw you."

Spencer returned the inspection. "I can't say as I remember seeing you, sir."

"Me 'n another brother of Charlie Mae's, Sander, followed her most every time she visited your shack in the woods. Sander said you were harmless and that the old lady was teachin' her to read. Sander wanted to learn to read real bad, and he figgered that if we left you alone, then after awhile, Charlie Mae could teach him. She done that."

Spencer looked startled, and his eyes went back to Charlie Mae, but Irwin wasn't through speaking his piece. "After you was gone, me and Sander used that old shed of your'n to plan a way to escape our pa, who was right ornery. I'm thankin' ya for all the stuff we made use of."

"I'm sure Grandma would be pleased to know that the things we couldn't take with us were helpful to you," Spencer said politely, sounding a little uncertain. He turned again to Charlie Mae. "Will you be staying long enough for us to catch up on all that's happened since we last saw each other?" Casting an uncertain look at the two young men standing behind her, he added, "Folks back in Missouri and Illinois had no use for us Mormons, and I got awful lonesome until I found Charlie Mae. She was the only friend I had."

"Folks like our pa didn't treat ya square." Irwin's voice was gruff, and he turned away abruptly. Charlie Mae watched him make his way to the wagon he drove. She was still discovering there was more to Irwin than she'd ever guessed.

"I expect we'll be moving on in a day or two. We only stopped to purchase water barrels," she told Spencer.

"Captain said he made arrangements to trade some of his goods for perishables for us and dried grass and clover for the mules. He figures if everyone eats good for a few days and we carry feed for the mules in one of the empty wagons, we'll be in better shape when we cross the Humboldt Basin, so we'll be stayin' here two more days. He plans to pull out come Thursday morning," Chester said.

"That stretch of desert is bad," said Spencer. "We hear tales from folks of wagons getting mired in the sand and oxen going crazy of thirst. Word is not many wagon trains get through without losing a few animals and people." Spencer nodded his head as he seconded the captain's assessment of the trail ahead.

"I mean to get both across that stretch." Captain Walker had walked over and joined in the conversation. She sensed his emphatic statement was more than his familiarity with the nightmare stretch of trail. He was thinking of Sylvia.

* * *

SPENCER ARRIVED AT Charlie Mae's wagon the next day while she was clearing away lunch and coaxing Abby to take a nap beside her mother. Sylvia smiled a little too brightly at the boy. She'd voiced her reservations earlier about having any more to do with the Mormons than absolutely necessary, but she'd reluctantly given permission for Charlie Mae to walk with him.

"Take Andrew with you," she said. "His papa is much too busy to watch him while Abby and I rest."

Charlie Mae agreed, and the three set off toward a creek that wandered through the Mormon city. As they approached the edge of the encampment, Mr. Rags escaped Miss Bonnie and ran toward them. Charlie Mae threw her arms around the black-and-white bundle of fur and buried her face in his soft coat. Andrew, too, was pleased to see the dog, and begged to hold the leash that had slipped from his caretaker's hand. Spencer introduced himself to Mr. Rags and indicated his approval of the friendly little dog.

"Don't worry," Charlie Mae called to the woman who was hanging back, looking concerned. "We'll look after Mr. Rags for a bit."

At first they walked in silence with Andrew and Mr. Rags trailing a few steps behind. At length Charlie Mae asked about Spencer's journey from Nauvoo. She was appalled to learn of the hardships the boy had endured but was cheered by his description of the Anderson home and the treatment he received there.

"The Andersons never had any boys of their own to care for, so they've been right glad to have me," he assured her. "Sister Anderson was Grandma's friend a long time ago, and living with her is almost like having a grandma of my own."

"My life is much better now, too," Charlie Mae confided. "Things got frightful bad living with Pa and his new wife. Most of my brothers left, and Irwin had made up his mind to leave too, then Agnes's son took to bothering me, so Irwin took me along when he left." She told him about their journey downriver and how they came to be crossing the continent with a freight company.

Talking with Spencer was as easy and natural as it had been when they were children. They sat on a grassy bank beside the stream Spencer called City Creek. They found much to talk about, and Spencer asked her about her plans for the future.

"Irwin and Chester plan to look for gold when we reach California," she said. "And I'll be going along. I wish you were coming too."

"Brother Brigham says that God has appointed this place for the gathering of our people. He says we'll do better staying here than by going off to the gold mines."

"It seems to me the Mormons are building a fine city here, but gold would surely help you build it faster."

"Might be faster and might not. Brother Anderson says that looking for gold is a fever, and when men find it, they're never satisfied. They keep wanting more. He agrees with Brother Brigham that we should stay right here where God put us."

"Sometimes I think God doesn't know where I am or care much what happens to me. It seems to me He wasn't around much while I was growing up." Charlie Mae felt a pang of guilt. She hadn't read from Granny's Bible for many weeks, and she'd almost given up saying prayers.

"God was watching over you more than you knew. I suspect He had a hand in Irwin deciding to take you with him when your stepbrother tried to hurt you. God always knows where we are, and He cares about us even when we don't pay Him no mind. After Grandma died, I felt powerful alone until Sister Anderson told me to read Romans 15:14 in the Bible. I've studied that verse a lot, and it comforts me knowing God cares enough about me to make certain that a whole book got written just so people like you and me can know He hasn't forgotten about us. We just need to be patient and take hope for the future."

"I remember reading that, but I haven't thought about it lately. I'll look it up again when I get back to camp."

Andrew took off his shoes and rolled up his pant legs. He sat on the grass, dangling his feet in the water. After a few minutes, he slid into the stream to splash and play with Mr. Rags, who joined him in the shallow water. For a moment Charlie Mae wished she were young enough to join them, but it wouldn't be fitting for a grown woman of seventeen.

While keeping an eye on her young charge, Charlie Mae noticed that Spencer cast frequent glances toward the child. Once he cautioned Andrew not to wade farther than a nearby tree he pointed out. His concern touched something inside Charlie Mae, confirming her sense that her old playmate was growing up in a responsible manner. Spencer was just a lad, but he seemed more grown up than his years.

"Which route will your wagons take when they leave here?" Spencer asked.

"I don't know. There's been some discussion concerning both the Hastings and Hensley trails. Those who have been over the trails say we're early enough that there's no reason to take the longer route."

"If you have any say in the matter, advise your captain to head north, following the lake around the north tip until he cuts across the California trail. The route around the southern end of the lake, Hastings Cutoff, is a bad trail. Wagons as heavy as the ones on your train sink to their axles in the salt, and there's no way to get them out. Few men or animals survive a hundred miles of salt desert followed by the Humboldt sink, especially in August, when the temperatures are at their highest."

"I'll tell Captain Walker what you said. He came this way last year, so he already knows many of the pitfalls."

After a time, Charlie Mae noticed that the sun had moved farther toward the west than she'd expected. "We best be getting back," she said. "Andrew, Mr. Rags, come now."

Andrew groaned but obediently stepped out of the water. Mr. Rags followed after only a few short barks that seemed to be begging his young companion to return to their game.

"Look at you," Charlie Mae scolded the boy. "What will your mother say when she finds you're all wet?"

Mr. Rags chose that moment to give his coat a vigorous shake. Andrew laughed. "Now you're wet too, Miss Charlie Mae."

"Indeed I am." Charlie Mae looked at the damp splotches on her shirtwaist.

Spencer laughed. "In this heat you'll be dry by the time we reach your wagon."

Their clothes did dry before they reached the circle of wagons. Miss Bonnie came to meet them, and Andrew reluctantly yielded Mr. Rags to her. Charlie Mae had gotten used to the outlandish dresses the women from the pink wagons wore, but she noticed Spencer's blush and his eagerness to be on their way when she attempted to introduce the two.

Chester joined them before they reached their wagon, and Spencer bid Charlie Mae farewell.

"I'll come again tomorrow afternoon," Spencer promised as he waved to her before retracing his steps. She watched until he was out of sight before turning back to Chester and the chores that awaited her. It wasn't until she lay on her quilt that night, trying to sleep in the sweltering heat, that she remembered the ruby. She'd forgotten to ask Spencer if he'd kept it.

13 ∾

MORNING BROUGHT A flurry of activity, and Charlie Mae was disappointed to learn that Captain Walker had finished his business early and planned for them to be on their way by mid-morning. She had hoped to see Spencer again before the Walker train broke camp.

"Cookie was able to purchase all the garden produce we can use before it spoils," Captain Walker told her. "He left a bag in your wagon along with a basket of early apples. He said they weren't quite ripe but plenty ripe enough for making a cobbler."

She wished there was a way to get a message to Spencer, letting him know they'd be leaving earlier than anticipated and to tell him good-bye, but everyone was busy. There were numerous tasks involved in resuming their journey, and each member of the party had assigned tasks, including her. She took down the cooking shelter and arranged her pots in the wagon and on hooks outside of it. Clothing she'd washed the previous day needed to be gathered from an improvised clothesline strung between the wagons.

Sylvia took the children for a short walk to enable Charlie Mae to work faster. Sylvia wasn't up to going far, and they scarcely seemed to start their walk when they returned. It seemed just minutes later that Captain Walker ordered the drivers to take their positions.

Both Charlie Mae and Andrew opted to start their day's journey on foot. Abby insisted she wanted to walk too. Sylvia yielded to her demands, placing her daughter's small hand in Charlie Mae's before climbing inside the wagon.

As Charlie Mae watched Sylvia disappear inside the wagon, she felt some of her concern for the woman fade. Resting for a couple of days combined with eating the appetizing dishes Charlie Mae had prepared for her and using herbs from the Mormons' gardens had done Sylvia a great deal of good. Charlie Mae was glad the captain had stopped; she just wished they could stay one more day.

They'd only gone a short distance when a rider was seen attempting to overtake the wagons. Giving instructions for the wagons to keep moving, Captain Walker and one of the scouts rode back to meet the slim figure on an oddly patterned horse.

"Indian horse," she heard one mule driver shout to another.

"Naw, that ain't an Injun paint," the second driver called back.

Charlie Mae lifted Abby in her arms as a precaution should it be necessary to quickly place her in the wagon.

"Stay close," she warned Andrew, seeing Captain Walker and the rider angle toward them as the scout dug his heels into his mount's side and urged it back to the front of the train. He passed them in a whirl of dust.

"It's Spencer," Andrew shouted. He took off at a trot toward the approaching riders. Before she could call him back, she could see the boy was right. Something lifted in her heart, and she grinned widely as Spencer slid from the back of the mottled gray horse. The captain touched a finger to his hat and rode on past to the front of the wagon line. Andrew grasped Spencer's hand and danced beside him as the youth made his way toward Charlie Mae.

"When I heard your wagons had pulled out this morning, I borrowed a horse from Brother Anderson," Spencer told her as he fell into step beside her. He kept a grip on the horse's reins, and the animal stopped docilely beside him.

Charlie Mae couldn't resist casting frequent curious glances toward the strangely patterned horse. It was like no horse she'd ever seen before. In the dime novels she'd read, horses showing that much white in their eyes were always wild or crazy. And she'd never seen a horse before that appeared to have been splashed with a bucket of whitewash. And it had vertically striped hooves.

"I wanted to send you a message, but everyone was too busy to carry a note to you." Taking her eyes from the horse, she looked at the gangly youth.

"What kind of horse is he?" Andrew tugged on Spencer's shirt tail to get his attention. He asked the question Charlie Mae was uncertain she should ask.

"Appaloosa."

"Appa-what?" Charlie Mae asked.

"Appaloosa. They make good stock horses. Brother Anderson got him off a trapper who said he got him from a Nez Percé north of the Humboldt."

Charlie Mae barely controlled a shiver. She'd heard some of the drivers talking about the Nez Percé, and she hoped they didn't meet any. The drivers claimed the Nez Percé were extremely dangerous.

"Uh," Spencer looked down at his dusty boots, then sideways toward Charlie Mae, "I thought about you many times as we made our way to Salt Lake. We had some real hard times, and I was awful lonesome, missing Grandma and you. I kept that big red rock you gave me in my pocket and I'd rub it with my fingers. It reminded me that somewhere in this big world I had a friend, and it made me feel better."

"I'm glad it helped." Charlie Mae felt a lump in her throat. Before she could ask if he still had the stone, he reached for her hand. Her fingers closed around a small square object. It felt like wood and was slick on all but one of its sides. That side was rough, as though something had been carved into the wood. She couldn't see past the child in her arms to examine it.

"I have to get back," Spencer said. "I've got chores to do, but I made that box for you. I hope it will help you on your journey—

like your rock helped me on mine." He stepped toward his horse. "Oh, I almost forgot." He reached inside his shirt and pulled out a tattered book. He looked toward her as though uncertain what to do with it. She stood with Abby in her arms, grasping the box he'd given her in one hand. He smiled sheepishly and tucked the book into her apron pocket. "Sister Anderson said to thank you for being kind to Grandma and me, and she said I should give you this and tell you to pray about it."

"Thank you." Charlie Mae smiled. "Your grandma already gave me a special gift. I always wanted to thank her for teaching me to read. I can't tell you how much it means to me and to my brother, Sander. Even Irwin has learned his letters and can read simple words now. I'm glad you're safe and happy, and if you ever get to California, find me."

"I'll do that." He swung into the saddle and touched his hat in almost the same gesture Captain Walker had used. He tugged on the reins, turning the Appaloosa back toward Salt Lake City. She waved, as did the children, but she wasn't certain he saw the gesture. While watching him grow smaller and disappear in the dust behind the wagons, she slipped the wooden box into her other apron pocket to be examined later. A wave of sadness swept over her, far stronger than any she had felt on leaving her childhood home behind.

* * *

THE MULES WERE rested and set a fast pace, tiring Charlie Mae and the children before they had gone far. They climbed aboard the wagon and settled down to watch the houses and farms slide by. The loads had been redistributed to lighten each wagon and to place an extra one or two water barrels in each. A well-traveled road stretched north from the city, and both the men and the mules were anxious to use it to move faster than was their usual pace.

The sun shimmered off the lake in the distance, and they passed several small towns and farms. Occasionally a dog barked or children waved as the wagons rumbled past. The heat was intense, even with the canvas sides of the wagon rolled up, and Charlie Mae was glad Captain Walker had decided to take the Hensley Salt Lake Cutoff instead of heading due west across a hundred miles of barren salt lands. She played simple games with the children and helped Andrew draw his letters on his school slate for a time, but in the heat, the children grew lethargic and drifted to sleep.

She too, drowsed, then remembering the book and the box Spencer had given her, she pulled them from her apron pockets. She wasn't surprised to discover the book he'd given her was a well-worn copy of the Book of Mormon. She'd heard just enough about the Mormon book to be curious, and she welcomed it as a means to help her pass the tedious hours when she was confined to the wagon.

The box was made of polished pine with thin strips of leather for hinges. She estimated that it was about three inches on each side and less than two deep. The lid bore a painstakingly chiseled picture of a bird perched on a blossom-covered tree branch. Running her fingers over the little bird, she wondered if Spencer had chiseled it himself. It had a delicate quality that told her there was talent behind the simple design, and she regretted that there was little chance she would see him again or discover if he possessed an artistic flair.

She tugged at the lid, discovering that its snug fit would ensure that the box couldn't be accidentally jarred open. When she managed to pry the lid up, she was astonished to see the ruby she'd given Spencer on the day he and his grandma had been driven from their home. It still burned like a live coal.

Touching it gently brought back a flood of memories. Her eyes grew damp at the picture that came unbidden to her mind of her own father pulling the trigger—killing an unarmed man. She saw the loose brick in the fireplace beside which she'd struggled since a small child to cook for her father and brothers. Those images faded, and she realized the ruby was especially dear to her because Spencer had treasured it.

She remembered Miss Louisa's ruby ring. There was little doubt in Charlie Mae's mind that the stone she now cradled in her hand was also a ruby. It was much larger than Miss Louisa's and wasn't set in a gold ring, but she felt certain it was far more valuable. She knew almost nothing about jewels, but if her suspicions were correct, possessing the ruby made her a wealthy woman. If she sold it, she could buy . . .

No, she wouldn't sell the ruby, not ever—unless she and Irwin were starving and they had nothing else. But Irwin was going to find gold and become a rich man. She too would search for gold, and if Irwin let her keep her findings, she would have the gold fashioned into a ring worthy of the ruby. It would be far grander than Miss Louisa's ring. But even if she didn't find any gold, she wouldn't sell the ruby. She would keep it always to remind her of her dear friend.

She considered showing the stone to Irwin and Chester, but a strange reluctance to do so overcame her. For now anyway, the ruby would be her secret. As she placed the stone back in its box, she noticed that the box was lined with soft velvet, and a folded piece of paper lay at the bottom of the box. She withdrew the paper, closed the box, and tucked it back into her pocket until she could find a secure hiding place for it.

Unfolding the lined sheet of foolscap, she noticed first that it was covered with beautiful script, and she recalled Spencer carefully drawing his letters when they'd studied together at his grandma's house. No matter how hard she'd tried, she'd been unable to form her letters as beautifully as those made by the younger boy.

With her hand, she smoothed the page and began to read.

Dear Charlie Mae,

For five long years, I have hoped to see you again. It brought me great joy when Brother Haslam told me a young woman on a passing wagon train was asking about me. I knew it could be no one other than you. My pleasure was doubled when I saw you.

A long time ago a friend of Brother Anderson's looked at the stone you gave me and was quite alarmed that such a gem should be in the hands of a boy. He assured Brother Anderson that the stone is a large ruby and of considerable value. The Andersons found a secure place for me to keep the jewel and said that it was mine to do with as I pleased. We were all puzzled concerning how a young girl, the daughter of a poor farmer, obtained the stone, but as there was little likelihood of seeing you again to return it to your keeping, the Andersons were comfortable with my keeping it.

I'm returning it to you now both because I think you had no understanding of its value when you gave it to me and because it truly gave me great comfort to know that someone cared about me enough to give me something of such beauty. It is my prayer that it will bring you comfort and assurance also. My foster parents expressed their approval of my decision to return the ruby to you. It is also my prayer that one day you will know that the book Sister Anderson gave you is of far greater value than the ruby, not just because it was first Grandma's, but because of the message contained in its pages. Please pray about it.

Your friend always,

Spencer Pascal

She read the letter again then refolded it to tuck inside the book. With the book spread across her lap, she thumbed lightly through its pages, noticing that it fell open of its own accord at numerous places. She suspected those places marked pages Grandma Pascal had turned to frequently, just as Granny's Bible opened easily to those sections she'd asked Charlie Mae to read again and again. Going back to the beginning of the book, she discovered a name, Clarissa Rogers Pascal, printed in neat script on the first page.

Touching her finger to the inked name, she thought of the tiny woman. Mormon or not, she had been a good woman, and Charlie Mae would read the book out of respect for her memory. She wondered why Spencer hadn't chosen to keep his grandma's book for himself. She knew he'd loved the woman.

She began to read and didn't think it strange that as the story unfolded, the brothers took on the appearance and mannerisms of her own brothers, though at times, she wasn't certain whether Nephi was more Sander or Irwin.

* * *

THE MULES MADE twenty or more miles a day as the train moved north. Water and grass were plentiful, and fresh produce could be obtained from settlers in the small outposts, though at a higher price than Cookie or Charlie Mae considered reasonable. Captain Walker merely laughed when they voiced their complaints to him.

"We're on our way to California to do the same thing—charge as much for our goods as the gold miners will pay. The Mormons know folks who've lived on beans and biscuits for three months will pay most anything for fresh produce, milk, eggs, and cheese. We're just fortunate to be the first train through and able to find an abundant selection."

Once past the Brownsville settlement, the route became more rugged, and fresh produce was no longer available. They forded the

Bear River without much trouble and continued on with the terrain becoming drier and more arid as they began angling west again. Crossing the Malad River took the better part of two days, and they encountered their first livestock loss when one of the mules broke a leg as it stumbled against a boulder midstream. To save the rest of the team, the mule was cut free and washed away to be dashed against the rocks.

Not trusting his family to the lurching wagon on the crossing, Captain Walker ferried them across the river on his horse. Once Irwin had reached the opposite bank, he returned for Charlie Mae on Sugarplum.

Two seasons of California-bound wagon companies had cut the trail deep, and because it was the way Captain Walker had traveled east the previous year, the heavy wagons moved west with few problems, though Charlie Mae was cautioned to watch for snakes whenever she and the children walked beside the wagons.

Stark rock formations, thick gray brush, and patches of Juniper trees created a seemingly endless vista beneath blue sky and the burning heat of summer sun. The heat and dust caused great misery, but she repeatedly heard the warning that the worst was yet to come.

At a point known as the Twin Sisters, the cutoff they'd taken merged with the more established California Trail, and the route veered to the south, following the murky waters of the Humboldt River. As a water source, the river was a major disappointment, being low and muddy.

Sometimes Charlie Mae despaired of ever reaching California. Day after day the journey continued over dusty trails and through brush, following down deep, narrow canyons and up rugged mountain sides. Sylvia became weak again and rarely strayed from her bed, and the children became fretful. The animals grew lean, and injuries to men and stock seemed to come more often. When the sameness of her days and the horizon became almost unbearable, she found herself stealing moments to gaze at the ruby, drinking in its beauty.

Coming upon a meadow where grass and water were abundant, the captain ordered the water barrels refilled. They stayed for two days to rest and make needed repairs. Then it was on to a barren wasteland of dust in which Charlie Mae's shoes sank to their tops. It became essential to cover their mouths and noses with bandanas, and Sylvia's condition grew worse. At night Charlie Mae was too tired to walk with Chester.

It was late afternoon on a hot, early August day when Captain Walker signaled for an early halt. The muddy river had disappeared, and the notorious Humboldt Sink was upon them. He announced that they would make early camp and start across the forty-mile desert before sunrise the next day. Charlie Mae climbed onto the wagon seat and stared in dismay at the shimmering sand before them. Waves of heat rose in columns that seemed to shift and sway. It was a frightening sight.

Her motions were slow as she began supper preparations. Halfway through, she heard Captain Walker speak her name. There was a note of concern in his voice. She turned to face him.

"Cookie's ill. You'll have to prepare enough supper for the whole company."

"But your wife, the children . . ." She claimed no false modesty when it came to her ability to cook for a dozen folks, but she couldn't fathom preparing food for several dozen men.

"I'll see to them and send someone to help you cook."

Chester and Irwin arrived shortly with the huge kettle Cookie used for beans and fetched the supplies from the cook wagon. While trying to multiply the ingredients needed for biscuits, she heard Captain Walker clear his throat again. She cast him a quick glance and stifled a gasp. Two women from the pink wagons, including Miss Bonnie, stood beside him wearing aprons.

The pink wagon women pitched in with supper preparations, scraping the last of the potatoes and stirring the various kettles. They laughed and joked with the men as they dished up heaping plates for them before filling plates for themselves, and there was a generally jovial air about the camp. Charlie Mae sent frequent, nervous glances toward the Walker wagon, where Sylvia lay, and she expected her mistress to poke her head around the canvas to order the women away. When she didn't, Charlie Mae's concern for Sylvia grew.

She noticed that Chester and Irwin undertook caring for the children for her, and both children seemed pleased with the young men's attention. There was no sign of the captain. She assumed that after arranging supper for the men, he'd gone to look after his wife.

14 ♋

Nevada, 1850

A PALE SILVER moon rode high in the sky, and stars stretched from horizon to horizon in every direction when Charlie Mae snapped the reins, urging Sugarplum and his teammates forward. Irwin had moved the big mule to the lead wagon carrying Sylvia and her children, which Charlie Mae found herself driving. Cookie lay in fevered delirium on the straw tick of the wagon Irwin drove, oblivious to all around him.

The mules stepped lively, and it seemed they were making great progress until the sun came blazing into view. It didn't take long for their black hides to turn shiny with sweat, then caked as the clouds of dust hovering around them turned to pale mud.

Heat waves shimmered in the distance, and rivulets of muddy sweat stung Charlie Mae's eyes and stained her dress. As instructed, she kept a water bladder at her side and took small sips from time to time. Controlling the urge to gulp the water as her thirst became nearly as great a trial as hearing Sylvia's groans and her feeble pleas for water. Her gratitude was as great as if her own thirst had been quenched when Captain Walker leaped from his horse to her wagon and made his way to Sylvia's side to dribble water between her parched lips.

When the heat was at its most unbearable level, Captain Walker called for camp to be set up. There was no fresh water or grass for the mules, but each driver hand watered his mules a ration from the barrels. Irwin and Chester took care of her team while she set out leftover beans and biscuits from the previous evening's meal. The men carried their own canteens of water, and the captain declared there would be no fires and no coffee until they'd completed the forty-mile crossing.

Charlie Mae checked on both Cookie and Sylvia. Using handkerchiefs moistened with a few drops of water, she wiped their faces. Taking pity on the children, she used a few more drops of her precious water to wash their faces and insisted they eat her last, shriveled potato.

She lay down beside them and drifted to sleep.

Leaving Sylvia and the children sleeping, Charlie Mae responded sluggishly to Captain Walker's call for the train to resume its journey as night fell. She settled onto the high box seat of the wagon and was glad their wagons were pulled by mules. Oxen were stronger but slower, and horses needed more water and grass than mules. Each small advantage mattered in the cruel land around them. She signaled for the mules to move forward. She agreed with Captain Walker—they couldn't finish with this stretch of the trail too soon to suit her.

The sun set in a brilliant display of color as they moved west. Another clear sky made night travel possible, and the train moved on. Sometimes she found her head nodding as she struggled to keep her team following Captain Walker's lead. Sometimes she talked to Sugarplum to keep herself awake. Under ideal circumstances, it was possible to cover twenty miles in a single day's journey, but the deep sand made pulling the heavy freight wagons difficult and slowed their progress. Frequent stops were required to free wagons and animals from the sand's grasp.

Each time the train stopped, Charlie Mae held her breath as she checked on Cookie and Sylvia, fearing one or both might no longer be breathing. She was hard pressed, too, to find sufficient jerky, tins of peaches, and cold biscuits to feed the men without a cook fire. There was little grumbling over their meager fare as most of the men were more thirsty than hungry, and all were eager to pass through the sink as quickly as possible.

By the second day, Abby clung to her, refusing to leave her side. She was whiny and lethargic, adding to Charlie Mae's concern. Andrew was older and more secure in his perch beside Irwin, but Charlie Mae worried the smaller child seated beside her might slip from the box and fall beneath the heavy wagon wheels, so she tied her apron around the little girl and fastened it to a nail behind the seat.

On the second day, as the wagons pulled into their customary circle for a few hours' rest, she climbed slowly down from her high perch. "Stay in the wagon," she told Abby and left the child whimpering as she moved on cramped limbs to the front of her team. She started with Sugarplum, loosening the straps of his harness. A hand reached out to lift the heavy array of leather and buckles from her hands.

"I'll take care of your mules," Chester said. She looked up at his face which was begrimed with thick, salty dust. His attempt at a smile was a brief widening of the slash that cut across the gray mask. "You got other chores."

She suspected she would have cried from sheer gratitude if she could have mustered enough moisture for tears. "Thank you," she whispered in a choked voice.

Her mules became part of his charge from then on, and her regard for Chester grew as he assumed responsibility for watering and harnessing her team along with the dozen mules that pulled his double wagon. When she ached with fatigue and could barely manage the chore of climbing up and down from the wagon, he was there to assist her.

Captain Walker's face grew grim, and his voice cracked as he urged the train onward. He spent time he should have been resting holding Sylvia while he coaxed her to swallow the trickle of water he pressed to her lips. Sometimes he sat beside her with his head bowed and his lips barely moving. Charlie Mae suspected she wasn't the only one who had taken up praying. On the occasions when Charlie Mae's eyes met his, she saw the fear he struggled to hide from the men.

Cookie was another matter. By the second night, his fever broke, and he managed to sit up for a few minutes, and on the third night, he made his way to the wagon seat where Charlie Mae sat, untied Abby, and placed her on the lumpy bed behind them before settling himself weakly beside her. The following day, a mule sagged in its harness, bringing the rest of its teammates stumbling to their knees until the animal could be cut free and dragged from the trail. The animal brought up to replace it balked, causing considerable delay.

On the fifth day, Charlie Mae was expecting Captain Walker to declare a halt about midday so that the party could sleep for a few hours as had become their habit. Instead he urged them to move on. Before long the mules perked up and began to move faster. Some teams were too far spent to increase their pace and were passed by swifter animals.

Cookie climbed onto the wagon seat again, shifting Abby to Charlie Mae's lap as he took over the reins. He was none too soon. The four mules pulling the wagon broke into a trot, then a mad dash. A patch of green appeared in the distance, and the race was on. Big Sugarplum showed his determination to be first to reach water, and the other three mules followed his lead. Cookie sawed at the reins, attempting to slow the mules, and Charlie Mae clung to Abby with one hand and clutched the seat with the other. Behind her, Sylvia was tossed from one side of the mattress to the other.

They reached the spring without mishap, but some were not so lucky. One wagon lost a wheel, and another mule sank in the traces, unable to rise while the other mules fought to free themselves.

The moment the mad dash halted beside a pool of water, Charlie Mae stumbled to Sylvia's side. Sylvia's moans indicated she was still alive, and Charlie Mae patted her face and hands with a generous helping of the fresh spring water Captain Walker fetched for her.

Captain Walker ordered camp set up near the straggling trees that grew around the spring, and Charlie Mae prepared the first cooked meal since the night they had begun crossing the dreaded Humboldt Sink. Men freed the mules still stuck on the desert, and some of the stronger animals were used to help the crippled wagons reach camp.

The children revived quickly, but when Charlie Mae carried a plate of stew to Sylvia in the wagon, she discovered Captain Walker there. Together, they bathed the semiconscious woman and forced a few spoonfuls of broth into her mouth.

"I'll stay with her while you eat and tend to camp duties," Charlie Mae offered.

"Thank you," he mumbled and turned away reluctantly.

Alone with the sick woman, Charlie Mae bathed Sylvia's face again and spoke softly to her, assuring her the awful desert was past. She refrained from mentioning that the jagged Sierra Mountain range loomed ahead of them. Sylvia's breath came in shallow gasps, and twice Charlie Mae leaned closer to assure herself that the other woman was still breathing.

She had lost her own mother when she was not much older than Abby, and she retained little memory of her. Granny had done her best, she supposed, but it hadn't been like having a mother. She'd often thought her childhood and entry into womanhood would have been much easier if she'd had a mother to protect and guide her. Her heart broke to think of dear little Abby growing up motherless.

Her thoughts went to Sister Pascal—though she'd known her only a short time, the woman had made a significant impact on her life. Spencer's grandma had hugged her and prayed over her in a way Granny never had. It occurred to her that Grandma Pascal would pray over Sylvia if she were present.

Charlie Mae thought about praying. She hadn't prayed much in her life, but Grandma Pascal had taught her how, and she'd done it a few times when she figured she was in more trouble than she knew how to handle. This seemed to be one of those times. Besides, praying certainly wouldn't hurt Sylvia. She knew her friend considered herself a Christian, and she insisted her children pray each night before climbing into bed, so she likely wouldn't object to someone praying over her.

Kneeling the best she could on the lumpy mattress, Charlie Mae screwed her eyes shut and began to pray. She remembered to give thanks for their safe passage across the sink before asking the Lord to bear in mind how much Sylvia's little children needed their mother. After she said amen, she remained on her knees with her eyes closed for several minutes. When she opened them, Sylvia was watching her.

"Are you feeling better?" Charlie Mae asked. Sylvia didn't answer, but the smallest hint of a smile slightly lifted one corner of her mouth before she closed her eyes again.

* * *

IT WAS LATE, and the sky was filled with stars again when she finished scrubbing the last of the pans and set them in their places. Cookie had helped prepare dinner but had looked so tired by the time the meal was served, she'd offered to do the clean up alone. Miss Bonnie and Miss Maude pitched in to help, only leaving when Chester suggested they find their wagon and get some well-deserved rest. Irwin volunteered to escort them. Chester lifted into place the heavy cast-iron pot Charlie Mae and Cookie used for beans and stews.

"Charlie Mae, it seems I ain't seen much of you for a powerful long time," he said as she clipped her wet dish rag and towels to a line strung from the cook wagon to the canopy sheltering the fire. The fire had died down to mere coals. He took her hand and led her to a large rock near the fire ring.

They sat for some time, enjoying the faint warmth from the coals. Charlie Mae didn't think she'd ever understand how the days they'd just endured could have been so unbearably hot, yet at night she'd shivered beneath her shawl.

"Seems all we could think about out there was how miserable we were and how we had to keep moving." She acknowledged how little they'd interacted, even though he'd been there to help her with the heavier work. They'd spoken little and spent no time alone.

"You were busy takin' care of sick folks and tendin' children—and you weren't accustomed to drivin' mules," he said. "But I did some thinkin' while I was sittin' there on that wagon. When we get to California, me and Irwin have plans to head into the mountains to do our lookin' for gold. With the supplies and wages Captain Walker has promised the three of us, and old Sugarplum, I expect we'll be set to build us a cabin and stay the winter. Unlike some folks, we won't have to winter over in Sacramento or in one of the camps."

"It'll be nice to have a cabin. I was fearing we would have to pitch a tent and move on right often." She admitted to herself that she'd grown tired of traveling and was looking forward to the time when she'd have her own floor to sweep and a real stove.

"Charlie Mae . . ." He paused so long she thought he might have forgotten what he meant to say. "I liked ya the first day I saw ya. You're purty and kind and . . . if ya don't find me too objectionable . . . would you think about marryin' me before we head into the mountains after gold?"

Her heart fluttered, and she couldn't avoid a small gasp. She'd suspected for some time that Chester was courting her. Not having had any prior experience with courting, she wasn't certain whether he was just lonely for the companionship of other young folks like her and Irwin or if he sought more than friendship.

"I promise I won't hit you or treat you bad the way Irwin says your pa did. I ain't got much now, but I'm strong, and I know how to work. You'll never go hungry, and if me and Irwin strike it rich like we aim to, I'll build you a big house, and you can fill it with all the fancy woman fixin's you like."

"I'd be happy to marry up with you," she stammered, ducking her head with a sudden bout of shyness. She'd thought more than once about what she'd say if Chester asked her to marry him. He was a good man and kind to her. He made her feel safe and protected in a way she'd never before experienced. She didn't reckon she'd find a better man.

"Charlie Mae?" She raised her head. Awkwardly he cupped her cheeks in his big hands, leaned forward, and lightly brushed her lips with his. "Thank you. I'll do my best to make sure you're never sorry you agreed to be my wife."

* * *

MORNING CAME TOO soon. Charlie Mae stretched and yawned. Then she remembered. She was engaged to be married! She could hardly wait to tell Irwin and Sylvia. Thinking of Sylvia, she scrambled into her dress and hurried to the other wagon.

Peeking inside, she saw that her friend was still asleep. She climbed inside to kneel beside her and was relieved to hear Sylvia breathing more naturally than she had for a long time. Taking care not to awaken her, Charlie Mae left the wagon to begin breakfast preparations. Cookie was there before her, seemingly his old self. Instead of preparing a separate meal for the Walker family, she pitched in to assist in preparing enough for the entire company.

Captain Walker addressed the group assembled for breakfast, saying they would remain where they were for another day. "Many of the wagons need repairs, so get out the grease buckets, boys. Tomorrow we'll start climbing, and I want every wagon in the best shape possible and the animals fed and rested."

Charlie Mae took advantage of a day off from traveling to wash a few items for her and the children. Andrew ran happily about camp, but Abby stayed close. She appeared content to dabble a handkerchief in Charlie Mae's wash bucket and help her compile the ingredients for a dried apple cobbler. Charlie Mae caught occasional glimpses of Chester and Irwin, but they didn't come close enough to exchange words with her.

It was almost lunchtime when Sylvia awoke. Though still weak, she accepted a few spoonfuls of broth. Little Abby fussed about her mother, patting Sylvia's face with her damp handkerchief and crooning unintelligible songs in her ear. She refused to leave her mother's side, so Charlie Mae took lunch to her. There was something that touched an empty spot in Charlie Mae's heart to see the little girl's devotion to her mother and awakened a vague sense that she'd once shared that same bond with her own mother. She dismissed the feeling as fancy.

When both of her charges were fed, Charlie Mae left them sleeping while she joined Cookie in setting out lunch for everyone else. She lamented that it had never seemed the right moment to share her news with Sylvia.

Lunchtime never afforded an opportunity to talk to either Chester or Irwin. She tracked down Andrew and made certain he got something to eat, and she read to him for a time from one of his mother's books. Her ability to read had vastly improved as had her grammar.

When Andrew set off to play again, she stroked the bird Spencer had carved on the wooden box with her fingertips and wished she could tell Spencer how much his gift meant to her and that she and

Chester were going to be married. She thought her young friend would be happy for her. Then she read from Grandma Pascal's book until Abby awoke and it was time to prepare supper. Sylvia seemed much better, so she left the little girl playing quietly in the wagon beside her mother while she built up the fire and set out her kettles.

Captain Walker was so pleased with his wife's improved condition that he fixed plates for himself and his family, and he and Andrew joined Sylvia and Abby for supper in their wagon. Between Sylvia's improvement and finally getting past the Humboldt Sink, there was an air of festivity around the campfire that night.

As he often did, Chester waited to be one of the last ones to fill his plate so that Charlie Mae would soon be free to join him with her own plate. She sat beside him and looked around for Irwin.

"Have you seen my brother?" she asked.

"Um, he's busy right now." Chester looked down at his plate and his ears turned red. She attributed Chester's discomfort to the possibility he'd already told Irwin about their engagement and had asked him to give them a little privacy. She didn't mind, but she had been looking forward to telling her brother herself.

"Did you tell him . . . ?"

"He knows. Since your pa ain't here, I figured I ought to let your brother know my intentions." She supposed that was only right.

Chester hung around while she and Cookie cleared away the dishes and leftovers. They talked for awhile after Cookie retired, then before his own departure, Chester kissed her again. She was making her way to her wagon when she heard Irwin speak her name in a low voice.

He stepped out of the shadows. "Charlie Mae, I expect you and Chester have got your plans all worked out."

"We're getting married as soon as we can find a preacher after we reach California."

"I'm glad you didn't let what happened back there in Pa's barn sour you on marrying. Chester's a good man, and he'll do right by you."

A lump came to her throat. Irwin cared about her even if he didn't say the words.

"I know he's a good man, and I'm looking forward to being his wife. I'm anxious too for this journey to end and for the three of us to strike out on our own. He said the two of you are planning to build a cabin. It'll be awfully nice to have a home of our own."

"Yes, from what I hear, there ain't much gold being found anymore in the lower valleys, so we're going to have to go higher, and the winters are fierce in the mountains. I don't want to have to travel back down to the valley as soon as we get there, and I don't relish spendin' the winter in a tent." It still amazed her when her brother strung more than a few words together.

"I reckon you're right." She took a step toward the wagon. Irwin clasped her arm, halting her steps.

"There's something else you need to know."

"What?" Surely he wasn't going to tell her something bad about Chester or that they were leaving her behind.

"I'm getting married too."

"Married? But who . . . ?" She knew perfectly well she and Sylvia were the only two ladies in the company.

"Bonnie McFarland and I are tying the knot soon as we can."

"You mean Miss Bonnie?" In the dim light, Charlie Mae saw her brother nod his head.

"But Irwin . . . Sylvia said . . ." She couldn't believe Irwin planned to marry one of Miss Louisa's girls.

"I know. Women like the ladies in the pink wagons are shunned by most folks. Sylvia has good cause not to want her children exposed to women with loose morals, but Bonnie ain't like the other women. It ain't her fault she's traveling with Miss Louisa and the others."

"Then whose fault is it?" How could Irwin even consider marrying Miss Bonnie after the things he'd said about Pa when he married Agnes? Irwin didn't get worked up about many things, but loose women and Pa were the exceptions. He'd made it clear he had no use for either.

"She grew up in an orphanage, and when she turned fourteen, Miss Louisa paid the man who owned the orphanage some money to turn Bonnie over to her. For almost two years, she has been doing laundry, mending clothes, fixin' hair, and runnin' errands at Miss Louisa's place in Charleston, but Miss Louisa said things are going to change when they get to California. Bonnie is growed up now and awful pretty, so Miss Louisa aims to make her do the things the other girls do."

"How do you know all this?" Charlie Mae wasn't ready to accept Miss Bonnie's story.

"Sometimes we talk when I take the scraps you give me to Mr. Rags."

"When Deke got married, you said you weren't ever going to marry."

"That was because I was still angry at Ma for leavin' us, even if Pa was a hard man to live with. For a long time I forgot all the good things about our ma, but spendin' time with you and Bonnie got me rememberin' how Ma baked cookies and read stories to us. She allus saved a piece of bread for me to hide in my pocket when Pa made me miss dinner. She didn't go nowhere without you. I started thinkin' Granny was right, and Ma wasn't the loose woman Pa said she was. After awhile I knew she wouldn't just go off and leave us. I'm pretty sure she's dead, and iffen she's dead, then she couldn't help leavin' us. That eases my mind about marryin'."

"You're not thinking Miss Bonnie might go off after you get her away from Miss Louisa?"

"She said she'd never leave me unless she died, and there's no way anybody can promise they won't die."

"Maybe she made up that story about being an orphan to get you to feel sorry for her."

"I'd know if she was lyin'. You forget I been livin' around the biggest liars in the country most all my life." His voice was bitter.

She nodded her head. Their pa, their older brothers, Mr. Sawyer, Agnes, and Agnes's boys weren't the least bit interested in the truth or being fair.

"I thought you liked Bonnie and would help us." There was disappointment in his voice. "Bonnie is gentle and sweet, just like our ma was, and she deserves a better chance than what Miss Louisa has planned for her."

"I do like Miss Bonnie, and if what she told you is true, then she does deserve a chance for a different life. She's been good to Mr. Rags, and she was a real help to me when Cookie was ill. It's just Sylvia. I don't think she'll believe anything good about any of those women, not even Bonnie, any more'n Pa would believe anything good about the Mormons."

"That's part of the reason we're going to need your help."

"If Bonnie doesn't want to work for Miss Louisa, why doesn't she just leave when we get to California? Why do you have to marry her?" It was hard to change her rosy dreams of just her, Chester, and Irwin spending the winter in a cozy cabin. She'd been looking forward to taking charge of her own home.

"She can't just leave." A note of exasperation crept into Irwin's voice. "How would she live? Ain't hardly nobody hires a pretty woman who is all alone to work for him 'cept for one thing. Besides, Miss Louisa ain't going to let her go without a fight. Even though Bonnie has worked for her for free for two years, Miss Louisa figures she owns her, bought and paid for just like some slave."

Charlie Mae's shoulders slumped. She could see Irwin had no choice really. He had a tough exterior, but there was a softer place in his heart that compelled him to help those in trouble. Bonnie's situation, she figured, wasn't too much different from her own. If Irwin hadn't helped her escape a similar fate, her future would be as dismal as the one Bonnie faced.

"What do you want me to do?"

Some of the tension drained from Irwin's shoulders. "We don't have it all worked out yet, but when we're ready to leave the wagon train, we'll move quickly, so be ready."

"I assume you won't be announcing your engagement."

"No, we'll let you and Chester take all of the attention while we avoid being noticed."

"I'm glad I won't have to tell Sylvia."

"It'll be all right," Irwin promised. "Don't treat Bonnie any different, and don't mention anything about our plans to anyone."

"Not even Chester?"

"Chester already knows, and I wouldn't ask you to keep secrets from him. Now you best get some sleep. We'll be moving on in the morning."

She watched him walk away and felt a stab in her heart for him. He deserved better than marriage to a woman who touched his heart but didn't capture it. She stirred uneasily, wondering if her engagement, too, was based more on expediency than love. She denied the thought. She truly cared for Chester, and he'd demonstrated his devotion to her many times.

* * *

BECAUSE OF THE excitement her upcoming marriage garnered throughout the camp, Charlie Mae paid little attention to the early portion of the train's climb up the steep switchbacks of the Sierra Mountain pass. With shade and abundant water, Sylvia showed improvement and began leaving the wagon for short periods again when they paused for a midday meal or camped for the night. She tired quickly, but it encouraged both Charlie Mae and Captain Walker to hope for the best. Learning of Charlie Mae's upcoming marriage seemed to be the boost Sylvia needed to make her want to get well.

The two young women spent hours discussing what Charlie Mae should wear and what supplies she would need to set up housekeeping in the cabin Chester and Irwin planned to build. Sylvia went so far as to offer Charlie Mae a blue satin gown she claimed no longer fit her. Charlie Mae stared at the dress in astonishment. It was the most beautiful gown she'd ever seen, and when she tried it on, she felt much the way she'd felt that day long ago when Sister Pascal had put her white baptism dress on her. It was too long for Charlie Mae, but she set to work shortening it and taking in the waist during the tedious hours she spent riding inside a wagon.

Charlie Mae found frequent opportunities to visit Mr. Rags and to observe Miss Bonnie. Even after three months on the trail, the other girl always dressed in beautiful gowns and tied her hair back with a ribbon each day. She noted that the girl's dresses were never as revealing as those of the other women who worked for Miss Louisa. However, she suspected Bonnie used rouge to brighten her lips and cheeks.

The first time Charlie Mae went in search of Mr. Rags after Irwin's confession, she felt ill at ease with the other girl until she noticed that Bonnie appeared to be just as nervous as she. There was little opportunity to talk as Miss Louisa or one of the other women always seemed to hover nearby whenever Charlie Mae put in an appearance.

The climb grew steeper, and Charlie Mae grew nervous about staying in the wagon as it jolted and lurched near steep dropoffs and threatened to roll backward should the sure-footed mules falter. Instead, she chose to walk most of the time. Andrew walked with her, and she alternated between allowing Abby to walk and carrying the little girl. On the most difficult days, Irwin unhitched Sugarplum from the cook wagon, substituting another mule from the small herd of replacement animals that followed behind the wagons, so that Charlie Mae and the children could ride on the mule's wide back.

Progress was slow, making keeping up with the wagons easier than when they'd traveled across flatter terrain. Captain Walker rested the mules a couple of days near a large lake before continuing on. The air was fresh and clean, and the vista was the most beautiful Charlie Mae had ever seen. Charlie Mae's spirits rose higher in anticipation of setting up a home in a cabin in those mountains.

One evening as she and Chester strolled beneath mammoth fir trees with Mr. Rags, they happened on Miss Louisa and two of the women who worked for her. They were poring over a piece of brown parchment Louisa had spread on the ground. The madam called to them.

"Mr. Gafton," she addressed Chester, "finding gold is a risky business, and I believe the greater fortunes are to be made in providing services for the miners. When we reach Sacramento, I'll be in need of a strong man to set up my tent and to tend to the heavier tasks in my business. I'd be pleased to offer the position to you."

"Thank you, ma'am, but I've plans to marry and form a partnership with my wife's brother." Chester appeared uncomfortable with the offer.

"I think I can guarantee to fill your pockets with gold much faster than kneeling in cold streams can. As for marrying, I'm sure Miss Charlotte would be much happier living near other people and the shops that are springing up in cities such as Sacramento and San Francisco. I could even offer her a position caring for my girls' wardrobes and cooking for us and our guests." Miss Louisa's offer of a position for Charlie Mae appeared offhand, but something about the appraising look in the madam's eyes brought a chill to her heart.

"Our plans are made, and I ain't lookin' to change them."

"You can't be planning to take Miss Charlotte to those mine camps or drag her with you into the mountains to live! I can offer her employment and look out for her until you return if you insist on looking for gold."

Mr. Rags barked and pulled at his leash. Charlie Mae knelt to hush him and didn't hear Chester's answer, but it didn't matter. She knew Chester would refuse it. Working for Miss Louisa was something she'd never agree to anyway, even if Chester did.

Lowering her eyes to avoid the calculating look she'd glimpsed in the other woman's eyes, Charlie Mae focused on the parchment. It took a moment for her to realize it was the drawing of a large space, possibly the tent Louisa had mentioned to Chester. An open area near the entrance was labeled SALOON. Behind it were six smaller squares with a larger rectangle at the end. The large rectangle had an L in its center, which probably meant that was Miss Louisa's office or perhaps where she would live. Curious, she glanced at the smaller squares. There was an initial marking each of those spaces, too. B, J, A, M, V, and C. Bonnie, Jerusha, Alice, Maude, Victoria, and . . .

She clutched her fiancé's arm. "Come, Chester. Sylvia will be expecting me."

"What's the matter?" Chester asked when they were alone again, and he was hard pressed to keep up with her rapid steps. "You know I ain't going to change my mind about going with Irwin."

"It's just a feeling I had." She stopped to face Chester. She stood twisting her apron between her hands. She told him about the drawing and the conclusion she'd drawn. "There are plenty of men in California she can hire to set up her tent and run her errands. I suspect she has a plan to force me to work for her."

"You're pretty enough." He grinned then stared at her incredulously when he realized she was serious. "But you ain't that kind of girl."

"I don't think that matters to Miss Louisa. According to Irwin, Bonnie isn't that kind of girl either."

Chester frowned and flexed his heavy biceps. "If she were a man, I'd punch her in the nose."

"Do you think she's been polite and nice to me ever since we first met to get me to trust her?"

Chester put his arms around her, and she felt safe in the shelter of his strong body.

"That's probably why she agreed to keep Mr. Rags, though Miss Bonnie has been the one really lookin' out for him. I think we better find Irwin." A deep frown replaced his usually cheerful countenance.

"You don't think Bonnie . . . ?"

"No, I don't. Near as I can tell, Bonnie don't belong with that outfit."

Chester walked Charlie Mae back to her wagon, where they found Irwin already rolled in his blankets beneath the wagon. When Chester told him they needed to talk, he joined them beside the smoldering campfire. He listened patiently while Chester and Charlie Mae told him about Miss Louisa's offer and the conclusions they'd drawn.

Irwin scratched his head and looked dubious. "I don't know. It could be a genuine offer. I'll ask Bonnie what she thinks. Give me Mr. Rags's rope, and I'll take him back. Could be I'll get a chance to talk to her. Then again, it might be a few days before I'll be able to catch her alone. Up to now, Miss Louisa has encouraged Bonnie to be friendly to men, but lately she's been watching her more closely." His last statement brought the old scowl to Irwin's face.

After Irwin left with the dog, Chester took Charlie Mae's hands in his and stood looking at her. She thought he was going to kiss her again, but he just looked at her for several minutes. Finally he said, "We've probably got this whole thing wrong, but I can't help worryin'. I ain't never seen a prettier gal than you, and I've been worrying for some time about keepin' other men from gawkin' at you and tryin' to take you away from me. But since you mentioned what you saw on that paper of Miss Louisa's, I been thinkin' about how much she likes expensive things like that ring of hers and how she's likely thinkin' she could get rich a whole lot faster if she had you workin' for her. You're probably safe enough for now with

Irwin and Cookie driving the Walker family wagons and me and Captain Walker close by most of the time, but it might be a good idea to stay close to your wagon unless me or Irwin are with you."

* * *

NEARLY FOUR DAYS passed before Irwin invited her to sit beside him on the wagon seat while he drove. He didn't say much for a long time, but Charlie Mae was accustomed to long stretches of silence from him. Several times he glanced behind him as though assuring himself that Sylvia and Abby were asleep. She supposed he'd arranged for Andrew to sit with Cookie, since the boy no longer napped during the afternoon. She smiled, thinking of the young boy who had changed from a timid child who clung to his mother to a sturdy, fearless young scamp who kept Charlie Mae chasing after him.

"Charlie Mae," Irwin said in a low voice to avoid being overheard, "Bonnie says Miss Louisa told them all that a new girl would be joinin' them soon. She said, too, that Miss Louisa has been giving Mr. Rags special bits of meat and paying him more attention than usual."

"I don't understand."

"Bonnie thinks Miss Louisa is planning to use your dog to trick you into going with her."

Charlie Mae swallowed hard and glanced back at Sylvia. "Doesn't she know you and Chester would come after me?" Her voice ended on a slightly uncertain note.

"We would," he hastened to assure her, "but I suspect she's got connections in Sacramento we know nothing about. She probably figures she could hide you until you have no choice but to work for her."

"I'd never . . ."

"Don't say you'd never become one of her girls. None of us knows for sure what we'd do if hungry enough or if someone we love is threatened. That might even be why she's being nice to Mr. Rags. She might threaten to hurt him bad if you don't do what she wants you to do."

"I wish Sylvia would let Mr. Rags stay here. The children love him, and now that the other dogs know him, they don't bother him anymore."

"I've been thinking about that. Chester could keep Mr. Rags now that the dog ain't sick no more. We could tell everyone that since you two are gittin' married, Chester wants the dog to get used to mindin' him."

"You think I really am in danger, don't you? That it's not just my imagination?" Charlie Mae looked down where the mules were kicking up a cloud of dust that lingered between the traces.

"I can't say for certain, but Bonnie says Miss Maude has a husband back in Richmond who thinks she drowned while he was away on business. Miss Louisa called at her town house claiming to be her papa's cousin. After sharing tea together, Miss Louisa begged Maude to show her the city. Maude became sleepy while riding in Miss Louisa's carriage, and when she awoke, she was miles away in a darkened room, her clothes were missing, she was covered in bruises, and Miss Louisa let her know she'd been seen throughout the city with a gentleman of questionable reputation. The carriage was found overturned in a swampy area with a few of her garments still inside. She was told she had entertained a dozen gentlemen, and even if she ran away, her husband wouldn't take her back after all she'd done."

The story brought a gasp to Charlie Mae's lips. "How can someone who seems to be so nice be so cruel?"

"I told you they are wicked." She turned to see Sylvia sitting up. Clearly she had overheard at least part of their conversation. Charlie Mae wondered how much.

"You should have come to me the moment you suspected that woman had designs on you." She scrambled closer to the wagon seat.

The wagon lurched over a rock, and Irwin scowled at the mules before meeting Charlie Mae's eyes with obvious concern in his.

"I shall tell Captain Walker he must leave those women and their gaudy pink wagons to make their way on their own. Until we are shut of them, you must never leave my side." Sylvia gripped Charlie Mae's arm.

Irwin's eyes flooded with pain, convincing Charlie Mae his feelings for Bonnie weren't based on compassion alone. Somehow Charlie Mae would have to convince Sylvia not to act hastily. Irwin wouldn't leave Bonnie behind. Neither could he abandon his post with the Walker train, thus forfeiting his wages and gold-hunting stake.

15 ᴏ₎

"I DON'T THINK there's anything to worry about until we reach a large town or gold camp," Charlie Mae said over her shoulder to Sylvia. "We may be mistaken about Miss Louisa's intentions, but even if our suspicions are correct, she's not likely to try anything until we reach a large enough settlement."

"My husband should be informed at once," Sylvia said.

"Please wait until you can speak to him privately. If everyone knows of our suspicions, it might cause trouble," Charlie Mae urged.

"Miss Louisa's agreement with your husband, ma'am, calls for her to pay the captain a bonus for the company's early arrival in Sacramento. We're well ahead of any other overland wagon train, and he stands to lose money if Miss Louisa pulls out of the company," Irwin noted.

"I might persuade the captain to allow the two of you to leave early," Sylvia suggested. "You could leave quietly and be miles away before that woman knows you've gone."

"When we leave, Chester Gafton will leave with us," Irwin reminded her. "He won't stand for Charlie Mae leaving without him, as they've plans to wed soon's they meet up with a preacher."

"And that would leave us short two drivers," Sylvia finished for him. The prospectors who had ridden with the wagon train were almost all gone. They'd broken away as singles or in small groups to begin searching for gold along the streams they'd passed since beginning their descent toward the Sacramento Valley. Sylvia was quiet for several minutes, apparently deep in thought before speaking again. "I shall think on it and discuss the matter with my husband privately. Until we come up with a solution, Charlie Mae, you must stay within sight of this wagon at all times unless escorted by your brother or Mr. Gafton."

"Yes, ma'am," Charlie Mae agreed without telling her the three of them had already decided that was the best course.

"I surely do appreciate your concern for my sister," Irwin added.

Sylvia lay back down, exhausted. Charlie Mae and Irwin looked at each other. Sylvia's tongue could be sharp, but she would be of little physical use if Louisa attempted to overpower Charlie Mae.

Charlie Mae found sleep difficult that night. She wasn't concerned so much for her immediate safety. Captain Walker's two children slept beside her on the feather tick, and both Irwin and Cookie had spread their bedrolls beneath the wagon. Chester and Mr. Rags slept beneath a wagon midway between her and the pink wagons. Mostly, she felt restless and anxious for the journey to end. She reached inside the coarse cloth bag that held her few possessions. Her hand rested on the small box Spencer had given her. Opening it, she brushed her fingers across the smooth surface of the ruby. There wasn't enough light to see the stone, but she gained comfort from merely touching it.

* * *

IT BECAME INCREASINGLY common to meet small parties headed east. A few were prospectors who had given up and were returning home. There were hunters and trappers and even a few Indians. Some were Mormons who had served as scouts for wagon trains the previous year, and some were immigrants headed toward Salt Lake City who had reached the West Coast aboard ships. Most rode horses or walked, leading pack animals, so sighting wagons coming up the trail late one afternoon excited Charlie Mae's curiosity.

The smaller train, on seeing the long line of freight wagons coming toward them, pulled aside into a flat area beside the trail to let the larger train pass. Charlie Mae counted six wagons pulled by oxen, at least a dozen horses, seven or eight women in calico dresses walking beside the wagons, and a surprisingly large number of men and boys. Peeking from the wagons were several small children. Captain Walker and one of his scouts reined in their horses beside the eastbound travelers while his own wagons continued west.

Not much time passed before Captain Walker caught back up to his convoy of wagons and passed the word that they would be making camp at the first suitable camp site. He paused beside first Cookie, then Charlie Mae, to inform them he had invited guests from the other wagon train to dine with them.

"If you've enough of those dried apples for a cobbler, we might share a treat with a few of the leaders," he suggested as he rode beside her for a short distance. She'd noticed the look of concern on his face the past few days when she caught him watching her, which he seemed to be doing more often than in the past. As soon as the wagons rolled into their accustomed formation for the night, she poured the last of the dry apple slices into a large bowl and covered them with water to soak until she was ready to make the cobbler.

While she browned meat and sliced onions into the sizzling fat, she became aware of a whispered conversation going on behind her. A glance over her shoulder confirmed that Sylvia and the captain were engaged in a heated discussion. It wasn't the first such argument between the pair in the past few days. She had a pretty good idea that she was the subject of their arguments. She hoped Sylvia wasn't insisting on ejecting the pink wagons from their midst. If Bonnie were forced to leave, she feared Irwin would abandon their plans in order to follow her.

The next time she looked toward the Walkers, their heads were close together, and they both seemed pleased with whatever solution they had reached. She hoped she, Chester, and Irwin would be equally pleased.

Charlie Mae was lifting golden biscuits from one of her large iron kettles when she saw a troop of people, including women, scrambling down the trail on foot. Captain Walker and some of the mule drivers stepped forward to greet them. In minutes, the captain ushered a gentleman who appeared to be in his fifties, and two younger men with the younger men's wives into his family's dining area. Abby clutched Charlie Mae's skirt and stared wide-eyed at the strangers.

One of the women carried a plump toddler on her hip. When the child saw Abby, she squealed, demanding to be set down. Her mother obliged, and the little girl lurched toward Abby. Confronted with the friendly baby, Abby at first resisted her overtures, then succumbed to her smiles and giggles. Sylvia and the child's mother smiled indulgently, and after a few minutes Sylvia returned to her wagon for a pair of Abby's rag dolls. Soon the little girls were playing contentedly near the wagon while their mothers were engrossed in conversation.

Andrew begged to be allowed to join Irwin and Chester at the larger cook fire, where most of their guests were gathered. Charlie Mae knew very well his real intent was to play with a couple of boys near his age who had accompanied their fathers. To her surprise, Sylvia approved and waved her son on his way. There was no time to wonder about Sylvia's sudden complacency.

While dishing up the meal, Charlie Mae learned that the two younger couples and four other couples with their children had arrived from Australia two months earlier by boat and that they were Mormons on their way to Salt Lake City. Their ship, which carried mostly men and boys seeking to make their fortunes in the California gold fields, had sailed into San Francisco bay to unload passengers and supplies before continuing on to San Bernardino, where a new Mormon colony had been established a year earlier. Most of the crew had abandoned the ship to become prospectors, leaving the ship's captain unable to continue on. The Mormon families had decided they would continue on to Salt Lake rather than turn south to San Bernardino.

Sylvia surprised Charlie Mae again by not appearing the least affronted to find herself entertaining Mormons. In fact, she seemed quite taken with the women who spoke with charming Australian accents.

"What of the other men in your party?" Captain Walker asked. "Did they arrive in California by boat as well?"

"No, they're mostly young men whom Brigham Young found to have too much time on their hands, so he sent them to California last summer to scout out possible locations for new settlements and to work for some of the large ranchers who have lost their ranch hands to gold fever. Elder Grayson," the older man nodded to a man twenty years his junior, "is a surveyor, sent to examine possible town sites. President Young sent me along as their leader."

"Bishop Westover and I, with our young helpers, were just beginning our trek back to Salt Lake City when we met up with the Australian immigrants. We helped them procure wagons and stock, which are in ample supply as the miners have no need of them and are anxious to sell all they have to obtain a stake for gold mining," Elder Grayson said.

"Right glad we were to find some of our own folks what knew the lay of the land and could give us the latest news from the Mormon authorities." One of the Australian gentlemen nodded his head and beamed at those gathered around him. "We were pleased to have Bishop Westover take charge of baptizing our Bobby as well."

"What's the trail like 'tween here 'n' Salt Lake?" the other man asked. "We've heard some fearsome tales."

"Difficult." Captain Walker launched into a summary of their experience crossing the dreaded Humboldt Sink. "This time of year is always hot and dry, but the heat seemed particularly bad this season. We were fortunate to be carrying extra water barrels."

"When we crossed last summer, our party consisted of just men on good horses. This year we will be moving slower since we've wagons with women and children. Is there any chance you'd consider selling some of the barrels you won't be needing for the rest of your trip?" Bishop Westover asked.

"I think something could be arranged." There was something about the captain's benign smile that told Charlie Mae that he had some sort of deal in mind.

The men continued discussing the trail in both directions while the women conversed quietly to one side. Charlie Mae finished her plate and rose to dish up the cobbler. As she did so, she wondered about the possibility of sending a letter to Spencer with one of them to let her friend know of her pending marriage. Behind her, she heard Captain Walker ask, "Is bishop an ecclesiastical title or your name?"

She heard a chuckle, then Bishop Westover's deep voice explained, "Brother Brigham called me to be a bishop a couple of years ago, and I was kept right busy with a ward—that's a congregation—down at the south end of the valley, until he called me to accompany Elder Grayson and his young assistants. He said there weren't no sense in releasing me 'cause I'd still be carrying out bishop duties."

"We've a young couple looking to get married. Could you marry them up proper?" Hearing Captain Walker's question, Charlie Mae dropped the spoon she was using to dish up the cobbler. It clattered and banged against the kettle before falling into the fire. She came close to setting her sleeve on fire as she stooped to fish the spoon out of the hot coals, straining as she did to hear the Mormon bishop's answer.

"I reckon I could," the bishop responded. "I performed two weddings in Sacramento earlier this summer."

"Good. I'll go fetch the groom." Captain Walker rose to his feet.

"Come, dear. I think you'll want to change your dress." She hadn't been aware of Sylvia's approach. Her friend's arm came around her shoulders. Numbness took over, and Charlie Mae allowed Sylvia to lead her to the wagon.

Once inside the wagon, Sylvia pulled out the dress they had decided earlier would be perfect for Charlie Mae's wedding. Her trembling fingers made unbuttoning the gown she wore nearly impossible. Giggling, Sylvia tackled the buttons for her and helped her step out of her plain muslin gown. The rustle of blue satin caused Charlie Mae's limbs to tremble and her mind to turn to mush.

"You do want to marry Chester, don't you?" Sylvia whispered.

"Oh, yes, but I hadn't expected . . ."

"Preachers are hard to come by out here, and I bet he reckoned getting you two married tonight might solve two problems—finding a preacher and keeping you safe from that horrid Miss Louisa." The gown slid over Charlie Mae's head, and Sylvia tugged it into place before starting on the row of buttons that ran down its back.

Charlie Mae's head reeled, and she struggled to take in what was happening. Trying to make sense of the details involved in beginning their married life while still with the wagon train caused her to blush. On the other hand, Captain Walker was probably right. There was no telling when they might find another preacher, and she would feel safer with Chester beside her at night.

Sylvia removed the pins that held Charlie Mae's hair in a snug bun at the back of her head and brushed out the long pale frizz, shaping the curls into ringlets. With a few deft swipes of the brush, she piled some of the curls into sausage-like rolls high on her head, pinning them in place and allowing a few long curls to fall in cascades down her back.

"There. You look lovely," Sylvia whispered.

"Thank you," Charlie Mae whispered back, hoping Sylvia was right. She did want to look her best for Chester.

"Charlie Mae, are you ready?" She recognized Irwin's voice. It held a note of impatience.

"We're coming," Sylvia announced, giving Charlie Mae a little push toward the opening at the back of the wagon. Irwin was there to assist her in climbing down. He took her arm and began walking toward the fire where the whole camp seemed to be gathered. At first she watched her feet and listened to the unaccustomed rustle of her full satin skirt. When she gathered enough courage to lift her head, she saw Chester standing beside Bishop Westover. He'd changed into a clean shirt that was pulled snug across his broad chest, and his hair was slicked into place. He looked just the way she felt, both happy and scared. He reached for her hand, and she clung to it.

Bishop Westover began in a low voice as though merely conversing with them. He asked if they were both certain they wanted to marry, and he explained that those who marry took upon themselves a serious responsibility to care for each other through good times and bad. He cautioned them to be loyal to each other and suggested they make a practice of praying together each day. He moved easily into the marriage vows, and first Chester then Charlie Mae spoke their responses.

Never having attended a wedding before and having only Sander's books and Sylvia's descriptions of lavish weddings she had attended to go by, Charlie Mae was startled by how quickly the ceremony was over. With a kiss, she became Chester's wife. A loud hurrah sounded, reminding her that the entire camp had gathered to watch them marry. Even Miss Louisa and her girls gathered a little apart from the men. She knew her cheeks were scarlet, but she had no time to dwell on her embarrassment.

The drivers descended upon Chester with shouts, handshakes, and vigorous thumps on his back. Captain Walker shook Chester's hand and spoke to him briefly in low tones that didn't reach Charlie Mae's ears over the shouts of the men. Then she, too, was caught up in a flurry of well-wishers as Sylvia and the women who had joined them for dinner fluttered about her. Both Cookie and Captain Walker kissed her cheek, which brought a chorus from the drivers demanding the same privilege. Chester insisted they back off and took her hand to draw her into the darkness beyond the wagons.

They walked for a few minutes until they were beyond the light from the campfire before settling on a log. From outside the circle of wagons they could see several fires burning brightly, illuminating the camp like a stage. Chester placed an arm around her shoulders and drew her close. His kiss had made her heart pound. She wished these few minutes alone with him could go on for a long time, but she had responsibilities.

"I should go back," Charlie Mae said. "If the cooking pots aren't cleaned promptly, they're almost impossible to scrub clean."

"Cookie promised to do them tonight. He said he's paying you back for helping him out when he was sick. You don't need to worry about anything. Irwin and Cookie are going to bed down under my wagon with Mr. Rags, and the captain promised to keep the children with him and his wife tonight." She felt her cheeks burn, understanding the arrangement would leave them the privacy of the cook wagon.

They watched the celebration continue without them. When the fires burned low, Bishop Westover and his party drifted back to their camp a mile or more up the trail. Sylvia gathered up her children and disappeared inside her wagon. Captain Walker, assisted by

Irwin, unloaded a barrel from one of the wagons. He then called for the men to each bring a cup. Drinks were distributed to all.

Charlie Mae was surprised to see that Captain Walker was allowing Miss Louisa and her girls to mingle with the drivers. He even offered them drinks, which they readily accepted. In the revelry, she lost sight of Irwin. Her awareness of his longing to openly claim Bonnie mixed with her own wedding doubtless caused him some pain.

"It's time." Chester helped her to her feet, and still holding her hand, he began walking rapidly through the trees. Each time she had to stop to free her dress from the shrubbery that caught at it, he bent to help her, but he seemed impatient to be on their way.

She struggled to keep up. "Where are we going?" she panted when it became obvious they were leaving the camp behind.

"I'll explain in a minute," he whispered back. "I think it's safe to walk on the trail now, so we should be able to move more quickly."

Two shadows loomed out of the darkness. Before she could scream, Chester placed his hand over her mouth. "It's okay. They're just Irwin and Bonnie. Captain Walker said he'd create a diversion after our wedding so they could sneak up to the Mormon camp and get hitched too. I didn't figure you'd want to miss it." Her already full heart seemed to explode with joy.

Bishop Westover and two other men were waiting when they stepped into the other camp. This ceremony was even more brief than Chester and Charlie Mae's had been. When it was over, Bishop Westover handed Irwin a piece of paper similar to the one he'd given Chester earlier.

"When you get to Sacramento, take this to the recorder's office," he instructed.

"Thank you." Irwin shook the Mormon's hand, and Chester followed suit before the four young people started their hike back to camp. When the campfires came into view, Irwin stopped. Placing a hand on his sister's shoulder, he said, "Charlie Mae, I've no regrets about takin' you with me when we left Pa's farm, and I've tried not to ask too much of you, but there's something I'm needin' now."

"I owe you. I'll do whatever you want me to do." With her hand in Chester's and a general sense of a bright future before the four of them, she felt amenable to whatever favor he might ask.

16 🖎

CHARLIE MAE TOOK a deep breath then stumbled while climbing into the cook wagon, setting the box of cooking utensils and tin plates that hung on the back of the wagon clattering against each other. Chester fumbled trying to assist her, knocking two tin tubs together, which made a resounding racket. Catcalls and laughter rang out from the crowd still gathered around the campfires as the newlyweds clumsily scrambled inside the wagon.

Charlie Mae sank onto the mattress that filled almost the entire floor space of the wagon, burying her face in her hands. In the dark, Chester felt his way to her side. After a moment, he asked, "You ain't cryin', are you?"

"No." She smothered a giggle in her hands. "But tomorrow I'm going to be too embarrassed to look anyone in the eye."

"Sylvia will go easy on you, but I expect I'll be in for it. You're a good sister to agree to help Irwin and Bonnie sneak back into camp."

"Do you think Louisa noticed that Bonnie left the celebration early?"

"Bonnie told Louisa she had a headache and was going back to their wagon. Captain Walker planned to keep Miss Louisa and the other women too busy to notice her absence."

"Captain Walker was certainly busy to plan all this."

"Actually he started putting it all together soon's he stopped to talk to that Mormon preacher. Sylvia wasn't too happy at first about havin' a Mormon preacher come to supper and do the honors, but he convinced her it was the only way to keep Louisa from gettin' a chance to force you into her line of work. I don't think he told her about the second wedding."

Gradually the laughter and bawdy songs stilled beyond their canvas walls. Charlie Mae yawned. It had been a long and eventful day, and it was well beyond the time she usually found her bed.

"Chester," she whispered. "I can't unfasten my dress. Sylvia did it up for me, but I can't reach all of the buttons."

"I expect I can handle a few buttons," he whispered back.

* * *

California, 1850

THE WEATHER GREW warmer again as the wagon train dropped into the Sacramento Valley, but it wasn't the intense heat they'd faced earlier. Though the long journey had tired everyone, including the animals, there was an air of rejuvenation, knowing their journey was finally coming to an end.

Tents and shanties were sprawled for miles along the Sacramento River, and the harbor was clogged with abandoned vessels. A smattering of sturdy buildings, many of them government offices, sat at the center of the chaos along with a few brick or stone buildings. The squalor and confusion that met their eyes sent Sylvia to her bed with a headache.

Camp was set up for the last time on the edge of the settlement, and Captain Walker arranged for the men to serve as guards in shifts throughout the night. Knowing the period of greatest danger to both Charlie Mae and Bonnie had arrived, Chester insisted that Charlie Mae sleep inside the cook wagon with the children instead of beneath the wagon with him as had become their usual arrangement. Irwin volunteered for guard duty near the pink wagons to be certain Louisa didn't quietly pull her wagon out of camp now that they'd reached their destination.

Unable to fall asleep, Charlie Mae mentally reviewed the meager belongings she kept stuffed in one small bag. She didn't own much—just two muslin dresses and the satin one she'd been married in, which Sylvia had insisted she keep, her warm shawl, a couple changes of small clothes, Granny's Bible and Grandma Pascal's Book of Mormon, and the small box Spencer had given her. She wished it weren't necessary to leave the wagon train so abruptly with no chance to linger in Sacramento. Her boots were nearly worn through, and it would be nice if she could have a new pair made before setting off for the mountains. She didn't know exactly when they would leave, but she expected it would be within the next couple of days, depending on how soon Captain Walker could spare Chester and Irwin. When she did finally fall asleep, she was awakened several times by unfamiliar sounds coming from beyond their camp.

The sky was just beginning to turn light when Charlie Mae heard Chester whisper her name. She crawled to the end of the wagon and poked her head outside.

"Get dressed," he whispered. "Captain Walker paid me and Irwin our wages and helped us load the supplies he promised us on Sugarplum. He gave me your wages too and suggested we light out of here before anyone starts stirring."

She nodded her head and withdrew to dress. It only took seconds to don her dress and gather up her bag. Before leaving the wagon, she knelt to press a kiss against each of the children's cheeks. She paused a moment, wishing she could bid Sylvia farewell.

"Hurry," Chester whispered. She handed him her bag, which he set on the ground, before lifting her down. Then carrying the bag in one hand and clasping her hand in the other, he led her to the edge of the encampment. They walked rapidly until they reached a cluster of trees and bushes that grew near the river. The

trampled ground and scarcity of grass told her it was a well-used
rendezvous spot.

A short yip preceded a bundle of fur that leaped toward her.
Mr. Rags's rope leash was fastened to a nearby tree.

"Shh," she cautioned as she knelt to hug the dog.

"It's about time," Irwin growled, handing Sugarplum's reins to
Chester. "Best Charlie Mae puts on Sander's pants afore I get
back." He took off at a lope, back the way they'd come.

"Where is he go—? Oh. How does he plan to get Bonnie away
from Miss Louisa?"

"He's hoping to catch her alone when she visits the privy. He
didn't tell me the particulars, but we better do as he said about
gettin' trousers on you before someone comes along and sees you."

Picking up the pile of clothing her brother had left near the
spot where he'd tethered the mule, she recognized the pants and
shirt she'd worn when she and Irwin escaped Pa's farm early last
spring. While Chester kept a watch out for anyone who might
wander into the grove, she changed into Sander's clothes, finding
them a little tighter than when she'd worn them before.

"I'm dressed," she announced. Chester turned around to
survey her critically. Without saying a word, he peeled off his
tattered, misshapen vest and handed it to her. It was many sizes
too large, but she gratefully pulled it over her shirt and tied its
leather strings.

"Better keep the hat on too." He handed her a battered felt hat
that looked suspiciously like one she'd last seen on Cookie's head.
While she stuffed her hair inside the hat, Chester attached her bag
to the bundle already on Sugarplum's back. Suddenly he stiffened.

"Somebody's comin'. Sit on that log over there, and keep your
head down. Don't say nothin'."

Charlie Mae placed a hand on the leather collar Chester had
made for Mr. Rags, who was making a low, throaty growl, signaling
that a stranger was approaching.

"Howdy," a voice called as a disreputable-looking old man came into view.

"Nice day," Chester responded. Peeking between her fingers, Charlie Mae observed the old man in baggy pants and an oversized, long coat with bulging pockets. He appeared in need of a shave and a haircut. A bath probably wouldn't have hurt him any either. His rheumy red eyes kept straying toward Sugarplum in a way that made her uneasy.

"You from that big freight train over there?" he pointed in the direction of the Walker camp.

"Who's askin'?" Chester challenged the man.

"Name's Claude, and I wuz just curious, seein' so many mules. Most folks ride horses or drive oxen."

"That so?" was Chester's brief response.

"What's a matter with your friend? He don't seem none too sociable." The stranger pointed to Charlie Mae, and she ducked her head lower.

"The kid's sick. Figured we best steer clear of folks 'til he's feelin' better. We passed a wagon train a few days back with folks sick with cholera. I'm hopin' he didn't catch it." Chester looked so serious, she was hard pressed not to laugh. Instead, she made a retching sound deep in her throat and leaned closer to the ground.

The stranger took a step backward. "I reckon I better be on my way." He nearly ran from the grove.

Neither she nor Chester moved for several minutes, then Charlie Mae flashed Chester a grin. Chester smiled briefly before turning toward the camp with a worried expression on his face.

"What do you suppose that man was doing out here?" she asked. "He didn't look like a miner."

"He looked to me like a man well acquainted with trouble. Men like him nose around other folks' camps lookin' for things to steal. He was plain salivatin' over a wagon train that looks as well outfitted as the captain's. He likely keeps himself in liquor and grub by snatchin' things other folks set down."

"Do you think he'll be back?"

"Not for a while. He'll find another place to sleep until it comes dark again."

"I wish Irwin would hurry."

"He said if he ain't back by the time the sun is full up, we should head north, and he and Bonnie will catch up to us."

"They're married. Why can't Irwin show their marriage paper to a lawman and have him demand that Louisa turn Bonnie over to him? It isn't decent to force a woman into an immoral life."

"Problem is, when Miss Louisa paid the orphanage keeper for her, she had papers drawn up sayin' Bonnie's an indentured servant. For five years, 'til Bonnie's nineteen, Miss Louisa owns her, and she can't work for anyone else or get married without Miss Louisa's permission."

Charlie Mae gasped. "Does that mean their marriage isn't legal?"

"Miss Louisa will likely claim it ain't legal, and there's no tellin' what a judge might say."

"It appears to me no one's paying any attention to what Bonnie wants. Or what God says is right."

"Get down again. Someone else is coming," he hissed, pointing to the log which was still deep in shadow. With her heart pounding, she settled onto the log, hunched over with her face resting in her hands.

"Chester!" It was Irwin who arrived out of breath. "Bonnie has disappeared. Louisa is packed and ready to move out, but there's no sign of Bonnie."

"How could she just disappear?" Charlie Mae jumped to her feet and ran to her brother.

"More likely Louisa has hidden her." Chester slammed a fist into his opposite palm. "We'll have to find a way to search her wagon."

"Miss Louisa is ranting and raving, insisting every wagon be searched. If she hid her, she's putting on a good act."

"I'll bet it's just that—an act," Chester fumed.

"I've got to get back and do another search. I have to find her before Louisa does. I only came back to warn you to be on your way."

"We can't leave without you and Bonnie," Charlie Mae protested.

"You have to. Louisa noticed that both of you are missing. She thinks you've taken Bonnie with you, and she's offering a hundred-dollar reward to anyone who goes after you and brings Bonnie back. I fear it's a trick to snare you, Charlie Mae."

"All right, we're leaving." Chester reached for Sugarplum's reins. "We'll follow the American River for four days, then cross it to make our way north. When we find a good place to hole up, we'll wait for you."

"If you have to leave a message anywhere, address it to my brother, Sander, so it don't fall into the wrong hands." With that, Irwin disappeared into the brush and was lost to sight almost immediately.

Chester yanked on Sugarplum's lead rope. The animal resisted until Charlie Mae took the rope from his hand. The mule followed docilely behind her as they wended their way through the trees and brush growing along the riverbank. Mr. Rags followed close on their heels. They'd put close to a mile behind them when they struck a wagon track. They debated the wisdom of following an open trail but finally decided that they ran the greater risk of drawing attention to themselves by skulking in the trees.

Walking was easier now, and they put a couple of miles between themselves and the wagon train before stopping beside a small stream to eat a breakfast of leftover biscuits Chester found in one of the packs. They had hot tea with their biscuits made from water from the stream heated over a small fire.

"I know what Irwin said, but I still think we should be helping him find Bonnie," Charlie Mae said. It just didn't seem right to leave Irwin to deal with the problem alone.

"I've been thinking about that," Chester admitted. "I don't feel right about leaving him to search for Bonnie alone either, but I don't want you near Miss Louisa. I'm not taking a chance she might grab you and hide you away somewhere."

"There's something I never told you," Charlie Mae began hesitantly. "I've been waiting for the right time. Maybe this is it. Over there in my bag is a wooden box with a big red stone in it. That boy I visited with back in Salt Lake kept that stone for me for more than five years then gave it back when we met up with him. He said his stepfather told him the stone is a valuable ruby. It's bigger and worth a whole lot more than Miss Louisa's ring she's so proud of. We might trade the ruby for Bonnie."

"Where'd you get a jewel like that?" Chester was more skeptical than shocked by her revelation.

"I'll tell you on the way back to help Irwin find Bonnie."

"Miss Louisa is more likely to trick you than bargain with you. She stands to collect a lot of gold by tradin' you and Bonnie to the miners. You're worth more to her than any old jewel, and she'll be after you quick if she sees you."

"Not likely she'd recognize me dressed like this."

"Anyone who looks close is gonna know you ain't a boy," Chester argued. "And anyone who knows me is gonna take a closer look at any stranger they see with me. And what if your hat gets knocked off?"

"Seems we're both needing better disguises," Charlie Mae mused aloud.

"Even with better disguises, it'd take us 'til noon to get back there."

"We can ride Sugarplum. Without his pack, he can move a lot faster than we've been walking."

"It might work, but we can't just leave our stake."

"Find a place to hide the packs, and we'll leave Mr. Rags to guard them. I saw something where we turned off the trail that might help with our disguises. Oh! I'll need the coffee pot." She pointed to the pot they'd used to heat water for their tea sitting on a rock beside the small fire Chester had built.

Before collecting berries and bark from several different plants and nut hulls that lay on the ground, Charlie Mae removed a few items from her bag. She tied the big ruby in one corner of her handkerchief and tucked it in a pocket of her overalls along with the two five-dollar gold pieces Chester had said were her wages. She then removed another clean handkerchief and a towel, which she set near the fire.

She knew that walnut hulls produced a black dye and that nuts that grew near her childhood home in Arkansas produced a buttery pale tan. She wasn't certain what color she'd get from the unfamiliar nut hulls scattered across the clearing, but with the blackberries she'd discovered, she expected the color would be dark.

Carefully holding her treasures in a large bandanna, she carried them to the pot that still held a small amount of tea. Adding the hulls and berries, she stirred the concoction with a twig for several minutes, then nestled the pot among the coals to let it simmer.

When Chester returned from hiding their supplies, he was muddy, and twigs were stuck to his hair and wet clothing. "I don't think it will be necessary to leave Mr. Rags to stand guard. I found a place by wading upstream where high water has cut away the bank and formed a small cave. It was a tight squeeze, but I got everything in, then walled up the front with rocks and mud to keep animals out."

"Good, I didn't feel good about leaving Mr. Rags behind."

"How're you going to change our appearances? You still look the same to me." He looked dubious.

"Granny taught me how to dye wool. I reckon we can dye our hair the same way." She picked up the pot and beckoned for Chester to follow her. When she reached the creek, she swished the pot in the cool water for several minutes before instructing Chester to bend over the water."

"Keep this over your face so none gets on your skin," she instructed, handing him her handkerchief. Still looking skeptical, he followed her instructions. Slowly she poured the thick sludge over his head then used her fingers to massage it into every strand. When she was satisfied, she took the handkerchief, and it was Chester's turn to dump the thick, wet pulp onto her head.

"Save some for Mr. Rags," she instructed.

It soon became clear it was much harder to work the mixture into her long curls than it had been to saturate Chester's hair. When he finished daubing at it, he backed off a few steps to survey his handiwork and began to laugh. "You sure enough look different, but I ain't so sure puttin' that mess in your hair is going to keep folks from starin' at you."

"We're not done yet." She turned to smear the last of the dye on Mr. Rags's white spots. The dog shook himself, splattering Charlie Mae. Then with a yelp, he veered toward the stream.

Charlie Mae rinsed out the coffee pot before rinsing both her hair and Chester's.

Chester's brown hair darkened nicely to a deep auburn, but as she worked on her own hair she discovered the reason for his laughter. Her blond locks were now a flaming red. Putting her hands to her face, she fought the tears that persisted in running down her face.

"Don't worry, Charlie Mae, honey. I think I can fix it. Can't do nothing about the color, but I can make it so's no one'll guess you're a girl." He hurried back to Sugarplum to fetch a blanket he'd pulled from their pack, thinking they might need it if they were delayed returning for their supplies. "Take off your shirt and drop your britches." When she obeyed, he wound the blanket around her. When he finished, he refastened her shirt and vest.

Next he instructed her to wind her hair in a tight braid atop her head. With his pocket knife, he pulled a few bottom strands loose then sawed off the ends leaving short, stubby spikes protruding from beneath her hat.

"Don't lose that hat," he cautioned her.

"I won't." She jabbed one of the pins that had held her hair earlier through the felt, securing the hat to her thick coil of braids. "Let's be off," she said, turning toward Sugarplum.

Chester seemed to hesitate, and she glanced back toward him. "Charlie Mae," he said, sounding a bit sheepish. "Every night afore we go to bed, you say your prayers. I told you I ain't much for prayin', but this might be a good time for one of them prayers."

17 ❧

THE SUN WAS straight overhead when they stopped at a ramshackle stable and made arrangements to leave Sugarplum while they proceeded on foot. The stable was empty save for Sugarplum and the talkative owner, who stumped about on a wooden peg.

"Don't get many critters this time of year," the owner said. "Most folks head for the mountains and the rivers soon's they get here. When it turns too cold to pan, the miners will be coming down, and they'll be looking for shelter for their beasts whilst they visit the gamin' tents. Then I'll take my pay in gold dust. Make a right decent living, I do."

"I'd appreciate it if you'd give our old mule some oats," Chester said. Mr. Rags sniffed at the man's wooden leg and growled low in his throat. Charlie Mae tugged at his collar.

"Stay with Sugarplum," Chester ordered the dog, and Mr. Rags curled up in the straw at the big mule's feet.

"What's that on your dog's coat?" the stable owner said, giving Mr. Rags a nervous glance.

"Caught a rabbit a ways back," Chester said. "He ain't too friendly, so stay back a bit when you put oats out for the mule."

Charlie Mae almost corrected Chester, but she'd promised him she wouldn't say anything around folks they met. But there wasn't anything unfriendly about Mr. Rags, and the streaks of red down his white chest were as misleading as the large red freckles Chester had informed her dotted her face from when Mr. Rags had shaken his coat, spraying her. When they were far enough from the stable not to be overheard, she confronted him on that fact.

"More'n one man has thought twice about takin' what ain't his when he met a dog guardin' that piece of property," Chester informed her. She thought about that for a few minutes before deciding Chester hadn't exactly lied. Mr. Rags had caught a rabbit a few days back, even if he'd had to make due with a strip of jerky today. And with so many strangers about, it might not hurt to let on that Mr. Rags didn't take kindly to strangers.

They stopped in the grove of trees where they'd hidden earlier that morning. Not many wagons remained in the meadow before them. The few still in camp were preparing to pull out.

"Captain Walker said he'd purchased a building and some land near the Sacramento River last year before he returned to Ohio for his family and supplies," Chester said as they watched the wagons make ready to leave. "He planned to check on it this morning and set some of the men to fencing in a big field for his mules."

Charlie Mae nodded her head. Sylvia had informed her that they intended to live in a couple of upstairs rooms above her husband's business until they could arrange to have a house built. She and the children were probably already there.

"I don't see Irwin anywhere," she whispered.

"He probably went with the captain or he might have followed Miss Louisa. We better trail along after these wagons and see if we can learn anything."

Charlie Mae was glad she was accustomed to walking as they followed behind the wagons for what seemed a considerable distance. As they walked, the tents alongside the streets gave way to wood and log structures and a few brick, stucco, and stone buildings. Construction seemed to be underway everywhere they looked, but thankfully the people they passed paid them little attention.

They entered a street where a flurry of activity was taking place around a two-story building of some size. Pausing behind a shed, they searched for Irwin or the captain, neither of whom were in sight. While they were wondering if they dared approach one of the drivers, they noticed a couple of familiar figures coming toward them.

"Cookie," Chester whispered when the old man and Andrew drew near.

"Chester?" Cookie looked around furtively. "That Miss Louisa has offered a reward for anyone who finds you and Miss Charlie Mae." His eyes took in Charlie Mae and moved on. Suddenly he swung back toward her, his eyes bulging. "You-you . . ."

"Yes, but don't tell anyone," she whispered back.

"Did you get in the poison ivy, Miss Charlie Mae?" Andrew asked.

"No, I'm hiding."

"But I can see you."

"Can you keep a secret? I don't want anyone else to know I'm here. That's why I'm dressed funny. If someone sees me who doesn't know me as well as you and Cookie do, they'll think I'm someone else."

"That's a funny game. I won't tell anyone except Mama. She's been crying all morning 'til her head hurts something fierce. She said she did something bad, and she can't tell anyone but you. You have to talk to her."

"Oh, dear. What shall I do?" She turned to Chester. "I don't dare go to her."

"Please, Miss Charlie Mae," Andrew whined.

"Look, Andrew," Chester knelt to look the boy in the eye, "if you can get your mama to go for a walk with you, you could bring her here."

"She'll probably tell me to go away."

"Will you try?"

"Yes, sir." He turned about, marching resolutely toward the warehouse.

"I best go with him," Cookie said. Chester caught his arm before he could take more than a step.

"Do you know where Irwin is?"

"Captain sent him with a wagonload of Miss Louisa's whiskey and that big tent of hers." He hurried off after Andrew who was nearly to the warehouse.

"Irwin likely volunteered to deliver Miss Louisa's freight," Chester suggested, "so's he would know where she's settin' up her place. That way he can see if she's hidin' Bonnie."

"How are we going to find them?"

"We'll have to tour the outer edges of the city, seeing as the inner portions are composed of mostly permanent buildings." He looked discouraged. "Best we get started."

"Wait, I think Sylvia is coming." Charlie Mae noticed a woman leaving the warehouse.

When Sylvia reached them, she seemed startled by Charlie Mae's appearance but quickly embraced her. Sylvia's eyes were red and swollen from tears.

"I've been so worried." She pressed Charlie Mae's fingers tightly. "I think I made a terrible mistake. One of that horrid madam's girls came by the wagon early this morning. She asked for you and was terribly agitated. We heard someone coming, and I panicked because I knew you'd gone with Chester and didn't want anyone to know. I figured she was the young woman I heard you and your brother discussing who wants to get away from that business, so I suggested she hide in the empty water barrel sitting beside the cook wagon. She climbed in, and I fastened the lid."

"Where is the water barrel now?" Charlie Mae couldn't keep her voice from revealing her excitement.

"That's what I'm trying to tell you." Sylvia expressed annoyance with the interruption. "The barrel wasn't one of the extra water barrels as I had supposed. It was the whiskey barrel my husband opened the night you two were married. One of the men, on lifting it and discovering it felt full, set it on the wagon with the barrels Irwin was to deliver to various establishments, including that vulgar woman's."

"Oh, no," Charlie Mae groaned. "She won't know Irwin is the driver and that she only need tap on the barrel to gain his attention."

"She's most likely unconscious from the fumes by now," Chester muttered. Louder, he asked, "Do you know where the wagon was headed?"

"I heard someone say Miss Louisa purchased a piece of property just north of where the Sacramento and American Rivers meet. All of the businesses along there were washed out in spring floods and new businesses are operating out of tents until a flood dyke and permanent buildings can be constructed." Sylvia wiped at her eyes.

"Mrs. Walker, do you have any idea how long it's been since Irwin left with the wagonload of barrels?" Chester asked.

"It was just before Cookie drove us here, and we've been here long enough to unload our wagon and lie down for a rest, though I had not closed my eyes yet." She turned to Charlie Mae. "Dear, you must stay with me while your husband goes after your brother and attempts to rescue that poor girl."

"Thank you for the information and your kindness in hiding Bonnie, but I must go with Chester. It may not be safe for him to return here to get me." She kissed Sylvia's cheek before hurrying away beside Chester.

They walked as rapidly as possible, and Charlie Mae appreciated Sander's britches. She could have never walked so fast or far in her usual dress and petticoats. They passed the stable where they'd left Sugarplum and Mr. Rags. Chester suggested they collect the animals, and Mr. Rags seemed particularly pleased to see them. Chester rubbed muddy water on the dog's ruff to darken it once more before boosting Charlie Mae to the big mule's back and clambering on behind her. They set off at a trot.

They knew they'd found the right place when they spotted a large tent being raised in the midst of dozens of smaller tents and wooden shacks. Five women in fussy, full-skirted dresses flitted about among several dozen men who were eagerly assisting with raising the tent or offering advice. A row of barrels sat a short distance from the center of activity.

"I don't see Irwin," Charlie Mae said in a low voice as they watched from behind a dilapidated fence that looked as though the first puff of wind might blow it over.

"I doubt he's gone far."

"Even if we get to the barrels without being detected, how will we know which one to open?" She continued to worry.

"There ain't no way to tell without lookin' inside, but we best figure out a way to start opening them soon. I don't know how much air is in one of them barrels, and Miss Bonnie has been in one most all day."

"If we knew which barrel is the one we're looking for, you could try to buy it from Miss Louisa with my ruby."

"I don't think it's a good idea for either of us to show ourselves," he said.

"If you were to sneak over to those bushes on the far side of the lot, I could stay here and create some kind of diversion on this side," she offered. "Once everyone's attention is over here, you could start opening those barrels."

"I'm not leaving you here by yourself." Chester was adamant. "There must be another way to get to those barrels."

"I'd like a peek in those barrels meself," a voice said from behind them. Startled, they turned to see the wizened old man who had been watching the Walker camp early that morning sitting astride a shaggy donkey. They'd been so engrossed in studying the lot in front of them, they hadn't noticed his arrival.

"Been near two years since I last tasted real whiskey." There was longing in the man's voice, but Charlie Mae felt little sympathy for him. Since her experience with Pa and his drinking, she had little respect for anyone who turned to liquor. "I could stir up a ruckus over here like the boy suggested if you'd leave just one of those barrels for me pleasure."

"We only want one. The rest are yours if you can beat the rest of this bunch to them." Charlie Mae lowered her voice and pretended to be friendly even though she feared the man's eagerness for the whiskey would give them away.

Chester showed no patience for the old man. "Be on your way," he growled.

The old man smirked and sent Charlie Mae a knowing wink.

"Come on, we better get as close to those barrels as we can." Chester nudged Sugarplum, and they began a circuitous path through the miners' and hucksters' shacks until they reached the far side of the clearing where the tent was almost in place.

They tied Sugarplum's reins to a sapling before creeping forward, staying low enough to stay hidden by a thick growth of willows and low shrubs. They'd almost reached the clearing when they spotted a figure kneeling beside a pile of debris left from the spring flood.

"I 'spect that's Irwin," Chester whispered.

Charlie Mae recognized her brother too and began working her way toward him. Irwin looked alarmed for a moment before he recognized them.

"I thought you were taking Charlie Mae someplace safe," he growled at Chester.

"We found out something you need to know," Chester whispered back. "Bonnie's in one of those barrels, and she's likely passed out by now."

"What?" He started to rise, but Chester reached out to pull him back down.

"We'll explain later, but right now we need to concentrate on thinking up a plan to get her out," Charlie Mae added. "I wanted to start a diversion on the other side of the tent, so Chester could sneak over here and check the barrels, but he wouldn't let me."

A sharp yap brought Charlie Mae's head up. Mr. Rags was pawing at one of the barrels.

"I think we know which barrel to check," Irwin stated in a grim voice. "Charlie Mae, stay with the mule while Chester and me go get Bonnie."

Charlie Mae picked her way back to Sugarplum. Several times she glanced back over her shoulder. She wished Chester had agreed to let her create a diversion. As soon as he and Irwin left their hiding place, someone would see them, and Bonnie wouldn't be the only one in danger. She suspected Miss Louisa would order her employees to shoot rather than surrender Bonnie to them. She still thought that returning to the other side of the clearing to create some kind of disturbance would be the safest way to free Bonnie.

She nervously paced to the edge of the clearing and back. If she could find a way to get everyone's attention focused on the other side of the clearing . . . a scream or maybe banging together some wash tubs she remembered seeing. She wasn't sure what kind of distraction she could provide, but she'd do something. She couldn't just stand by and do nothing while Chester and Irwin risked their lives. Making up her mind, she hurried from the trees and along the narrow street to the back of a shack on the other side of the tent.

Peering around the side of the shed, she counted six men with tied-down guns and one wearing a dark suit with a ruffled shirt.

Sudden darkness enveloped her, and her arms were wrenched behind her back. Her attempts to scream were stifled by thick fabric covering her head. She struck out with her feet in a vain attempt to free herself.

"Now, now, girlie," a voice cackled in her ear, followed by searing pain in her head. She lost consciousness briefly. The next thing she knew, she was sliding downward, and she could smell dirt and sawdust. Her hands were bound, making any effort to cushion her fall useless. She landed with an uncomfortable jolt. She had no idea how long she'd been unconscious, but she suspected it hadn't been long. A familiar woman's voice reached her. "Which one did you manage to locate, Claude?"

"I figure she's the yeller-haired one, though she's died her hair red. She was with that big bloke from the wagon train."

"And how did you get her away from Mr. Gafton?" Louisa asked in a bored voice. Clearly she doubted the man.

"I seen 'em this morning in the trees by the Walker camp. The yeller-haired one was dressed like a boy and pretendin' to be sick. When I saw them again, I knew the kid was really the gal you was lookin' for, so I follered 'em. Got her alone not far from here and brought her to ya." She could hear the satisfaction in the man's voice.

"If she's Charlie Mae, you can bet Chester Gafton is nearby," Louisa warned.

"I ain't worried about him. Just gimme my money, and I'll be gone."

"I always inspect the merchandise before I buy," the madam said smoothly. Seconds later, the blanket covering Charlie Mae's head was ripped away, and she found herself glaring at Miss Louisa. "My, my," the woman seemed to be laughing at Charlie Mae's appearance, "I'll have to do something about that awful hair and those freckles. Of course, repairing the damage you've done to yourself will come out of your wages. It would have been so much simpler if you'd accepted my first offer."

Charlie Mae did the most unladylike thing she'd ever done in her life. She spit at Miss Louisa, hitting her right on the beauty spot at the corner of her mouth. In turn, Louisa slapped Charlie Mae so hard her head seemed to ring. Louisa turned about to place several bank notes in the old man's hand.

He looked at the money and swore. "You said a hundred," he whined.

"That was for both of them," Louisa snapped. "I don't see that ungrateful girl, Bonnie."

"You didn't say nothin' about catchin' Miss Bonnie too," Claude complained.

"I'm saying it now. Go get Bonnie, and you'll get the rest of your money." Louisa sat in an elegant chair behind a small table, dismissing the man with a wave. She picked up a pen, dipped it in ink, and began to write something in the register before her.

The old man stood fuming, his face turning red. "It ain't fair. I done what you said."

Miss Louisa slid open a drawer in the table and withdrew a pistol, which she pointed at him. "Go," she repeated.

The old man strode from the tent with all the dignity he could muster. Charlie Mae's heart pounded inside her chest. She was more afraid of Miss Louisa now than ever. Somehow she had to get free, and if she couldn't get free, she still had to create a distraction so that Irwin and Chester could free Bonnie. She moved her hands, trying to loosen the cord that bound them behind her back.

A repetitive sound from outside seemed to be annoying Miss Louisa. She rose to her feet and without a backward glance at Charlie Mae, left the canvas-walled room. In moments she could be heard shouting instructions to the hapless workmen.

Thinking this was her chance, Charlie Mae managed to draw herself upright. She looked around, searching for a way out, but there was only the one flap where Miss Louisa had exited and through which she might return any minute. Dropping back to the dirt floor, she attempted to wriggle beneath the heavy canvas. She knew someone was likely to spot her the moment her head or legs emerged on the other side of the canvas, but something within her urged her on. She couldn't wait meekly for the fate Miss Louisa planned for her.

As she moved her head from side to side, dirt filled her mouth and something sharp scraped her face. At last she managed to burrow her way beneath the canvas far enough to see the other side and not far away, the row of barrels. Beyond the barrels she knew Chester and Irwin waited—unless they'd already found a way to free Bonnie. Several workmen pounded stakes nearby but hadn't yet noticed her. She drew her legs beneath the canvas and prepared to stand. Running would be difficult with bound hands, but somehow she would do it. She could only pray that Chester would see her and come to her aid before any of Miss Louisa's men could overtake her.

An explosion sent her sprawling facefirst on the ground. Wood and debris flew around her, and the stench of smoke filled the air. For a moment she thought the blast had robbed her of her hearing. Then screams and shouts penetrated the thickness inside her head.

"Fire!" someone shouted, and Miss Louisa's workers ran toward flames that were shooting skyward from the burning canvas. She struggled to her feet, but finding running impossible, she stumbled and staggered toward the barrels.

"And there's our diversion!" she wanted to shout. She saw Irwin crouching low as he raced toward the barrel Mr. Rags was still scratching and pawing. Chester suddenly burst from the trees, looking startled, and dashed past Irwin, heading straight for her.

Just before Chester reached her, she saw Irwin with Bonnie's limp form in his arms, racing for the trees with Mr. Rags at his heels. Chester didn't even pause as he swept her up and followed Irwin.

"The whiskey," she gasped. Chester seemed to understand. He carefully set her on her feet long enough to roll a barrel into the trees. "Figure we owe him." He panted as he pushed the barrel toward a sandbar at the river's edge where it would be safe if flames spread across the grass. She started toward the spot where she'd left Sugarplum, but in moments Chester swooped her up and set her on the mule.

Irwin had left his team and wagon a short distance from where Sugarplum was tethered. By the time Charlie Mae and Chester caught up to her brother and sister-in-law, Irwin was leaning over Bonnie, fanning her face and urging her to breathe.

"Drive! We've got to get out of here. If Louisa doesn't catch us, the fire will," Charlie Mae shouted to him while Chester was busy releasing the rope that bound her hands. When she was free, she leaped onto the wagon and took Irwin's place beside Bonnie, pushing him toward the wagon seat. Reluctantly, Irwin settled on the driver's box and shook out the team's reins.

The wagon began to move, and Mr. Rags leaped aboard, settling in beside Bonnie. Irwin gave the mules their heads, and the wagon surged forward in a mad race for the road before the fire could cut them off. Chester raced beside them on Sugarplum.

The fire was spreading fast. Several other tents and shacks caught fire, and confusion reigned on every side. Charlie Mae looked up just long enough to see a line of flame creeping toward the whiskey barrels. A whistling sound sailed over her head followed by Chester's shout, "Keep your heads down!"

A second shot hit the back of the wagon seconds before a series of explosions shook the ground beneath the mules' running feet.

18 ⟋

THE WAGON LURCHED and swayed. Charlie Mae held her ear to Bonnie's face, trying to discern whether or not she was breathing. The stench of whiskey was thick and nauseating on Bonnie's skin and hair, bringing unpleasant associations to Charlie Mae's mind. One of the wagon's wheels dropped into a hole then jerked free, wringing a faint moan from the unconscious girl. Charlie Mae's hopes soared.

"She's alive!" she shouted. Irwin urged the mules to greater speed.

As the wagon took a corner too sharply, Charlie Mae was left scrambling for something to hold onto and to keep Bonnie from flying out of the wagon. They catapulted onto a quieter street, and Irwin let the team of mules run for several more blocks before reining them in to a more sedate walk. Suddenly he shouted, "Whoa!"

Charlie Mae was surprised to see they had stopped on the street that led to Captain Walker's warehouse. Chester urged Sugarplum next to the wagon where he conversed with Irwin briefly before leaping from the mule's back to the wagon box. Irwin moved just as quickly, taking Chester's place on the mule. Chester scooped up Bonnie, placing her in Irwin's arms, before turning to Charlie Mae.

"Jump!" he shouted, taking her hand and leaping with her to the road. He slapped the nearest mule's rump, sending the team running toward the Walker compound while he and Charlie Mae with Mr. Rags at their heels sprinted toward the narrow space between two large buildings. They paused to catch their breath, and she noticed that Sugarplum and his riders were already out of sight.

Slowly they began picking their way east, planning to reach the American River well past the confusion they'd left at the juncture of the two rivers. Charlie Mae glanced at Chester's face several times with quick, nervous gestures. His mouth was set in a firm line, and his jaw was thrust out as though ready to challenge anyone who got in his way. He hadn't said a word yet about her escapade. She'd never seen him really angry before, and his silence worried her. She didn't speak either until she noticed a sign on a building that said RECORDER AND ASSAYER.

"Is that place just for recording claims?" she asked.

"I suppose so." Chester seemed puzzled by the question.

Charlie Mae pulled papers from her pocket and handed them to him. "One is Irwin's. Go see if we can record our marriages. I'll stay out of sight with the dog."

He hesitated, and she quickly promised, "I won't leave for anything. I'll be right there." She pointed toward a narrow alley. Before he could respond, she dodged into the alley to wait. In a much shorter time than she had anticipated, Chester was back with a wide grin on his face, his good nature seemingly restored. He handed the papers back to her.

"The clerk wasn't even interested. Just wrote down what's on the papers in a big ledger before handing them back to me. I guess that means you're stuck with me for the rest of your life, so don't you never run off again."

She smiled, glanced around to be sure they were alone, then kissed his cheek.

"You scared me back there," he mumbled. "I thought you were with Sugarplum 'til I seen ya running toward me."

"I'm sorry." Instinctively, she ducked her head and scuffed her shoe in the dirt, half expecting a blow, though Chester had never struck her. Only Pa, and occasionally Deke or Clyde, had shown displeasure with their fists. "I wanted to help, but I should have kept a better watch. That old man with the donkey caught me and took me to Miss Louisa. If she hadn't been so greedy, he wouldn't have blown up the tent," she explained in a rush.

"That old man? And I left him a barrel of whiskey," he finished on an angry note of regret.

"Don't begrudge him the whiskey," Charlie Mae said. "He did provide enough distraction to free Bonnie."

"Did he clout you on the head, or did you get that in the explosion?" He touched a tender lump on the side of her head.

"It doesn't matter. We best be on our way." She became conscious that they had lingered in the alley longer than they should have. The shadows were growing long, and businesses were closing for the night.

He grabbed her hand, and they began walking again. "We'll talk about this later," he grumbled before leading her from the alley.

The sky was dark, and her stomach was complaining when they reached the river again. Charlie Mae sank down on a patch of grass overlooking the water. Chester sat beside her. A loud rumble told her he was as hungry as she was.

"Do you suppose anyone is following us?" she asked.

"It's hard to tell. Soon someone will start looking to settle the blame on anyone they can."

"I heard shots. Why did someone shoot at us if they didn't know we did anything?"

"Some folks shoot in the air or fire at anything that moves when they get excited. Someone saw us getting out of there fast, which might have made us look guilty."

"There was an explosion."

"Coulda been the whiskey or more dynamite. Miss Louisa can't be sure we had anything to do with it, and no one else knows us. Even if she catches that old guy, he can't lead her to us. Anyway, he was only interested in whiskey. If she sends someone to hunt us down, it will be because she suspects we had something to do with Bonnie's disappearance."

"I hope Bonnie is going to be all right. How long do you think it's going to take us to catch up to her and Irwin?"

"They can move faster on Sugarplum than we can walk, but I suspect Irwin will stop as soon as he thinks it's safe. Bonnie needs to rest, and she likely needs food and water more'n we do." He stood. "Best we keep walking, and we ought to keep an eye out for them too."

Charlie Mae stood slowly. Her body ached. She was tired and extremely hungry, but there was no sense complaining. Complaining would only make Chester feel bad about something he couldn't do anything about. Besides, she didn't hurt any worse than after one of Pa's beatings.

It seemed they'd walked for hours in the dark when Chester nudged her toward the side of the trail. She could make out a faint path leading into a thick copse of trees, but she wasn't certain she could take another step. She stumbled, and Chester placed an arm around her to lend her support as they climbed a gentle incline. Once they were well off the trail, Chester sat at the foot of a large tree and settled her between his legs with her head resting against his chest. The night was cooler than the day, but with her husband's arms around her, she wasn't cold. She was asleep before she could think of anything else to worry about.

It seemed she'd just fallen asleep when she awoke curled in the grass. Chester's heart no longer beat beneath her ear. She could hear water running nearby, and the air was decidedly much cooler.

"Chester?" She sat up abruptly. He was gone. It wasn't yet light, and she was alone. Panic swamped her senses then faded away. She wasn't completely alone. Mr. Rags lay at her feet, his eyes following her every movement. Besides, Chester wouldn't leave her alone in this strange place. Chester was a good, caring man, and though she'd had little reason to trust many people in her life, she trusted Chester. He may have gone to answer nature's call or to scout out the area. He'd be back.

She surveyed the dark shapes and forms around her with wary, nervous eyes. Then she did the only thing she'd learned offered comfort in times of stress. She knelt to pray.

Hearing a sound behind her, she whispered a hasty amen and jumped to her feet. Chester burst into the clearing. There was just enough light to see his finger pressed to his lips. She reached for him. His hand met hers, and he led her deeper into the trees to crouch in a jumble of thorn-covered bushes. Mr. Rags stood before them with his legs braced and the hair on his neck standing stiffly at attention.

After what seemed a long time, the dog relaxed his stance, lowered his body to the ground, and appeared to drift back to sleep. Charlie Mae faced Chester, wondering if she dared ask aloud what had happened.

"I heard what sounded like approaching riders, so I went to the trail to check," he said. "When I got close enough to see the trail, there were half a dozen men coming up from the river just ahead of where we left the trail. Four were riding on a wagon pulled by a team of horses. Two more men on saddle horses rode beside the wagon. As far as I could tell, they were all carrying rifles. Something about them made me uneasy."

"They might be headed for the gold fields, just as we are," Charlie Mae suggested, but she didn't believe they were quite like her and Chester. She'd heard of roving gangs who stole other miners' caches of gold and sometimes their claims. She couldn't deny the sense that came over her that they'd had a close call. She suspected Chester and even Mr. Rags shared the feeling.

The close encounter left them both anxious to find Irwin and Bonnie, and they agreed to push on at once. They'd only taken a few steps when Charlie Mae stopped.

"Chester, which way is the river?" she asked.

"That way." He pointed down the slope.

"I think there's a spring behind us then. I could hear running water when I woke."

"If you're thirsty, we'll be close enough to the river to get a drink in a few minutes."

"No, let's find that spring." She darted back toward the sound she'd heard earlier then paused to wait for Chester to catch up.

It took only a few minutes to find where a trickle of water seeped through a crack between two large rocks at the foot of a small bluff. It fell several feet to form a small pond before it continued on its way to the river. Charlie Mae knelt to eagerly scoop the cold, clear water into her mouth. After quenching her thirst, she backed up to give Chester access to the tiny stream of water.

Feeling greatly refreshed, she watched Chester, and her eyes lit on something just beyond where he knelt. "Look!" she pointed.

"What?" His eyes scanned the bottom of the pool. "Is it gold?"

"Something better." She laughed and reached to pluck a handful of green. "Cookie showed me watercress when we crossed a mountain stream a few weeks ago. It's edible, and if you remember, we all ate it for lunch one day pressed between cold biscuits." She took a bite of the wet, green leaves in her hands.

Looking a little uncertain, Chester reached for a few sprigs and took a small nibble. "Doesn't taste too bad," he conceded, "but I reckon I'd have to eat an awful lot of that stuff to get full." He took a few more bites and grinned. "Reckon if we keep eatin' them greens, we'll start brayin' like mules?"

Charlie Mae laughed. "I hope not, but if you'd like some berries to go with your watercress, there's a bush just like the one I used to make our hair dye from just behind you. They look like blackberries."

"Reckon they're safe to eat?" Chester eyed the berries hungrily.

"I noticed birds eating them when we stopped yesterday," she told him. "Seems to me that if they're safe for the birds to eat, they might be all right for us."

"That ain't always a true sign, but I'm willing to give it a try." He reached for a plump blackberry, thrust it in his mouth, and chewed. Charlie Mae watched anxiously.

"Delicious!" he pronounced with a wide grin, and they both filled their hands with the juicy, ripe berries. Even Mr. Rags stuck out his tongue to delicately draw a few berries into his mouth.

Exercising caution to stay well behind the group of men they'd seen earlier that morning, Charlie Mae and Chester made their way along the trail until they reached the place where they'd turned around the previous day. They were relieved to find that the men they'd seen earlier weren't occupying the spot, but there was no sign of Bonnie and Irwin either. After some discussion, they decided to leave their packs hidden for the present, since they couldn't carry them anyway without Sugarplum, but Chester visited their hiding place to retrieve some of their cooking supplies.

Once their stomachs were filled, they leaned back to wait. Chester told Charlie Mae that before they'd parted, Chester had given Irwin instructions for finding them and their equipment. She fell asleep, and when she awakened, the sun had moved far to the west, and Chester was sitting on the bank of the stream trailing a fishing line in the water. The dog lay beside him, seemingly asleep. When she approached Chester, he drew a willow branch from a shallow pool with a grand gesture to display three plump trout.

"We'll dine in style tonight!"

"One for each of us," she said with a laugh. "Though I'm not sure we should feed Mr. Rags fish."

"Don't worry. He ain't interested in fish. He already caught a rabbit and wolfed it down for his supper. I tried to talk him into saving you a piece, but he refused." Mr. Rags thumped his tail and looked up at her.

She smiled, glad that Chester was back to his usual cheerful, teasing self. She was preparing to sit by him when Mr. Rags leaped to his feet with a low growl. Chester's eyes met hers, his smile gone, and they swiftly gathered the few items they'd carried to the little glen. She glanced at the dog once and saw him lean his head to one side as if listening, then streak across the clearing toward the trail.

"Come back, Mr. Rags," she whispered as loudly as she dared. The dog ignored her, and she turned to Chester.

"Don't call him again," he whispered. He took her arm to draw her deeper into the trees.

"But . . ."

"He's better equipped to avoid being caught than we are." He pulled her down beside him to crouch in a tangle of thick grass and shrubs. Time seemed to slow to a crawl as they waited for the danger to pass and the dog to return.

Finally they heard the sound of someone approaching. Chester grasped Charlie Mae's arm, ready to flee.

"Chester? Charlie Mae?" a tentative voice called.

They both leaped to their feet and burst into the clearing almost simultaneously. Irwin sat astride Sugarplum with Bonnie pressed against his chest and held in place by one arm. He looked gray and exhausted. Chester reached up, and Irwin passed Bonnie to him then slowly climbed down while Chester placed her on the grassy hummock where he and Charlie Mae had sat a short time earlier. Mr. Rags barked with excitement before settling beside Bonnie.

Charlie Mae gave Sugarplum's long head a quick embrace before leading him to the stream for a drink. When the mule had his fill, she secured him to a sapling that grew on the edge of the grassy clearing. When she was sure the animal's needs were met, she hurried back to assist Irwin in caring for Bonnie.

Chester was just returning from the stream with a wet handkerchief, which he handed to her brother. While Irwin bathed Bonnie's face and spoke soothingly to her, Chester built up the fire, and Charlie Mae began mixing corn cakes to go with Chester's fish. She gathered more berries, crushed them with sugar, then diluted the syrup with water for Irwin to spoon into Bonnie's mouth.

While they worked, Irwin explained how he'd left the trail the previous night for one of the first thickets of trees and shrubs he'd found growing beside the river. Clean air and abundant water had helped Bonnie regain consciousness, but she'd been too weak and tired to go on. He'd spent a long time massaging her cramped muscles. Several times rowdy groups of men had passed by their hiding place, too close for comfort, and he hadn't dared lower his guard to sleep.

Knowing they must put some distance between themselves and the city before the sun came up, they'd started out again as soon as Bonnie felt brave enough to attempt it. They were both feeling faint from hunger, and he could scarce keep his eyes open when they left the trail again to work their way deep into a thicket of willows that grew close to the river. Their hiding place provided plenty of water but little grass for Sugarplum and nothing for the two of them to eat.

Bonnie struggled to sit up after swallowing half a tin cup of the sweetened berry mixture. She managed to eat a corn cake and a good portion of one of the fish before leaning back against the nearest tree and closing her eyes again. Both men and Charlie Mae finished the rest of the food.

Suddenly Bonnie began to cry. Irwin, who was sitting beside her put an arm around her and drew her head against his chest. "Are you still hurting?" he asked.

"It's not that. Though every muscle and bone I've got is aching." She gulped back her tears the best she could. "No one has ever been so nice to me before in my whole life. The Carters who ran the orphanage were always mean. Miss Louisa treated me pretty well most of the time, but she reminded me every day of how she expected me to pay her back for the food and clothes she gave me." She swiped the back of her arm across her eyes.

"It's all right, honey. You don't have to talk about it." Irwin attempted to comfort her, and Charlie Mae wondered where he'd learned to say nice things to a woman. He sure hadn't learned it from Pa.

"I want to tell you and them . . ." She indicated Chester and Charlie Mae with her head. "Miss Louisa set the others to watching me every minute once we reached the Sacramento Valley. I think she suspected I might run away. I always dreamed of being a real lady with a husband and children of my own. I used to talk about my dreams until I understood what Miss Louisa's plans were for me. I knew if I became one of her girls, I'd never be anyone's wife or mother, and I'd likely die from some shameful disease."

"Hush! Miss Louisa ain't never gettin' her hands on you again. You're my wife, and after I git rich, we'll build us the biggest house in California and have as many young'ns as you please. We'll have a fancy carriage and a matched team of horses to pull it too," Irwin promised.

She smiled weakly at him. "I was so scared I'd never see you again. When I woke up yesterday morning, I was alone except for Miss Maude, and she'd fallen asleep. I figured it was the only chance I'd get to escape, but I didn't know where to go. I knew which wagons belonged to the captain's family, and I took a chance that Charlie Mae might help me. I didn't expect the captain's missus to hide me."

"Sylvia's a good woman. She was raised to be a lady, so sometimes she sees things differently from how other folks do," Charlie Mae said.

"I didn't dare make a sound when someone picked up the barrel I was in," Bonnie continued. "I pushed the plug out of the side of the barrel, but I passed out from the whiskey fumes and so little air anyway. It was terribly hot in there. I would have died, or Miss Louisa would have caught me if you hadn't rescued me." She snuggled closer to Irwin, burying her face against his chest.

"There's an old man with a burro and a thirst for whiskey you'll need to thank if we ever run on to him again," Chester told her in a dry voice. Seeing Bonnie's puzzled look, Charlie Mae filled in the rest of the story.

"That was a blamed fool thing to do." Irwin glared at Charlie Mae. Tears pricked the back of her eyes. She knew she'd acted foolishly, but she didn't need Irwin to tell her so. She'd done it for him and Bonnie.

Chester put his arm around her. "She acted a bit impulsively, but ain't she the bravest woman you ever met?"

"I think you were brave." Bonnie smiled at her.

Irwin ignored Chester's reminder that Charlie Mae's action resulted in Bonnie's freedom. "This is a comfortable spot, but it's a little too close to the public trail." He looked around critically. "It's time to move farther inland and set up our tents. We need to get up early tomorrow to start our journey to the mountains." His gaze returned to Charlie Mae, and he seemed to soften. "I'll see if I have an extra pair of trousers Bonnie can wear tomorrow."

"Good idea," Chester agreed. "It might be safer not to draw attention to the fact she's a woman, but I'd suggest she give the hair color a pass."

19

Sierra Nevada Mountains, 1850

CHARLIE MAE AWOKE one morning to find that the air had turned crisp. If her calculations were correct, September was nearly over. She looked over at the unfinished cabin and sighed. Irwin and Chester spent every day wading in cold mountain streams while putting off completing it. They'd started with good intentions and had finished the first four tiers of logs before Irwin found his first nugget. So while Chester and Irwin picked specks of gold dust from their washing pans and dreamed of a big strike, the four of them were still living in tents. Should snow come early, they would freeze to death, and there was no place for Sugarplum to take shelter.

She approached Chester while they were eating breakfast. "Did you notice how cold the air is this morning?" she asked.

"Yes," he said while eating, "we don't have much time left before the streams freeze."

"You don't have much time to finish the cabin either." Her voice betrayed her frustration more than she intended.

Chester looked up startled. "But the gold—"

"Will still be there after we've frozen to death," she said. He merely grinned at her show of temper.

"It'll soon be too cold and wet to sleep outdoors," Bonnie said, meeting Irwin's eyes. She'd recovered from her ordeal in the barrel, and she and Charlie Mae had become close friends with the younger girl losing some of her shyness.

When they'd first arrived in the high mountain valley and had decided to make it their home base, both young women had tried their hand at panning for gold but hadn't met with success. When their husbands abandoned work on the cabin, they'd continued to daub mud in the spaces between the logs and do all they could toward the construction of their home, but recently they'd acknowledged there was nothing more they could do until Irwin and Chester cut more logs and placed them in position. Charlie Mae had determined to broach the subject, and Bonnie had agreed to back her up.

"You promised we'd spend the winter in a cabin," Charlie Mae reminded the two men. "But it's beginning to look like we'll still be in a tent—under ten feet of snow!"

"I reckon the girls are right," Irwin conceded with a show of reluctance. "This morning, I noticed a mess of black clouds building up to the north. It's getting so we're cold and wet all day, and I'd like to be warm and dry at night. Best we get a roof on the cabin."

"All right," Chester grinned at Charlie Mae, "we'll work all mornin' on the cabin, if you and Bonnie will start collectin' stones for the fireplace. It's about time you two took a turn standin' in that cold creek. This afternoon Irwin and me will look for gold while you two catch up the chinkin'."

Charlie Mae sighed. As hard as she and Bonnie had worked evenings to correct Chester's and Irwin's speech, Chester had made little progress. Irwin, on the other hand, had been warned by Sander that success in the business world would require him to be able to read, write, and speak properly, and he'd made considerable progress. Bonnie reinforced his progress by pointing out that rich people didn't talk like country people, and Irwin was determined to become rich.

"Do you really know how to build a fireplace?" Charlie Mae asked Chester.

"Drivin' mules ain't the only thing I ever done. Before I started drivin', I worked at a lot of odd jobs for Captain Walker and some other folks." Chester chuckled as though remembering himself as a boy who had taken on any job that added a few coins to his mother's purse.

Charlie Mae and Bonnie agreed to the bargain, and before the breakfast dishes were finished, the men were swinging axes in a thick stand of trees nearby. With Sugarplum's help they set the logs in place. It didn't take the two young women long to discover that the smoothest stones were found in the swift creek water that ran a few yards below their tents.

Charlie Mae hated stepping into the cold water and feeling it rush against her legs, threatening to trip her while sharp stones bit into her bare feet. Bonnie was equally lacking in enthusiasm for the task, but she gamely rolled up her pant legs and daintily followed Charlie Mae into the water. When all of the suitable stones nearby had been heaved onto the bank, they wandered farther downstream, selecting stones and tossing them to the bank. They would carry them to their cabin site later.

For three days, they followed the pattern established that day. The two young husbands spent their mornings working on the cabin while the women hunted suitable stones for the fireplace. Afternoons saw the men disappearing up the stream with their washing pans while the women added their stones to the growing pile beside the cabin. When they finished hauling the stones, they mixed mud and grass to form a thick mortar to stuff in the cracks between the logs.

An ear-piercing scream startled Charlie Mae on the fourth day so much that she lost her footing and tumbled into the swift current of icy water. She came up spitting, freezing, and completely drenched. "Bonnie!" she called. When there was no answer, she screamed her sister-in-law's name louder. Lifting one foot after the other, she struggled against the current toward the place where she'd last seen Bonnie. The water tugged at her, threatening to trip her with each step.

To her right she heard the sound of something heavy thrashing its way toward her. Either their screams had attracted a large wild animal or their husbands had heard their cries and were rushing to their rescue. She hoped it was the latter.

Charlie Mae reached Bonnie first. She was leaning against a large boulder with water rushing past her knees, completely oblivious to everything around her. Her entire focus was on something she held in her hand.

"What is it?" Charlie Mae gasped as she closed the distance between them. Bonnie didn't answer. She might not have heard the question due to the roar of a series of small waterfalls formed by a stairstep of boulders directly ahead of them.

Closing her arms around Bonnie, Charlie Mae attempted to lead her friend to the creek bank nearest their camp. Bonnie appeared startled, resisted for just a moment, then allowed Charlie Mae to lead her. Just as they reached shore, Irwin and Chester burst through the brush carrying the rifles that had been part of their pay for driving the freight wagons.

"Are you hurt?" Irwin shouted. He rushed toward the two girls and placed his arms around his wife to help her out of the water.

"What happened?" Chester looked Charlie Mae over. After helping her from the stream, he pulled off his thick flannel shirt and placed it around her wet shoulders.

"L-look!" Bonnie opened her tightly clenched fist. The sun glinted off a large gold nugget lying on the palm of her small, work-roughened hand. It was roughly the size of a lima bean and was by far the largest nugget any of them had seen thus far.

Irwin picked up the nugget almost reverently. He examined it then bit down on it. "It's gold," he affirmed in a hushed whisper.

His face lit up and he stumbled over the words as he demanded to know where she'd found it.

"Just beyond that rock." She pointed to where the water swirled around the boulder she'd been leaning against a few minutes earlier. "I picked up a smooth, black-and-gray rock to toss onto the bank. When I turned back, I noticed something shining in the sand where the rock had been, so I bent over to pick it up. The minute I held it in my hand I knew it was gold." Her face glowed with excitement.

"Wahoo!" Irwin shouted. He picked up Bonnie and twirled her around, ending with a loud kiss on her mouth before setting her back on her feet. "Stay right here! We'll get our pans," he yelled before he and Chester took off running toward camp.

"Oh, dear, they'll never get the cabin finished now." Charlie Mae sank down on a fallen log. Gingerly, she picked at her cold, wet pants, attempting to pull them away from her shivering skin.

Bonnie sat beside her, still looking stunned. She ignored her own wet clothing. Her attention focused on the nugget Irwin had returned to her. She whispered, "We really are going to be rich, aren't we?"

"I'd rather be warm," Charlie Mae muttered.

Neither man paid the women much attention when they returned with their mining gear. They immediately waded into the cold water with their pans and began scooping up sand and small pebbles. Charlie Mae and Bonnie watched them for a little while before wandering back toward the unfinished cabin. They each carried one of the rocks they'd pulled from the stream.

As near as they could tell it was midday. They changed into dry clothes, prepared lunch, and waited. When the men didn't return, they ate by themselves. After eating, they checked on the progress that had been made that morning. They counted nearly a dozen logs felled, but none had been added to the almost-completed cabin walls. A tall stack of thin saplings meant for the roof rested beside the fireplace rocks. They spent the afternoon carrying the rocks they'd thrown from the water that morning to a spot near the opening left for a fireplace.

When they finished their tasks, they began preparations for supper. It was well past supper time, and the sun was long gone when Chester and Irwin came dragging into camp. They were tired, wet, and cold, but their spirits were high, and they had a noteworthy accumulation of gold flecks.

After eating, Irwin said they had some things they needed to talk about. "Before we left Sacramento," he began, "we didn't have time to gather supplies beyond those Captain Walker gave us as part of our wages. We're going to need more food, warmer clothes, and more blankets to survive the winter. With the nugget Bonnie found today and the gold dust and nuggets we've collected so far, we know this is a good spot, and we need to register our claim. To do that, Chester and I need to go back down to the valley."

"We talked about it this afternoon," Chester said. "We don't like leaving you here by yourselves, but we figure it could be more dangerous to take you with us. What we have in mind is to take a week to finish up the cabin so you can move inside before we go. We'll take Sugarplum." Charlie Mae suspected the decision to finish the cabin before leaving was Chester's idea. Though he dreamed of making a big strike, he wasn't as obsessed with getting rich as Irwin.

"If we start out for Sacramento a week from today," Irwin continued, "and tend to our business as fast as we can, we'll be gone two weeks, three at the most. We don't dare take more time than that, or we might not make it back before snow blocks the trail."

"I still have the gold pieces Captain Walker paid me. You can use them to purchase supplies," Charlie Mae offered.

"Irwin and I still have our wages too," Chester pointed out.

"I figure we can buy what we need with the gold dust we've found," Irwin said. "We don't plan to take any nuggets with us, especially that big one." Bonnie frowned. "It might draw attention to our claim. You should keep that for a good-luck piece."

Charlie Mae thought of her own so-called good-luck piece. The giant ruby fascinated her as much as it ever had, though Chester refused to consider it as more than a woman's bauble. She had to admit that it certainly hadn't brought her luck. She was the only one of the four who hadn't found a speck of gold.

The men were true to their word. They were up before the sun the next day, pushing and tugging the logs into place and attaching the roof beams. Charlie Mae and Bonnie fetched and hammered until the roof began to take shape, then they wove willows, grass, and mud between the poles. By the end of the week, Chester had finished the fireplace, and Irwin had erected a lean-to on one side of the cabin for Sugarplum and a covered space for storing firewood. A small, square privy sat a short distance behind their new home as well.

With the cabin finished, the men went hunting, bringing back a couple of pheasants and a deer.

The two couples spent the last night before Irwin and Chester's departure inside the cabin. Charlie Mae was thrilled to have a roof over her head, and the first meal she cooked indoors brought cheers when only a small amount of smoke made its way inside the one-room structure. They used the canvas from one of the tents to separate half of the room into two bedrooms. They laughed at the absence of furniture, and Charlie Mae fell asleep making plans for spending a cozy winter inside the small house with Chester, Irwin, and Bonnie. She refused to allow herself to think of Chester's departure.

Charlie Mae stood with Bonnie at the cabin door the following morning and waved until their husbands were out of sight. A deep silence seemed to fall over the clearing as Chester and Irwin disappeared over a hill, and some of the daylight seemed to disappear from Charlie Mae's life. She'd never been without the protection of her brother or Chester since running away from the farm. Keeping their eyes averted to hide their tears, the two women set to organizing their equipment and supplies. Using some of the leftover log ends and bits of wood from the cabin's construction, they devised stools to sit on and hammered shelves in place against one wall. In the afternoon, they began searching for dry firewood to fill one side of the attached shed.

For almost two weeks, Charlie Mae and Bonnie worked at cutting grass and piling it near the cabin for Sugarplum to eat through the winter. They'd both had experience chopping firewood, so they took turns chopping downed trees into chunks suitable for their fireplace. Occasionally they took their husbands' gold pans to the creek to sift through the sand and small pebbles, but without any luck. Each night, well before dark, they barred themselves inside the cabin with Mr. Rags.

Chester had warned Charlie Mae against allowing the dog out at night. "He might attract a cougar or bear if left out," he'd said. "I don't doubt Mr. Rags would die trying to protect you and Bonnie, but you'll be perfectly safe inside the cabin, and there ain't no sense putting your dog at risk."

"Charlie Mae?" She awoke one night to Bonnie's scared whisper. "Someone's trying to get in."

Sitting up in her bedroll, she could see nothing in the stark blackness, but she could hear a shuffling outside their door and a deep rumble coming from Mr. Rags's throat. She made her way to the dog on her hands and knees. She tried to keep him still and quiet and wished the cabin had a window to let in a little light and to enable her to peek out. She wished too that Chester and Irwin had left one of the rifles behind, though she'd never shot a gun and wasn't sure she'd know how to go about it. One thing was for sure: she vowed that when Chester got back, she was going to learn.

"Maybe it's Irwin and Chester," Charlie Mae said. She could tell Bonnie didn't really believe that, but she was trying to keep Bonnie from knowing she was scared too. She suspected Bonnie knew as well as she did that if their husbands had arrived, the men would shout for them to unbar the door even if it was the dead of night, and Mr. Rags would be barking and dancing about to show his excitement.

It was a long time before the shuffling and scratching stopped and Mr. Rags settled himself in his customary place before the door. Charlie Mae returned to her bed, and Bonnie crawled in beside her, still too afraid to sleep alone.

When morning came, Charlie Mae opened the door with extreme caution. They didn't find any tracks large enough for a bear, but to their annoyance they discovered that some creature had gnawed off the axe handles.

"Porcupine!" Charlie Mae said with disgust. Her disgust was mostly for herself because she hadn't remembered to move the axes inside the previous night. There were nibble marks on one of the shovels as well, but fortunately it was still usable.

Unable to chop wood, they decided to spend their day panning for gold and were rewarded with a few grains of the shining metal. It was Charlie Mae's first success at the venture, and she carefully added the few bits of gold to the box that held her ruby. On an impulse, Charlie Mae showed the fiery red stone to Bonnie, who nearly choked on seeing the fabulous gem.

"Where did you get it?" Bonnie gazed at the ruby in awe. She didn't question if it was real. "May I touch it?" she practically stammered.

"Certainly." Charlie Mae handed the jewel to Bonnie, who carried it to the door where the light was better.

"See." Bonnie pointed to the perfect six-point star that seemed to glide fluidly at the center of the stone. "Louisa talked a lot about jewels—especially the ruby. She said a ruby, cut so that the star is visible, with a silky sheen to its surface and a deep red color, is the most valuable of all jewels."

"I thought it was a hot coal when I first saw it," Charlie Mae told her. "I was amazed when it didn't burn me."

"The fire within a ruby burns many ways." Bonnie looked pensive and sad. "They are a symbol of great passion and power. Louisa said rubies are found in kings' crowns and are used as a symbol between two people who love each other endlessly." She stood still, examining the stone for several long minutes. When she spoke again, her words were bitter. "Louisa didn't acquire that ruby ring she flaunts from a long-ago love. I first saw it at the orphanage when I was a small child. Mr. Carter said it was on a ribbon placed about my neck when I was left at the orphanage door. He said it would be mine when I reached sixteen. He also threatened that if I didn't work to earn my keep, the ring would be sold to pay for my room and board."

"Oh, Bonnie." Charlie Mae hugged her sister-in-law. "Did he sell it to Louisa?"

"I think he gave it to her to keep safe for me until I turned sixteen. Mr. Carter was mean and demanding, but he set great store by honesty. Of course, there was no ring on my sixteenth birthday."

"That ring should be yours."

"I can't prove that. Besides, she has another ring with a red garnet in it. She might easily claim it was the one intended for me. If there's any truth to her story, it may be the one given her by the young man who courted her. Anyway, it doesn't matter now. If I went to the law to demand the ring, she'd claim it was payment for breaking my indentured servant contract."

"Your mother must have been a woman of some consequence to have owned that ring," Charlie Mae assured her.

"As a child, I imagined my mother was the daughter of wealthy parents whose lover died in some glorious battle before he could return to wed her and claim me and that one day my mother would come for me. As I got older, I became convinced that no matter her station, I would only be an embarrassment to her. I don't hate her or despise her for what she did, but I wish she had loved me enough to give me to a childless couple who might have come to care for me."

"She did make certain you were in an orphanage where you were educated and weren't beaten."

"I'm sorry." Bonnie looked contrite. "Mr. Carter was harsh and required strict obedience with no allowance for childish mistakes. He never showed any fondness for any of the children in his charge, but he did require us to read the Bible for two hours every day and to learn to speak properly. I always thought a mother would show more kindness."

"I have only the vaguest memory of my mother," Charlie Mae confided. "I think she loved me, and Irwin said she did, but she didn't leave me any better off than your mother left you. I swore when I was eleven and saw my pa shoot an unarmed man just because he didn't like the man's religion that if I ever married, I'd pick a man that would make a good pa." She hesitated then asked, "You do think Chester would be a kind pa, don't you?"

"Are you going to have a baby?" Bonnie grinned with excitement.

"No, at least I don't think I'm in the family way, though I don't rightly know much about woman things like that. I was just thinking I'd like to have children, and I think Chester would be good to them if I died early like Granny and Irwin said my ma did."

"Of course he'd be a good pa. Irwin would make a fine pa, too."

"I used to think Irwin was like Pa because he frowned a lot and drank too much 'shine, but I learned different." Charlie Mae returned the ruby to its box and hid it in one of the secret compartments Chester and Irwin had fashioned for hiding their gold inside hollow spots they'd discovered in a couple of logs they'd used for the cabin walls. Then linking arms, the two women set out for the stream again to pan for gold, though they were convinced there were no places left within sight of the cabin they hadn't already scoured, and they were too nervous to stray farther away.

The backbreaking work produced few results, so they turned over a few stones in hopes of finding nuggets. That task proved fruitless too. They enumerated the days since their husbands left and made plans for the celebration dinner they'd prepare when Irwin and Chester returned, which they felt certain would be any day. By their calculations, their men had been gone sixteen days, and it was now late October. A cold breeze blew, and fallen leaves from the few trees and the bushes that lined the creek rustled beneath their feet and floated atop the rushing water.

Something struck the water near where Charlie Mae stood. She looked around, seeing nothing alarming. She heard another splash, then a deluge of water poured from the sky.

"Run for the cabin!" Bonnie shouted.

They ran awkwardly, clutching the pans, which they didn't dare leave behind. Mr. Rags streaked past them to reach the cabin first, where he pawed at the door, anxious to find shelter. Charlie Mae fumbled with the latch then thrust the door open, letting Bonnie pass before her. The dog nearly tripped her in his eagerness to get inside.

Charlie Mae continued to hold the door slightly ajar to help Bonnie find the lantern and light it. Once the flame caught, she closed and bolted the door. When she turned around, she discovered she was not only shivering with cold, but also standing in a mud puddle. Removing her shoes, she padded her way to the fireplace to stir up a fire. She'd gotten adept at burying coals each morning when they left the cabin so that it would be an easy matter to add little curls of wood shavings and kindling to heat the cabin quickly when they returned.

Once the fire was burning well, she retired to the section of the cabin she and Chester had claimed to change her clothes. She considered donning a dress. She hadn't worn one since leaving

Sacramento. But she decided pants would be warmer and more practical. She and Bonnie prepared a simple supper without saying much, but Charlie Mae knew Bonnie was worrying about Irwin just as she was thinking of Chester. She hoped they'd had time to find shelter before the storm struck.

They went to bed that night with the sound of rain beating against the cabin and wind howling as it blew against the cabin. Sleep didn't come easily, and twice Charlie Mae climbed out of bed to add wood to their fire and to kneel to pray for Chester and Irwin's safety. In the morning, they opened their door to a world of white.

20 ⤶

"SNOW!" CHARLIE MAE didn't notice the way it sparkled in the early morning light nor the fantasy sculptures and frosted trees that stretched as far as she could see. All she could think of was Chester and Irwin. They hadn't made it back before the snow fell. They might even be stranded, cold, and miserable somewhere without shelter. What would she and Bonnie do if they had to spend the winter alone in an isolated cabin with limited supplies? Her practical nature wished she'd spent more time drying berries and salting fish instead of searching for gold.

"It's beautiful," Bonnie whispered in awe. "I know we saw a few patches of dirty snow in crevices when we crossed the Sierras, but I've never seen anything like this." Being from the South, snow was a new experience to her.

Charlie Mae had grown up in Illinois and was quite familiar with snow. She kept her worries to herself as they watched Mr. Rags jump and roll in about six inches of the white fluff. Bonnie fashioned snowballs in her hands and threw them in the air for the excited dog to catch. It wasn't until they carried buckets to the stream to fill with water that Bonnie began to understand the gravity of the situation.

Walking down the slope to the stream, Bonnie began to slide. Before she could catch herself, she crashed through a thin layer of ice to land in the water. Charlie Mae hurried after her but practiced more caution as she made her way down the slope. The water was shallow where Bonnie had fallen through, and she had regained her feet by the time Charlie Mae reached her side. Crying and shaking, she struggled to step ashore but kept sliding back until Charlie Mae wrapped an arm around a tree that grew next to the stream and extended her bucket toward Bonnie for her to grasp.

Bonnie's nearly frozen fingers couldn't grasp the pail, and she resorted to looping an arm through the bucket handle. Once Bonnie stood trembling on the icy bank, Charlie Mae instructed her to hurry back to the cabin to change her clothes and warm herself by the fire.

Charlie Mae debated whether or not she should accompany Bonnie to make certain she reached the cabin quickly, but they needed water. She retrieved Bonnie's bucket then dipped both pails, one after the other, through the hole in the ice to fill them before beginning a careful, circuitous trip back up the slope. When she reached the top, she hurried as fast as she could manage without sloshing the precious water from the buckets.

Before Charlie Mae reached the cabin, she saw Bonnie huddled against the door. The girl lacked the strength to lift the latch with her wet, numb hands. Hurrying to her side, Charlie Mae set down the heavy buckets and lifted the latch, then helped Bonnie inside. She stripped off the freezing young woman's wet clothing, bundled her in a blanket, and set her in front of the fire before adding more wood to it and returning to the doorstep for the buckets of water.

The remainder of the morning was spent tending to Bonnie's needs and preparing a steaming broth from the drippings left from the pheasants their husbands had bagged before their departure. She added a pinch of dried wild onion she'd gathered while hunting for a place to build their cabin and a handful of rice. The addition of biscuits would take care of both lunch and supper. She thought longingly of the vegetables they'd purchased in Salt Lake and hoped that when Chester returned he'd bring seeds so she could plant a garden in the spring. Mostly she worried. The possibility that Chester and Irwin would be unable to get through with supplies was a frightening prospect. How would she feed Bonnie and herself? What if Bonnie took ill from the morning's mishap? And how could she search out enough firewood without an axe to keep them warm through a long, cold winter?

Something splattered near her feet. She glanced up in time to narrowly avoid a trickle of muddy water. Another thin stream ran down the closest wall. Snatching up a pan, she thrust it under the larger drip. Soon every bucket, pan, and tin can she could lay her hands on was employed in a frenzied attempt to keep their food supply, bedding, and clothing dry.

Bonnie moved from her perch beside the fire to her bed, and Charlie Mae checked on her periodically. She seemed to be sleeping soundly, and the roof over her bed was dry at the moment, so Charlie Mae took the opportunity to retire to her own side of the canvas divider. There she knelt to ask God to protect her husband and brother and help them to return to the cabin. She also expressed her concern for Bonnie and asked that she not suffer from her fall into the half-frozen stream. Should her sister-in-law become ill from exposure, Charlie Mae feared she'd not know how to care for her. She pleaded too that the cabin roof would hold until the men returned and could repair it.

When she finished praying, she sat on her blankets for a long time, considering their situation. Praying had restored her faith that their situation wasn't hopeless. She felt certain God had helped in their escape from Miss Louisa, and that had looked pretty near impossible. She berated herself for allowing the excitement of embarking on their long-planned adventure to distract her from making adequate preparations. She couldn't blame her plight entirely on Chester and Irwin's delay in finishing the cabin while they searched for gold, either. She'd also spent time searching for an elusive fortune and dreaming when she should have been picking berries and digging roots. She should have paid more attention to making their roof stronger as well, instead of merely wishing to be done with the task. She'd had the responsibility for storing winter supplies for many years and should have known better. But it did no good to think of what she hadn't done. She needed to decide what to do now.

In Illinois, the first snowfall didn't last long. She hoped the same was true in California. If God gave them a second chance, she would do all she could and encourage the others to look first to their survival. Gold could wait.

Bonnie awoke a few hours later, seeming none the worse for her icy dip in the creek. She was appalled at the sight of buckets and pans of dirty water dotting the cabin floor. Wrapping a blanket around her shoulders for a shawl, she opened the cabin door for a trip to the privy and stared in amazement. Almost all of the snow was gone with only patches lingering beneath the larger trees and farther up the slopes of the small valley. The sun shone brightly, though there was an icy edge to the breeze that swept past them. Charlie Mae said a silent thank-you to God for keeping Bonnie well.

"I don't understand." Bonnie looked bewildered. "I thought winter had begun."

"It has," Charlie Mae informed her. "Most of the time, the first few snowfalls melt quickly. But soon the snow will stay, and with each storm it will get deeper. We need to be better prepared."

"It was so pretty," Bonnie said with regret.

"I think we need to talk about the things we need to do to get through the winter." Charlie Mae broached the subject again when they returned to the cabin.

"You mean like fixing the roof?"

"Yes, and tying ropes from the cabin to the privy and from a tree at the top of the slope to the tree beside the pool where we fill our water buckets so we can get water when the trail is slippery."

"All right, I can see where the ropes will help, but how are we going to fix the roof?"

"I think we need more grass in our chinking mixture. I wish Chester and Irwin would come. They might know something more we can do." Charlie Mae's shoulders sagged. "We need to cut more grass for Sugarplum and collect more wood, too. We've used up almost all of the wood we put in the shed."

Over the coming days, the two young women cleaned the muddy splotches from the cabin and emptied the buckets and pans. They made a thicker mud and grass mixture to patch the leaks in the roof, attached ropes to assist in reaching the stream for water and pulling themselves back up, scavenged for wood, and caught a few fish. The days grew cooler, and the nights were far colder. They found the edges of the pool where they gathered water rimmed with ice each morning, and as a precaution, Charlie Mae suggested they fill the water buckets each evening. Night and morning they watched the sky, dreading another storm. At least a dozen times a day they gazed down the trail hoping for a glimpse of their husbands.

One morning, they surprised a large elk helping itself to their supply of grass. Their excited cries frightened it away, and they spent the remainder of the morning moving the grass beneath the shed's roof. They began gathering firewood from the forest to restock their dwindling supply.

On one of their return trips, they noticed something different as they approached the cabin. A gray donkey peered from the door of the lean-to, and the cabin door stood open.

"Someone's in the cabin," Charlie Mae whispered.

"Irwin . . ."

"No." Charlie Mae grasped Bonnie's sleeve, drawing her to a halt. "I don't know who it is, but it's not Chester and Irwin." Bonnie peered around Charlie Mae for a better view.

Unsure whether they should proceed, the women hesitated. Not so Mr. Rags. He suddenly erupted in a fury of barking and lunged toward the cabin. Neither Charlie Mae nor Bonnie dared call him back for fear of revealing their own presence.

Shouting and swearing erupted from the cabin accompanied by Mr. Rags's frenzied barking. A sudden yelp of pain convinced Charlie Mae the stranger had struck or kicked her dog.

"Hurry, Chester!" Charlie Mae screamed. "Bring your gun. Someone has broken into our cabin!"

A short, squat figure charged from the cabin. He quickly freed the burro and left the clearing at a run, leading the animal by a short rope. Charlie Mae stared after him open mouthed.

"He's gone!" Bonnie sagged against her. "I thought sure he would come after us when you shouted. How did you . . . ?"

"I don't know. I didn't even think about it. I just knew I had to make the intruder believe a man with a gun was hurrying toward the cabin."

"Whatever made you say it, it worked." Bonnie began running. "Poor Mr. Rags."

Remembering her dog, Charlie Mae ran too. They reached the cabin together and rushed inside.

Mr. Rags lay near the fireplace. He raised his head and whimpered. Charlie Mae rushed to his side while Bonnie closed the door and dropped the bar into place. In the sudden darkness, Charlie Mae could see little, but it only took a moment before Bonnie stirred the fireplace coals and added a small log. Flames licked at the log, and Charlie Mae ran her fingers over Mr. Rags's ribs. She couldn't tell if anything was broken, but the dog licked her hand and slowly began to revive.

Bonnie found the lantern and lit it. She brought it closer and knelt beside Charlie Mae. She, too, ran her hands over the dog's furry body then buried her face in the dog's thick black coat. When she lifted her head, Charlie Mae could see tears coursing down her cheeks.

"I know he's your dog, but sometimes I pretend he's mine too." She sniffed before going on. "I don't know what I would have done if you hadn't found him and let me care for him. Miss Louisa promised Captain Walker she and her girls wouldn't entertain any men until after she left the wagon train, but some of the mule drivers would sneak over after everyone else was asleep. I was so afraid she would make me . . . but dear Mr. Rags shared my blankets every night and threatened to wake the whole camp if anyone attempted to disturb me. I think that's why she tried to wean him away from looking after me once we reached the valley."

"Oh, my!" Charlie Mae didn't know what to say.

"And he was someone I could talk to . . . I don't think I can stand it if that man has hurt him badly."

"I think he's fine. Probably just had the wind knocked out of him, and he may be sore for a few days. But Bonnie, it's all right if Mr. Rags is your dog too. We can share him." They embraced each other and sat with the dog for a long time until Mr. Rags pulled himself up and made his way to the spot before the door where he usually slept. He curled up on an old shirt Chester had left there for him.

Charlie Mae stood and turned slowly, once more thinking of the intruder and wondering why he had entered their home uninvited.

"Bonnie!" she gasped, drawing the other woman's attention away from the dog. It appeared the man had been looking for something. Their clothes and supplies were scattered about, and their attempts to patch the leaks in their roof had been pulled out, leaving grass and twigs scattered on the floor.

Bonnie looked around, seeing all Charlie Mae saw. "He was looking for gold, I expect," she fumed. "Irwin told me about men who try to make their fortunes by stealing gold from other prospectors."

"Chester told me the same thing. He said prospectors who find gold have a hard time hanging onto it because of thieves. He said some steal it at gunpoint, some by selling supplies for exorbitant prices, and some by getting the miners drunk, then cheating them out of their gold."

"Miss Louisa said she could earn more gold with girls and liquor than any of the fools who dug it out of the ground would ever see." Bonnie began moving about the cabin, checking to make certain her nugget and Charlie Mae's ruby were still in their hiding places. She expressed satisfaction on finding them safe.

Charlie Mae had a difficult time falling asleep that night. She hadn't said anything to Bonnie, but she'd noticed that some of their meager supplies were missing. Their intruder had come looking for more than gold. Every sound set her nerves on edge and left her fearful of another intruder, either man or beast. Bonnie was restless too. She got up several times to check on Mr. Rags and eventually moved her bedroll next to Charlie Mae's. They avoided speculating on when their husbands might return. More than three weeks had passed, and neither young woman wished to express her fears.

When she judged it to be morning, Charlie Mae crept to the door, lifted the bar, and opened it a crack. It wasn't fully light out yet, but it was more morning than night. A slight movement caught her attention, drawing her eyes to a buck standing at attention at the edge of the trees. Mr. Rags brushed past her to push the door wider and limped across the clearing. The deer disappeared into the forest, but the dog paid it no mind. He went about his usual morning routine, conveying the message there was nothing near for the women to fear. Charlie Mae watched him for several minutes then concluded that if the dog felt comfortable taking his morning stroll, it must be safe for her and Bonnie to visit the privy and get on with their morning tasks.

The sky was overcast, and a bitter wind blew down the valley. The ice on the creek was thicker, and it took longer to haul water for the day's needs. For a short time they hunted for firewood, but after the previous day's events, they feared wandering far from the cabin. Besides, Charlie Mae's shawl was little protection from the cold wind, and Bonnie found that wrapping herself in a blanket left her hands nearly useless. Using Mr. Rags's injured leg as an excuse, they elected to spend the afternoon inside the cabin patching the holes in their leaking ceiling.

"Hello, the cabin!" A shout broke the silence. Bonnie and Charlie Mae looked at each other, and Charlie Mae could see that Bonnie trembled with fear. She glanced toward Mr. Rags and was surprised to see him standing on his hind legs, pawing at the door. Instead of growling, he made a soft whimper.

A shout came again.

"Charlie Mae! Bonnie!"

"They're back!" It was almost a sob. Charlie Mae fumbled with the door but finally managed to lift the bar and jerk it open. Bonnie rushed past her. Tripping over each other and Mr. Rags, they dashed outside in time to see their husbands and Sugarplum, heavily laden with two panniers and a huge pack, approaching the cabin.

"Chester, oh, Chester!" Laughing and crying, Charlie Mae flung her arms around him and felt his answering embrace.

"It's starting to snow." He brushed specks of moisture from her check. "Hurry inside where it's warm while Irwin and me free Sugarplum from his load."

She paused to pat the mule and kiss her brother's cheek before returning to the cabin, where Bonnie joined her in the open doorway. As the men carried their purchases to the door, the two women scurried about finding places to stack the supplies. Chester paused to open one bundle then straightened to drape a heavy coat over each of the girls' shoulders.

Charlie Mae prepared supper from a large ham, and while Irwin and Chester wolfed down biscuits and peach cobbler made from canned peaches, she and Bonnie listened to the men recount their adventures.

"Captain Walker was pleased to see us," Irwin said. "He'd just made a deal with a ship's captain to purchase the ship's entire cargo for the store he set up in that warehouse. He was fair with us and allowed us first choice of all the supplies on our list. He even suggested a few things we hadn't considered."

"I'm certainly pleased with the coat you brought me." Bonnie leaned closer to Irwin. "It's been difficult fetching water and firewood wearing a blanket."

"We got wool pants and long johns for all of us too." Chester grinned, and Bonnie blushed.

"I wish I'd added a window to your list," Charlie Mae spoke wistfully. "I've discovered I don't like being unable to see out before opening the door. And it would be good to know if the sun is shining."

"That's one of the things the captain sent special for you at Sylvia's suggestion," Chester assured her. "There are four small panes of glass wrapped in a bolt of cloth she thought you might use to make curtains and new aprons."

"I'm not handy with a needle, but I helped Granny make shirts and mend pants," Charlie Mae said.

"I can sew," Bonnie said enthusiastically. "You take care of the cooking, and I'll make curtains."

"We'd just begun our return trip when we got caught in a snowstorm," Chester said.

"We set up our tent in the shelter of a grove of pine trees to wait it out. It was a difficult time, but we were glad the two of you were safe and snug inside this cabin," Irwin added.

A large splatter of mud landed on Irwin's plate. He stared at his plate in dismay before turning his gaze upward while the girls giggled. Looking up, he caught the next splatter in his eye. This time Chester roared with laughter, just before a chunk of mud and grass lost its precarious hold to drop on his head.

* * *

Salt Lake City

SPENCER PAUSED IN setting posts for Brother Anderson's new corral. With the addition of two new colts last spring, there was need for a larger enclosure. He lifted his eyes to the mountains in the west and felt a longing that had come to him more often of late. He was a man now, fully grown, and he dreamed of seeing the other side of those mountains. He'd heard tales of the great ocean and strange trees, of distant lands and foreign tongues—all things he wished to see before settling down with a man's responsibilities. Some men as young as he had already been called to serve missions, and he longed to be among those called to carry the gospel to distant shores. Some had struck out on their own seeking gold and adventure in California.

He sighed and resumed pounding nails. Sister Anderson did not want him to leave; she was adamant that his place was with her and Brother Anderson, who were growing old and needed Spencer's assistance. He was like a son to them. The Andersons weren't truly his parents, and he was no longer a child needing their support, but he felt a moral obligation to assist them as they had assisted him and provided him with a home when he was orphaned.

"Hello, young Spencer!" A voice broke through his thoughts. He looked up to see the familiar figure of President Young.

"Afternoon, sir."

"I stopped to visit with Brother Anderson and inquire after his health," the president reported. "I saw you and knew at once that you are the answer to the problem I have been trying to resolve. There is a need for young men to serve as couriers between far-flung gatherings of Saints. Brother Anderson has informed me that you are a steady young man and that you are particularly skilled with horses. I am in need of a young man who is mature in nature to carry dispatches between the settlements."

"I'd be glad to help," Spencer said.

21 ✑

THE STORM DIDN'T last long, and as soon as it ended, Irwin and Chester tackled repairing the roof and installing a window near the front door. With Sugarplum's help, they hauled logs from the woods and used their newly acquired saw to rip crude boards for a plank floor and to make rough shingles. They constructed a table and four chairs that only wobbled a little. They replaced the canvas that separated their sleeping chambers with a wooden partition and built rough beds from lodgepole pine and ropes. Chopping firewood became a continual task, adding it not only to the bin next to the mule's stall, but also forming a stack that reached higher than the lean-to beside it.

Sometimes Charlie Mae noticed one or the other of the men staring toward the creek, but they continued to work doggedly on finishing the cabin and making it tight and comfortable for the winter. She suspected the early storm had frightened them as much as it had her. She kept busy too, organizing their food supply and salting the fish Chester brought her.

Irwin was an excellent marksman, and a few days after their return, he shouldered his rifle and disappeared, to return a couple of hours later with several ducks and a pair of geese that hadn't yet traveled south. The birds were a welcome addition to their diet, and Charlie Mae saved the feathers with the intention of eventually making mattresses for their beds.

One morning, with half a foot of snow covering the ground and the sun shining brightly, Chester and Irwin persuaded the girls to dress in their warmest clothing and accompany them on a hike up the valley to a small lake they had discovered. Laughter and teasing made the day one that would always linger in Charlie Mae's memories.

By mid-December, snow was piled around the eaves of the house, and it was almost a daily task to clear a path to Sugarplum's stable to feed him and to fetch wood for the fireplace. Some days the window was covered with snow, requiring gentle scraping to permit light to pass through the panes. Charles and Irwin took over fetching water. They chopped blocks of ice from the frozen stream and set them in buckets before the fireplace to thaw.

When blizzards howled around the cabin and snow threatened to bury them, it became difficult to tell night from day. January and February passed with few days they could escape outdoors. On the occasional day that it didn't snow, the men trudged through the snow searching for game, and if Irwin felled a deer, they used Sugarplum to drag it back to the cabin.

Bonnie sewed curtains for the cabin, aprons for herself and Charlie Mae, and new shirts for Irwin and Chester. She'd been pleased to discover that the bundle of fabric protecting their precious glass window was not the only fabric or sewing supplies Sylvia had insisted Irwin and Chester purchase with their gold dust. A spot close to the fireplace to take advantage of the additional light furnished by the flames became her favorite place to sit.

Charlie Mae did most of the cooking, and she spent a great deal of time reading her scriptures. With little to do most days, the others frequently invited her to read aloud to them, especially from the New Testament. After reading the New Testament from cover to cover twice, she asked if they'd like to hear the Book of Mormon.

"What?" Chester asked in shock. "Where did you get that wicked book?"

"It's not wicked," she said defensively.

"I've heard it's full of witches and devils. Throw it in the fire," he demanded.

"I won't," she stubbornly said. "When I was much younger, a kind lady used the Book of Mormon to teach me to read. She was my friend Spencer's grandmother, and when we passed through Salt Lake, he gave me her book. It's dear to me because it was hers."

"It won't hurt none for her to keep it," Irwin noted. "But we don't have to listen to it. She can read the other part of the Bible."

After some consideration, Chester agreed.

Charlie Mae turned to the Old Testament and began to read. Bonnie and Chester had received little more religious training as children than Irwin and Charlie Mae had. They found all of the "begats, cubits, and Isaiah" more of a struggle than they'd bargained for. After a few days, Chester reluctantly suggested, "Maybe we ought to give the Book of Mormon a try. I been thinkin' about it, and it don't appear readin' it hurt Charlie Mae none."

It didn't matter to Irwin, and Bonnie was content to let him decide, so Charlie Mae retrieved the book and began at the beginning. To Chester and Irwin's surprise and her amusement, they particularly enjoyed the wars and battles which led to exciting discussions about people who couldn't get along with each other. Bonnie had little to say about the book, but when Charlie Mae's voice grew tired, she offered to read for a spell.

By the beginning of March, there was concern about fuel for the lantern lasting until they could make another trip to Sacramento or to one of the other communities that had sprung up in the wide valley. The wood pile was growing low, and the pile of grass for Sugarplum was gone. Storms were less frequent, so after feeding Sugarplum a measure of oats each morning, Chester began tethering the mule outside where he could paw through the snow for the last bits of grass he found beneath it. Everyone's spirits were buoyed by patches of new grass and the buds that began to appear on the trees.

Irwin returned to the cabin one morning with two buckets of water sloshing over their tops to announce that a narrow crack had opened in the creek and a slender stream of water was moving again. The news was met with cheers. The men were anxious to resume panning for gold, and the women were equally anxious to give their clothing and bedding a thorough washing.

As the days turned warmer, the stream became a source of concern. Sometimes a loud cracking sound could be heard, signaling that the ice on the lake was breaking up, and the creek ran deep and full, carrying chunks of ice and debris in a mad race to the valley below. The snowfall had been heavy through the winter, and with the first signs of spring, the creek threatened to overflow its banks. The water rose past the sandbars, and the steep slope became the new banks of the stream. Each day the surging current grew closer to the top of the small ravine.

One day as Charlie Mae walked from the cabin, she noticed that the water had begun to subside. The others accepted the news with relief, but as the day advanced, they began to notice that the water was slowly diminishing to a mere trickle. Toward evening they stood looking over the deep channel cut by the previously raging spring runoff and were amazed by how quickly the high water had ended. They stood ten or twelve feet above the now-tame trickle of water that ran over a visible bed of rocks and sand.

Chester and Irwin helped their wives down the sharp bluff that had so recently been merely a steep slope. Curiosity drew them to the streambed.

"Look!" Charlie Mae screamed with excitement when she spotted her first nugget. It wasn't as large as Bonnie's, but after picking it up, she quickly spotted two more.

"I heard about spring runoff carrying bits of gold to new resting places or exposing previously buried nuggets," Chester said as he examined the nuggets and confirmed they were real. He and Irwin clawed their way up the bank and raced to the cabin for their gold pans.

Bonnie found a small nugget, and it was while she was showing it to Charlie Mae that an explosion ripped the spring afternoon quiet. The two young women stared at each other, perplexed.

Mr. Rags began a mournful howl, and a deep rumble shook the ground.

"Run! Run!" Both Irwin and Chester began shouting as they charged from the cabin toward the nearly dry streambed.

"Maybe it's a bear!" Bonnie shrieked as she searched for the rope they'd used to pull themselves up the slope when it had been slippery from snow and ice. It was gone, torn away by the earlier high water.

"Grab my hand." Irwin lay at the top of the slope, reaching his arm toward her. Charlie Mae gave Bonnie a boost, and Irwin caught her wrist. He dragged her squirming, struggling body up the muddy cut until she disappeared over the rim. Even jumping, Charlie Mae could not reach Chester's hand.

She looked about for a more gradual slope, but there wasn't one unless she crossed the creek and climbed a bank half as high as the one before her. She leaped, trying to catch her brother's hand, which reached farther than Chester's, but her grasp fell short. Behind her, she heard a loud noise that seemed to be drawing closer. Chester's head appeared above her.

"Grab hold!" he shouted. Something dangled from his hand. She caught at it, tangling one hand in thick wool. She felt her feet jerk off the ground, and she began to slide up the muddy embankment at a dizzying speed. Feeling her hand begin to slip, she tried to grasp the fabric with her free hand, but to no avail. Her face collided with the wall of mud and rocks, leaving her spitting mud, and she felt herself sliding backward.

A hand caught the sleeve covering her flailing arm about the same time her toe found a protruding root. In seconds she was lying facedown in a puddle of mud and soggy pine needles. Chester didn't allow her to rest. He pulled her upright and began running with her in tow. He paused only long enough to release the catch on Sugarplum's shelter before following Irwin and Bonnie up the hill behind the cabin. The mule passed them, running as though chased by a demon.

A deafening roar filled the valley, and she turned to see a massive wave of water below them, pushing trees and boulders before it, sweep down the valley. Winded and aching, she sank to the ground to watch in horror as the monstrous wave shot toward the cabin, turning at the last moment to spill over the far bank. Then more slowly, the water crested over the bank she had scrambled up moments before. It swirled around the cabin, leaving it an island.

"Pray it holds," Chester whispered as he settled beside her. "If the cabin goes, so will our supplies." He took her hand, and they sat without speaking until the light faded and the water became a silvery gleam, barely visible below them. As long as they sat there, the cabin was still standing, though she thought it might be leaning a little.

"Charlie Mae! Chester!" Irwin called to them. "There's a place up higher where we can shelter for the night." She'd hardly given a thought to the other couple as she and Chester had watched the devastation that had so nearly claimed her life.

Chester helped her to her feet, and she moaned as the movement brought pain to her abused muscles. He kept an arm around her as they stumbled their way toward Irwin. She'd taken several steps before she noticed Chester wasn't wearing pants, only long johns and a coarse-weave cotton shirt with long tails. She remembered the wool she'd clung to as he pulled her to safety.

"Your pants!" she gasped.

"Well," he sounded embarrassed, "like fools, Irwin and me left our coats in the cabin when we grabbed our gold pans. We didn't want to get them wet. When I realized Irwin couldn't reach you, my pants were all I could think of to reach you with."

"Thank you." She kissed his cheek. "You saved my life."

"I should have realized sooner that the drop in water was a sign of a blockage farther upstream." He sounded apologetic, and she snuggled closer to his side in an effort to assure him she didn't hold him responsible. "I wouldn't want to live if you'd been caught by the flood when the water broke free." His voice was filled with emotion.

They spent a cold night huddled together under a rocky ledge, half hidden by two large pine trees. Both women shared their coats with their husbands, and they welcomed the added comfort when Mr. Rags crawled into their midst.

As soon as the first gray light of dawn began to peer over the mountain, the two couples scurried down the hill to see if their cabin was still standing. To their immense relief, it still sat in the clearing. A sea of mud surrounded it, the fireplace chimney had toppled, and one corner hung over a chasm cut by the water. Sugarplum stuck his head out of the open door of the shed, waiting for his daily ration of oats.

"We better get out what we can," Chester said with a sigh.

"You can't go in there," Charlie Mae objected. "It looks like it might fall down any minute.

"We have to," Irwin added in his blunt fashion. "We won't survive another night without a fire and food."

Reluctantly she watched the two men make one trip after another, wading through the mud to the cabin and returning with their arms full. Charlie Mae was pleased to see that on their first return trip both of the men wore the long overcoats they'd purchased on their trip to Sacramento.

"The water didn't get more'n a foot deep inside the cabin," Chester informed her. He handed her his rifle, and she was glad he'd placed pegs above the fireplace for the two guns. He laid a piece of canvas filled with canned goods, plates, and her skillet on the ground. "We can use this to carry our supplies to a higher spot."

The food they'd kept on shelves was safe, as were the clothes they'd hung on nails hammered into the log walls. Their precious supply of sulfur matches had remained dry in their can on the shelf above the fireplace. The beans and flour stored in bags on the floor were gone, while rice and cornmeal sat safely on shelves. Two chairs, a bucket, Bonnie's sewing supplies, the saw, several items of clothing, and most of their blankets had disappeared through a hole in the cabin floor where it hung over the chasm. More items would have likely followed had the table not tipped over, partially blocking the hole.

Charlie Mae sat on one of the remaining chairs and wept when Chester handed her the canvas bag that held her two precious books and the small wooden box Spencer had carved for her ruby. The little box also held Chester's largest nuggets. Remembering the nuggets she'd discovered just before the deluge of water had struck, she drew them from her pocket and added them to the treasure trove in the little box. They were without a roof over their heads and short on supplies, but they weren't destitute for funds if they had a place to spend them.

When Irwin checked the shed, he found that the tin bucket holding the last of Sugarplum's oats had kept the feed dry, and the axe with its new handle and the shovel hanging on the wall were safe. After gathering everything salvageable from the cabin and shed and carrying it to dry ground, the four young people shared a can of peaches before carrying their belongings to higher ground. Several times Charlie Mae looked back with tears in her eyes at the forlorn cabin that had been the first home she and Chester had shared.

That night as they sat around a warm fire and discussed their situation, they decided against building another cabin or returning to Sacramento. It would soon be summer, and they believed they would be fine in a canvas tent until the summer ended. Then they would make their way down to the valley to spend the next winter.

None of them relished thoughts of another winter in the high mountains.

"If we don't take time to build another cabin, there will be more time to search for gold," Irwin pointed out. "With all the money we'll get for our gold, we can build fine houses in Sacramento next winter."

Keeping warm and dry became a daily challenge as spring rains added to the discomfort of sharing a tent. The men and Bonnie bounced back quickly from the ordeal, but Charlie Mae's aches persisted, and she had little energy. After nearly two months in the tent, she deeply regretted agreeing to live in it for nearly four more months.

Chester grew more concerned for her health each day. After discussing the matter with Irwin, he determined to find better shelter and more convenient access to water before leaving the women alone while he and Irwin worked the stream. He set off one morning on Sugarplum and returned late that afternoon filled with excitement.

"There's a spring to the south of the lake in a small cleft in a rock cliff. It's situated on a plateau safely above the lake with plenty of timber nearby. It wouldn't take long to construct a log shelter there using the cliff for one wall." They discussed the matter far into the night. When morning arrived with another drizzling rain, they decided to move to the location Chester had found.

Anxious to shoulder her share of the work, Charlie Mae prepared breakfast, and though she didn't feel well, afterward she trudged to the stream to scrub the dishes and skillet. Working her way down to the water that was still high but no longer flooding, she followed a trail Chester had carved in the steep bank. When she reached the water's edge, she sat on a flat stone to scrub the skillet with sand. She thought longingly of a real stove and a dishpan.

She found herself wondering what day it was and if her birthday was already past. She remembered her previous birthday with a smile. At last she rose to her feet, remembering she had work to do. She gathered up the skillet, cups, and plates and began the arduous climb back to the path leading to their camp. Midway she saw little spots dancing before her eyes and felt a strange sense of dizziness overcome her. Fearing she might fall, she sat down abruptly and lowered her head to her knees.

After a few minutes, the dizziness disappeared and she continued on, though a slight queasiness in her stomach made her regret eating fried corn cakes for breakfast. On reaching camp, she said nothing about being ill but helped store their belongings in Sugarplum's panniers.

They each carried a bundle as they walked beside the mule. The early-morning rain had cleared, and the sun shone brightly, promising a pleasant journey. By the time they reached the lake, Charlie Mae's bundle had grown heavy, and her footsteps lagged. Bonnie slowed her steps to walk beside her.

"Are you all right?" Bonnie asked. "If you need to rest, I can ask Irwin to stop for awhile."

"I'm fine," Charlie Mae answered. "I've just never recovered from nearly drowning then freezing while waiting for morning to come." She didn't mean to sound peevish, but the words came out that way. Most of the time Bonnie's sweet acceptance of their hardships endeared her to Charlie Mae, but lately she'd found too much niceness as irritating as Chester's sense of humor and Irwin's determination to get rich.

"I think it's more than that," Bonnie said tentatively. "You're not eating much, and several times I've thought you were about to lose the little you had eaten. And you're always tired. Could you be increasing?"

Charlie Mae stopped abruptly to stare at Bonnie. "You mean I might be sick because I'm going to have a baby?"

"Most women are tired and have stomach trouble when they start out. They have to visit the privy real often too."

Charlie Mae's face flamed.

"You are, aren't you?" Bonnie giggled and hugged her friend. "Have you told Chester?"

"But I don't know . . . How do you know so much?" Charlie Mae struggled with doubt and mounting elation.

"Some of the girls at the orphanage knew a lot about babies, and Maude and the others at Miss Louisa's place talked quite frankly about such matters."

Charlie Mae remembered a long-ago brusque explanation Granny had given her about the changes in her body. Her heart filled with delight. "Please don't tell Irwin until I get a chance to get Chester alone."

"I'll take care of that." Bonnie laughed. "I'll go walk with Irwin and send Chester back to walk with you."

22 ∾

"ARE YOU SICK? Do you need to rest for a few minutes?" Chester had dropped back to walk beside Charlie Mae. "Bonnie said you needed me."

"I'm not sick—not the way you mean anyway." She bit her lip and struggled to find the right words. "I think I'm going to have a baby."

"A baby!" He whooped so loudly that even Sugarplum turned to look at him. Irwin started to turn around, but Bonnie caught his arm. After a second's hesitation, she stood on her toes to whisper in his ear.

Chester picked up Charlie Mae and whirled her around, then stopped to carefully set her back on her feet. "What do you mean, you think? Is something wrong?"

"I don't think so. I just don't know much about having babies."

"Can't say that I know a whole lot either, but with four sisters and working around rough men since I turned fourteen, I picked up a few things. Some of it is likely plain wrong, but if we put our heads together, we might figure out the important parts."

"Bonnie said she knows the most important parts." She grinned at her husband.

"You told Bonnie first?" Chester appeared hurt.

"She figured it out before I did and told me."

* * *

THE PLANNED SHELTER became a cabin, and it took shape much more quickly than the first one had, though it was larger and divided into three rooms. The middle room became a common room while the smaller rooms on either end were bedrooms. A separate shelter for Sugarplum was erected by leaning cut logs against the cliff face. Without the saw, they couldn't put a proper roof on the cabin and had to settle for thatch. Expecting the cabin to only serve their needs through the summer, they didn't bother constructing a fireplace, and they planned for food preparation to take place outdoors.

Charlie Mae moved about in a daze. As closely as she and Bonnie could figure, the baby would arrive in November, and they planned to be in Sacramento long before then. At quiet moments, Charlie Mae found herself thinking about her own mother. She wondered if the woman she didn't remember well had been happy to discover she was having another baby when she learned Charlie Mae was growing inside her. She hoped she'd been pleased to have a daughter after four sons.

The men made one more trip to their first cabin to retrieve the window and bed frames that had miraculously survived the flood waters. Seeing that the tabletop was still intact with only a few gouges, they retrieved it too. Irwin retrieved his cache of hides from several deer that he'd shot through the winter. When they returned to their wives, they reported that part of the cabin roof had fallen in, and more of the fireplace had crumbled.

That afternoon Charlie Mae and Bonnie collected pine boughs to soften their beds and covered them with hides before moving their bedrolls to the new cabin. They fussed with turning the cabin into a home while the men disappeared with their gold pans, returning only when it grew dark.

Charlie Mae's nausea came only fleetingly and disappeared entirely before the days grew hot. Chester approached his search for gold with greater diligence. His impending fatherhood impelled him to search longer and harder than he had the previous summer, and his efforts paid off with a growing accumulation in the little leather bag he used for holding his dust and the small nuggets he found.

With few tasks commanding their attention, Charlie Mae and Bonnie began accompanying their husbands to the various streams that fed the small lake. Some days they worked as a foursome, and on others they separated into pairs. On the days they searched separate streams, Mr. Rags raced between the two couples, uncertain which to accompany.

A great deal of laughter accompanied their panning expeditions, though at first both Irwin and Chester expressed concern for Charlie Mae's condition. Before long they accepted her ability to keep up and were pleased with the additional amount of gold dust they were able to accumulate with their wives' help. Bonnie became adept at panning, but the constant stooping limited Charlie Mae's success. As the summer progressed and Charlie Mae grew heavier, she frequently gave up on seeking gold and filled her bonnet with berries instead. Other times she sat on a rock or log near Chester, and while he carefully sifted the sand and pebbles in the bottom of his pan, they talked and dreamed of their child and the house they would one day build. They disagreed on whether they should settle in Sacramento or return the next year to search for gold. Chester insisted he must find as much gold as possible while Charlie Mae thought they had enough to buy a home somewhere and start a small farm or business.

They occasionally met other prospectors and invited a few to share supper with them, but mostly they were alone. Other than longing for a real house with a cook stove, Charlie Mae was content, and she thrived on the love and attention Chester showered on her and thanked God each night when she knelt to pray for the life Irwin had invited her to share with him when he ran away from Pa. She was grateful too for Bonnie, who had become the beloved sister she'd once dreamed of having.

One day, Bonnie asked if she could borrow Charlie Mae's Bible.

"Of course. I keep it on the shelf Chester built for me above our bed. You can read it any time you like."

In the coming weeks, she often found Bonnie poring over the Old Testament, and she noticed her kneeling beside her bed on several occasions. She suspected something was troubling her friend and hoped she would confide in her, but the days went by, and Bonnie said nothing.

As summer drew to a close, the nights grew cooler, and they began to make plans for their return to the city. Charlie Mae was growing increasingly awkward, and Chester feared she would soon be unable to walk the distance their journey would require.

The men agreed at last that it was best to return to Sacramento early for the winter, where they would be assured of finding a woman's help for Charlie Mae when her time came. Irwin, more than Chester, had acquired a significant amount of gold dust and was anxious to find a safe place to keep it. In Sacramento they would also be able to acquire supplies and equipment for the following summer.

"The baby will be able to come with us next summer when we come back," Chester said to Charlie Mae. "We've found enough gold to feel certain there's a rich vein near here, so we don't want to move on to another valley. Irwin thinks we should invest in better equipment so that we can accomplish more with our time."

"But won't Bonnie and I be in danger if we go to Sacramento?"

"It's not likely we'll meet Louisa again. We didn't want to bring up anything about that woman when we returned to you and Bonnie last fall, but some of the mule drivers we saw told us she and her girls moved on to San Francisco."

Learning they weren't likely to meet Miss Louisa eased some of Charlie Mae's concern. She'd long since stopped looking over her shoulder, fearing Pa or Cletus might come after her, but Miss Louisa had taken their place.

The morning of their departure, they gathered their remaining supplies, their pouches of gold dust, and Charlie Mae's treasured books along with the box that held her ruby and the larger nuggets she and Chester had found. They began their journey slowly and made frequent stops to allow Charlie Mae to rest.

From a bluff a mile from their first cabin, she picked out its familiar shape with its sagging roof and felt a wave of nostalgia. She appreciated the newer cabin, but it didn't hold the memories the first cabin did. She turned to see tears on Bonnie's cheeks. Putting her arms around the other woman, she whispered, "We'll never forget it."

"It was the first place I could call home."

"It was the same for me. I don't think either Irwin or I ever thought of Pa's house as home."

Bonnie remained melancholy and withdrawn for several days then awoke one morning violently ill, yet she smiled and looked smugly pleased with herself. When she was ill again the next day, she announced that she, too, was going to have a baby.

Charlie Mae hugged her sister-in-law, and the two young women spent many hours planning the wonderful times the cousins would have together. Irwin developed a definite swagger.

"I was jealous that you were having a baby and kept hoping I would become pregnant too," Bonnie whispered to Charlie Mae. "I remembered that woman in the Bible you read about—Hannah was her name. She prayed, and God sent her a baby. That's why I asked to read your Bible, so I could read that story again. I feel just like Hannah; God answered my prayers. From now on I'm going to pray every day like you."

Bonnie's morning sickness was far worse than Charlie Mae's had been and required frequent stops. She grew so weak that room was made for her to ride part of the time on Sugarplum's back.

Their slow journey to Sacramento ended on a cold, rainy day. They went straight to Captain Walker's business to inquire whether he might be aware of a house they could rent.

"Excellent timing," he said as Chester asked about available housing. "I had a house built last spring, and Sylvia and I just moved into it, leaving the apartment over the store empty. In the spring I'll need more storage space, and my plan is to convert the apartment for that use, but for the winter I'd hoped to make the space available to someone who would watch the store and mules at night. If you and Irwin would like the job, you can have it and the apartment."

"We accept your offer," Irwin said, not waiting to inspect the apartment. His major concern was to find a warm place with a roof over it where Bonnie could lie down.

The captain turned to Charlie Mae. "Sylvia will be pleased to hear of your arrival. She has fretted about you since you left."

"I shall be pleased to see her and the children again." She smiled warmly at him.

Little time was wasted in carrying their supplies up the narrow flight of stairs to the apartment above the store. The apartment wasn't large, but it afforded them more space than they were accustomed to, and they were pleased to find it had two bedrooms.

"Look!" Charlie Mae clapped her hands in delight. "There's a stove with an oven." After discovering the stove, she scarcely glanced at the rest of the apartment.

Chester seemed uncertain why the stove should please his wife so much, but Irwin displayed one of his infrequent grins and promised Chester that he was in for a pleasant surprise. The men disappeared while the women decided which of the two bedrooms each couple would claim and unpacked their few belongings. They returned a few hours later, loaded down with purchases and looking pleased.

Bonnie opened the door to see the two men struggling up the staircase with beds and mattresses they'd bought in trade for some of their gold dust. Chairs, a table, and two pie pans followed.

Charlie Mae was anxious to visit Sylvia and share the news of her approaching motherhood. She'd missed Andrew and Abby, too, and hoped they remembered her. At the first opportunity, she set off for the Walkers' new home, following the directions the captain had given her. The sun was shining, and they were enjoying the walk in spite of Charlie Mae's awkward gait and Bonnie's queasy stomach.

"Oh!" Bonnie suddenly stopped short. Charlie Mae followed her sister-in-law's gaze to a pair of fashionably dressed women. Ruffles and flounces ran from their necks to their hems. Graceful bustles ended in short trains. Lacy parasols were held by gloved fingers. The older of the two women looked with disdain at Charlie Mae with her bulging abdomen and Bonnie in her over-large overalls. The younger woman swept her skirt safely away before it could brush against their worn boots.

Suddenly the older woman stopped. She frowned on recognizing the two young women. She looked them up and down, and her lip curled in a sneer. "Look at you! And to think I offered you everything." She grasped her companion's arm and swept away with an air of haughty superiority.

Charlie Mae barely managed to restrain her giggles until Miss Louisa was out of sight. The unexpected encounter had been nothing like she'd feared. "I don't think we have to fear her anymore," she sputtered. Bonnie recovered from her surprise more slowly. She glanced over her shoulder several times as they continued on their way.

Sylvia was appalled at the sight of Charlie Mae and Bonnie when they called on her. "You must get rid of those pants at once," she insisted. "And I have a recipe for a lotion for your faces. Whatever possessed you not to wear bonnets?" she fussed at them.

"We tried to put on dresses before coming to call," Charlie Mae defended. "Bonnie's only dress was ruined in the whiskey barrel you hid her in, and I couldn't squeeze into either of my dresses, which also proved too small for Bonnie."

"It's fortunate I saved my dresses from my last confinement then, though John disapproved of the space they took up on our journey. If either of you are handy with a needle, they will likely need some adjustment, since I am taller than either of you."

"Sewing is one of the skills I was taught at the orphanage," Bonnie said, ducking her head. She was still a little reserved around Sylvia.

Charlie Mae thanked Sylvia, though she wasn't certain she wished to give up wearing pants completely. She had found definite advantages to the male attire, even though she could no longer button her trousers.

Andrew, on seeing Charlie Mae, shouted and flung himself into her arms. Abby smiled but hid behind her mother's skirt. It took a while for her to warm to her usual exuberant hugs and chatter.

* * *

NOVEMBER HAD BARELY arrived when Charlie Mae awoke in the middle of the night to a painful knot in her abdomen that seemed to grow and expand until she thought she might burst before it faded away. She turned to Chester, but finding his side of the bed empty, she remembered it was his night to patrol the captain's property. Sacramento, they'd discovered, was plagued with an abundance of unsavory characters, including women such as Miss Louisa and her girls.

She had almost returned to sleep when she felt the rising pressure coming again. She lay still, waiting for the sensation to ease then slipped out of bed. She paced the floor, traveling to the window to see if she might catch a glimpse of Chester and then went back to her bedside. The contractions came at even intervals but were not coming on top of one another as Sylvia had warned her would be the case when she was about to deliver.

With her mind rushing from elation over her baby's imminent arrival to alarm over the increasing intensity of the contractions, she debated awakening Irwin and sending him for Sylvia. When the first rays of morning light began to creep inside the apartment, she made her way to the kitchen to begin breakfast preparations. Hearing footsteps on the stairs, she turned to greet Chester. He stepped through the door just as a crushing pain left her gasping for breath and stumbling to grasp the corner of the table for support.

"Charlie Mae!" Chester reached for her. He swept her up in his arms and carried her back to bed. Bonnie, wearing a voluminous flannel nightgown and with her hair in a bedraggled braid down her back, charged into the bedroom with Irwin right behind her, hitching up the suspenders on his pants.

"I'll go for Sylvia," Irwin shouted when he learned that his sister's time had come. He dashed back to his bedroom to find his boots. Seconds later he was heard clomping down the stairs.

"I'm sure there's plenty of time." Charlie Mae moaned. "Sylvia said Andrew took all day and half the night." She grasped Chester's arm, gripping it hard as another contraction washed over her.

"I expect we should get ready, just in case," Chester told her. "No two mares are the same, and it's likely the same for ladies." He and Bonnie hurried out of the bedroom to wash their hands and arms, and Bonnie set a kettle of water to heat for a warm bath for both the mother and the baby as Sylvia had earlier instructed.

Charlie Mae screamed for Chester. He returned to the bedroom in time to grasp his son, who arrived with an impatient howl. Charlie Mae's whimper turned to a soft giggle at the sight of her big, strong husband's shocked face as he lifted the wiggling, squalling infant into the air.

"If that don't beat all!" Bonnie stared at the scene a moment before hurrying forward to wrap a piece of warm flannel around the small body before tucking him in the crook of Charlie Mae's arm. Struggling to remember every detail Sylvia had shared on the births of her babies, she tied the cord and snipped between the two knots with her sewing scissors. Chester knelt beside the bed, unable to take his eyes off of his wife and their newborn son.

Sylvia arrived and banned Chester from his wife's room. She advised Bonnie of the particulars of washing the baby and bundling him securely in a warm quilt. They had to change Charlie Mae's gown and bedding. Unsure of what she was supposed to do with the baby while attending to the new mother, Bonnie thrust the squirming bundle into Chester's arms before hurrying back to the bedroom to attend to the tasks she'd been assigned.

When she returned for the baby, Chester stood near the warm stove with the infant in his arms and a pleased smile lighting his face. Bonnie reached for the baby, but Chester ignored her outreached arms. Instead he walked to Charlie Mae's bedside, where he personally settled the newborn at her side and earned Sylvia's disapproval when he refused to leave while his son received his first nourishment.

When all of the commotion settled down, and Sylvia had left for her own home, Chester drew Charlie Mae's hand from beneath her quilt. He slid a gold band on her finger. "There wasn't time or opportunity to get you a ring before we got married, but I made a vow that night that my first gold nugget would go for a wedding band for you. It was finished two days ago."

She had another surprise waiting for her when Chester lugged a rocking chair into the room and set it beside the cradle he'd spent much of the winter constructing and polishing to a fine hue. She'd never seen such fine furniture before. "You should be opening a wood shop, not panning for gold," she told him as she ran her hand across the smooth surface of the chair.

She leaned back in the chair with Daniel in her arms. She'd never expected to be so happy. She looked at the ring then at her husband before glancing down at the sleeping baby. She had much for which to thank God.

* * *

THE WINTER PASSED quickly with the four adults doting on baby Daniel. The weather remained mild with frequent rainstorms and an occasional light dusting of snow, but the two couples were warm and comfortable with plenty to eat. Charlie Mae was happy baking and preparing meals with all the commodities available to her and the use of a real oven. Bonnie stitched dresses for herself and Charlie Mae and shirts for everyone, taking particular delight in creating a wardrobe for Danny and for the baby she felt sure would arrive in June.

The men spent considerable time discussing their plans for expanding their search for gold. Many of the streams that branched off the Sacramento and American Rivers were panned out. A few big strikes had been made, but most of the prospectors were turning to other pursuits or chasing rumors of gold in other places. Farms and orchards were expanding across the Sacramento Valley and along the length of California. More families were moving west, and California had become a state. It became apparent to Charlie Mae that in spite of her longing to establish a permanent home, the men would return to the valley at the earliest opportunity. Besides, Captain Walker would soon have need of his apartment.

One night as they sat around their supper table, Irwin glanced at Bonnie, appearing uncomfortable. "We need to get back before claim jumpers take over our valley," he said.

"I don't think I can travel," Bonnie interjected.

Charlie Mae knew her sister-in-law didn't want her baby born in the rough mountain cabin, yet she worried as much as the others did about the looming deadline to vacate the apartment.

Irwin laid out the facts of their finances to them. "We have enough gold dust to see us through the rest of the winter," he said, "and to purchase supplies for the summer. If Bonnie is unable to travel, we can use the larger nuggets to rent a small house and purchase just half of the equipment we'd been planning to buy. Charlie Mae will have to stay with Bonnie, and by being careful, you women will be all right until we return in the fall."

"What about my ruby?" Charlie Mae offered. Some time during the long previous winter, she'd shown the stone to Irwin and had told him how she'd come by it. "It should bring enough to purchase a house and supplies for Bonnie and me. Then you won't have to cut back on the mining equipment you need."

Chester and Irwin looked at each other. Finally Chester said, "We'd like you to keep your ruby for an emergency. As long as we can make it without trading that gem, we both think that is what we should do."

"But—"

"Accidents happen," Chester interrupted. "If I should meet with an accident as my father did, I'll be happier knowing you have the means to take care of yourself and to feed Danny. If I hadn't been almost grown when Pa died, Ma and my sisters would have had little choice but to work for someone like Miss Louisa, and that would have killed Ma." Charlie Mae had known of Chester's reluctance to sell the jewel, but she'd never considered that he thought of it as a kind of insurance for her. She felt a lump in her throat. She was fortunate indeed to be loved by such a good man.

As spring approached, Irwin and Chester grew restless to return to the mountain, and little Daniel became cranky. Evidence of a sore mouth suggested his first teeth were about to break through. Charlie Mae and Mr. Rags were anxious to spend more time outdoors too and to shake off the last signs of winter. Only Bonnie seemed content to rest and conserve her energy.

Chester built a small cart, a kind of pram, for outings with Daniel, and one bright April morning Charlie Mae left the apartment with Daniel and Mr. Rags for a stroll through the nearby streets. Trees were blossoming, and the city bustled with new construction. Danny clapped his hands and crowed his enthusiasm for the outdoor adventure. As it grew close to his feeding time, Charlie Mae turned the cart back toward the apartment.

A for-sale sign caught her eye, and she glanced at a narrow, two-story house that fronted almost on the street. She stepped closer to peer through a broken window. One large room that was completely bare save for a large stove and a few shelves was all she could see. Curious, she stepped to the side of the house and noticed that the house sat on a deep lot and the room she'd viewed had been added on after the original construction. A small window at each end of the upper story of the main part of the house suggested there was space for at least two bedrooms in the attic.

Daniel began to fuss, but as she hurried back to the apartment, she couldn't get thoughts of the house out of her mind. An idea began to take shape.

That evening, Charlie Mae prepared a special meal. She baked rolls and prepared Chester's favorite peach pie. Saving some of the bread dough she'd used for rolls, she formed cinnamon buns, knowing Irwin had a soft spot for the treats and would welcome them for breakfast the following day.

"What's the occasion?" Bonnie asked, eyeing the results of Charlie Mae's baking frenzy.

Charlie Mae looked around to be certain the men couldn't overhear before whispering in Bonnie's ear, "I have a plan for how we can stay in Sacramento without sending our husbands off short on supplies."

Charlie Mae waited until Chester and Irwin had both taken the edge off their appetites to announce, "I found a house today."

Both men turned their attention to her, and she told them about the house she'd seen while taking the baby for an outing.

"I know which house you mean," Irwin said. He was shaking his head.

"We already looked at that house," Chester said, obviously hating to disappoint her. "The owner wants more for it than we can afford."

"What if we paid the owner as much as we'd planned then paid more each month until it was ours?" Charlie Mae didn't seem deterred by their lack of enthusiasm.

"How could we do that?" Irwin scoffed. "We won't have any more gold until we return in the fall."

"I've been thinking. There's a kitchen range in that house. I saw it through the broken window. And Sacramento is full of men without wives to bake for them. I like to bake. I could turn that large room at the front of the house into a bakery. I think I could earn enough to pay for the house."

Chester looked at her like she'd lost her mind, but she hurried on. "I've noticed that a number of respectable women are taking in laundry or running boarding houses. A bakery wouldn't be any different."

To her surprise, Irwin didn't immediately condemn her suggestion. Instead he appeared thoughtful. He sat for a long while, staring at the bite of pie on his fork. "Maybe we should think on it, Chester," he finally said. "Charlie Mae sure can cook."

The next day, Chester and Irwin made inquiries about the house and returned to report to Charlie Mae that the owner was agreeable to accepting the terms she'd suggested, but the bank insisted that they put up some kind of collateral until all of the payments were made.

Another argument ensued over the ruby, but Charlie Mae eventually prevailed.

"You'll have to make a payment each month to that new bank in the center of town or you'll lose your ruby," Chester cautioned.

"I can make it work; I know I can," she told him, putting more confidence in her voice than she really felt. She'd never undertaken so great a venture on her own before, not even when she ran away from the farm. Even then she'd had Irwin to make decisions and protect her from disaster. If she made a mistake this time, the fault would be all hers.

In the coming days, whenever the weather would permit, she bundled Daniel in his cart and walked to the house that would soon be her home and her business. Chester accompanied her the first time to repair the window and check the chimney, then she spent her time scrubbing and preparing the house for occupancy.

The days were slipping away, and there was little time left before Chester and Irwin would leave when she finished preparations to move to the house. She purchased a modest amount of flour and baking supplies from Captain Walker, and when they were stored on her shelves, she looked around with pride. Everything was in place to begin her new venture. The lengthening shadows reminded her she needed to hurry back to the apartment before darkness fell. Chester and Irwin had both warned her that the streets were not safe for an unescorted woman after dark.

As she pushed the cart carrying baby Danny, her mind continued to go over her calculations. She'd have to bake a dozen loaves of bread each day to begin with, and when word of her business got around she could . . .

"Ma'am, could you help me?" She hadn't seen the stranger approach. She looked apprehensively toward a tall, blond man who blocked the boardwalk. She was almost a block from the apartment, making it doubtful Chester or any of the men working for the captain would hear her if she screamed.

While eyeing the man's well-cut suit and polished boots, she clutched the cart handle tightly, prepared to run if he moved a step closer to her.

"I'm looking for a man who left a letter for me close to two years ago. He indicated a Captain John Walker might know where he could be found. The directions I received indicated Walker might establish a business in this area. If you are acquainted with this part of town, could you perhaps direct me to Captain Walker's business?"

Slowly she lifted her eyes to the man's face, noting the neatly trimmed sideburns and the pale curls that crept beneath the man's hat. He was young, and when he doffed his hat and smiled, her breath caught in her throat.

"Sander?" she gasped. He looked puzzled for just a moment, then his smile widened.

"Charlie Mae?"

She nodded, and with a whoop, he swept her into his arms.

23 ✑

CHESTER ROSE TO his feet, revealing a frown on his face when he saw Charlie Mae approaching Captain Walker's compound arm-in-arm with a handsome stranger—a stranger who was holding Chester's son in the crook of one arm. He started toward them only to be passed by Irwin, who tore past him running as fast as his long legs would go. Chester arrived in time to rescue Danny from being crushed between the other two men as they embraced and thumped each other on the back. When there was a pause in their exuberant greeting, Charlie Mae made introductions before hurrying inside to prepare lunch.

Sander was lavish with his praise for the lunch she served them. When they finished eating, the men leaned back in their chairs to talk. Irwin and Sander spent some time catching up, and Irwin told Sander of his and Charlie Mae's escape from Pa and the claims they'd filed in a mountain valley in the Sierras. Sander expressed interest in their claim and explained that when he'd left the farm, he'd traveled east and found work on a large plantation run by a man with an interest in a small college. He'd helped Sander get accepted at the school. After two years at the school, he'd been offered a job with a consortium of bankers interested in western development, including mining and railroads. He'd been living in

San Francisco for a year, and this was his third trip to Sacramento, where Irwin's letter had finally caught up to him.

"We'll be leavin' by the end of the week to work our claim," Irwin told Sander. "You're welcome to go with us."

"I'm afraid I can't," Sander declined. "I've hired on as an assistant to the vice president of the company and will be needed in San Francisco for a few months, but if you leave me directions, I could take leave and make my way there in July."

"Bonnie and I could show him the way," Charlie Mae volunteered.

Sander looked questioningly at Charlie Mae then turned to Irwin. Irwin explained their quandary. He and Bonnie didn't want to be apart, especially with their child due to be born in a couple of months, but their future depended on him and Chester returning to their claims as soon as possible and leaving their wives on their own for a few months.

"I can check on them each time my employer's business brings me to Sacramento," Sander offered. "Then when I'm free in July, I'll escort your families to your camp."

Irwin explained they would also be moving in a few days, and Sander made note of the new address. Irwin also spoke of Charlie Mae's plans for opening a bakery.

"Fortunes are made from just such ventures." Sander turned to Charlie Mae. "I've thought of you often and hoped you'd find a better life. I never appreciated how hard you worked back on the farm until I had to take care of myself. And had you not taught me to read, I wouldn't have gained acceptance at school. I wished many times that I might show my appreciation. Do you have the capital needed to purchase supplies?"

"I don't expect to make a fortune, but I think I can make a successful bakery," she told him. "I'll begin with just a dozen loaves of bread and use whatever I earn to buy more supplies. If my business fails, we won't be without a roof over our heads." She told him about the ruby locked away in a bank vault until she finished paying for the house.

"Where did you get a ruby?" he asked.

"Do you remember the night you and Irwin followed Pa and our older brothers to Nauvoo to burn out the Mormons?" She didn't wait for a response. "You already know I followed you that night and saw Pa shoot an unarmed man. You saw me creep up to the dead man, but you didn't see me discover the ruby lying on the ground."

"Pa let you keep it?"

"Pa didn't know. I was a child, and I thought it was some kind of magic coal that didn't burn out. It was many years before I discovered that my coal was really a ruby. Chester wants me to keep it for insurance after I pay off the bank loan, but I will sell it if I need to."

"Chester's right. You shouldn't sell the gem. Just promise me that if you must sell it, you'll contact me before you accept an offer."

* * *

THREE DAYS LATER, Bonnie and Charlie Mae bid their husbands a tearful farewell. Chester, too, wiped tears from his eyes as he said good-bye to Charlie Mae and Danny.

"Take care of Mama," he whispered in his small son's ear. Danny's face crumbled, and he, too, cried as though he understood the separation about to take place. Charlie Mae couldn't help remembering their last separation when she and Bonnie had stayed behind in an incomplete cabin as winter threatened to separate them from their husbands and needed supplies. Being apart had proved far more difficult than she'd expected. She wished with all her heart that this separation was not necessary.

When the men were gone, she looked around their new quarters, reminding herself that she faced different circumstances from that previous separation. Their house was snug, and there was ample space for a garden. Wood was stacked high near the back door of the shop, a clothesline stretched between two trees in the backyard, and both the house and the shop's pantry were stocked with supplies.

Bonnie had claimed the main-floor bedroom as climbing stairs had become an almost impossible feat for her. Charlie Mae slept in an upstairs bedroom in a bed that seemed far too large without Chester. On a table beside her bed rested her Bible and Book of Mormon. The other upstairs room held Danny's small bed and the rocking chair Chester had made for her to sit in to feed the baby and rock him to sleep. She ran her hand over the smooth wood, marveling at the workmanship. It was nothing like the crude furniture Chester and Irwin had hastily made for their mountain cabin. If Chester ever got tired of searching for gold, he could surely make a comfortable living making furniture.

Her thoughts turned to a rosy dream of the future with Chester building a carpentry shop behind the house. After a day of building beautiful chairs and tables, he would join her and their children at the dinner table, where the aroma of fresh bread from her bakery mingled with the scent of new wood. She pushed the dream to the back of her mind. She could dream later; now was the time to get to work.

Before dawn the morning after Chester departed, she began mixing two batches of bread and setting the even dozen loaves on a table to rise. While the bread was rising, she returned to find Danny stirring. After dressing and nursing him, Bonnie and Danny accompanied her to the tidy kitchen that lay between their living quarters and a larger room where Chester, Irwin, and Sander had placed planks on saw horses to form tables and benches for her customers. The first six loaves of bread were ready to go in the large oven.

While the bread baked, Charlie Mae turned her attention to making pies with frequent interruptions to pick up dropped toys for Danny and to laugh at his antics. Once the aroma of baking bread began to fill the shop, Bonnie covered the sawhorse tables with cloths, and Charlie Mae prepared a pot of coffee and set out mugs. Before she finished placing a sign in the door announcing fresh bread for sale, their first customer arrived. He gave her two five-dollar gold pieces for three loaves of the hot bread. She held the coins in her hand in semi-shock long after he departed. She'd received as much money for three loaves of bread as she'd earned in the four months she'd traveled with the Walker wagon train.

Customers arrived quickly after that. Some purchased whole loaves of bread, and some paid four bits for a single slice slathered with butter. Her pies disappeared just as quickly. By lunchtime the pies and bread were gone, and she had to remove the sign from her door.

The second morning, she doubled her output and added two kinds of cookies. As her reputation spread, she experimented with other baked goods and was continually astonished by the success of her small business. Each day she closed her shop at noon with her shelves bare. Her afternoons fell into a pattern too. She took a brief nap with Danny, then set out for a brisk walk with him in his cart. Some days Bonnie joined them on their walks, and at least once a week she found it necessary to stop at Captain Walker's business to acquire more supplies. Occasionally they visited Sylvia and her children. Abby adored Danny and was more than pleased to share her toys with him.

By June, Bonnie was nearing the birth of her own child and was far more awkward than Charlie Mae had been before Daniel's birth. Danny was crawling and attempting to pull himself up, making keeping him safe and out from under Charlie Mae's feet while she worked a challenge for both Charlie Mae and Bonnie.

Each evening when she settled in the rocking chair beside Danny's bed, she always felt a tug of sadness that Chester wasn't there to see how quickly his son was growing and changing. There was something satisfying about holding Danny's warm, chubby body close, but she sensed her enjoyment would be greater if Chester were nearby to share her pleasure in their child.

Charlie Mae grew as anxious as Bonnie for the arrival of the other woman's baby. Each morning she expressed hope that it would be the day and went to bed disappointed in the evening. The wait dragged on Bonnie even more.

One morning, just as Charlie Mae set out her sign, a young couple greeted her. She recognized Spencer Pascal at once. His bright red hair was darker now, almost devoid of its earlier flaming color, but the green of his eyes hadn't changed nor had his warm smile. He was dressed in buckskins and towered over the slender, dark-haired woman who stood beside him.

"Good morning," he greeted her. "I couldn't resist the opportunity of looking you up to introduce you to my bride while I'm in California. Charlie Mae, this is my Pamela, who arrived in San Bernardino last fall. President Young sent me there with correspondence late last year with instructions to winter over. I met with a group of Saints near Sacramento this spring to serve as a guide and will be leading them to Salt Lake through the new settlement at Carson Valley. Pamela and I were wed just two months ago."

Charlie Mae and Pamela exchanged shy greetings before several eager buyers approached expressing their eagerness to purchase bread.

"Oh, my!" Charlie Mae was suddenly flustered. "Please come inside. "You must think I have no manners. Please be seated while I tend to my customers." She hurried to the counter where she exchanged warm loaves of bread for pinches of gold dust or silver coins.

A line formed at the counter where her bread and pies were displayed. Several times she had to dash to her kitchen for more of her baked goods. There was no time to do more than occasionally smile and shrug her shoulders toward her guests.

Her morning rush was interrupted by a frantic tugging at her dress. Pausing, she glanced to the side, where she saw Bonnie with tears streaming down her face. Daniel was screaming in her arms. Her baby strained toward her, and Charlie Mae scooped him up with one arm to rest him on a hip.

The moment Danny left Bonnie's arms for his mother's, Bonnie sagged against the counter, holding her abdomen. Clearly, her time had come.

"Mrs. Gafton, I been waiting a long time," one of her regular customers whined.

"I want two loaves and a pie today," another shouted.

"I heard you bake cookies on Wednesdays."

Charlie Mae looked around in bewilderment, uncertain where to turn first.

"I'll get a midwife." Spencer was suddenly at her side. He disappeared through the front door.

"I've been watching the way you do things," Pamela whispered. "I'll take care of your customers while you take care of your friend."

Bemused, Charlie Mae placed her free arm around Bonnie to lead her back into the house. Mr. Rags met them at the door and followed them to the bedroom with his tail drooping between his legs.

"Get back in bed," she told Bonnie, "while I settle Danny. She set the baby in his chair and tied a dishtowel around him to keep him from falling off, then handed him a cookie and a string of wooden thread spools to keep him occupied.

She returned to the bedroom to find Bonnie attempting to change her sheets. She finished the task for her and helped Bonnie into a clean gown before her friend would lie down. Once Bonnie was back in bed, Charlie Mae hurried back to the kitchen to check on Danny. To her dismay, he'd managed to grasp the tablecloth, sending breakfast dishes crashing to the floor. Milk and oatmeal were everywhere.

She didn't know what to do. Bonnie needed her, her son was ready to be nursed, she'd left a complete stranger to deal with her customers, and there was a mess to be cleaned up.

She'd have to nurse Danny quickly then put him in his bed. He'd cry, but it was the only safe place for him. She freed him from his chair and reached for the buttons on her dress just as a soft tap sounded at the door. Without waiting for an answer, Pamela poked her head inside.

"Everything is gone," she said. "I locked the door and pulled the shade. I hope that's all right."

"Yes, thank you."

Pamela entered the room, carrying the box in which Charlie Mae kept her day's cash. "Where shall I put this?" It was difficult to hear the question over Danny's insistent demands to be fed.

"Inside that cupboard will do," Charlie Mae said, then continued preparing to feed her baby, but a moan from the bedroom caused her to hesitate.

"Take care of your baby. I'll stay with your friend," Pamela offered.

"Thank you again. She's my sister-in-law, Bonnie. I won't be long." Soon Danny's cries were silenced, and Charlie Mae could hear the murmur of soft voices coming from Bonnie's bedroom. She tried to relax, but she couldn't avoid worrying. She needed to send someone for Sylvia. Spencer had gone for a midwife, but she'd neglected to tell him they hadn't been able to find one. There was only a choice between a doctor who lived in shanty town and drank too much and Sylvia, who would tell Charlie Mae what to do.

Danny was almost asleep when another tap sounded at the door. Charlie Mae straightened her clothes and hurried to answer it. Mr. Rags got to the door first. He whined eagerly and scratched at the door. She opened the door to Spencer and an older woman who bustled straight toward the bedroom where Bonnie's cries were growing louder. Mr. Rags sniffed at her skirt and let her pass. Spencer bent to pat the dog. Mr. Rags wagged his tail.

"I'll take him for you." Spencer held out his arms, and Charlie Mae relinquished her son to her childhood friend.

"His bed is at the top of the stairs on the left," she whispered before hurrying to be with Bonnie. Mr. Rags followed Spencer and the baby up the stairs.

Time took on a surreal quality as Charlie Mae hurried to do the midwife's bidding. There was no chance to question where Spencer had found her. Bonnie's pains seemed far more intense than those she had suffered at Daniel's birth. Twice Charlie Mae left the birthing room to feed Daniel and was vaguely aware that the kitchen had been straightened and her floor scrubbed.

Darkness had settled and lamps were lit when the midwife asked her to call Spencer into the room. Bonnie lay exhausted, no longer screaming as her body twisted in pain. Without being told, Charlie Mae sensed poor Bonnie lay near death. Tears welled in her eyes. After all she and Bonnie had been through, she couldn't bear to lose her dear sister.

The midwife and Spencer conversed quietly while Charlie Mae knelt beside Bonnie, bathing her face with cool water and whispering encouragement. After a moment, Spencer knelt beside her.

"Mrs. Riggins," he said in a soft voice to Bonnie. "Your little one is in need of help to be born, and you have exhausted your strength. You are both in need of God's help. Would you like me to give you a blessing to help you through this difficult time?"

It was impossible to tell if Bonnie answered yes or no, but she seemed to nod her head just a little.

"I think she wants you to go ahead with the blessing," Charlie Mae said. "Bonnie is a good woman, and she believes this child is an answer to her prayers. Neither Bonnie nor I were raised with much religion, but we've read the Bible and the Book of Mormon you gave me. I think she wants you to ask God to help her."

Spencer placed his hands on Bonnie's head and spoke a few fervent words, pleading for life and strength for both Bonnie and her infant. Kneeling beside her sister and friend, Charlie Mae didn't see what the midwife did, and she was still clinging to the prayer Spencer had voiced when Bonnie cried out, then lapsed into unconsciousness. A few seconds later, a limp, silent baby girl was thrust into Charlie Mae's arms.

Charlie Mae spanked the baby's bottom. She'd heard that was the usual way to start an infant breathing. Getting no reaction, she rubbed the infant's chest and back. Spencer leaned across her to blow gently in the child's mouth. Feeling a slight quiver, she urged Spencer to continue blowing air into the baby's lungs. At last their efforts were rewarded with a faint, mewling cry. Tears splashed down Charlie Mae's cheeks and onto the baby as she wrapped her in one of the small quilts Bonnie had sewn for her baby.

With the baby held tightly in her arms, she turned back to the bed where Bonnie lay.

"She's sleeping," the midwife said. "She'll be all right but will need a lot of rest for a few weeks." She turned to the baby and examined her closely. "Give the little one a warm bath, then wrap her snugly. When you've done that, you'll have to rouse her mother enough to feed her."

The midwife reached for the cloak she'd thrown aside when she'd first entered Bonnie's bedroom. "We must be on our way," she said more to Spencer than to Charlie Mae. "It's nearly morning, and Elder Jacks said we would be leaving at dawn. Come, Pamela."

Charlie Mae realized the midwife spoke with an accent reminiscent of some of the English people she had met since her arrival in Sacramento, as did Spencer's wife. Her easy familiarity with both Spencer and his wife suggested she was part of the group of Mormons headed toward Salt Lake.

With a flood of gratitude, she attempted to thank the woman. "I think Bonnie would have died without your help."

"'Twasn't me but the Lord's that did it," the woman said. "I've lost more than one lass with milder complications. Watch her close for bleeding, and make certain she nurses her babe as often as possible for a time. If her milk doesn't come in, and it sometimes doesn't after a delivery such as this, you shall have to take over nursing both babies."

Charlie Mae set the baby beside her mother and hurried to the cupboard where Pamela had placed her cash box. Extracting four five-dollar gold pieces, she pressed them into the midwife's hand, refusing to listen to her protests.

"My brother, Bonnie's husband, would give you the entire box. She is that dear to him," Charlie Mae insisted. "Surely you don't wish me to incur his anger by failing to pay you."

"It wasn't the visit I planned." Spencer took her hand. "But I feel the Lord had a hand in bringing us here today. And should President Young send me this way another time, I shall surely stop by to visit with you and your husband."

"Thank you for caring for my son." Charlie Mae pressed her cheek against Pamela's.

"He's a fine boy. I hope I shall one day have one just as fine." Moments later Spencer, Pamela, and the midwife were gone.

Charlie Mae spent the remainder of the night alternating between praying, sometimes in gratitude, sometimes for continued help, and listening for her three charges. She was aware that the dog stayed by her son's small bed and was glad for his vigilance. As light filled the small house, she brought Daniel's cradle downstairs to keep him close while she cared for Bonnie and the fragile new baby, and she placed a sign on the bakery door saying the shop was temporarily closed.

24 ⌒

CHARLIE MAE GAVE a coin to a boy to carry a message to Sylvia the next day, and her former employer arrived a little after noon to take charge of the household. She was put out that she hadn't been notified earlier but was pleased to sit with Bonnie and rock her newborn daughter while Charlie Mae caught up on some badly needed sleep. In the coming weeks, she came frequently, but it fell to Charlie Mae to care for the two babies and Bonnie most of the time.

Reopening her bakery became an impossible task, and Charlie Mae became concerned about her payment to the bank. With their anticipated stay in the mountains, she needed to have enough gold and coins on hand to finish the payments. Long after the other members of her household were asleep one night, she carefully counted the coins she'd accumulated. There was far more money in the box than she'd thought. By including the few nuggets she'd found, there was just enough to finish paying for the house.

Bonnie's health steadily improved until she could take over the primary care of her daughter, whom she named Susannah. Susannah was a quiet, pleasant baby who seldom fussed. Danny was entranced with her, and both Charlie Mae and Bonnie had to watch that his busy little hands didn't become too rough for his smaller cousin. Little Susannah was just four weeks old when Sander arrived, ready to visit Irwin and Chester's valley.

Neither Charlie Mae nor Sander was convinced Bonnie should undertake such a journey after nearly losing her life in childbirth and with such a fragile, young baby, but Bonnie wouldn't be swayed. She couldn't wait to show Irwin his daughter, and she missed her husband. Charlie Mae missed Chester, too, and allowed herself to be persuaded to undertake the journey.

Within hours of his arrival, Charlie Mae asked her brother to accompany her to the bank with the bag filled with coins and gold dust. He was pleased but expressed his astonishment when he saw the amount of profit she had made. He was further astonished when he saw the jewel his sister reclaimed.

Charlie Mae was embarrassed to admit she had no funds left with which to purchase a few items for their journey. Bonnie offered her large nugget but reluctantly agreed to let Sander purchase the supplies they would need when he insisted she should keep her nugget. He suggested that both Bonnie's nugget and Charlie Mae's ruby should remain in a safety-deposit box at the bank, but Bonnie meant to keep the nugget, which she considered a good-luck charm, with her on their return to the mountains. Charlie Mae had missed her ruby and refused to part with it again so soon after regaining it. She placed it back in the box Spencer had made for it and hid the box at the bottom of the bag that held Danny's diapers.

Sander had brought horses for both women and a pair of pack mules to carry supplies and the tools he would need to evaluate Chester and Irwin's claims for his employer. He fashioned a sturdy sling that went over Bonnie's shoulder for carrying Susannah, and he used a length of thin rope to secure Danny in front of Charlie Mae. Traveling with two infants necessitated stopping more often than he would have liked, but Charlie Mae was pleased with his patience. Danny seemed perfectly happy riding a horse and sleeping in a tent while Susannah slept contentedly in her sling other than when she needed to be fed. After the first few weeks, she was showing signs of developing a healthy appetite, and fortunately, Bonnie's milk supply was keeping pace with her daughter's growing appetite.

The trail showed signs of heavier use than it had the year before. Though both women wore pants, it was more difficult to conceal their gender, and Sander took pains to secure camping spots away from the trail that were also easily defendable. Mr. Rags was quick to alert them anytime a stranger approached. They met few prospectors, but the ones they did happen on seemed tired, disillusioned, and shabbier than those from the previous two seasons. Charlie Mae suspected some of the drifters they passed were merely opportunists looking to get rich off someone else's hard work.

The day they entered the valley, neither woman could conceal her excitement. At the lower end of the valley, they passed their first cabin. The roof had fallen in, and the entire structure leaned more precariously toward the chasm that had been dug even deeper by another spring runoff. Charlie Mae told Sander about the weeks she and Bonnie had spent there alone and the day they'd fled the raging spring flood.

They arrived at the cabin against the cliff near sundown. A corral and shed now stood to one side of the cabin. No one was close enough to hear their greetings, so they unpacked the animals and turned them loose inside the corral before making their way inside the cabin. Charlie Mae was quick to notice that a considerable number of changes had been made. A fireplace now filled one end of the cabin, and a second window had been added. Planks covered the dirt floor, and rough shingles made the roof rainproof. A ladder led to a loft that looked out over the larger room. It was evident Chester and Irwin had anticipated the needs of their families. Sander claimed the loft for his bedroll.

"We're home!" Charlie Mae whirled around with Danny in her arms, making him giggle. She set him on the floor while she helped unpack their supplies and the personal items they'd brought with them. He crawled about, happily exploring and getting underfoot.

A shout from outside brought up her head, and Mr. Rags began barking wildly. She snatched up Daniel and ran from the house with Bonnie and little Susannah right behind her. Coming over the rise was old Sugarplum traveling at a rapid, lurching pace. Chester held to his lead rope while Irwin sprinted ahead.

Charlie Mae passed Irwin and launched herself into her husband's arms. They held each other and cried until Danny pushed at Chester, demanding his share of attention. Chester lifted his son high until he giggled and drooled on his father's shirt.

"He's so big," Chester marveled, looking him over carefully.

"He crawls and pulls himself up to stand already." There was pride for her son's accomplishments in her voice. "He looks more like you each day with those square shoulders and that little cowlick in his brown hair. His cheerful temperament has been a constant reminder of you, too." Her words brought a noticeable swelling to Chester's broad chest.

"He has your green eyes." Chester looked from the baby to her and back.

Gradually they became aware of Irwin and Bonnie standing nearby. Irwin looked up with a proud grin. "Come meet my daughter." He motioned to Chester then gave Charlie Mae's shoulders a one-armed hug.

* * *

IT WAS GOOD to be back in the mountains. Charlie Mae missed her more-efficient kitchen back in Sacramento, but being with Chester again more than made up for it, and seeing his pleasure in his son brought joy to her heart. She couldn't help comparing the bond between Chester and little Daniel with her own painful childhood and fear of her father. Irwin seemed to take his cue from Chester rather than their father in the way he related to his own child, which pleased Charlie Mae.

Most mornings they arose early; packed pans, shovels, and a screening device on Sugarplum's back; and headed up one of the creeks that fed into the lake. Irwin carried Susannah in her sling while Chester carried Danny on his shoulders or allowed him to sit on Sugarplum's back while he walked beside the mule with one hand gripping the small trousers Bonnie had made for the boy.

Some days the women spent most of the day watching over their babies while the men panned for gold. On other days they took turns watching both children and wading into the cold water to do a little panning of their own. Sander studied the area Irwin and Chester favored and concluded there was likely a vein nearby. Both Irwin and Chester had found numerous nuggets as large as bird eggs in the water near the spot Sander selected. With great anticipation the men dug into the rocks and dirt with picks and shovels.

Almost a week's work resulted in a pleasingly heavy bag of gold, but the vein they sought was elusive. At last they decided to give the spot one more day, and then they would look for another possible site.

"We found it!" rang through the air one September morning within a short time after Chester took his first swing with the pick. Charlie Mae and Bonnie were picking berries but heard his shout and rushed to examine the find. They arrived to find Chester and the Riggins brothers kneeling in the creek, furiously chipping at the rock bluff that rose on the opposite side of the stream. When Chester saw Charlie Mae and Daniel, he rushed across the creek to swoop them up in his arms for a crazy dance in the shallow water.

"Put me down!" Charlie Mae laughed.

"Down." Danny mimicked his mother while giggling over his father's antics.

Over the next few days, the men accumulated several pounds of what they hoped would prove to be high-grade gold. Sander performed a test with acid and smiled broadly at the results.

A week later the find petered out. Irwin particularly voiced his disappointment, but Sander told him not to give up. "It's not unusual to find small veins near large veins. You have enough gold now to live comfortably for many years. There's still time before winter sets in to discover whether there is a vein large enough to justify setting up a mine."

That evening the three men discussed whether they should return to Sacramento earlier than originally planned to have their find assayed or to continue searching for the main gold vein. Sander, who needed to return to his job, had planned to return alone but was now anxious for the company of the others on the return trip.

"I'll begin arrangements for a backer to begin mining operations." He laughed. "But the nuggets I found, I plan to keep." He held out his hand, displaying four nuggets each larger than the big one Bonnie had found their first season.

"We'd like for you to be a full partner," Irwin offered. "Chester and I discussed making you a partner earlier this summer. We filed claims on most of this valley a year ago in all four of our names. Then before we left Sacramento last spring, we added two more claims; one in your name and one for little Daniel."

"Is that legal?" Charlie Mae asked. She was uncertain whether an infant or a woman could own property.

"The man at the claims office didn't stop us, and when we get back, we'll file on the rest of that canyon in little Susannah's name," Chester said.

It was decided that they would leave in three days' time. That would give the women time to prepare for the journey, and the men would spend two more days panning and making certain the markers outlining their claims were in good repair.

Daniel voiced his objections when Chester prepared to leave without him the next morning. He held out his arms to his father, then when that didn't bring the desired results, he let go of the chair he clung to and tottered across the uneven floor.

"That's my boy! He's walking!" Chester shouted with glee. Both he and Charlie Mae rushed toward the boy. Chester lifted him high and hugged him tightly. After several minutes of praise for his son's accomplishment and with obvious reluctance, he passed Danny to his mother. It took all of Charlie Mae's powers of persuasion to soothe the disappointed little boy who wanted to go with his pa.

Returning to the cabin that evening, all three men wore looks of concern.

"It looks like someone has tampered with our markers near our first claim below the old cabin," Irwin explained.

"There are signs of digging near the rapids, about where Bonnie found her first nugget," Chester added. "We found a campsite too, but it doesn't appear to have been occupied for several weeks."

"We put the markers back where they belong, but it's a good thing we'll be starting back right away," Irwin added. "Whoever moved the stakes did it because he found color in the creek there. He'll now try to beat out our claim."

"As soon as we reach Sacramento, I'll notify my employers to begin arranging to purchase the land as well as for bids from various mining companies," Sander said. "They'll want to meet with you to make arrangements for a partnership or an outright buyout. Unless someone in the registrar's office is crooked, the company's attorneys will stop anyone from taking over your claim." Sander attempted to downplay the seriousness of the situation.

It was a more sober group who met at breakfast the next morning. Even the babies seemed to sense the undercurrent of tension. Danny swatted his bowl of cereal from the table to the floor, and Susannah whined and fussed.

"We're just gonna get the screen and shovels," Chester explained when he kissed Charlie Mae good-bye. "We should be back by noon, and if you an' Bonnie have our packs ready to load on the mules, we'll start out this afternoon."

* * *

"I THINK I'LL go meet Irwin," Bonnie said as she finished packing the last of the items she would need for Susannah during their trip in her saddlebag. The two women had spent the morning sorting their belongings into packs for Sander's pack animals and selecting those items which needed to be kept close at hand in their saddlebags.

"Are you sure you should go alone?" Charlie Mae said. "I'd go with you, but I haven't finished preparing lunch. Besides, Danny just fell asleep, and his disposition will be much better if his nap isn't disturbed."

"I'll be fine," Bonnie assured her. "I'll probably meet Irwin before I get far. He's anxious for us to be on our way."

"Chester, too," Charlie Mae said. She turned to adding the finishing touches to the double-sided leather bag she'd purchased two months earlier in Sacramento. In one side she put diapers, a change of clothes, and foods that would help keep Danny from fussing during the long ride. On the other side, she put her scriptures and several items she wanted to have available for quick access. When she finished, she added her bag to the mound of bundles and supplies piled in front of the cabin for the men to form into packs for the mules.

Back in the cabin, she completed lunch preparations and checked on Danny. He lay sprawled on his back in his bed with his small hands resting palms up on either side of his head, his pudgy fingers almost touching the thatch of thick brown hair that matched his father's. Charlie Mae smiled as she watched her son sleep, and as always, her heart swelled just a little bit with the love she felt for him.

Lifting her eyes, she remembered the little wooden box holding her ruby and several large gold nuggets that she'd hidden behind a cleverly concealed section of one of the bedpost logs. Shaking her head at her forgetfulness, she removed the box from its hiding place and dropped it into a pocket in her baggy trousers. With one last glance at her sleeping son, she hurried from the cabin to add the treasure box to her saddlebag.

She'd taken a few steps when four riders burst into the clearing. Before she could retreat to the cabin, one of the riders leaped from his horse to grab her arms. She screamed for Chester while the ruffian forced her arms behind her back in a painful position, and when she attempted to scream again, he shoved a dirty cloth in her mouth. One man remained mounted and held a rifle pointed toward her while the other two began pawing through the packs heaped in front of the cabin.

Charlie Mae kicked and struggled to free herself. The man holding her cursed and slammed his fist into her temple, leaving her reeling and struggling to remain conscious. *Danny is in the cabin sleeping. I have to stay conscious for his sake.*

She fought the pain that exploded inside her head and the darkness that threatened to overtake her. She was conscious enough to understand that the men were looking for Irwin and Chester's stash of gold dust. They ripped open the bags and bundles she and Bonnie had packed and kicked aside the kettles and cans in which the men had hidden their nuggets and gold dust without bothering to look inside them.

"What's this?" One of the men held up a rock with a spidery vein of gold running through it.

"Ore, you fool," the man holding the rifle retorted. "Just as I suspected. They hit it big." He tossed a leather saddlebag to one of the men on the ground, and the two men began feverishly gathering up the pieces of rock with veins of gold that Sander had selected to take with them. When they finished, one of the men kicked clothing, diapers, and quilts into a pile, dumped kerosene on them, and set them afire.

Charlie Mae's heart filled with despair. Frantically she searched the edge of the clearing, hoping her husband and brothers would arrive in time to save some of their belongings.

"If they have ore, they have nuggets," the mounted man snarled. "Find them!"

One of the men started toward the cabin, and Charlie Mae increased her struggles. She no longer cared about her burning clothes and blankets. Though her thoughts were blurred with pain, instinct told her she must get to Daniel before the robbers awakened him. He would scream if confronted by strangers, and she didn't want to know what the men might do to silence him.

A black-and-white blur streaked toward the man entering the cabin. Hope filled her heart as Mr. Rags launched himself toward the intruder. The man screamed, and behind them came the spitting sound of rifle fire. Charlie Mae watched in horror as her dog crumpled in a bloody heap in the doorway. Tears of sorrow piled atop her pain, and her fear for her son increased. The robber staggered backward, clutching at his throat. Blood dripped from his hands. Mr. Rags's heroic effort hadn't been entirely in vain.

The mounted thief shouted for the others to hurry as the injured man groped his way to his horse and struggled to pull himself into the saddle.

"Hurry! Someone might have heard that shot," the leader yelled. He rode closer to Charlie Mae and pointed his rifle at her.

"Tell us where the gold is hidden or you'll get a bullet too!" he shouted.

The man holding her shook her violently. She sputtered, unable to speak with the rag in her mouth. She pointed toward the scattered possessions strewn across the ground where the cans labeled peaches and milk held gold. Angrily, her captor shoved her to the ground and picked up two kerosene lanterns. One after the other, he hurled them at the cabin. The man who had lit the clothing and blankets on fire grasped one corner of a burning quilt and hurled it toward the kerosene-splattered doorway.

Jerking the rag from her mouth, Charlie Mae screamed, "My baby!" The man closest to her blocked her from running to the cabin. *If I gave him the ruby, he might let me go,* she reasoned in her desperation to reach her son. Thrusting her hand in her pocket, she drew out the small wooden box. She extended it toward him, and as she'd hoped, he grabbed it from her. Dodging his foot, she began to run. She had to reach Danny.

"What's in the box?" someone shouted.

"Chunks of gold! Big ones too," she heard the man shout.

"Don't let the woman get away!"

She'd almost reached the door where flames licked up the wooden doorframe. Something hit the back of her head hard, then bounced through the flames ahead of her. She went down. Pulling herself to her knees, she began to crawl toward the burning inferno that had been the cabin. *Danny! She had to get to Daniel.*

"Someone's coming!"

"Let's ride!"

Behind her were shouts and confusion, but her attention was focused on reaching Danny. Someone ran past her. One more shot rang out as Chester burst through the flames ahead of her. The last thing she saw before blackness claimed her was the flames reaching out toward her husband's falling body.

25 ❧

THROUGH SWIRLING BLACKNESS, she saw Pa raise his rifle. There was a terrible sound, and a man fell. She ran toward him, and somehow he changed. It wasn't the man in Nauvoo trying to escape the burning building who lay in the grass. It was Ma lying so still, with only her petticoat fluttering in a stray breath of wind.

SHE AWOKE TO shrill screams, barely conscious that they were coming from her own throat. "Mama!" She struggled to sit up. Memory crashed its way through the fog blurring her senses. "Chester! Danny!" She fought off the arms restraining her.

"I'm sorry, so sorry." Bonnie was weeping. A baby's cry reached her ears, and she strained to see. Her hope was dashed when she recognized Susannah, not Danny, lying in the grass beside Bonnie.

Turning her eyes to Bonnie's face, she knew with a terrible finality there was no reason to ask about Chester and Danny. They were gone. She turned slowly toward a smoldering pile of rubble where flames still licked at the heaviest logs, which was all that was left of the cabin—all that was left of her reason for living. Cold blackness stole inside her heart. Slowly she rose to her feet, shaking off Bonnie's restraining hands. She began walking, and clouds of darkness closed in, narrowing her focus to the glowing red coals, drawing her to them. A flash of déjà vu hinted that once before she'd walked toward shining embers that were all that was left of a terrible act. She'd almost remembered then, that night in Nauvoo, but now she knew Ma had died just as Chester had, with a bullet in her back.

Sander had found her and led her back to the house. She'd been a small child, and the memory had dimmed, never to be spoken of. Now she wasn't a child, and she did not want to live without Chester and Daniel. She should have died too. But for the object that struck her down, she would be with them. She knew with a strange, detached certainty that the object that had hit her was the box Spencer had carved for her ruby. Hysterical sobs bubbled up in her throat. The evil men who had taken all she loved most had murdered them for a few lumps of gold and had flung a ruby valued beyond tens of thousands of dollars into a funeral pyre. The heat from the blaze seemed to call to her with promises of joining her husband and son. Heat seared her face, and yet she didn't feel it.

"No!" Sander snatched her back before she could take another step. Irwin stepped forward to fold her in his arms.

"Chester would want you to live," he whispered. Tears coursed down Irwin's face in an unfamiliar display of loss.

"I can't," she sobbed. "I want only to be with them." Her bones seemed to melt, and she fell limp in her brother's arms.

Blackness came and went. Sometimes she heard Irwin's and Sander's voices, and she was aware at some level of Bonnie's efforts to get her to swallow a few sips of water. How much she heard and understood didn't matter then, but when morning came and the sun's rays failed to warm her, she knew her brothers had taken their rifles and set out to follow the thieves. When they returned, they reported that they had found the one who had run afoul of Mr. Rags lying in a pool of blood, felled by a single shot to his head and left beside the trail by his companions. Fearing the thieves might double back and find the women alone, the brothers had returned.

Charlie Mae sat with her back against a tree, her head bowed, neither seeing nor thinking, as her brothers searched for Chester's and Daniel's bodies among the ashes of the cabin. When they were ready, she stood beside the graves Irwin and Sander dug. Into one went Chester and Daniel. Into the other went the pitiful bits of bone that were all that was left of Mr. Rags. Sander read from what was left of Charlie Mae's scorched books of scripture that he'd found trodden and torn by the raiders' horses. When he finished, Charlie Mae knelt beside the marker her brothers erected over the grave to whisper a last good-bye.

* * *

SHE CHOSE TO ride Sugarplum when they left the scene of so much tragedy, though both of her brothers attempted to persuade her that one of the horses would be far more comfortable than the mule. As though in a trance, she rode until the old cabin came in sight. A flood of memories brought scalding tears to her cheeks. Sugarplum pricked up his long ears and turned his steps down the familiar path. He halted in front of the door that had once led to his lean-to. From faraway, Charlie Mae thought she heard the rumble of Chester's laughter.

Leaning forward, she patted Sugarplum's neck and spoke softly. "Thank you. This should be my last memory of this valley." She slid from the mule's back and took a tentative step toward the cabin.

"It's not safe to go inside," Irwin said from beside her as he took hold of her arm to prevent her from entering the badly deteriorating cabin. She'd been oblivious to the others who had followed Sugarplum into the clearing. She stopped and let memories of better times offer solace to her aching heart.

A commotion disrupted the peace of the cabin setting. Sugarplum reared and threw his broad rump against the lean-to, which fell, adding its weight to the pressure tugging the cabin toward the creek at the bottom of the chasm. The rumble of logs cascading down the steep slope frightened the horses and pack mules, generating shouts and frantic tugging at ropes and reins to bring the animals under control. A cloud of dust arose as rocks and dirt tore loose from the steep bank down which the logs thrashed their way to the bottom. Out of the chaos scurried a fat porcupine and her half-grown offspring.

Charlie Mae reached for Sugarplum's reins. Speaking in quiet tones, she subdued his antics. The dust settled, and she looked to where the cabin had stood. Only a few logs remained, and there was no remnant of the fireplace Chester had so lovingly built.

"Look at this!" She heard the excitement in Irwin's voice. "We were living right on top of it!" Irwin's voice was charged with awe, and she thought she detected a note of regret as well.

"If this vein extends any distance back into the mountain, you're a rich man." Sander clapped Irwin on his back.

"We all are," Irwin's voice was humble, and she saw tears in his eyes. "If only Chester had seen this."

Irwin and Sander covered the rich vein of gold unearthed by the falling walls of the log cabin with dirt to conceal it from anyone who might pass by. Charlie Mae paid them little heed. She saw only the collapse of her home, the place where she'd laughed and played with Chester and where their son had been conceived.

She remembered little of their journey back to Sacramento. The days and nights were much the same. Only later did she learn how carefully Bonnie had rationed their food because so much had been spoiled by the raiders and that her brothers took turns sleeping in front of the tent that had been salvaged for the two women to share. The brother not sleeping served as a guard over their camp. There weren't enough blankets, and the few pieces of clothing that hadn't burned were used for diapers for Susannah.

They met other prospectors who told similar tales of stolen gold dust, burned possessions, murder, and stolen stock. Comparisons produced similar descriptions, and rumors spread of both lawmen and vigilantes pursuing the murderous trio of outlaws.

Within days of reaching Sacramento, Irwin and Sander hurried on to San Francisco, leaving Bonnie to look after Charlie Mae. By the end of September they were back with loaded wagons, mining equipment, and five armed guards who planned to stay in the valley to guard it until representatives of the largest mining company in America could arrive in the spring to begin mining operations.

This time when the brothers left, it was with the promise that they would return before winter snows closed the mountain pass to their valley. Before departing, Irwin sat down beside Charlie Mae on the back porch where she often sat staring sightlessly toward the mountains.

"Charlie Mae, I made some decisions while in San Francisco," he said, taking her limp hand between his warm palms. "The mining company is paying us a huge sum upfront for the right to mine our claim. They're forming a partnership with us, as well as assigning us stock which will pay us dividends as long as the mine is in operation. I sent a packet of bank notes with one of the mining representatives who is journeying east to deliver to Chester's mother. Sander wrote her a letter telling her about your marriage, little Daniel, and about Chester's and Danny's deaths. He also told her that if ever she is in need, to contact him, and he will see to her welfare. I also made arrangements for a house to be built in San Francisco overlooking the bay."

She made no response, and he kissed her gently on the cheek. "I brought you this." He placed a heavy, leather-bound Bible in her hands. "Perhaps it will help."

She caressed the leather with her hand. She missed Granny's well-worn book of scripture. The torn pages Bonnie and her brothers had salvaged for her were dear, but she was glad to have the new book. She thought longingly of the other volume of scripture. It had often seemed to speak to her more clearly than Granny's Bible had, and a faint whisper deep inside her now suggested that its words, if only she could remember them clearly, would offer her a small measure of comfort.

In the coming days, her appetite didn't improve, and she took no interest in the changing leaves or in Susannah's newest accomplishments. She never ventured into the small bedroom that had been Danny's, but occasionally she opened the book Irwin had given her and stared at the pages.

Bonnie sent for Sylvia, and the two women fussed over Charlie Mae, urging her to eat and to order new dresses. They took her on outings and spoke in glowing terms of the house being built in San Francisco, but nothing lifted the gloom that burdened her. Only little Abby seemed to be able to penetrate the lifeless core around her heart.

The little girl climbed onto Charlie Mae's lap and asked, "Did you make cookies today?"

When Charlie Mae merely shook her head, Abby brushed Charlie Mae's damp cheek with her tiny fingers. "Tomorrow you'll bake cookies?"

Charlie Mae promised she would. Stirring up the batter and dropping round balls of dough onto a cookie sheet awakened something within her, and the next morning she left her bed early to mix bread. While the bread was rising, she kneaded more dough and scrubbed counters and shelves. This became the pattern of her days. Her former customers welcomed her joyously, and she could almost pretend while she labored in her shop that Chester was merely away and would soon be returning and that little Danny was upstairs asleep in his bed. Then night would come with an almost unbearable reminder of all she'd lost.

Irwin and Sander returned to report that the mining company's men were safely installed in the valley and that they would spend the winter there constructing several cabins and a mining office. In the spring, they would begin widening the trail to make it better suited to wagon traffic. In time, if the gold vein ran as deep as expected, they would likely construct a rail spur.

They said, too, that a vigilante posse had caught up to the three remaining men who had killed Chester and Danny and had promptly hanged all three of them. Learning of the raiders' violent end brought her no satisfaction. In truth, she'd given them little thought. The only effect the news had on her was one of regret that they'd been dispatched by a lawless mob such as Pa, Deke, and Clyde had ridden with.

She looked up from the mound of dough she was kneading.

"I remembered," she said in a soft, emotionless voice. Her brothers looked at her questioningly and she went on. "Pa shot our ma. Ma and I were sitting in a grove of trees near a pond, and she was reading to me. She heard him coming, and she hid me. He didn't find me, but he found her. He tore the book from her hands and threw it in the water. When she turned as though she meant to rescue her book, he shot her in the back. After he carried her away, I stayed in the woods until Sander came calling my name."

Irwin looked uncomfortable. "Pa said she ran off, and I believed him until Bonnie made me question his story. I was angry with her for leaving me, so I tried to make Pa like me, but it was no use. I was almost sixteen when I figured out it was Pa's fault she left."

"I think I always knew she was dead," Sander said. "Granny knew it too."

* * *

IRWIN WAS ANXIOUS to move his family to San Francisco, and he was eager to watch over the construction of the house he'd commissioned and for Bonnie to select its furnishings. Sander had business to attend to there as well. All three were upset when Charlie Mae announced her intention of remaining in Sacramento.

"The house I'm renting isn't as large as the one Irwin is having built," Sander told her, "but there is plenty of room for them and you to stay with me while their house is under construction. Once

Irwin and Bonnie move into their house, I would be pleased to have you stay with me if that is your preference. When you're ready, we'll begin building our own house."

"You know we want you to live with us," Irwin countered, and Bonnie seconded his offer.

"I love you all and appreciate all you've done for me," Charlie Mae said, attempting to soften her refusal, "but I truly wish to stay here. My bakery is here, and I can support myself."

"You don't need to run that shop," Sander protested. "Irwin and I agreed you should have Chester's share of the mine."

"I don't want it," she said, her voice breaking. She knew no way to explain her aversion to any part of the rich gold strike Chester had searched for but hadn't found before his death. The gold ring he'd placed on her finger was the only gold from those prospecting days she wished to keep.

Sander and Irwin argued and Bonnie pleaded tearfully with her, but she did not change her mind. At last Irwin promised to transfer his part ownership of the house and shop to her, and Sander vowed he'd set her share of their new wealth aside in a separate account in case she changed her mind someday. Bonnie promised to return often to visit and made one last plea for her to go with them.

Before her family left, Charlie Mae touched her forehead to Sugarplum's long head one last time and in a choking whisper admonished him to mind Irwin.

* * *

San Bernardino, 1853

SPENCER PITCHED HAY to the horse he'd ridden on the last leg of his journey. It was the best horse he'd ridden on the entire trip. Brother Anderson's horse, with which he'd left Salt Lake, was a good animal, but he'd never seen anything like this one before. He patted the cinnamon-colored mare's nose before putting up the fork he'd used.

Leaning against the top rail of the fence, he studied the mare. His thoughts drifted to Pamela and his newborn son. He was anxious to be with them again, yet he felt reluctant to return to Salt Lake. Between Pamela and Sister Anderson, he felt completely useless—like a bone caught between two dogs. It wasn't only his desperate need for a job that had pushed him to accept this courier assignment. Now that he had a wife and a child, he wanted to establish a home of his own. He appreciated all the Andersons had done for him and their eagerness to include Pamela in their household, but he wanted his own place, and he'd hoped to find employment that would pay enough to enable him to move his small family to their own home.

"Mr. Pascal?" He turned, surprised to see a stranger address him by name. The stranger, who appeared to be particularly well-dressed, held out his hand. "My name is Joshua Williams, and I inquired after you when I realized you have an eye for fine horses."

"The mare isn't mine, though I wish she were. I only picked her from a corral of animals available to express riders such as myself."

"Do you have dispatches you are contracted to carry east?" the man inquired.

"No. My instructions are to winter over in Southern California and carry a report back to Salt Lake City in the early spring."

"Would I be correct, then, to assume you might be available for an expedition into Mexico to buy horses? There's a good-paying market for horses up and down the coast."

* * *

Sacramento, 1853

FOR A LONG time, it seemed strange to Charlie Mae to be alone. She'd never really been completely dependent on herself before. She worked long hours in her bakery, constantly adding new items to her list of wares, and she frequently walked to the bank to add more coins to the growing sum there, though she was indifferent to the total. At night she fell into bed exhausted. The only days she didn't rise before dawn to begin mixing bread were Sundays and the day that should have been her son's first birthday. She didn't venture out looking for a church on Sundays but spent all day reading the Bible Irwin had given her. In the front of that book she wrote Chester's name and her own, then beneath them she added Daniel's, fearing that if she didn't record their names and the dates they were born and died, generations to come wouldn't know the two people who mattered more to her than life.

It was on the second anniversary of her son's birth that she finally opened the door to the little room across the hall from her own and stepped inside. The cradle, with its smooth wooden slats, and the rocking chair, were just as she'd left them. A few items of clothing Danny had outgrown were neatly stacked in a drawer of his bureau. His few toys and the remainder of his clothing were gone. Seating herself in the chair, she slowly rocked back and forth, remembering the feel of his sturdy body cradled in her arms and the sweet, milky smell of his hair. Her mind filled with pictures of her little boy's eagerness to be born, to crawl, and those determined first footsteps to his father and the world beyond the cabin. With thoughts of Danny came memories of Chester's solid dependability, his belief in her worth, and his eagerness to set forth on a new life with her and Irwin. In whatever trials he faced, he'd found something amusing. Shame overcame her. Neither Chester nor Daniel would have crawled into the dark hole her life had become.

Sitting in the once-familiar room, Charlie Mae's motherly heart refused to accept the finality of her baby's death. Surely, somewhere he still existed, and one day she would hold him in her arms again. Somewhere Chester waited for her. The first peace she'd known in almost a year came, bringing her an assurance that there was a reason she did not die with her husband and child.

She sat for a long time, thinking and remembering, then she rose to her feet and crossed the hall. She gathered up her clothing, her Bible, her blankets, and her few possessions to move downstairs to the empty bedroom there. She rearranged every stick of furniture in the little house until there was little resemblance to the house it had been. When she finished, she thought, *Charlie Mae belonged to Chester and Danny. I will be Charlotte now.*

Sylvia came to call a few days later and expressed her approval of the changes Charlotte had made. Sylvia, too, was about to embark on changes in her life, she explained. The captain's business had flourished greatly, and he had plans to sell his store at a considerable profit and expand his freight hauling business to San Francisco and the larger settlements that had sprung up around the large bay there. There was money to be made hauling gold for the successful mining ventures, too. Construction had already begun on a mansion that would perch atop a hill, giving Sylvia a magnificent view of the city and the bay.

Soon, only Charlotte was left in Sacramento, and one day after another held the same bleak routine.

Irwin and Sander arrived on a windy March day without old Sugarplum, who was getting on in years. Bonnie and little Susannah had stayed behind as well, since Bonnie and Irwin were expecting another child, and Bonnie wasn't feeling well. Charlotte was eager to hear their news and pleased to learn that Sander was courting the daughter of one of the financiers constructing a railroad to link the larger California cities. The brothers planned to help in the development of their mine and return to their homes well before Bonnie's baby was due. Sander proudly announced that he was no longer an aide to the vice president of the company but had been promoted to a management position. Charlotte couldn't help noticing with a hint of regret that the two fashionably dressed young men who spoke with hardly a trace of their country roots were almost strangers to her.

26 🌀

Sacramento, 1854

CHARLOTTE HAD PACKED a new, sturdy carpetbag for her trip to San Francisco. She'd purchased it especially for the occasion. A tap sounded on her door. Unaccustomed to visitors, especially in the evening, she peered out the window before releasing the latch. A man stood on her doorstep. His shoulders were hunched and his head lowered, yet there was something about him that seemed familiar. Cautiously, she opened the door to find a pale, gaunt man who, in spite of his shaggy beard and hair, was no stranger. Spencer Pascal stood framed in her doorway.

"Spencer! Come in." Charlotte reached for his arm, drawing him inside the house. "Dinner's almost ready, and I would be delighted to have a guest to share it with me." She took his hat and ushered him to the table then bustled about setting another place and dishing up the simple meal she'd prepared.

He picked up his fork but sat listlessly without making an effort to eat.

"What happened? Are you ill?" His clothes were shabby, and the spark she'd always admired in his eyes was gone.

"No, I'm not ill. Not in the usual sense of the word," he clarified. "If sorrow and self-loathing are an illness, then I lie at death's door."

"I don't understand." She watched his face, not understanding the emotions mirrored there.

"My Pamela gave birth to a son a week before I was to carry dispatches over the southern route to San Bernardino. When I arrived in the settlement, I was told of a trader who was seeking caballeros to drive a herd of horses north from Mexico to San Francisco. Being in need of funds and still making our home with the Andersons, I eagerly offered my services, thinking to earn enough to establish a home of our own. The gentleman paid handsomely, and I agreed to return with him and his men for a second herd he was bringing up from Mexico. When I reached San Francisco the second time, I discovered a letter waiting for me that had left Salt Lake just two weeks after my own departure from there. I learned my wife had died of childbirth complications."

"I am so sorry." Charlotte reached across the table to touch his hand. He gripped it as though it were a lifeline.

"I didn't know she was ill. She was tired and weak, but I thought that was normal. I should have been there. How can I go on, knowing I failed her?" His face twisted in anguish.

"Don't blame yourself. Pamela wouldn't. I've no doubt she knew you were doing all you could to provide for her and your child." Charlotte spoke in soothing tones, knowing firsthand the grief her childhood friend was experiencing and that he would hear little of what she said.

"I should have known she needed me."

"You couldn't have known."

"We had so many plans and dreams, so much we meant to do together. I never gave any thought to either of us going on alone. How shall I bear living a solitary life until we are together again in God's kingdom?" He buried his face in his hands and wept.

Charlotte sat in stunned silence for several minutes. *He expects to be reunited with Pamela in heaven? My own hope of living with Chester and Daniel again might be possible—or are we both clinging to a desperate fantasy?*

"Spencer," she said, once more reaching out to touch him. "Will you see your wife again?"

"Yes, I have no doubt of that. It's one of the truths taught by the restored gospel that families are meant to be eternal. God Himself instituted marriage as an everlasting covenant."

"And my baby . . . will I have my baby again?" Charlotte's cheeks were awash with tears as she gripped Spencer's arm and stared into his eyes.

"Your baby?" Spencer appeared puzzled, then understanding spread across his face. "That dear child is gone, too? I didn't know. Tell me what happened."

With frequent stops to wipe her eyes and control her wavering voice, she told him of the tragedy that had befallen her family. When she finished, he made an awkward attempt to apologize for burdening her with his pain when she had such a great load of her own.

"I'm glad you came," she said. "I've not been able to speak of those terrible events, not even to my brothers or to Bonnie. I tried to close off that part of my life and pretend it never happened. I even *became* Charlotte, believing Charlie Mae died with Chester and our son, but nothing returned any light to my soul until you spoke of one day being with Pamela again."

Far into the night, they talked and consoled each other. Spencer explained more about the eternal nature of families, and Charlotte listened intently. When he learned the fate of the Book of Mormon he had given her, they shared memories of Grandma Pascal, whose book it had been. He took his own copy of the book from his pocket and gave it to her with the assurance that he could easily obtain another one when he returned to Salt Lake.

"What about your son?" she asked him, thinking it strange that he'd never mentioned the baby. "You must be anxious to return to him."

"In truth, I've given him little thought," Spencer admitted. "I know nothing of babies. When he was born, Pamela's aunt, the same midwife who delivered your sister-in-law's infant, and Sister Anderson, who has been a second grandma to me, took over his care. They made it clear my stumbling attempts to hold or comfort him were far from adequate and that the nursery was not a man's province." He hung his head as he continued. "In my darkest hour after reading the letter sent by Brother Anderson, I blamed my innocent child for his mother's death."

"If all you claim is true concerning marriage, one day you'll have to face Pamela when she asks how you raised the son she gave you," Charlotte reminded him. "If I had died instead of Chester, I would be greatly concerned that Chester should take personal charge of Daniel."

Spencer hung his head and conceded that she was right.

Morning was not far distant when Spencer took his leave. He intended to ride hard in hopes of catching up to a small group that departed three days earlier, heading for the Sierras and on to the east. Charlotte added to the rations of food and water he carried with him and knelt with him for a brief prayer before bidding him farewell.

Back in her kitchen after he'd gone, she debated finding her bed or beginning the first batch of bread. The bread won out. Through the hours she labored in her shop, her mind went over all Spencer had taught her. When at last she closed the shop, she stumbled to her bed, where she quickly slipped into her first uninterrupted night's rest since the deaths of her loved ones.

* * *

ON A CRISP October morning, Charlotte boarded a coach for the eighty-five mile journey to San Francisco. Sander met her and whisked her away to Irwin's home, where she arrived too late to assist with the birth of Bonnie and Irwin's second daughter.

Victoria, unlike Susannah, arrived with little trouble and with a healthy set of lungs. After shedding her cloak and bonnet,

Charlotte settled in a chair beside Bonnie with the day-old infant in her arms. Susannah, with her thumb in her mouth, peeked shyly at Charlotte from the far side of her mother's bed.

Cradling the newborn in her arms brought a lump to Charlotte's throat. Victoria's hair was a little darker than Susannah's, though not as brown or as abundant as Danny's had been, but there was something about the little face and bright green eyes that brought an ache to arms that had been empty too long.

The days passed in a swirl of catching up, with Charlotte touring the rapidly growing city, meeting Sander's bride-to-be, and attending to the needs of Bonnie and her two small daughters. She could almost envy Bonnie and her brothers' elegant homes with their graceful furniture, lovely fabrics, and modern conveniences.

Sylvia called one day and insisted on taking Charlotte to lunch at a newly opened tea room followed by shopping for a more fashionable wardrobe. They talked, and Charlotte even laughed at some of the more absurd hats her friend insisted she try on.

Sugarplum trotted toward the fence to greet her when Irwin walked her behind his house to a pasture where the old mule grazed along with a pair of fine saddle horses and four sleek carriage horses. She patted his nose and fed him an apple while whispering her regrets that she couldn't keep him in Sacramento.

As rain and fog settled in over the city, Charlotte knew it was time to return to Sacramento and her shop. Irwin and Sander trotted out all of the old arguments to persuade her to stay, but the life they'd chosen wasn't for her. She assured them she'd had a lovely visit and she'd come again, but she wished to be back in her own house, baking bread and taking walks along the riverfront. And so it was that, attired in one of her fashionable new gowns, she boarded a steamboat for a much quicker return trip to Sacramento. The tempo of the rain increased, and she scurried under the cabin roof for shelter. As she did so, she looked back to wave to Sander. Behind him she saw a familiar figure. Even with the rain pounding on the deck and nearly obscuring her view, she recognized Miss Louisa scurrying aboard the ferry.

She knew the moment the madam recognized her but was surprised when the woman approached her.

"Hello, Charlie Mae," Louisa said cordially as though greeting an old friend. "You're looking well." She eyed Charlotte's new traveling suit. Sylvia had insisted it suited her perfectly.

"Hello." Charlotte nodded her head in a brief gesture, meeting the woman's eyes with neither deference nor fear. Shock registered slowly as Charlotte observed the heavy makeup that hid a black eye and a large bruise that spread from the corner of Louisa's mouth across one cheek.

Louisa merely shrugged. "It happens," she said. "I hear your life didn't work out too well and you've found yourself alone. I'd repeat my offer of employment, but considering the fact that both of your brothers are now wealthy and that your sisters-in-law are on that narrow-minded little committee determined to drive businesses such as mine out of San Francisco, it wouldn't be wise. Of course, if you find yourself lonely and simply want a diversion, look me up." She handed Charlotte a neatly embossed card before strolling away with a practiced swagger.

Charlotte watched Louisa walk away and felt a kind of pity, sensing that Louisa was even more alone in the world than she. Once she'd despised and feared Louisa almost as much as Pa, but now she wondered what hope and tragedies had led an intelligent, beautiful woman to choose a life of degradation and abuse over a husband and family. Had fate or greed driven her to sell herself?

She looked out over the gray water, watching the mist swirl until it obscured the shoreline. Once she would have felt alone, but now memories softened by time brought a smile to her lips, and as she often did, she sensed that Chester was not too far away. The fog came closer, enclosing her in trailing wisps of white. A quiet peace filled her heart, assuring her that not only was Chester near, but so also was her Heavenly Father. She remembered the words Spencer had taught her years ago. "He knows where I am."

* * *

THE LITTLE HOUSE seemed to welcome Charlotte, and she was glad to be home again. She spent two days scrubbing and carrying in supplies before she opened her bakery again. Her customers welcomed her with enthusiasm, and she settled back into the life she'd made for herself, though she went out more frequently—to concerts, the opera, and on occasion a play.

Rain fell frequently, and occasionally it turned to thick, white flakes that covered the ground before quickly melting. One such morning, Charlotte stepped outside her door to see a light blanket of white covering everything in sight. With a rush of pain, she remembered wrestling in the snow with Chester in the cabin clearing, treks to the creek holding tightly to a rope, and snuggling beneath a quilt with her young husband while the wind and snow howled around the cabin. A terrible loneliness settled over her, and she found the prospect of spending all her years baking bread for strangers and spending her evenings eating solitary dinners nearly unbearable.

That afternoon when she finished her day's work, she trudged up the stairs. She opened doors left closed for more than a year. Dust lay heavy on every surface, but slowly she sorted through the few items Chester had left behind. He'd owned little, and there were only a few shirts that he'd thought unsuitable for the mountains and a thin packet of letters from his mother. She determined to give the clothes to one of her customers who might have need of them, but she'd carry the letters downstairs to store in her trunk with the few mementos she'd collected through the years.

She paused outside Danny's room, then gathering her courage, she stepped inside. She brushed aside an occasional tear as she gathered her son's few items of clothing that hadn't accompanied them to the mountains. She stroked a quilt Bonnie had lovingly stitched for him, which she'd thought too fine for the journey to the cabin. She carried the quilt and the small pile of clothing downstairs. She'd decide later whether she could bear to part with them.

She returned one last time to her son's room. Her eyes settled on the chair Chester had made while they awaited Daniel's birth. Stepping closer, she knelt, resting her clasped hands on the seat where she'd sat so many times to nurse her baby. A compelling urge to pray came over her.

"Father," she pleaded, "I miss them so much. Are they happy? And is it true that there is a way we can be together again?"

When she finished praying, she decided to take the chair downstairs and place it beside the fireplace. It was by far the most comfortable chair in the house, and she found it more comforting than painful now to remember the hands that had so lovingly made it for her.

That night she dreamed of standing beside a wide meadow, watching Daniel and Chester playing some kind of game. Danny was bigger, and as he ran across the flower-strewn grass, his laughter trailed behind him. Chester caught him up, and he giggled. She wanted to join them but couldn't. She became aware of another little boy, one who watched wistfully and longed to join in the game. Her heart went out to the child, but when she reached for him, she awoke.

The dream came again two more times before the arrival of spring. She wondered if God sent the dream to her to assure her that Chester and Danny were safe and well. That thought brought her comfort. But the other child in the dream puzzled her. *Could the child left out of the game be herself?* she wondered. *Was he a warning that there were things she needed to do before she could join her family?* Each time the dream came, she pored over her scriptures, rereading the verses Spencer had pointed out to her.

Spring brought with it an air of expectancy. Something was about to change, though she wasn't sure what. She aired the upstairs bedrooms and had a larger bed installed in the smaller one. She purchased quilts and made the house ready for the arrival of her brothers, whom she suspected would soon pass through Sacramento on their way to the mine. Everything was ready in case their wives and children accompanied them.

When Sander and Irwin arrived, they were alone. Sander's wife was facing the early months of her first pregnancy, and Bonnie feared caring for her two small daughters would be much too difficult without the support of another woman. Her brothers stayed only a day, as they were eager to see the progress that had been made since their last visit to the mine. They promised a longer visit in the fall.

Charlotte turned her attention to spading up a garden plot and tending the plants through the spring and into summer. Lacking family to share the garden's bounty, she gave many of her vegetables to her customers, and often she left a picking of peas or a dozen ears of corn on the doorstep of one of the shanties she passed during her frequent walks.

As the days grew hotter, she often found herself looking east toward the mountains. Shutting out the painful memories, she made plans for the dinners and comfortable visits she would have with her brothers when they returned in the fall. Perhaps she would even accompany them to San Francisco for a short time. She awoke early one morning and rushed to begin her routine. When she opened the door to her bakery, it wasn't her brothers who greeted her.

"Spencer!" She looked up at the tall man. He looked far better than the last time she'd seen him, but there was a perpetual sadness in his eyes, and something in his bearing spoke of greater maturity. "Come in," she invited. "I'll bring you some breakfast."

She sat near him, and he ate as they exchanged tidbits of news. He and four elders intent on traveling to the Pacific Islands to proselytize had begun their journey as soon as word arrived that the pass was open, Spencer told her. There was still snow at the higher altitudes, but he hadn't found the trail unduly difficult for a small party without wagons. She learned that Brother Anderson had been ill much of the winter and that he and his wife had decided to move farther south to take advantage of the milder climate around the new settlement of St. George. The elderly couple would be leaving Salt Lake City at summer's end.

Charlotte told him about her visit to San Francisco and her new niece.

She closed her shop early that day and packed a lunch for the two of them. With the basket on Spencer's arm, they strolled through the city until they reached a grassy spot beside the river. The sun beat down, but a breeze off the river brought cooler air. Charlotte pulled a blanket from the basket to spread on the ground, and when they were seated, Spencer plucked a long stem of grass, shredding it between his fingers while he stared out at the wide expanse of water.

"Is your son well?" she asked, sensing that something in the atmosphere had changed from the easy camaraderie they had shared all morning.

"He is pale and much too coddled, I fear," Spencer said. "Sister Anderson and Pamela's Aunt Jessica mean well, but they are at constant odds over his care, and I'm left on the outside, not knowing what to do. I've come to love him dearly, but I fear he shall never learn to walk, for one of them is forever carrying him about, and he has become somewhat spoiled."

"Oh, dear!" She didn't know what to say to offer him encouragement.

"To complicate matters further, Sister Anderson wishes to take him with her when they move to St. George, while Aunt Jessica is equally adamant that she will assume responsibility for him after their departure."

"They both seem intent on cutting you out of his life."

"They don't mean any harm to either of us. Just the opposite. They're quite certain they're relieving a helpless male of an impossible burden and offering great love to a motherless baby they both truly love. Aunt Jessica never bore children of her own, though she has probably brought a hundred or more babies into the world. And I've been Sister Anderson's lone chick since I was a lad."

"What are you going to do?" She wrinkled her brow, trying to think of wise advice to give him. Her instincts warned that the child belonged with his father and that Spencer must take a more active role in his upbringing.

"I felt confused and unsure until one night as I knelt beside my bed, praying for the wisdom to do what is best for little Jacob. A window seemed to open, and I thought I saw Pamela weeping for our son. I begged her to tell me what to do, but I couldn't make out the words she spoke. Sometime later I awoke, still on my knees. Feeling stiff and sore, I crawled into bed and lay for a long time wondering if what I had seen was real or merely a dream. At last I fell asleep. When I awoke, it was your face I saw before me, and I knew what I should do."

"I don't understand . . ."

"I think it was a prompting that I should get away for a time to think the situation through carefully and seek your advice. My son's future depends on the choice I make. I became even more convinced that I should seek you out when I learned that day of the missionaries' need for a guide. I promptly volunteered. What better way to think the matter through than to visit with you?"

"I don't know that I can offer advice on such a delicate matter."

"You, more than anyone else, understand me. You were my only friend when I was a lonely child, and you've suffered a similar fate to mine. Thoughts of your friendship have comforted me many times through the years."

"I, too, have cherished our friendship. I shall think on the matter," Charlotte promised.

* * *

SPENCER FOUND LODGING nearby, and the days seemed to speed by as he appeared each morning to assist her with her customers. He joined her for the long strolls about the city, and they frequently carried a lunch and sought out a shady spot in which to share it. Twice they sat on a blanket spread on the ground to listen to the newly formed city band. Sometimes they talked about that distant time when they were children.

"Did you know my father was part of the mob that drove your people from Nauvoo?" she asked one day. "He was one of those who burned your grandma's little house, too."

Spencer was quiet for a long time. She watched as he stared from their sheltered place across the river. When he spoke his voice was mild. "It's difficult not to hate those who caused so many people so much grief. Yet hating your father would not bring Grandma back, and I'm not sure I'd want to go back to Nauvoo at this time if I could. I like the West. Hating him and men like him, I fear, would merely distract me from the problems I face now. The Savior instructed that we should forgive those who do evil to us, but when Grandma died I found forgiveness difficult. I cried myself to sleep many times and had nightmares wherein I saw her shivering in that cold grave. I'm not sure I've achieved the ability to completely forgive yet, but I no longer feel the rage I once did."

"I feel that way about a woman who once threatened my happiness with Chester." She explained about Miss Louisa. "I saw her again some months ago. I'm not certain whether forgiveness is the right way to describe what I feel for her now. If I feel anything, it's pity."

"I don't feel pity for those who brought about Grandma's death, but I no longer wish to retaliate, and I'm content to leave the matter in God's hands. I think that's a step on the way to forgiving." He hesitated a moment then went on. "I don't hold your father's prejudices against you. You've never been anything but fair and kind to me."

"You're far more forgiving than I am," Charlotte told him. "Forgiving Miss Louisa is a simpler matter than forgiving Pa." Her voice turned bitter. "In a way, he was responsible for your grandma's death, but he was directly responsible for murdering a man who was trying to escape from a burning building in Nauvoo. I saw him shoot that man. He shot my mother too. I'll never forgive him, nor will I forgive the men who killed Chester and little Danny." Her shoulders shook with the force of her emotion.

Spencer's arms came around her, holding her while she cried and raged against her father for all his cruelties and for the stark injustice that had taken her husband's and son's lives. He said nothing but held her until her emotional storm was past and the sun was sinking beyond the river.

"I'm sorry," she said at last and scrambled through her pockets looking for a handkerchief. Spencer handed her his own. She wiped her eyes and blew her nose.

"Don't be sorry," Spencer soothed her. "Anger and outrage have to be released before healing can begin. Grandma taught me a long time ago that our enemies only win as long as they have a hold on us. You physically escaped your father's hold a long time ago, but not until you accept in your heart that he can no longer hurt you will you be able to pity then forgive him. Neither he nor the men who killed Chester and Danny can hurt you now. Your anger and hate can't touch them either. Those feelings hurt only you by keeping you from moving forward with your life."

"What life? I get up every morning, bake bread for strangers, then sleep in my cold, lonely bed each night. I should have died with the two people who loved me more than anyone or anything else."

"Over and over I have wished that I might have died with Pamela," Spencer admitted. "But of late, I've come to believe that life matters and that she wasn't the only one who truly loved me.

You convinced me that my son needs a father, and I've come to believe that God has more in mind for me than an empty, cold existence. I think He has more in mind as well for the little girl who once tiptoed fearfully about her father's house, struggling to be perfect to avoid a beating."

After drying her tears, Charlotte leaned on Spencer's arm—it felt so natural as they made their way back to her house. From halfway down the block, she became aware of a light burning in her kitchen. Her first fearful thought was of fire, but she soon became convinced that a lantern had been lit.

They approached the house quietly, and Spencer insisted that she conceal herself behind the tree that grew beside the door while he checked for an intruder. Pulling her skirts closely about her, she watched in apprehension as Spencer reached for the door. It opened suddenly, and Irwin stood framed in the doorway.

"Who—?" both men began, and Charlotte rushed forward.

"Irwin, why are you back so soon? And where is Sander?" She looked around for her other brother.

"I'm here." Sander stepped forward.

"Haven't I seen you before?" Irwin looked at Spencer as though trying to place him.

"We met some years ago when you journeyed through Salt Lake." Spencer extended his hand. "I'm Spencer Pascal."

"The redheaded Mormon kid Charlie Mae used to run off to meet back in Illinois?" Sander slapped his hand against his thigh and chuckled. "How'd you two ever meet up again?"

Irwin ignored Spencer's hand, and Sander reached past him to shake it. "Come on in," he invited.

While Charlotte set a cold supper on the table, the three men talked in stiff tones, and she learned that her brothers were returning to San Francisco to finalize arrangements for a railroad spur. Two weeks later, Irwin would return to the mine for a short time while Sander took care of matters at his company's offices.

"Would you mind if I accompanied you on your return to the mine?" Spencer inquired of Irwin.

Irwin studied him for a moment, glanced at Charlotte, then nodded his assent.

27 ∾

CHARLOTTE WAS SURPRISED by Spencer's interest in the mine. To date, he'd shown little interest in gold, though he'd alluded to some difficulty in supporting his family. She was also surprised by how much she missed him after he and Irwin rode away.

She thought often of their long talks concerning their losses. They'd talked, too, of the Book of Mormon, and Spencer had explained many things that had been unclear to her. Remembrance of their discussion on forgiveness plagued her, and she found herself frequently on her knees seeking a means of letting go of the anger and painful memories.

One of her customers spoke of a young woman who had given birth to twins in one of the shacks near the river. Finding she was unable to get thoughts of the young mother, living in poverty with two small children, out of her mind, Charlotte set out with a basket of bread and the little pile of clothing that had been Daniel's. She found the girl and spent the remainder of the afternoon cleaning the small home and doing all she could to make the new mother comfortable. She learned the girl had worked in an establishment much like Miss Louisa's until her babies' father had persuaded her to live with him. He had abandoned the girl a few months later, leaving her with no means of support.

When Charlotte finally began the trek back to her own house, she felt a new determination to do something with her life. Without

Irwin's assistance, she could have found herself in the same situation as that young mother. Without Chester's love, the birth of her child would have been a sorrowful event instead of the joyful blessing each moment of Danny's brief life had been. The informal education she'd received from Sister Pascal and Sylvia along with the baking skills Granny had taught her had helped her take care of herself. She'd been blessed more than she'd supposed. She started making plans to speak to Sander about using some of the money he'd set aside for her from the gold mine's profits to benefit young women who found themselves in desperate circumstances.

September came, and the trees by the river began to turn gold. She paused on her walk, enjoying the spectacle of the turning leaves and the sun shining across the gray water. A faint breeze cooled her cheeks, and she felt alive. Her mind was filled with the spectacular reds and golds interspersed with the deep green of fir trees in the mountains. She remembered the way the sun slanted across the crystal clear lake. For the first time in two years she could see Chester and Danny near to bursting with laughter and exhibiting a passion for life without experiencing crushing pain. Though their time together was short, she was glad for every minute they'd shared.

Catching herself humming a few days later, Charlotte shook her head. Just because Spencer and Irwin were due back any day was no reason to behave like a young girl, and just because Irwin had said they'd return the first week in September, there was no reason to believe this would be the day. Nevertheless, she prepared a pan of cinnamon rolls and donned one of her newest dresses after closing the bakery for the day. She'd scarcely removed the rolls from the oven when she heard a tap on her door and looked up to see Irwin and Spencer entering her kitchen.

Irwin enveloped her in a hearty hug and burned his fingers lifting a cinnamon roll from the pan she held. Spencer stood back, appearing a bit awkward. As soon as she could free herself from her brother and the pan she held, she stepped to his side, impulsively brushing his cheek with her lips.

After staying one night, Irwin was anxious to be on his way. He'd missed Bonnie and their little girls. He didn't even consider it an extravagance to pay the extra charge for taking his horse and pack mule on the ferry. She handed him the letter she'd prepared weeks ago to give to Sander.

Spencer accompanied them to the ferry in order to escort Charlotte safely back home, but once Irwin was on his way, his steps and hers turned toward the river path where they'd walked many times before. When they reached the spot where they'd picnicked before his journey to the mine, Spencer's steps halted. Leading her to a favorite grassy spot, he seated her and sat beside her. After a few moments he said, "The mountain passes will soon be filled with snow. I miss my son and find I'm anxious to return to Salt Lake before the Andersons depart for St. George. Brother Anderson has offered me his small farm at a reasonable price, and I need to settle the arrangements."

"I shall miss you greatly," she said with real regret, finding it difficult to conceal the tears that threatened to fall.

"I don't think we are meant to part." He picked up her hands and held them in a firm grip.

"I don't understand . . ."

"I think you do. I'm asking you to marry me, to be my wife and a mother to my son."

Her mouth opened, but no words came out. Finally she gasped. "But we don't love each other."

"I think we have always loved each other." He lowered his voice. "I don't expect to take Chester's place in your heart, and I shall always love Pamela, yet since we were children there has been a bond between us. The first time I saw you lying in the mud and forest debris, I think I knew we were destined to support and comfort each other through life's trials."

"I'm not a Mormon, and I'm older than you." She continued to protest, though his words had touched a response deep within her.

"You're only a little older, surely no more than a year or two." He smiled, and she saw a trace of the little boy who had rescued her from hurt and sorrow so many years before.

"As for being a member of the Church, I suspect our faiths are far more similar than dissimilar. I'll not pressure you to be baptized; you will have all the time you need to decide the matter." She didn't miss the confidence in his voice that revealed his certainty that she would accept his faith. In all likelihood she would. The Book of Mormon was already one of her greatest treasures and the source she turned to most often for peace and comfort.

"Your son . . . ?" She didn't know how to voice her uncertainty concerning becoming the boy's stepmother. Then she recalled her dream. *Could Jacob be the child she wished so desperately to help?*

"A boy needs a mother." Spencer's words were a reminder that he'd grown up without one, and the pain in his voice revealed the sorrow that circumstance had caused him. "And a man needs a wife—one he loves deeply."

Their eyes met, and she was through with argument. He was right. She did love him. There had always been hope and joy in their relationship. The future that had been a long, black tunnel widened to admit light and warmth. Loving Spencer would not be the same as loving Chester, but it would be rewarding and fulfilling in a different way.

Rising on her toes, she pressed a brief kiss to the corner of Spencer's mouth and felt new life stir within her heart. Her marriage would not be merely a means of passing time until she could be with Chester and Daniel. Her life would be filled with purpose again.

"Charlie Mae?" It had been some time since she'd been called anything but Charlotte. He appeared uncertain for a moment. He held out his hand. Nestled on his palm was the deep red of her ruby. He lifted it, and she saw that it swung from an intricate gold chain. Slowly he placed the chain about her neck. Instinctively, her fingers caressed the familiar stone.

"But how. . . ?" she whispered.

"Irwin took me to your burned cabin, and I spent days sifting through the ashes. This stone tied us together through all the trials we've faced, and something inside me urged me to search for it, though the task appeared hopeless at times. After I found it, Irwin gave me a handful of nuggets he said came from the stream where your first cabin stood. I fashioned the chain from them, hoping you'd see my efforts as a symbol of my love for you."

* * *

JUST AS SHE expected, her brothers protested her plans to marry a Mormon and move to Salt Lake, but they soon came around to a grudging acceptance of Spencer. Sander agreed to her plan to provide for abandoned and destitute women when she reminded him that she wanted no part of the gold that had enticed Chester and led to his death. She wanted only her profits from her bakery and the gold band Chester had given her.

Irwin broke off his protests with a burst of laughter. "I'd love to be the one to tell Pa his daughter is marrying a Mormon."

"Pa's crippled and spends his time tied to a chair, drooling on himself," Sander ended the laughter. "I stopped there on my way West to see if the two of you needed my help. I spoke with Deke. He said Pa was injured in a mysterious accident, most likely a bullet in his back, and that Agnes now controls the farm. Cletus and Dwight ran off a long time ago."

"Why didn't you say something before now?" Irwin appeared upset over the news.

"There didn't seem to be much point in stirring up old resentments when you'd both made a good new life for yourselves," Sander said.

"Is Deke all right?" Charlotte remembered that in his own selfish way, her oldest brother had helped her escape Cletus and the misery of living under Pa's roof.

"His father-in-law was close to losing his farm to the county for unpaid taxes. He and Sissy were talking about taking up a homestead farther west. He seemed older and less sure of himself than I remembered. And before you ask, he said neither he nor Pa had heard anything from Clyde."

* * *

ON A SPARKLING, clear late September morning, Spencer and Charlotte Pascal guided their horses up the steep trail leading to the pass over the Sierra Mountains. Three pack animals, including old Sugarplum, carried her pans, supplies, water bags, clothing, and the gifts her brothers and their wives had showered on them. Charlotte reined in her horse to look toward a mountain to the north.

As she gazed at that distant spot, she felt herself bidding Chester and Daniel farewell in a way she'd been unable to do when she'd knelt beside their grave on that fateful day they were buried. A slight breeze drifted toward her, seeming to say that their love would endure and that they would be together again someday. Until then she must value life and continue on the new path she had chosen.

Spencer stopped beside her. "Chester and your baby paid a terrible price for the greed of those men who attacked you. It's a marvel you were spared that day." He reached across the gap between their mounts to take her hand.

"I tried to reach them, but one of the outlaws hurled the box you carved for my ruby at my head. The blow knocked me unconscious just long enough for Irwin and Sander to arrive and to prevent me from entering the burning cabin."

"I'm glad you were spared." His eyes said much more. "I wonder why the thieves didn't take the ruby."

She turned to face him. "They were so focused on gold, they didn't recognize the worth of the ruby."

"I wonder how many times I've only seen the gold and overlooked the ruby in life." He smiled tenderly as they urged their horses onward, riding side by side.

After a few minutes she said, "I would have given my life for Chester and Danny, but with each day the conviction grows stronger within me that there is something only I can accomplish for them by living. Moments ago, as I looked at that distant peak that marks their graves, I at last felt at peace and received an assurance that Chester is pleased with the direction my life is taking."

"I never thought I would be happy again, but I feel great joy and peace this morning, too." Spencer leaned forward to kiss her brow.

"It's time to be on our way." Charlotte's lips curved upward in a playful smile. "We've a new life to discover together, and I've a new son to hold and love. If one day the Lord should bless us with a daughter, I will call her Ruby." Her hand went to the pendant that nestled at her throat.

About the Author

Photo courtesy of Olan Mills

Jennie Hansen graduated from Ricks College in Idaho, then Westminster College in Utah. She has been a newspaper reporter, editor, and librarian. In addition to writing novels, she reviews LDS fiction in a monthly column for Meridian Magazine.

She was born in Idaho Falls, Idaho, and has lived in Idaho, Montana, and Utah. She has received numerous writing awards.

Jennie and her husband, Boyd, live in Salt Lake County. They have five married children and ten grandchildren.

Jennie enjoys hearing from her readers, who can visit her website, www.jennielhansen.com, or who can write to her in care of Covenant Communications, P.O. Box 416, American Fork, UT 84003-0416, or via e-mail at info@covenant-lds.com.